DOUBLE FAULT

Also by Janice Simpson

Let Sleeping Dogs Lie (2012)

Murder in Mt Martha (2016)

A Body of Work (2018)

you will see mountains and seas in those eyes (2024)

DOUBLE FAULT

Janice Simpson

Published by Apsley Press

Maryborough Victoria

© Janice Simpson 2025

First published 2025

ISBN 978-0-6459158-0-8 (p)

978-0-6459158-1-5 (e)

All the characters in this novel are purely imaginary and have no connection to any living person.

For Des

SUNDAY

AFTER MONTHS of paperwork, to-ing and fro-ing between Melbourne and Sydney, Detective Senior Sergeant Brendan O'Leary had a search warrant for the Glenlyon property owned by Hubert Ramsay Krakauer. Heading north towards the Loddon River, SES volunteers—their orange uniforms cruel against the grey scrub and dried off grass—fanned out over a paddock. The smell of eucalyptus hung in the air. The only sounds were twigs snapping under foot and the occasional kookaburra jeering overhead.

Currently an inmate at the Metropolitan Remand Centre, Krakauer was due to face court on drug trafficking charges laid almost two years ago, after 80 packages of ecstasy pills with a street value of more than $300,000 were found in his possession. It still made O'Leary livid that Krakauer was granted bail by some civil rights do-gooder sucked in by his growing-up sob story. Drug-abusing parents. Bed wetting. Foster care. Bullied at school. Sexual identification issues. Released on just $5,000 security. Probably pulled the cash out of his shoe. Wasn't until August last year that he'd been picked up again, this time by Sydney traffic police, after he ran up the arse of some woman driving a Merc out of a city showroom. Officers opened up Krakauer's boot and found a USB stick. Links to the dark web revealed kiddie porn. When O'Leary watched some of the footage, he was pretty sure

1

that eight-year-old twins, kids who'd disappeared without trace from Beach Road in Beaumaris in 2015, were featured. The case stuck in O'Leary's craw. And then last week a child-size tattered hoodie and a pair of jeans were found in one of the old mine shafts that dotted Krakauer's Glenlyon farmlet. A keen local cop had made the discovery during a routine visit to investigate reports of a burn-off on a total fire ban day.

He sniffed at the air. Hot wind blowing steadily from the north. Anything was possible. Cap pulled low over a back-to-work haircut, he sat on a fallen tree branch in the shade, cooler than waiting in the caravan that had been towed on site and set up as a makeshift headquarters. Watched the search line move snail-like over the rough ground, until it dipped from view down to the river gully. He rubbed absently at his right thigh, thumb kneading a ridge of scar tissue through his jeans. Gazing up into a peppermint gum, he tried to pinpoint the magpie that had now joined the kookaburra. There it was, perched high in the crown, silhouetted against a brittle sky. He thought he could make out a nest, raised his phone to take a snap to show Zoe and Jack, his twins, when a shout from the direction of the gully had him on his feet. 'Shit,' he said, sitting down as promptly as he had risen, a sharp pain shooting the length of his right leg. He kept forgetting that sudden weight bearing was not an option. He craned his neck in the direction the sound had come from and saw two SES volunteers cresting the rise, trudging towards him.

'Think we've found something,' said the older bloke, heavyset, scarred cheek.

'Yeah,' said his mate.

'Bones,' said Scarface.

'Where?' O'Leary hungry, as if knowing the location could solve everything.

Scarface shifted on his feet. 'About a foot from a mineshaft entrance.'

'Yeah,' said his mate again.

'Probably been pulled out by animals.' Looking at the ground now. 'Or something.'

O'Leary felt a cold wave course through his guts. 'Cordoned it off?'

'That's what I told the blokes to do,' said Scarface.

'Nguyen still down there?'

'The little Chinaman seems to know what he's doing.'

O'Leary resisted landing a punch on the man's sun-damaged nose. Easy enough for him living in the city. Doubtless few Vietnamese had made their way to Glenlyon, a place on the Loddon River boasting not much more than a general store. And plenty of self-healing and yoga, if the community noticeboard was anything to go by. Not far from Melbourne, but could be a million miles from anywhere, like most of the discarded country towns dotted across the state. 'Might pay to get your people working in another direction,' he said instead. 'The area to the west of the house hasn't been done.'

The two men shuffled off as O'Leary got out his phone. 'What's it looking like?'

Detective Constable Sean Nguyen had been on O'Leary's team on and off for three or so years. 'It's human.'

'How much?'

'Top half of a small body.' He heard Nguyen draw in breath. 'No sign of a skull. Keep you posted.'

Flopped on her couch Angela Micelli was leafing through the day's paper, thick dark hair tied in a ponytail in an effort to keep cool. Outside the sun was sneaking in through gaps in the drawn curtains. She flicked pages until she located the weather report: *Thunderstorms expected to cross the city in the late afternoon but little to no rain expected. Hot and humid, winds south-easterly averaging to 40 km/h. Gale warning for waters east of Wilsons Prom. Fire danger: moderate to high in the west and northern districts. Maximum 38.* Sweat beaded on her forehead. A pedestal fan was whirring in the corner, moving warm air side to side. Her phone, lying on the coffee table, vibrated. She lunged at it, heart racing. Sighed. 'Ciao, Mumma.' A few moments passed before she was able to get a word in. 'I've already been for a bike ride this morning, so don't worry, I won't get struck by lightning.'

'And you no go to work today, Angela?'

'Not today. Nor tomorrow.'

'Only asking.'

Hearing the quaver in her mother's voice, she realised she was annoyed the caller was not the person she was expecting. She sat up straighter, made herself smile. 'Sorry, Mumma. Something else, that's all. The damned aircon's not working.'

'Ah, your papa and I say always you must find nice man. Have fun. Get married.'

Micelli held the phone out from her ear while her mother told her again why women like her needed a husband. 'Are you going over to Rosie's tonight?'

'Of course, Angela. I like to see my beautiful girls.' Micelli glanced over at the photo on her bookshelf: Rosie, Maria, Rita, Angela. The four Micelli girls, lined up in age order, dressed in identical pink frocks with wide pink hair ribbons trying vainly to hold back unruly curls. Rosie had recently taken to organising family get-togethers on Sunday evenings. With her husband Frank and their three children, she lived in a suburban mansion in Thornbury, a house Micelli privately referred to as the Pantelerri Palazzo because of its reliance on heavy colonnading, several Juliet balconies and a wide terrazzo-tiled verandah. She could think of nothing worse than traipsing across town from her seaside apartment in Altona to eat mediocre Bolognese washed down with a cheap pinot noir. And fending off questions from her sisters who shared their mother's view that fun equated to a few dates with a man everyone approved of, followed by a lavish wedding.

'You want your father and me to pick you up?'

Micelli rolled her eyes towards the ceiling. 'Okay, Mumma. I'll see you about six.' Another four hours to herself before they arrived, provided she resisted the urge to call her boss, Brendan O'Leary, who was back on the job.

She got up and walked down the hall to the laundry where Marbles was sprawled out on the tiles. A lazy fly buzzed round a bowl half-full of sardines in jelly. She tugged a load of laundry from the machine and piled it into a basket. Outside the concrete was so hot it burnt into her soles, forcing her to duck inside and slip on a pair of thongs.

At the clothesline she pegged out her things: work shirts, mainly white and cream; t-shirts – most white, one red and one black; jeans – two pairs; bike gear – lycra shorts and a few old jerseys; underwear – black and flesh-coloured. It made her grin to think what her mother would say about her failure to pre-sort the laundry into piles of coloureds, whites and darks. And her failure to peg socks in matching pairs.

She went back to the couch and picked up the paper, flicked through to the sports section. Her attention was drawn to a close-up of a blond man, grasping a tennis racquet in a sweeping back swing. His wide blue eyes were focused on a yellow ball still several centimetres from his racquet strings. The headline: *Kross shot will cut deep at the Open*. Reading further, she discovered that Markus Kross from Estonia was in town to contest the first of the grand slams for the year. He had already won a junior title in Melbourne. 'I love this place,' he was quoted as saying. 'In my city, Tallinn, it is beautiful, yes, but here it is long gold beaches and long roads with trees. I am full of motivation and want to achieve what I did here five years ago.' Typical. Talk up the city. Beat the local hero. Become the poster boy for thousands of teenage girls with sunburnt shoulders. Further down the page, a report about Julia Kneebone was doing the opposite, revving up animosity for one of the world's most successful players. Kneebone was reported as saying, 'Sure I'm here to win, but tennis, it's like, not my favourite. Now shopping, if we're talking like favourites, absolutely. But like, you know, I need to win to shop.' Micelli dropped the paper onto the floor in disgust. She picked up her phone, put it down again. When Brendan O'Leary went on sick leave she had taken over as an Acting Team Leader, fancy corporate-speak for a homicide detective who could take responsibility for an investigation. For the last four and a half months, give or take a few days, she'd been in charge. His recovery had taken longer than anyone had expected, and although she missed his clear mind and sharp eyes, his absence had given her a taste for what it was like to lead a team and get results.

When her phone started to jump and buzz on the table, she

lunged again. Cleared her throat. Saw the caller ID. 'Hello Brendan.'

'G'day, Ange. You staying cool?'

'Kind of,' she muttered, 'better if the aircon'd behave itself. What's up today?'

'Search underway since mid-morning. SES as far as the eye can see.'

'Oh.' She tried to keep her voice light, conceal the hurt that was stinging like a jellyfish. 'Thought you were going to let me know when operations started.'

'It's your day off, remember. You've been working like a Trojan the last few months. Anyway, I can handle it. Used to do it all the time before you joined me.'

She hesitated. 'Nothing to keep me in Melbourne, though.'

After a few more exchanges, he promised he'd be expecting her complete attention on the job, but not until Tuesday when she was due back.

She turned her face into the couch.

No call from David.

Dinner with the family.

The aircon on the blink.

And now, absolute confirmation that she was no longer in charge of a team.

Micelli's mother stood on the doorstep, silver hair brushed to fine silk cut snug round her face. She was mopping her brow with a lace-trimmed handkerchief, sun-spotted hands bearing witness to years in the sun. She wore a sleeveless black linen frock, amber beads picking up the colour of her sandals. 'Come in, Mumma. I'll be ready in a tick. Just got to clean my teeth.' She ducked into the bathroom.

'So messy, Angela. What happen if someone come to visit?'

'Who would visit me, Mumma?' she spluttered through a mouthful of toothpaste, bracing herself for what she knew was surely coming.

'You need husband, Angela. Your father and me, we sick of

seeing you live like this.'

Ten minutes later, dressed and ready to leave, Micelli threw an arm round her mother's shoulder and escorted her to the front door. 'What I need is a long holiday with plenty of beach and bike and beer. Not a husband. Come on, or we'll be late,' she said, 'and if we're late, the man on the white horse may have left before we get there.'

'What man? What you not tell me?'

Micelli pulled her mother outside, locked the door and walked her down the path to where her father sat waiting in the car. 'Ciao bella. You look lovely. Red suits you.'

She leant over and kissed him on the cheek. 'Let's go, Dad. Can't keep Rosie waiting a minute longer.'

The Pantelerri household was bursting when Micelli and her parents arrived. The women were gathered in the kitchen tossing salad, slicing bread, draining pasta. The men were outside on the patio, beers in hand, swapping stories of the week gone by. Micelli noticed her nephew, Nick, had joined the men. A shadow of stubble, brown eyes squinting into the late afternoon sun, fashioned hair tumbling over his brow.

'Hey stranger,' she said.

'Ange,' he said, eyes lingering on her, 'great to see you.' He swept his hand round to include his father, uncles, cousins. 'I need someone to deliver me from all this boredom.'

'Hey, punk,' someone said, but Nick was not to be interrupted.

'Can't wait for tomorrow and some action.'

'The tennis?' she asked, checking an incoming text on her phone. *Fed sq tix box 10.30 tmr xxx d*. She felt her face redden. Slugged down a mouthful of pinot.

Nick leant towards her, put his mouth close to her ear as if confiding a secret. 'I'm working in the bars this year.'

Now considerably taller than her, she was forced to look up at him. 'No more ball boy?'

'Too old, Ange. Besides, there's after parties and that sort of stuff. More interesting than locker room tours.' He took a swig of beer. 'What about you? Guess you're not lucky enough to be rostered on anymore?'

'Not now I'm in homicide, but I am going tomorrow.'

'You and—?' He left the question hanging.

'Now, now. No need to be cheeky. I'm still the best aunt you've got.'

Nick was referring to David Romano, whom she'd been seeing since their first meeting at a barbecue just after Christmas. He was in Australia for the tennis, marketing manager for one of the big brands, which one she couldn't recall. She wondered how Nick sensed she was planning on being with the New Yorker tomorrow. 'Will you be working Rod Laver arena?'

'Dunno yet, but I'll text if I am. You can have a drink,' he said, his left eyebrow rising, 'like on the house.' His next words were impossible to hear as rain hammered down, large drops pelting the pool into a froth and forcing everyone inside. So much for the weather forecast.

The sun had dipped into the west when the line search was called to a halt. All day to find a few more bones that might fit into the clothing found earlier, and two side-by-side child-sized mounds. Then in the last few minutes before dusk they'd located the largely decomposed body of an adult male that had been shoved headfirst into a mineshaft. Someone had concealed the entrance with branches and ripped-out gorse bushes. Brittle leaves and browned-off thicket heaped up ready for a match, like some careful farmer might do if he was clearing land in preparation for spring pasture.

O'Leary heaved his six-foot frame into the caravan and sat heavily on a bench seat. He fingered the St Michael's medal he wore round his neck, present from his mother, Kathleen, when he was laid up last year. 'This'll keep you safe, love,' she'd said, tears welling in her grey eyes, same colour as his. 'After this, no more hospitals, Bren. Promise me, won't you?'

He opened his notebook and wrote *Child* on the first line with a question mark beside it. Added, *if found clothing belongs to found bones*. On the next line, *Adult male, decomposed*, another line down, *Two mounds*. Perhaps graves, perhaps not. They wouldn't know until chief forensic investigator Rod Jones came to scan whatever was under the soil, now matted with leaf litter and dead grass. The person responsible, or persons plural he noted, must know this land. Know it like the back of their hand. And know that no one else was likely to stumble through it on an autumn mushroom hunt and kick over old bones. Or notice a decaying body, the stink of which must have pitched and swirled in the air for weeks if O'Leary's experience with the bloated carcasses of dead sheep was anything to go on. He wondered if something new would turn up in the morning, or if they'd found the total of the killer's handiwork.

There had to be a logic. And it had to be connected to Krakauer. He didn't think he was looking at some random serial killer or thrill seeker. More like someone who had to dispose of people when they were no longer useful. Child porn could explain the kids. There was also the stuff in a couple of sheds the Drug Squad would be interested in. 'Lot to sort through here,' he'd said, when he phoned Inspector Goddings, his boss at Homicide. 'Forensics'll have their hands full getting this lot excavated, bagged, sent to Macleod.'

'Make sure you do everything right,' Goddings said. 'I know you've got Nguyen with you, a good solid officer. I want all the i's dotted, all the t's crossed.' A few months back several cases had crumbled because some idiot cops hadn't sworn their affidavits. Goddings wasn't about to let that happen again. 'How's the leg, by the way? Holding up?'

O'Leary assured him he was in good health, and there was no need to worry on that account. 'SES's coming back in the morning. They're going downstream along the river.'

'Need divers?' asked Goddings.

'Not right now, but yes, we might later on. Wouldn't look good if we prosecuted and something else turned up later.'

'Rightio,' said Goddings. 'Sounds like we might have broken into Krakauer's child porn business at last. And a good job that is. Thanks to you.' His firm voice left no doubt in O'Leary's mind that he had his boss's full support and cooperation, dispelling worries he'd had while on sick leave.

O'Leary settled down to wait for Nguyen to return. Birds darted through the dusk, on the wing for the thousands of insects that were swarming round the arc lights set up by the SES. He'd read somewhere that the average bird needs to eat half its body weight each day to stay alive. He wondered what might happen if they ate too much, like the ones now gorging on flying ants and fat grey moths. He could hear beaks snap in tight staccato, yet the mass of moths and other visitors attracted to the lights didn't seem to be diminishing.

Harsh silhouette-bodies began to appear over the crest of the slope. Nguyen plodded towards O'Leary, his slight frame standing out from the shapes of the other searchers. On reaching the van, he grabbed a drink and sandwiches from an Esky someone had lugged to headquarters along with fold-up chairs and a gazebo. He pulled up a chair and plonked into it. Black hair plastered to his forehead with sweat, he twisted the top from a bottle labelled Organic Lemonade and swilled it down in one go. He peeled the plastic wrap from a round of sandwiches and began to munch through ham and mayonnaise, beetroot and lettuce. 'Not bad,' he said through a mouthful. 'Want one?'

'Nah,' said O'Leary. 'Already put on five kilos. If I don't watch it, I won't even be able to walk properly, let alone run.'

'You'll be okay, Boss,' murmured Nguyen. 'Seen you too many times before when things got—' His voice trailed off as a cockatoo screeched overhead, swooping into a dead tree where its mates were hanging like an old woman's wash of white handkerchiefs.

'Changed my mind. Is there a corn beef and pickles one?'

The sound of a car pulling into the driveway, followed by a door closing, broke into the evening racket of birds and insects. O'Leary watched a figure casting a long shadow climbing into overalls. Frank Sutcliffe had arrived and was getting ready to work.

'G'day Frank,' O'Leary called, getting up and stretching his leg, which had stiffened while sitting. Sutcliffe who looked fit and tanned as usual, was fiddling with the straps of a headlamp. 'Didn't get you off the boat, did we?'

Sutcliffe extended a hand. 'Brendan. Good to see you back on deck. Festival of the Sails on soon, but the crew can do without me for the moment, especially seeing I'm hosting various bods attending an international forensics and autopsy conference we're convening in Melbourne as from tomorrow. What about you? How's the family?'

The twins had spent the holidays with O'Leary while their mother, Claire, and her partner, Karen, had bush walked in Tasmania, a trip arranged and paid for long before the shooting. It'd worked out well, him being on sick leave and having time. Lazy summer days, the kids climbing into bed for morning stories, going to the beach, playing cards, watching movies on TV. 'Yeah, not bad thanks, Frank. Can't complain.'

They walked over to the caravan and climbed up the couple of steps. 'Professor Frank Sutcliffe,' said O'Leary introducing him to Nguyen, who was hunched over a laptop. 'State's senior pathologist.'

Nguyen jumped up, shook Sutcliffe's hand, offered him a drink. Declining the offer, Sutcliffe asked, 'Forensics here?'

'Rod Jones is over at the mineshaft,' said Nguyen. 'Been there for an hour or more.'

'Assume the body's in situ?'

'Ready to lift it out whenever you say the word.'

'Better get a wriggle on then. You coming, Brendan?' O'Leary and Sutcliffe walked the hundred or so metres to where arc lights were set up in a semi-circle. Sniffing the night air as if it might carry answers, Sutcliffe said, 'Pretty dry summer. Glad my family sold up our farm. I'd hate to be beholden to the weather, trying to turn sheep into money these days.'

'Yeah,' agreed O'Leary, thinking about his family's farm, his father's expectation that he as the eldest son would stay home, take over its running. O'Leary was pretty sure Kevin had never forgiven him for heading to the city, leaving him to work on until one of the younger sons showed an interest in potatoes. 'Can be pretty tough on the land.'

Every couple of seconds a camera flashlight went off. Swatting away insects, Sutcliffe squinted down a shaft. O'Leary peered into the hole. It may once have been the conduit for tonnes of gold-embedded quartz to be brought to the surface, making a fortune for the man who had dug it, but it could just as easily have been another false lead, dug in hope, abandoned in despair. The lights caught the gleam of what had been an expensive black leather shoe. Wedged about two metres down. Body twisted sideways where it had come to rest on a ledge. Grey suit. Soft stripe. Looked to be a silver-grey business shirt. Hard to tell after time and death had had their way.

'Rod? Room for one more?' Swift as a cat Sutcliffe glided down the ladder. O'Leary tried to kneel, ended up lying full stretch on the dirt, head hanging over the shaft entrance.

'Not a lot left of him, I'm afraid,' said Jones. 'Best come over here and examine his skull. Think you'll find the cause of death there.'

Sutcliffe pulled on gloves, before carefully positioning himself so as not to dislodge any of the markers the forensics team had placed near the body. 'Looks like a gunshot wound to the head,' he called up to O'Leary. He removed a small ruler from his top pocket, reached forwards to where the skull was resting on a protruding ledge of rock. 'Almost 10mm cranial perforation where the bullet entered. Approximately 12mm bevelling on exit. My guess is a handgun. Held close against the forehead. Teeth seem in good order. Not much else to see until we get him horizontal.'

'Any idea how long he's been down there?' O'Leary asked.

'Months, most likely. Hard to say.'

'No driver's licence in his jacket?'

Jones laughed. 'You remember the one we got out of the mineshaft near Dunolly? No head. No hands. But the silly buggers had left the victim's wallet in his back pocket. This crook was marginally smarter. Left us with a complete body far as I can see, but no ID.'

O'Leary listened intently until Jones and Sutcliffe began on the technicalities of moving the body out of the shaft. 'I'll leave you blokes to it.' He picked his way gingerly towards HQ. Once inside, he filled the kettle. 'How're the missing person files stacking up?'

Nguyen looked up. 'Until we know the approximate date of

death, it's going to be hard to narrow down.'

'Try missing persons from July onwards. Suit size 42, according to Jones. Armani, so can't have been short of a quid.'

'Age?'

'Sutcliffe reckons he's somewhere between late thirties and early forties.'

Nguyen scratched at a mosquito bite on his hand. 'If you're making a coffee, I'll have one. Any idea of height?'

'About 180 centimetres. How many does that leave us?'

'Give me half an hour and I'll tell you.'

O'Leary poured boiling water into mugs. 'Dunno which is worse. Cheap tea bags or catering-quality instant coffee.' He placed a steaming cup near Nguyen's elbow and left the van. Pulling a camp chair under one of the lights, he opened his notebook to a blank page, jotted *male – approx 40 – well-dressed – date of death?* Another line down, *HOW + WHY = WHO*. Part of the how seemed easy – gunshot wound to the head. But how had he ended up headfirst in a mineshaft on an out-of-the-way property near Glenlyon? Had he gone willingly with someone he trusted, or was he abducted, before a gun was held to his head and the trigger pulled? In fact, he could have been killed elsewhere and his body transported to the site. Why Glenlyon? He stopped scribbling. Took a swig from his mug and looked up at the ever-increasing insect population circling the lights. 'Found anything yet?' he called to Nguyen.

'Not yet. Filtering some info in the mispers database. The internet's not real quick in the country.'

Being at Krakauer's place was where the why came into it. Maybe the victim had a predilection for child pornography? Could even be someone in the dark web videos. But that only made sense if there was a blackmail opportunity. Drugs? Krakauer was deep into the trade. Could tempt almost anyone who wanted fast money. And certainly not going away despite the wholesale destruction of several drug gangs operating in Melbourne a few years back. Since then, there'd been many more quick to fill a gap in the market. Pseudoephedrine in soap powder imports from Vietnam. Butyl stuff coming in from China. Ships escorted into harbours by the navy. Raids on factories and houses. If he was to believe what the commissioners were warning, there were more drugs in circulation now than ever before. And tobacco. Another federal policy that had backfired. If he knew who the victim was, he might have a better idea of the reason why he ended up in a mineshaft. Beyond that, further thoughts eluded him. 'Think I'll turn in for the night. You right to lock up?' he said through the flywire.

He lumbered over to another caravan, this one set up by the SES. 'Just in case you need to stay overnight,' Scarface had said. 'Not flash, but it'll save you driving into Hepburn or Daylesford if you're out here late. Be lucky to get anywhere to sleep in them towns at this time of year, any rate.' O'Leary unlocked the door, shone his torch around. Three beds already made up. He chose the one furthest from the door, tested the mattress, firm as a rock. One hand against the overhead cupboard, he levered off his boots, shoved them against the wall. Stripping down to his underwear, he clambered in under a sheet.

A little over four months ago, a bullet had pierced his flesh, ripping apart thigh muscles, tearing them from the bone. Staring for days on end at the ceiling of a hospital room, he'd thought about a lot of things. Family stuff mainly. Stuff he'd put off thinking about for years. Now he was glad to be back at work, even if he was mainly restricted to sitting on his arse. 'Light duties' the force called it. He breathed deep. Tried to clear his mind.

Stretching out, he felt the familiar grab of muscle in his right thigh. He tried rubbing the cramp out with his fingers, cautiously repositioned his leg. No change. Struggling upright, he used both hands to knead his thigh. Finally the muscle loosened. He shuffled to the kitchen end of the van, checked the fridge. Bottles of water, soft drinks, a couple of beers. Deciding his mother's cramp remedy might help, he poured water into a glass, dashed in one, probably two, teaspoons of salt followed by a stick of sugar, swirled it round with a plastic spoon, swallowed it in one go. Taking a bottle of water, he padded back to bed.

Hearing the crunch of footsteps outside, he rolled over to face the wall, waited for Nguyen to open the door. Vaguely aware that a torch was being shone round, he buried his head under the pillow. Too many thoughts clamouring for attention. But one thought comforted him. No murder charges laid on Krakauer as yet, but this afternoon's discoveries made it seem like they were not far away.

MONDAY

O'LEARY TOOK a swig of tea. He lifted the lid on one of the plastic containers lined up on the bench near the stovetop. Individual packets of cereal. He turned a box on its side and read the spin. *Twenty-five per cent of the recommended daily intake of calcium and iron and half of the RDI for folate*. Should be good for something. He ripped open a box and let dried flakes of malty cereal drift into a chipped bowl. Yawning, he poured on milk.

'Morning Boss,' said Nguyen as he climbed up the steps of the van. 'Sleep well?'

'You're an early bird. Heard you come in last night, but didn't hear you get up this morning.'

'Heard me come in where?'

'Here.'

'I didn't. Slept on the bench seat at HQ. Thought it was easier. Didn't want to disturb you.'

O'Leary stopped eating. 'I distinctly heard someone come in after I was in bed and shine a torch.'

'Wasn't me. Must be those painkillers you're taking. Giving you hallucinations. Anyway, think I know whose body it is in the mineshaft.'

O'Leary scratched his head, frowned. 'Whose?'

'Vincent Valentino's.'

Tried to focus on the conversation. 'The same bloke that's a big

17

name in horse racing circles?'

'Yeah. Seems he left town in late August and no one's seen him since. I came across a report from the *Fin Review* about him going to China for business. His wife knows nothing about it.'

'You've rung her?'

Nguyen nodded. 'She listed him as a missing person last September. Course we'll have to wait for positive ID, but everything's pointing in that direction if her description's accurate. Same size Armani suit, similar colour. Black leather Prada shoes, size 11. Eighteen carat gold LaCroix watch.'

O'Leary got up, scraped his leftovers into the bin, squirted detergent into the bowl. 'She's not intending to come up here and identify him, is she?' he asked, swirling water into the sink, brushing the bowl clean.

Nguyen described his conversation with Adriana Valentino. She'd been matter of fact on the phone, not mincing her words when it came to describing the state of their marriage, apparently more or less arranged when they were teenagers. They'd had two kids, the eldest, a law student currently overseas for the summer, and the other staying with friends at Lorne. 'She didn't seem surprised that it might be her husband upside down in a mineshaft.'

O'Leary wiped the bowl, hanging the tea towel back on its hook. 'Really? A story we need to know by the sounds of it. Good work, by the way.' He placed the bowl in an overhead cupboard and shut the door.

'How long do you reckon before we can get a positive ID?'

O'Leary bit his bottom lip. 'If you mean forensically, depends what we've got on file. If we have to start from scratch, then a day? Maybe two? Call Mrs Valentino back. Make arrangements for her to meet me at the morgue this afternoon. At least, she'll be able to identify his belongings. If they are his, that is. But that still won't identify the remains.'

Nguyen nodded.

'And the other bones?'

'Sutcliffe says there's not much to go on.'

O'Leary slid onto a bench seat covered in beige vinyl, opened his notebook to the page he'd written on last night. *Bones. Two mounds waiting to be excavated. Adult male. But no clue as to whose bones. Are there bodies buried in the mounds?* He flipped the book closed, stretched his arms upwards then clasped them behind his neck. 'This'll take time. Got to get DNA samples from the remains,' he said, wiping sweat from his brow, 'and there might be more than one person whose bones we've found. Then we check the results against data already held, assuming there is something already stored. If not, back to square one.' He dropped his hands onto the tabletop.

'Do you think the mounds are where the missing Beaumaris kids were put?'

O'Leary grimaced. 'Good chance. Otherwise, it's more trawling through missing kids' files. Going on wild goose chases.'

Nguyen filled the kettle.

O'Leary opened his notebook again. His pen scratched words across the paper until they filled a page, then another. If it was his kids whose bones had been found, he'd want the cops to make a careful report. Something with enough details for a crime brief, but one that also understood the pain of it all. Then he caught himself. How could he know what the pain might be? He might have a better inkling if it fell to him to break the news to the parents. And he was pretty sure that would be a job for him. But know? No way. And he hoped he never would know. He patted his trouser pockets, then his shirt pocket. 'You seen my phone?'

Nguyen brought over a cup of tea. 'Nah. When did you last use it?'

Getting up, O'Leary ran his hands along the length of the seat, felt down the back. 'Yesterday, just before Sutcliffe got here. Remember, I phoned Goddings?' He lifted papers, ran his eyes over the table, opened the fridge. 'Thought I left it on the bench here last night along with my keys.'

'I'll ring it,' said Nguyen.

The phone rang out.

'Better duck over to HQ. See if I left it there. Call me in two.' O'Leary stepped down and half hopped, half stumbled over a hundred metres of parched ground to where the headquarters caravan was parked. Climbing into the van, he rechecked his pockets, turned over papers on the table, searched the back of the bench seat where he'd last been sitting. He stuck his head out the door, yelled across to Nguyen. 'Call me now.' He waited, yelled again, stumbled down the steps and back to the van where he'd slept.

'Did you call?' he asked on his return, breathing hard.

'Three times.'

O'Leary tossed bedding onto the floor, pulled the mattress away from the wall, shook down the pillow. He slid onto a seat, massaged his forehead with both hands.

'Thoughts?'

He raised his head, groaned. 'Worst case scenario?' A knock on the side of the van prevented him continuing. 'Yeah?' he said, opening the flywire.

'Found this over near the house.'

O'Leary snatched a plastic bag containing a phone from the hand of an SES volunteer. Turned it over. His all right. He recognised the scratch on the screen. 'Where'd you say you found it?'

'Near the house. We were line-searching the front garden and one of our blokes stepped on it. Show you where if you like.'

O'Leary followed him across the paddock to Krakauer's front fence and through the front gate. 'Just there, where that marker is.' O'Leary knelt down on his good leg, surveyed the scene. Left-hand side of the path, about two metres from the front verandah.

He limped over to HQ where Nguyen was hunched over a laptop, picked the satellite phone off the bench, tapped in Claire's number. 'G'day Zoe, love,' he said when his daughter answered, 'you ready for school yet?'

Her pert voice scolded him. 'Course not, Dad. It's still holidays, silly billy.'

He grinned, chatted a bit, asked for Jack.

'Dad, what happens if one of our chooks gets lettuce in her eye?'

'Well, Jack, to tell you the truth, I haven't been home for a day or two,' he said, hoping that his neighbour Bonnie had remembered to feed and water the two hens in his backyard.

He heard muffled giggling. 'She'd be called a chicken Caesar salad.' Jack's infectious laugh rumbled down the line. 'Get it?' he spluttered, 'a chicken sees-a-salad!' Not waiting for his father to respond, he resorted to spelling the word out, 's-e-e-s a salad.'

'You got me a beauty, Jack. Wait til I tell Ange. Hey Jack, if mum's there I'll have a quick word. Love you, Jack.' While he waited for Claire, Nguyen pushed a mug of fresh tea towards him across the table. It was one of those mugs that people get for Christmas with a cellophane packet of cheap chocolates inside. This one was emblazoned with a flurry of tiny red hearts falling as snow on Santa sitting in his sleigh. *Merry Xmas* it proclaimed. No reindeers in sight. Mustn't have been enough money in the job to do the whole panorama.

'G'day,' said Claire, still on a high from her Tasmanian bush walk judging by her tone. She assured him the school holidays were progressing well and not to rush back to town on the twins' account as Karen's mum was arriving within the hour to take them camping for a couple of nights.

'Where to?' He hoped his voice didn't betray the hurt her news had brought. It should be him taking his kids camping, not his wife's partner's mother.

'She's got a van down at Ocean Grove. Remember? I told you about it the other day.'

'They'll be inside at night, won't they? Door locked?'

'You sure you're okay with being back at work?'

O'Leary slurped on his tea, shot a look towards Nguyen who seemed to be wholly focused on a computer screen. 'Yeah,' he said slowly, 'just thinking about some of the stuff going on here, that's all.'

'Take it easy, Brendan. Karen's mum'll get the twins to phone you as soon as they get to the beach.'

O'Leary pushed the mug in circles on the tabletop watching the rising steam dissipate. Already too late, he knew that. 'Phone's not working properly in the bush.' His mouth was dry. 'Only got the satellite phone, Claire,' He wanted to tell her to call him immediately if she had the slightest hint of something being awry but couldn't think of how to say it. In the end he rang off, said he'd phone later. 'Anyone been over Krakauer's house?'

Nguyen raised his head. 'Forensics turned the place inside out. Hard drives, laptops, other stuff. Didn't you see the report?'

He nodded. 'Still. Might wander over.'

Nguyen turned back to the computer. 'I'll print a copy for when you get back. And,' holding up the bag containing O'Leary's phone, 'want me to send this to forensics?'

O'Leary closed his notebook and slid off the seat, taking his weight on the good leg. 'Yeah, that'd be good. Ring the Remand Centre, too, will you. Tell them I want to interview Krakauer this afternoon. Say four o'clock.' He half swung, half walked down the two steps before he poked his head back in. 'Do I need keys?'

'Not according to the SES. But you'll need these.' Nguyen handed him a pack containing gloves, a disposable overall and booties which he pushed into a trouser pocket.

Out in the paddock SES volunteers were trooping towards the gully, carrying tools, coils of rope, shovels, buckets. Buckets could be for the soil that would be removed from the mounds. Whenever that might be. Scarface sauntered past and waved. 'Good day for it.' O'Leary nodded and walked towards Krakauer's house.

Micelli eased on a pair of tailored navy shorts and a white linen shirt, jammed her phone between shoulder and ear, returned a missed call. 'Ah, it's you,' she said, when O'Leary answered. 'What's with the long number?' She listened as O'Leary explained about his phone.

'I'm worried that whoever took it might've copied my contacts.'

She filled a water bottle and threw it into her backpack along with sunscreen and a floppy hat. 'Have you told Nguyen? He's a phone wiz.'

He mumbled something but she didn't catch it.

'By the way, there's nothing online about Krakauer. Weren't the media informed?'

'Didn't need to be. They're camped at the gate. Binoculars, drones, TV trucks. You name it.'

She breathed in through her nose, out through her mouth, counted to three. 'You know as well as I do that by using the media we can alert people who might know something to come forward.' She located her wallet on the kitchen bench, checked for cash.

'Yeah, or alert them not to, more like it.'

No matter how many times they'd worked on cases together, getting O'Leary to make a statement or call a media conference was like getting a dog to the vet. 'Not going to buy that one, Brendan. Anyway, gotta go.' She rang off and tossed the phone into her backpack and zipped it closed. She closed up, took her bike from the shed and pedalled off down the street towards the beach, the sun's warmth on her back. Just past the Spotswood power station she craned her neck to see which side of the Yarra the punt was on. She was in luck, it was chugging across the river to the west. Wheeling her bike down to the dock she joined a ten-strong group of riders older than her parents, dressed in lycra and high-vis vests, propping up fancy e-bikes. 'G'day love,' said a man sporting a grey beard as long as Max Gawn's. 'Lovely day for a ride.' She nodded. Wheeled her bike onto the punt and stood it along the side rail. 'Beaut bike,' he said, following her on board. 'Get it for Christmas?' Peering at the front crankset, he ran a finger over the chain, bent down to get a closer look. She could see his white backside through his shorts as clearly as if he'd been wearing sheer black pantyhose. 'Doesn't look like it's gone far. Ride often, do you?' She moved to the rear of the punt, looked the other way, and was relieved when her interlocutor's attention was drawn to a battery problem by a fellow rider. When the punt landed she was first off, pedalling in the opposite direction to the group who were still arguing about which of the beachside cafés they should stop at for morning coffee.

Pulling up at Flinders Street Station she could see David Romano standing in the lee of the ticket box in Federation Square that was set up especially for the tennis. He was dressed in an open-necked checked shirt the colour of dried orange peel. On anyone else it would look horrible, but against his southern Italian skin it was perfect. Tan leather loafers. Beige shorts. No hat. 'Ciao,' she called, waving to him from across the street. Shrugging off her pack, then just as quickly putting it back on again when she felt the breeze blow icy-cold against her back. Her shirt was sodden. What had she been thinking? A change of clothes, at the very least. You're an idiot Ange, she said under her breath. As if he's up for more than a day at the tennis. Especially with a sweat-drenched cop whose only knowledge of the game is what she can glean from Sunday's paper.

'Ciao bella.' He galloped to the pedestrian lights and taking her by the arm, pressing a warm kiss on both cheeks. 'Hey—good to see you. You look great.' His grin displayed a set of teeth that must have set him back a few dollars at a fancy New York cosmetic dentist. She squinted up at him. 'And you've come by cycle. Very European.' His grin widened. He grabbed her bike and deftly steered it through the crowd strolling along the Yarra's edge, his other arm linked in hers. She was not accustomed to this level of chivalry.

Once inside the main arena, they found their seats, mercifully a little shaded. Blue plexicushion surface, retractable roof open to the Melbourne summer, expected to reach 37 degrees by midafternoon. Two Russian women were exchanging slugs from the baseline, each shot punctuated by loud grunting from one, high-pitched moans from the other. The blonde with the thick plait slapping against her back was winning handsomely. Match point, the victor thrust an obligatory fist in the air before running to the net to air kiss cheeks with her opponent. Next up, Markus Kross versus an Australian newcomer, Thomas Lilley.

'No chance,' gruffed Micelli's neighbour who was sporting a green-and-gold hat, a green-and-gold t-shirt emblazoned with a map of Australia, and clutching a green-and-gold flag depicting a boxing kangaroo. As far as she could see he was only missing the parallel stripes of green and gold zinc cream on his cheeks. 'Only 17, you know.' He flourished a copy of the morning's *Gazette* at her. 'Dunno why they persist in saying Aussies are going to win when they haven't got a hope.'

Micelli scanned the page, more picture than writing. 'Seems like the Estonian's the full bottle.'

David looked at her, eyebrows raised. 'Full bottle?'

She grinned. 'Means he's the expert.'

'Oh,' he said, nodding, 'kinda like it's all in there already?'

'Yeah.' She didn't know how to explain the phrase any better.

'Hey, want me to grab a soda before they start?'

Glancing at him sideways, aquiline nose, hint of dark stubble, soft eyelashes, she almost forgot the question. 'That'd be nice. Something cold and fizzy.'

An army of adoring fans dressed in green and gold, brandishing flags emblazoned with a boxing kangaroo, ran through chants in preparation for the match at hand. 'Aussie Aussie Aussie, Oi Oi Oi.' Not particularly motivating, Micelli reflected, but she couldn't help admiring their attempts to whip the crowd into a Mexican wave. The warm-up complete, the umpire called time. David scrambled up the steps and slid in beside her. 'All I could find.' He thrust a can of Coke at her.

She smiled. 'Thanks David. The Aussie won the toss. He's elected to serve.' She looked towards the northern end where a scrawny kid dressed in baggy grey shorts and a five-sizes-too-big yellow-and-grey-striped t-shirt was bouncing a ball with the flat of his right hand, racquet gripped like a club in his left. Down the southern end, a thickset blond dressed in white shorts and a shirt printed with blue flags was dancing from foot to foot behind the baseline, wholly concentrated on the first point. The chair umpire held up a hand, called something to the players. The Australian looked up, continued to bounce the ball with his palm.

'Who's that?' David whispered, indicating a tall man dressed in grey and pale blue who was making his way down the stairs to the front row, delaying the start of play.

Micelli looked over to see him squeezing past others towards a vacant seat in the middle of the row. 'Huh. Well, if it isn't our brand-new police minister, the Honourable Phillip Sinclair. In the President's Box, no less. Thinks he's smart, that one, but there's a few skeletons in his cupboard still to see the light of day.' David cocked his head enquiringly. She raised an eyebrow. 'You get to find out all sorts of things as a detective. Trouble is, you can't tell anyone.'

He ran a finger lightly up and down her forearm. 'I wonder if there's a way to make you talk.'

O'Leary scanned Krakauer's house from the front gate. Built sometime in the 1980s on top of a slight rise overlooking the gully, it was protected from the south by a row of cypress trees, dusty branches tracing arcs in the dirt beneath them. Two sheds, an old water tank on its side, an axe head buried in a chopping block in front of a woodheap. Dog kennel. A chain tethered to the ground with a rusted railway spike. Any dog tied up there wouldn't have had more than a couple of metres to walk in circles. He ambled round the house perimeter, fenced on three sides with star pickets and wire mesh, solid enough to keep a toddler confined. The front fence was a fancier affair made from cream-painted pickets, a few struggling shrubs planted at neat intervals along it. Lace curtains in all the windows, blinds pulled low. Impossible to see in. A rectangle of red brick, green iron roof, cream aluminium windows. Budget hadn't been wasted on an architect. The path to the front door was covered in leaves and debris from nearby eucalypts, dried off weeds drooped from the guttering and a gnarled rose bush struggled to produce a few pink blooms near the front door. He plucked the protective gear pack out of his pocket, donned gloves and booties, opened the front door.

The house was divided by a central passage. Beige carpet, lighter beige walls, natural timber trim. Doors open to the two front rooms. He sniffed the air. Woodsmoke? Fried bacon? Something astringent, too. Perhaps fly spray? 'Anyone home?' he called. More out of habit than expectation. Silence. He closed the front door behind him.

Black metal-framed double bed to the right; two singles, also black metal, in the other, no mattresses. He walked towards the double bed and over to the window where he tugged on a set of Venetian blind cords. Strips of light flooded in. Beside the double bed frame he could see where a night table had been, its feet leaving small square imprints in the carpet. No evidence of a bed side table on the other side. Perhaps a chair in the corner, judging by the width of the indents. A stain near the end of the bed, brownish-grey, like a cup of coffee had been spilt and no one had bothered to clean it up. Wardrobe along the length of one wall, rail, shelves and drawers all empty. The bottom shelf where shoes had most likely been kept was lined with newspaper. O'Leary bent as far as he could manage, read the date as Wednesday 24th January 2001. A full-length mirror was glued to the inside of one door. He examined the bedhead. In places the metal was scratched, but his eyes were drawn to the two sets of almost parallel lines etched into the paintwork, less than half a metre apart. He wondered why forensics hadn't removed the bed for testing as well.

The second bedroom was much the same, wardrobe built in, no other furniture except for the beds. He opened the Venetians, peered at the bedheads which appeared unmarked, pulled open the wardrobe doors. His eye was caught by an orange power cord dangling from the wardrobe ceiling, similar to three phase cords he'd seen in industrial workshops.

Continuing down the hallway he came to a bathroom on the right, opposite a toilet and linen cupboard. Another room on the left. When he opened the door two mice scampered across the floor, squeezed themselves under the skirting board and disappeared from sight. This room, similar to the other bedrooms, contained only a single bed frame. No Venetians. O'Leary pulled open the wardrobe. A few wire coat hangers, a pillow on the top shelf, and neatly folded into a corner, a sleeping bag. Why had they been left behind by forensics? He crouched down as far as his right leg would let him, put his nose into the space and sniffed. Mousey? Probably his imagination, but he thought he could detect a whiff of aftershave.

Returning to the bathroom where a towel was draped over a rail, he opened a mirrored wall cabinet. Tube of toothpaste, toothbrush, plastic disposable razor. He pulled back a plastic curtain onto a tiled shower recess. Floor dry. A bar of soap rested in a ceramic holder. He touched it. Something slimy adhered to his glove. The sort of sliminess soap gets when water has been allowed to settle around it.

He walked back down the passageway and out into the brittle

morning light.

'You got that report?' O'Leary said as soon as he stepped up into the van. 'There's either some slack investigation that's gone on, or someone's living at Krakauer's. They couldn't have missed a towel hanging in the bathroom, could they? Thing's damp, I swear. And the bed frames. Why didn't they take them away for testing?'

Nguyen raised his eyebrows. 'House was completely emptied according to this.' He passed over the report.

O'Leary heaved onto a seat and flicked through it. All mattresses removed plus bed linen; no results as yet. Carpets tested for bloodstains. Only one small area in the front double bedroom showed positive. Not conclusive as to the source of the blood, further tests underway. No blood detected on any walls or ceilings. A long list of video and camera equipment, tripods, lights, backdrops, as well as computer stuff. Fridge and pantry contents noted, photographed, removed. Bathroom cabinet emptied of contents – the usual shaving and hygiene stuff, muscle rub, painkillers, several prescription medicines including sleeping tablets and Valium. Chemical testing underway. No towel in the photos of the bathroom. Power cord clearly in view in the second bedroom. All wardrobes photographed before and after clothing removed and bagged. Inventory listed the usual men's stuff. No sign of a sleeping bag or pillow. Shoes and boots collected from outside, photographed, bagged. Everything sent for testing. A note that all personal effects most likely belonged to a male. Flicking to the last page, he could see no reason to doubt the professionalism of the team who'd carried out the examination. 'House needs another go-through. Get whoever's on field duty at Macleod to get here ASAP,' he said. 'And tell them to look for tyre tracks. I'd better get on the road. Wouldn't be a spare phone somewhere, would there? I can't take the satellite one with me.'

Nguyen opened a plastic container, rummaged through cords, chargers, batteries. 'Here,' he said, handing a phone to O'Leary along with its power cord. 'You can plug it in on the way to Melbourne.'

O'Leary turned it over in his hand. 'This the number?' He

pointed to a sticker on the back of the case.

'Guess so. But you can always check the number when it's got some charge in it.'

'Huh?'

Nguyen pulled out his own phone. 'I'll show you how.'

O'Leary felt the power as the new Falcon surged down the narrow gravel road then onto the Calder. He'd wedged a rolled-up towel behind the small of his back. Might relieve the pain in his leg. Acres of farmland dotted with beef cattle, sheep seeking shade under stands of straggly gums. On the main road in Woodend a bakery advertised award-winning vanilla slices. He pulled in under a line of old oaks, killed the engine. He took a number, waited in line, ordered coffee and one of the slices. A girl who was probably filling in over the school holidays brought his order to the table, belly falling over the elastic of her black leggings. She smiled. Wished him a good day. Would Zoe turn out like this? Makeup gummed on near perfect skin, blackened eyes weighed down by the longest fake eyelashes he'd ever seen. He ate the slice, flicked through a community newsletter. Good to see that Rotary was on the case, cutting grass for pensioners and delivering early loads of chopped winter firewood.

Back in the car, it was time to put the foot down. He was meeting Mrs Adriana Valentino at the morgue. Traffic was light on the highway. Bypassed Gisborne, skirted Diggers Rest, past the raceway, on to the Tullamarine. Steel gantries spread themselves over the lanes, scanning for transponders. No longer a freeway since a road construction consortium did its deal with the government. O'Leary winced at the signature shrieks as he sped past Pascoe Vale, Strathmore, the Flemington high rises.

Last time he was at the morgue was for an autopsy. Watching, listening. Now he was to walk a woman through the process of what was needed to identify a dead husband. Even if she turned out to be as cold as seawater in winter, as Nguyen had hinted, it'd be a first if she didn't want to lean on him. At least for a bit.

He eased the car into a park under the shade of a ferny Robinia behind the building, fished in the glove box for a packet of painkillers, swigged down a couple with the remainder of a bottle of Glenlyon mineral water. Despite the towel, needles of pain tracked down his right leg from hip to knee. He edged himself out of the car, leant against the back door, zapped the locks shut. Perhaps time to visit the Men's and see what damage time in the country had done to his demeanour. But Adriana Valentino was waiting in the foyer. Dark hair caught in a ponytail. Single strand of pearls knotted level with her breastbone. Grey silk dress, cut full round the hips. Legs the colour of burnt caramel, feet slipped into black high-heeled sandals.

'Mrs Valentino?' he said, walking towards her, hand outstretched.

She jumped slightly at the mention of her name. 'Mr O'Leary?' She accepted his hand, hers warm, nails lacquered pale orange. 'I'm a bit early, sorry. The run up was much quicker than expected. Happy to wait if you've got things to do before we—' She paused, swallowed saliva.

He took her elbow and guided her into a small room off the foyer, shut the door. 'Can I get you a coffee?' he asked, gesturing towards a low-slung chair.

She sat on the edge of the chair. 'Actually, I'd rather get the thing over and done with, if that suits.'

He nodded. 'Need to go through some details first, Mrs Valentino. Won't take long.' He waited while she pushed back into the chair. 'Got your licence handy?' he said as gently as he could. She rummaged in her handbag, opened a black leather wallet and handed over the card. The photo was her, more than five years ago according to the issue date. No real change apart from hairstyle. Birthdate tallied with what car rego records had turned up. He handed it back. 'Sure I can't get you a drink?' he offered again. 'I could do with a coffee.'

'Oh, if you're having one,' she said quickly. 'Black. Strong. No sugar.'

He took the chance to duck into the Men's. Ordered their coffees on the way back. Sank down into a chair. Watched her face.

'Stupid man,' she said, turning her head from side to side. 'I told him he was an idiot. But would he listen?' Her voice trailed off. There was a light knock on the door. A young woman wearing an intern's badge carried in a tray, placed it on the coffee table, clicked the door shut behind her.

'An idiot?' he asked, stirring sugar into his cappuccino.

'I told him not to have anything to do with his cousin. He's only ever been bad far as I can see. Knew it was something to do with money laundering.'

'Sorry, I'm not quite following. What was to do with money laundering?'

'His murder,' she said quietly, as if it hurt to say the word.

O'Leary shifted awkwardly, thought about hitting record on his phone. Didn't. Wanted desperately for the painkillers to kick in. 'Murder? What makes you think that, Mrs Valentino?'

'Well, his cousin of course.'

'Cousin?' asked O'Leary, realising that he was sounding like a half-wit by repeating her words.

'Surprised you don't know him. Greg Anson. Bad egg. Always was. Always will be.'

O'Leary's eyebrows shot up. Anson was last seen at Tullamarine five months ago and hadn't been spotted since. Drug dealer. Money launderer. Probably much more. 'You don't happen to know where he is by any chance?'

'I hope I never see that gutter crawler ever again.' She slammed her coffee down on the table. Her cheeks were flushed.

'Any idea what type? Money laundering, that is,' he said, pulling himself forward with the aid of the chair arm.

She furrowed her brow. 'You mean how did he get the money?'

He nodded.

'However, whenever and whatever. My husband loved money.' Her tone had edged away from the recent flash of anger. She sounded almost like she cared. 'Couldn't get enough of it. You'd think he would've known better, man of his age. Not like he's still in his twenties.' Standing up, she said, 'Can I see his things now?'

He straightened his tie, shepherded her out of the room.

The room he led her into was dimly lit, floor-length royal blue curtains draping two walls. No comparison to the cold neon and stainless steel of the autopsy rooms. A couple of chairs were arranged in a corner, either side of a pedestal that supported a vase of white liliums. A long table stretched along one wall. O'Leary motioned her over and drew back a cover revealing several plastic bags containing shoes, trousers, jacket. She picked up the bag containing the shoes, turned it sideways, examined the wear on the heels. Next she picked up a small bag containing a watch. 'This is his stuff. For sure.' Tears fell silently down her cheeks. She made no attempt to wipe them away.

Nguyen was eating an egg and lettuce sandwich, courtesy of the SES vollies, when O'Leary called, told him what Adriana had said. 'Can you get together a brief about Anson? Can't recall all he was up to when he crossed our radar last year.'

'Sure thing,' Nguyen said.

'Any progress at your end?'

'SES's been working in the gully, went over the front and back yards at the house. Nothing to report so far.'

Finishing his sandwich, he stepped outside. Checked his weather app: 34 degrees, northwesterly, chance of a thunderstorm. Drab clouds were gathering on the horizon. He hoped it was rain, not smoke. Watching a squall of white cockatoos screeching across the sky, he strolled over to the gully. Half a dozen men in orange overalls were by the river, some on hands and knees. 'Hey,' he called, quickening his pace. 'Found something?'

Several heads turned.

Scarface straightened his ample body, began ambling up the slope towards him. 'Better have a geezer. Could be the skull.' Nguyen joined the men. He could see a rounded shape protruding slightly from the earth. Small, yellowish, a bit like a stone. 'C'mon youse blokes, stake it and we'll keep going,' Scarface said, scratching his head. 'Makes you wonder.'

Nguyen was about to call O'Leary when his phone rang. Macleod office. 'Yep?'

A sergeant introduced himself. 'You wanted to follow up the Krakauer property report? I've talked to the techies. We've still got tests outstanding.'

'What ones?'

'Bio data stuff mainly. Fingerprints, hairs, semen, blood.' He ran through the items as if he was checking a shopping list. 'We're also running some tests on floor covering samples.'

Was that a yell from further along the creek? Nguyen turned to face the west, ears pricked. 'Look mate, I've gotta go. But we need another site inspection according to the boss. Email me the stuff that's still ongoing. And let me know where the semen and blood came from.' He scrambled down the rocky bank of the dry creek bed, started to run towards where Scarface was lying on his guts, hands outstretched in front of him. 'Is he all right?' he called to the men milling round.

'Think so,' said one. 'Tripped over a rock or something. Says he's hurt his ankle.' Nguyen knelt down beside the man, rolled him gently on his side.

'It's okay, mate. We're all first-aid trained.'

'Sure,' said Nguyen. 'Leave it to you, then.'

Back at HQ, he settled in front of a laptop, began to read the available data about Gregory Anson. Forty last birthday; reported to have worked as a baker's assistant, plumber's assistant, bookie's assistant; no known current occupation. Suspected drug manufacturer and dealer to the well-off; suspected murderer of Simon Thomson-Paton, a socialite drug dealer who wound up shot, body dumped at the Organ Pipes park; suspected murderer of Charles de Havilland, another socialite drug dealer, found dead in a Ballarat hospital. Charged several times with drug-related offences; always represented by lawyer Elise Lanigan.

Nguyen recalled his visit the previous year to Anson's house, how his girlfriend Christina was scared. Pictures there of a little girl. Her daughter, definitely. But not clear if the kid was Anson's child. Then Anson disappeared. Last seen at Tullamarine airport September last year. Could be anywhere.

The Metropolitan Remand Centre was settled on the western plains, ash-grey like the grasslands surrounding it. O'Leary pulled up in the car park, no shade anywhere. Reception area glassy, one of those slanted roof-things jutting out at the front, popular on government buildings in the nineties. Useless for keeping rain off, but someone must have thought they looked decent enough. Showed his badge to the officer on the desk and announced his appointment to interview Krakauer. 'Has he got legal representation, do you know?'

The officer beamed, showing off a row of stumpy yellowed teeth set into thick grey gums. He could smell the smoke. She bent her head, checked a computer screen. At least a centimetre of regrowth along her hair parting where mousy brown met intense auburn. 'Said he doesn't need it,' she said, looking up, rolling her shoulders, arching her back. Her shirt buttons strained over her bust.

O'Leary sighed. 'Is there a duty solicitor available?'

She picked up a phone, fingernails bitten to the quick, beamed again after a quickly concluded conversation. 'Yep. Follow Officer Gauci,' she said as gaily as if she'd won Tattslotto, pointing towards a whisker-thin man who had slid in behind the woman without O'Leary noticing. Together Gauci and he walked the length of reception, turned right, entered a secure area. Gauci showed him into a room furnished with a table, its edges chipped, and four chairs, one of which bore the faint texta remains of an ejaculating penis.

The door opened and a young woman clomped in. Black Doc Martens, black jeans, black long-sleeved t-shirt. She adjusted rimless spectacles by poking them back up the bridge of her nose with a forefinger. She held out her hand, clear brown eyes meeting his. 'Julia Greene. Haven't met before, have we?' He waited for her to take a seat before outlining what he wanted to ask Krakauer. 'Sounds kosher,' she said, pushing her spectacles up her nose again. 'I'll buzz to say we're ready.'

Krakauer walked into the interview room. Like the officer on reception, he too was beaming. O'Leary quelled an urge to slap the smile off his face, recalling their last encounter in Sydney when Krakauer had given him a history lesson about gold mining in the Glenlyon area before telling him how much he loved children. There was a smell, like sour milk mixed with cheap aftershave. He hadn't noticed it before. 'Who's this?' asked Krakauer. He pointed a slender index finger towards Julia. Another waft of aroma when he raised his arm. She stood, introduced herself, proffered a hand. 'Ah you legal beagles,' he said, his eyes twinkling like a benevolent uncle's on Christmas Day, 'think you're God's gift. But the day I need you will be a sorry day indeed. So, without further ado, get out.' He sat opposite O'Leary, smile gone, glaring straight ahead. 'Go on!' he repeated. 'Out!' The guard who'd followed Krakauer in, approached the table. Krakauer turned his head forty degrees, hissed in his general direction. 'I said get her out.' Giving her spectacles one last push, she exchanged glances with O'Leary and left the room. Krakauer leaned back in his chair and ran fingers along his bald scalp as if separating strands of hair. The smile returned. A good set of teeth. Too perfect to be his own. 'Ah, Mr O'Leary, it's always a pleasure to see you. More questions for me? What about this time, I wonder? You know I'm taking the stand in court this week?' Like a light switch, able to turn menace off and on at will.

O'Leary ignored Krakauer's reference to Friday's scheduled court appearance for drug dealing. Instead, reading from his notebook, he rattled off the first few questions on his list. No comment. No comment. No comment. When he got to the fourth question, Krakauer drew in a sharp breath, began to cough like a kid trying to convince his mother he was sick enough for a day off school. 'Vincent Valentino's a name I would remember. Never met him, as far as I know.' There was that smell again, more sour milk than aftershave.

O'Leary scribbled something in his notebook, broke the rhythm. 'He says he knows you, Mr Krakauer. Met you at the races. Said it was a while ago.' A lame attempt. Kept his fingers crossed.

'Does he now? And what races might that be? Dogs, cars, horses? There's a lot of races going round, Mr O'Leary.' Ran his fingers over his scalp again.

Keep him talking. 'Horses. Valentino's a bookmaker. Place bet on a nag called Wild Pansy, I think he said. Thirty to one. Says you cleaned up more than a hundred and fifty thousand from him.

Offered to show me his book.'

'A hundred and fifty! Bullshit! Maybe eight. If he's got a hundred and fifty written down you should go him for tax evasion.' Laughing now.

O'Leary furrowed his brow, consulted his notebook. 'You're right. My apologies. It was one hundred and fifty thousand for something else. Not the bet.' He could see red splotches beginning to creep up Krakauer's neck. 'By the way, there's a few of your old friends wondering how you are. Remember Gregory Anson?'

A long pause. More smiling. 'How's your brother by the way?' Krakauer's comment landed like a kick from a horse. Last year Stephen O'Leary had got himself mixed up with drugs; men now dead. O'Leary slowly breathed in, just as slowly breathed out, kept his eyes on his notebook. Krakauer sniggered. 'I doubt Mr Anson will be worrying about me anymore.'

Soft voice, like a counsellor. 'Why's that, Mr Krakauer?'

'Because he's dead. Or didn't you know? Got killed up New South somewhere. Car accident I believe. Thought the police would have been onto that.'

'Is that right?' said O'Leary thoughtfully, looking up from the notebook page that was swimming in and out of focus. 'Well, I'll pass that on. We'll probably want to lay a wreath.'

Loud laughter. 'You know Mr O'Leary, you're a very funny man. I'm beginning to like you.'

Back in his office on Spencer Street, O'Leary picked up the phone. 'Mrs Valentino? Sorry to disturb you. We need to go over some things. Any chance I might drop round in say the next half hour?' He checked his watch, noted the time on a clean page in his notebook and scribbled down her address. He shoved the phone in his pocket, fossicked under papers until he located the keys to the Ford. He took the stairs down to the basement, trying to give his leg a bit of a stretch before the drive to Point Cook. At least he wouldn't be far from home when he'd finished. Thinking about dinner made his guts gurgle.

From the carpark he turned left into La Trobe Street, the Bolte

Bridge shimmering in the distance. He grabbed for his sunglasses from the console. The early evening sun blasting against a windscreen smeared with insect bodies was making it impossible to see anything. Unusually he had the road almost to himself. Melburnians were still on holidays.

He cruised along the highway keeping an eye out for the exit Adriana had told him to take. He resisted the urge to speed after the hoon darting in and out of lanes in a low-slung purple Datsun 240 sporting a home spray-job, leaving behind a trail of exhaust smoke. A half-broken P-plate flapped from a piece of wire on the back bumper. A driver on the right gave a good blast when Hoon ducked in front, nearly running up the back of a delivery van. O'Leary waited for the response and was not disappointed when the predictable two-finger salute was shoved out through the driver's side window. He shook his head. Obviously had never been involved in an accident. Not yet.

Foliage hid the steel-ruler edges of the Valentino residence, succulents softened driveway rockeries. Nearby water lapped against reeds and water plants. O'Leary had not ventured to this part of greater Melbourne before. No plans to purchase property, no friends to visit, no murders to investigate. Up until now at any rate. He couldn't discount anything yet in this case, especially not the theory that Valentino could have been murdered in his home, then later transported to Glenlyon. That was of course if the body *was* Valentino's. Sure it was his clothes, but could be anyone's body without empirical confirmation. He'd been annoyed that other jobs had taken priority over the case. What had McKinnon from Macleod said when he'd tried to set up a forensic sweep of the family home? 'If the victim's been dead for six months, we're not going to find anything today that we won't find tomorrow.'

Grey silk had been swapped for yoga pants and a t-shirt. 'You'll have to take me as you find me,' Adriana said as she gestured for him to come in. 'Haven't come to grips with it all as yet.' He crossed the threshold, waited for her to deadlock the front door, followed her into a sitting room with a panoramic view over the lake. Wisps of high cloud tinged pink, flotillas of moor hens and ducks crossing the water, a lone jogger on the shoreline. 'Coffee?

Something stronger?'

'A cup of tea'd be good,' he said, choosing a black leather armchair, placing his notebook on a glass-topped side table.

She slid open a pair of cupboard doors to reveal a fully stocked bar almost as big as his kitchen. She filled a shiny kettle from a long-necked tap. 'Milk? Sugar?' she asked, getting a mug down from an overhead cupboard. 'Dunno if I can tell you much.' She perched on the arm of an easy chair, snapping at a hair elastic on her wrist. She seemed to have faded since the afternoon, lips no longer frosted with orange, hair loose over her shoulders.

'Lived here long, Mrs Valentino?'

'Call me Adriana. Mrs Valentino sounds weird. No one calls me that.' She tilted her head, gathered her hair into a ponytail and wound the elastic round it. 'Never really wanted to live here in the first place,' she said, flicking a few loose strands off her forehead. 'He said it'd be good for the kids. Course it wasn't. Spent all my time driving them here, there and everywhere. Not like anyone thought about that when they designed this estate.' She almost spat *this estate*, eyes blazing like she wanted to strangle the anonymous planners she was blaming for making her life hell. 'Can't wait to leave the place. You know we hardly saw each other? The house is so huge. We could've been in separate cities.' The kettle clicked off. She got up and attended to his tea. Poured herself a whiskey. No ice. No water. Carried over a tray and set it on the side table. Took a big swallow from her glass.

O'Leary fumbled in his top pocket, pulled out his phone and a pen. 'Adriana, when did you last see your husband?'

'You mean in this house?' At first she was laughing but he quickly realised that her mirth had turned sour. He retrieved a clean handkerchief from his back pocket, offered it to her as tears rolled down her cheeks. She shook her head, pulled a wad of tissues from somewhere inside her t-shirt, mopped at her face. 'Oh god,' she moaned. 'I didn't really love him you know. But he is the father of my children. And it was fun. Sometimes at least.' She paused. Smiling and sniffing at the same time. 'After he'd had a win, that was.'

'Horses?'

Her eyes took on a faraway look as she balled the tissues into her palm. 'Anything. Anything that moved. And some things that didn't. More tea?' Without waiting for his reply, she swallowed the rest of the whiskey, walked over to the bar and refilled her glass. 'As I said earlier, his cousin was the worst thing that happened to Vince. Hours they spent holed up in that office of his.' She gestured towards the front of the house. 'That's where I last saw him, before he headed out the door with Anson. Said he'd be gone for a few days. Never heard from him again.'

'Was that usual? That he'd go away for a few days?'

'Had been getting more usual,' she said, leaning back. She exhaled deeply. 'Said he had business to do. Deals, more likely. He always returned from trips flush with cash. He thought I didn't know. But he stashed it in that stupid safe he had installed in the office.'

'He told you the combination?'

She snorted. 'Vince may have been a good bookmaker but he wasn't the sharpest knife in the drawer. Only took me four goes. Knew it was going to be somebody's birthdate. Sure enough. His.' Laughing now. 'That's why it took four. Who'd be that stupid?'

He smiled. 'You definitely saw him leave the house? And didn't see him again?'

'That's right. Left with an overnight bag. Twenty-ninth of August. I didn't know what the so-called business was. Could have been property development.' She made a noise somewhere between a laugh and a sneer. 'Yeah. Good one, that was. Some property developer. Did this house and the one next door, and if we hadn't sold our other place and moved here, we would have gone broke.'

'How come you recall the date so clearly?' asked O'Leary, draining what remained of his tea.

She continued as if he hadn't spoken 'But if I was to put money on it, it wasn't the bookie business that sent him off with Anson.'

'Oh?'

She took another gulp from her glass. 'No. More likely the other business he was in.'

O'Leary waited a few moments for her to add more. When she

didn't, he asked, 'And the other business was?'

'Drugs. Fucking drugs. He thought I didn't know about that, either. Stupid dumb fuck of a man!' This time she sobbed loud enough to make him wonder if he needed to do anything.

He extracted himself from the armchair and pitched towards where she was now thrashing in her chair, balled fists scrubbing at her face. 'Adriana? Adriana?' He didn't know what else to say, her wailing filling the room, filling his ears with sounds he did not want to hear. Then just as quickly as she had begun, she stopped, righted herself and looked up to where he was hovering above her.

'Should we leave the questions for now?'

'I'm okay,' she said softly. 'Would you pour me another please?' She pulled the elastic from her hair and shook it free, no sign of the sixty-second tsunami that had wracked her just moments before.

O'Leary returned her glass, more than two fingers sloshing in the bottom. He settled back in his chair and picked up the notebook. Scanned what he'd written last. 'You said you saw your husband leave with Anson on the twenty-ninth of August. Why so clear in your mind?'

'Oh. It was his mother's birthday. We were meant to go out for dinner. Me and the kids still went. I made some excuse to Nonna about Vince. Can't recall what it was, now. Made so many over the last few years.' She turned herself in the chair, faced the window. 'He was doing okay you know with the bookmaking business, being introduced to the right people, enjoying himself. That is until Cousin Gregory crashed in.'

'Right people, Adriana? Meet any of them?'

She got up, came over to his chair and picked up the cup and saucer. She was so close he could smell the alcohol on her breath, feel the warmth from her body. 'Two. A flash redhead lawyer by the name of Elise Lanigan who thought her shit didn't stink. She and Vince were pally, too. Much too pally for my liking, if you get my drift.'

O'Leary felt a shiver run through him at the mention of Elise Lanigan. She and he had never been on good terms. He disapproved of the clients she chose to represent, including

Krakauer, who was on her list last year. No longer though, it seemed. 'You mean lovers?' he asked, regretting his words the moment they were out of his mouth.

Pouring herself another whiskey, she said, 'Probably. Vince never could resist a tart in heels.'

'And the other?'

'The Racing Minister.'

Frowning, he asked, 'Phillip Sinclair?'

'Yeah, that was him,' she said, her words slightly slurred. 'Tall, good-looking bloke. Met him at a Flemington cocktail party.'

O'Leary took the Westgate. He pulled up outside his Yarraville home where he'd parked his Celica for many years. Like a few other things since the leg injury, that car had gone and been replaced with a five-year-old Subaru, silver duco already looking like a dirty saucepan. He nudged the Ford in beside it. The adjoining park was full of people and dogs, some dogs sopping wet from a dip in the creek, others hammering after balls, leaping and twisting in the air, mouths open for the catch. Everywhere he looked, the ground was littered with a mantle of fallen leaves and brown grass. Over the road, Bonnie, hose in hand, was trying to coax life into a front garden that copped the full brunt of summer sun. Maggie, O'Leary's black-and-white Border Collie was there too, tail upright, fossicking round the base of an out-of-control bird of paradise planted long before O'Leary had moved into the neighbourhood. He swung his legs out of the car, stood upright before arching his back, hands pressed into the small. 'Hey girl.' The dog bolted to the front gate.

Bonnie lifted her head. 'She's been nothing but trouble you know, Brendan.' She patted Maggie before opening the gate to let the dog join her owner. Maggie's tail was wagging at a rate that could power a small engine, tongue hanging out pink and wet. O'Leary ruffled her ears, reached down to pat her belly. 'Don't know if she's as slim as when you left, though,' Bonnie said, ambling over. 'We had barbecue chops last night, didn't we love? But we managed to walk some of it off, I'm sure.'

He grinned, straightened up. 'Dunno what I'd do without you Bonnie. Much appreciated.'

'Oh, and I've fed the chooks. Think there's a couple of eggs, too.'

The dog followed O'Leary through the gate and up the overgrown path to the front door. A large cardboard box was sitting on the doorstep. A dozen bottles of Barossa red. Hardly the weather for it. He lugged the box into the kitchen, dumped his jacket on the couch, pulled a beer from the fridge. 'That's better,' he said, pushing open the doors onto the back garden. Folding himself carefully into a deck chair, he scratched behind the dog's ears, feeling her muscles ripple as he moved his hand over her back. 'Miss me, old girl?' She licked his hand.

Opening another beer, he wandered down to the chook house and collected four eggs. He placed them in a bowl on the bench and checked the fridge's contents. A half-finished bottle of white wine, the remains of a bag of grated cheese, some milk that smelled good enough and a cube of butter wrapped in foil, complete with a dusting of toast crumbs. Breaking the eggs into a bowl, he whisked them to a froth. Gas alight under a frying pan, he knifed in a chunk of butter, waited for it to sizzle. Upended the eggs. Careful spatula work round the edges until he was satisfied he could put the pan under the griller, watched while the sprinkled cheese melted into a molten layer. He gently turned the omelette out onto a plate. 'Pretty good tucker, even if I say so myself.' The dog's ears pricked even though she remained lying on the floor. He returned to the back deck. The first star was visible in the northeast. Venus. He couldn't remember how long he'd called Venus the morning and evening star. His mother, Kathleen, used to point it out to him when he was a kid, sitting on the front lawn on a hot summer's night, stars as clear as crystal in the Dunnstown sky. Now, Venus was about the only object he could see with any regularity, city lights competing too fiercely for serious stargazing.

Bob Marley's intro to *Be Happy* rang out from the kitchen. A snarl of pain coursed through his thigh as he raced inside, snatched up the borrowed phone. 'Yep?'

No answer.

He took the phone outside, hit redial.

'Hello.' A woman's voice. One he'd known all his life.

'G'day Mum,' he said, wondering how she'd got this number. 'It's Brendan. Sorry I missed you just now. How're you doing?'

'I'm alright, Bren. Be a lot better though if that brother of yours would get in touch every now and then.'

'Yeah, so you haven't heard from Stephen either, I take it.'

'Not a word. All the shops must be clean out of the card things you put in your phone.' She drew breath. 'He's a terrible one for communication, I'll give him that. Just like his father. Anyway, how's things with you, love? That leg getting better?'

He reassured her he was improving little by little every day, that the twins were well and enjoying a break at the beach, and that work was off to a good start.

'You want to be careful, Bren. Don't go overdoing it, now.'

He fed a morsel of leftover omelette to Maggie. 'How about I come up next Sunday? Bring the kids? Depending on work, of course.'

'That would be lovely. I'll do some lunch for us all.'

He rang off, still smiling. His mother never changed. Still loved him like she did when he was a kid, loved every one of her brood. Loved his twins like they were her own. Even still loved Kevin, O'Leary's father, who could manage days on end without once talking. He knew it drove his mother mad, a woman who liked nothing more than a good chat. It was more than fifty years now, and they continued to rattle along, Kevin out with the horses and Kathleen doing the garden and the house. Seemed to work. Certainly worked better than what he and Claire had managed. He still didn't understand how she could have been so ardent one minute, then announce in almost the next breath that she'd fallen in love with a woman.

Be Happy again.

Nguyen's voice on the line. 'You want the good news or the bad news, Boss?'

O'Leary grunted. 'Bad first.'

'Anson's death isn't listed as far as I can find.'

He scowled. 'We'd all be better off if that prick was dead. What's the good news?'

'Your phone's been locked and cancelled. Forensics have taken the stuff from Krakauer's house and are running urgent on it. And Sutcliffe was able to fit in the autopsy today after all.'

Shit. He'd forgotten all about Sutcliffe when he was at the morgue with Adriana. He could've called in, asked directly for the results. 'And?'

'Been dead for several months. Definite gunshot wound to the head. No other obvious injuries. Want the bullet details?'

'Match anything we've got on file?'

Nguyen chuckled. 'You sitting down? None other than Simon Thomson-Paton.' Thomson-Paton's body had been found dumped at the Organ Pipes National Park north-west of Melbourne months ago, gunshot wounds to the head. As yet, no one had been charged with his murder. Strong suggestions he'd been involved in a turf war over drugs.

O'Leary sucked in air. 'I'd better get back up there.'

'Not tonight, Boss. Sleep in your own bed.'

He watched a possum clamber into the pear tree. 'We'll need a full search organised for Valentino's place. By the way, we got anyone else working on this?'

'Nah. You'll be up tomorrow.'

'Might bring Ange. She's been in my ear. Give her something to do.'

'Don't be too hard on her Boss. When you were away, she was like—' Nguyen didn't finish his sentence.

Micelli's day at the tennis was winding down over oysters at Southbank. She sat at a balcony table with David Romano enjoying a breeze off the Yarra after the relentlessly hot day. Wafting upwards from the food court, fried chip smells mingled with the sizzle of kebabs. She sipped on a glass of chilled Prosecco, wondered if she could have another, seeing she still needed to ride home. And tomorrow was a workday. David was onto his second.

'Everything okay here?' asked a black-attired waitress. She picked up the platter of discarded shells bedded in rock salt and Micelli's empty glass, and melted into the background.

'You enjoyed today?' David's dark eyes scanned her face. 'It's a shame you can't go tomorrow.'

She twiddled a strand of hair between thumb and fingers. 'Umm,' she said thoughtfully 'I'll miss the showdown between Kariolakis and Jovac—' Her vibrating phone momentarily caught her attention. She looked back up, still twiddling her hair. 'Only my sister. She can wait.'

'You're not only missing tennis games tomorrow, Ange, as I'm scheduled to meet with one of the sport's development managers. Could be a very fruitful meeting that would see me in Australia much more regularly. Maybe even—' He raised one eyebrow, extended his chin, allowed himself a broad smile.

'Mmm,' she murmured, before glancing towards her phone, which was vibrating again. 'And if you were in Australia, whereabouts exactly would you be based?'

'Melbourne, of course.' He grinned, reached over and stroked her forearm very briefly.

Again, her phone vibrated. Her eyes darted to the screen.

'Hey, Ange.' His voice betrayed his hurt. 'Aren't I sufficient for a firebrand like you?'

She looked up, flicked her hair back. Firebrand? No one had ever called her that before, but she liked the sound of it. Probably her mother would agree, as she would definitely construe failing to find a husband a revolutionary act. But maybe—She left the thought hanging, as a text beeped. She picked up the phone and read, *URGENT! CALL NOW*. Groaning, she said, 'Sister Rosie seems insistent about something.'

'Why don't you give her a call?' Conciliatory now. 'Put her out of misery then we can get on with dinner in peace.'

'Yeah, good idea.' She pushed back her chair, stood up, walked over to the railing.

The waitress returned with menus, two glasses and a bottle of wine. 'I can recommend the butterflied sardines with a parmesan crust. Chef gave us a plate to try before service.'

Micelli dashed back to the table. 'Something's happened to Nick.'

David raised his eyebrows. 'Nick?'

'Rosie's son. We bought a beer from his bar at the tennis, remember,' she said, scrabbling her backpack out from under her chair.

David stood up. 'Anything I can do?'

But Micelli was already on her way. 'I'll call later.' She stepped quickly through the mess of tables and diners and was soon lost in the throng along the promenade.

O'Leary went back inside leaving the fruit bats and possums to feast on unripe pears in the back garden and poured himself a glass of wine. He found a can of dog food in the back of the pantry and scooped it into Maggie's bowl, watched her sniff it, lick the edges then eat it slowly, like she was telling him that a can of dog food didn't really cut it in comparison to Bonnie's dog barbecues. 'Back to Bonnie tomorrow old girl, so we better get you out in the park bright and early in the morning.' He turned on the television. News was full of tennis. Maybe five seconds to tell viewers that a body suspected to be that of missing property developer and registered bookmaker, Vincent Valentino, had been located. No details. Just the way he liked it. Soon the switchboards would light up. Might even harvest something. Especially seeing there was already a handsome reward for information.

'Time for bed, old girl,' he said to the dog, swallowed another couple of painkillers, shuffled up to his bedroom. Without bothering to turn on the light, he laid full stretch on the bed, recounting the previous night. Shadows from the trees in the park played softly on the walls. He hadn't dreamt it. Someone had been in the van. Torchlight, for sure. He had been facing the wall, sheet pulled up and over his shoulders. Was there a smell too? Faint trace of lavender. That would have been from the bed linen though. He squeezed his eyes shut, tried to visualise the scene. There had been the click of the door catch, the van had tilted momentarily as the weight of a body climbed in. Then the torch.

Had it swept from side to side? Down the length of the van? He couldn't be sure. Only on for a few seconds. But there had been a smell. Something oddly familiar.

He sat up, swung his feet onto the floor, turned on the bedside light. Maggie was where she always was, lying beside his bed, gently snoring. He bent and gave her rump a swift pat on his way to the ensuite. Opening a cabinet, he removed two bottles of aftershave, remnants from Christmases gone by, and three bottles of Claire's perfume that she'd forgotten when she packed her stuff and rushed off to Karen's. He screwed the cap off bottle number one and inhaled deeply. He repeated the process until he came to bottle four.

Bingo.

TUESDAY

ANGELA MICELLI was being pursued uphill by a bike rider insistently jangling a bell. The hill was getting steeper and steeper, the insistent ringing becoming increasingly threatening. She turned to see who was pursuing her, skidded to a stop and fell sideways off her bike. She woke on the floor, a sheet twisted round her like a shroud. She picked the ringing phone off the bedside table. 'Morning, Ange. Ready for me to pick you up for a trip to Glenlyon?' O'Leary's voice boomed into her ears.

'Oh my god.' She groaned, struggled into an upright position, squinted at the time. How had it become 6am already? 'I'm a mess, Brendan. Total fucking mess.' She tried to unravel the sheet from her sweaty torso.

'What's happened?'

She could hear the sharpness in his voice. 'Tell you when you get here.'

Marbles followed her into the ensuite, miaowed pitifully. Ignoring the cat, she stumbled into the shower and raised her face to the spray, let the full force of the water plummet over her. Clutching the shampoo bottle, she squeezed until there was no more liquid left. Raked fingernails back and forth over her skull, as if this might make things better.

Last night she had sat with her nephew, Nick, in the police room at Melbourne Park, listened while he tried to explain why a teenager had accused him of taking pictures up her dress. Rosie was there when she arrived, face runnelled with teary mascara, hair askew, one earring missing. 'They've had him in there for hours. Dunno what he's said or anything. I'm worried sick, Ange.'

When Micelli had finally been allowed in, Nick was consistently maintaining his innocence. The young constable questioning him had said politely, a smile on her face, 'Maybe so, Nick, but as I've said, what maybe ten times now, there is a photo of her underwear on your phone. And you can't seem to tell me how it came to be there.'

'And I've told you, also ten times, constable,' he had replied sullenly, 'that I dropped my phone and it must have taken a photo automatically.'

But when the constable turned to Micelli and calmly explained that there were several pictures on his phone, all taken up skirts, she had exploded. 'You had no right to interview him without a parent present. Or to go through his phone.'

'I'm 18 now, Ange,' Nick had said quietly.

Of course he was. And here she'd been, letting her emotions get the better of her, treating a fellow officer like dirt. What was it about this boy, man actually, that made her behave like a mother bear? He already had a mother. Didn't need another one. Especially an out-of-control cop. She had pushed her palms against the tabletop, willed herself to get a grip. Apologised. Knew that it wasn't enough.

When O'Leary arrived at her door, she let him in, filled the cafetière with water, explained the situation. 'Has he got a lawyer?'

'Rosie's organised that. Too late, but. They've already seen the other photos. I feel terrible, Brendan. I know he's 18, but he's just a kid, really.' She gulped, busied herself getting out mugs. 'You still off sugar?'

He nodded. 'What's Nick saying?'

'Doesn't know how the photos came to be there. Someone must have taken his phone. That sort of thing.'

'You'll have to tread carefully, Ange.'

She rubbed a hand over her face, massaged her eyebrows. 'Yeah. Shouldn't have barged in. But Rosie was almost hysterical.'

'Get any sleep?' He reached down and stroked Marbles who was rubbing against his legs.

'Not a lot.' She scowled. 'Feel like a three-day-old pork chop.'

He breathed in. 'There's a lot for you to do at Glenlyon. But I think you should spend the day here. You can go through a few files and stuff for us. That way you'll be on hand if the family needs you.' He took a swallow of coffee, screwed up his face. 'And you won't be getting any sleep today either, if you keep drinking this brew. Bloody hell, Ange, it's fierce.'

She almost smiled. 'What do you want me to do re Glenlyon?'

He walked over to the bench and filled a glass with water, drank it in one go. 'I'll get Nguyen to contact you. He's on top of what's needed. Anyhow, I'd better be on my way. They're digging the mounds this morning.' He put his cup on the draining board and gave her a quick squeeze. 'Families. More trouble than they're worth, sometimes.'

His comment reminded her of the trouble he'd been in a few months ago with his brother, Stephen. In with the wrong crowd. Driving cars for drug dealers. Transporting and sampling their drugs. Lucky to get off with a warning. And O'Leary, lucky to avoid an inquiry into how he came to be in a shoot-out at his brother's farm.

'Want me to run you to the station?' he asked.

'That'd be great,' she said, stifling the urge to hug him again, grabbing her backpack instead. 'Left my bike in the city last night. Hope it's still there.'

Once on the highway, O'Leary slipped the car into cruise control, set the radio to the national broadcaster, tried to focus on the news. Climate activists barricaded in a room at Parliament House in Canberra; three dead in a single car crash at Ouyen; an update on how the Aussies fared yesterday in the tennis. He switched channels. Sports commentators complaining about cricket;

presenters giggling furtively like school kids at innuendos; a weather update. Stabbed at the search arrow. Cohen's half-finished *Chelsea Hotel* startled him. Listened to the bit about giving head on the bed, her not needing him, not needing anything. What price love? His throat ropey with the idea. Too soon. Surely, too soon. *Hallelujah* saw him onto the Calder before his thoughts took over completely, the music providing little more than background noise.

Clouds puffed up on the western horizon, planed bottoms furled grey, fluffy white cumulus on top like a colossal pavlova. Seen them too often to seriously consider they promised a storm. Hopefully a storm for Krakauer, though, who was due to face court on Friday on charges relating to trafficking. He went over what else they knew about the scumbag. A charge for prostitution going back years, porn videos for paedophiles found on a USB in his car last year along with drugs ready for sale, but that's where their intelligence dried up. Or had dried up until Adriana Valentino had talked. And forensics had done some quick data matching. Up until now it'd seemed like Krakauer operated a one-man show, even though O'Leary and every other cop worth their salt knew that to be impossible. He must have had people who did things for him. And with him. Like starring in the porn, for one, unless he was the criminal equivalent of Renaissance man who could turn his hand to anything: casting, scripting, acting, video production, web uploads. Not to mention the drugs. That alone would see him dead if he didn't have the right connections. Chances were he was in cahoots with someone whose business it was to look after the drugs side of things, someone like Gregory Anson for example, leaving Krakauer free to take the leading hand in the porno stuff. Business partnership. Or partnerships. He put his foot down, felt the Falcon surging up the rise near the Gisborne turnoff. Maybe Nguyen would have some ideas. Some definite links were clicking into place. Thomson-Paton, drug dealer, body dumped virtually en route to Glenlyon. Valentino, bullet to the head in a Glenlyon mineshaft, bullet matching the one that killed Thomson-Paton. Then there was Anson, the slippery drug dealer, who'd disappeared from everyone and everywhere, just so happened that his disappearance was a few days after Adriana Valentino last saw her husband, who, she said was doing some sort of business with Anson. No paedophile links as yet. They'd come, though. He was sure of that.

The phone danced around in the console. He pulled over, tyres gripping the gravel, wondered who else must know this number. 'Yep?'

'That you, O'Leary?'

He recognised Goddings's voice.

'I want you to leave that Krakauer case on hold for a while. Not like anything's going to change much in the next few days.' He pinched the bridge of his nose, let Goddings continue. 'There's a job in the city. Something connected with a tennis player called Kross. Apparently his manager's been found dead in the Condor Hotel at Southbank.' He unscrewed the top on a bottle of water, took a swig. Listened while Goddings filled him in on the details to date. 'Need someone who can pull off a potentially international investigation. Eyes of the world on Melbourne at the moment. Sure you know this. You're the best man we've got. How soon can you be there?'

O'Leary almost laughed out loud when Goddings said he was the best man they had. Certainly hadn't said those words or words anything like that after the debacle at Dunnstown. What had changed, he wondered. Someone else fuck up big time? If they had, surely he would have heard about it through the rumour mill.

The thought of leaving the Krakauer case just as things were hotting up irked him. 'What about Ange Micelli?' he asked, explaining his planned work schedule. 'She'd be up for it, and she's not working on anything so important for the Krakaeur case that she couldn't drop it.' He didn't add that it would take her mind off whatever stupidity her nephew had got himself into.

'Rightio,' Goddings said slowly. O'Leary could almost hear his brain ticking over. 'She did a good job on that Dangerfield case, didn't she?' Without waiting for O'Leary to answer he announced, 'I'll call her now. Get the ball rolling. Then, when you're back in town...' The connection failed, leaving Goddings's words hanging in the air. Not a moment too soon, for O'Leary could predict what he'd say, get Ange to start and then he'd be asked to take over. He grinned, imagining the look on her face should such a scenario present itself.

The Condor Hotel dominated the waterfront, its glass and steel edifice reflecting the coffee-coloured waters of the Yarrra River. Micelli strode up to the entrance and homed in on reception, festooned with vases of red gladioli. A muffled conversation, a flash of her badge, a reedy man in red-and-gold livery emerged and directed her to the service lift. The ninth-floor corridor was decorated with glass shelves lit from above and more vases of red gladioli. She flashed her badge again to the pimply constable on duty outside a room recently occupied by Mr Alexei Azarov. Deep-pile carpet the colour of outback dust cushioned her footfalls as she walked slowly towards a king-size bed perfectly positioned to take in a view of the city. A painting of a reclining schoolgirl, straw hat pulled low over deep black eyes, nose pressed hard against a single daisy, stretched the length of the headboard. Not the sort of thing she would choose as up-market hotel decoration, even if the girl's dress did pick up on the dust colour scheme. She counted six pillows. The bedcover was crumpled on the floor, tangled snow-white sheets partially pulled over a man lying on his back, arms flung out to the side, open eyes staring at the ceiling. A condom was rolled onto his erect penis. She sniffed. Sex? Or was her nose playing tricks, telling her what her eyes were seeing? Perfume? Perhaps. Undoubtedly, something sweet lingered in the air.

Frank Sutcliffe greeted her warmly as he snapped on gloves. 'Morning, Ange. Good to see you again. All well with you?'

The phrase complete cock-up came to mind. Neither he nor the forensics team already at work needed to know the ins and outs of the Micelli family dramas. And some of that drama had ceased to be so critical in her life now she was in charge of an investigation. A high profile one too, connected to one of Australia's and the world's most important sporting events. 'Great to see you too, Frank.' She left his last question unanswered.

She surveyed the room. Like hotel rooms the world over, two bedside tables, an easy chair, wall-mounted TV the size of a small car facing a three-seater sofa. On the coffee table was a large white platter with what looked to be sushi leftovers. An uncorked bottle of Veuve Clicquot, one glass, half full. Micelli raised it to her nose. Smelt like the real thing. Three floor lamps and a small cabinet placed below a large mirror containing the minibar and tea and coffee making equipment.

The creamy marble bathroom was softly lit from behind a translucent glass panel etched with words she recognised as meaning water: eau, agua, wasser, aqua, air, and words in scripts she didn't recognise, different sizes, different fonts. Thick white towels stacked on chrome racks, toilet paper tipped to a point, complimentary toiletries artfully arranged on a glass dish, also etched with the water words.

Returning to the bedroom, she opened the closet. Chestnut-brown leather jacket, zippered front, an unopened leather duffel on the luggage stand. Two white robes loosely belted at the waist, two pairs of complimentary slippers, ironing board and iron, two spare pillows, an unopened one litre bottle of vodka. She laid the jacket over a chair and went through the pockets. Loose change, Australian and Euros. ID lanyard in the name of Alexei V Azarov. Passport of the same name. Photos might come in handy. Wallet. Two credit cards, some banknotes in both currencies, a business card in the name of Jason Woods, marketing manager for one of the major sponsors. Nothing written on the back. A phone. She opened the contacts. None. No missed calls. One outbound call. Local landline. She dialled the number. It rang out.

'Get this over to Macleod,' she said to one of the forensics dotted about the room. 'Need to know ID of last call out, phone's provenance. And any info from the apps he's got on it.'

Turning back to the bed, voice almost a whisper. 'Is that normal?'

'You mean—?' Sutcliffe nodded towards the dead man.

She felt warmth flush from her neck to her cheeks. A giggle escaped.

'Yep. More ups than downs, so to speak, Ange, in the violent death business. At least he died on a high.'

She exploded, tried to cover her laughter by coughing. Recovering somewhat, aware that several of the techies were looking her way. 'How long's he been dead, do you think?'

'Hard to say.' He winked.

Again she was overtaken by a fit of giggling.

He stood to his full height, took on the stance of an Oxford don, lowered his voice to a rich baritone. 'Many have never heard of Priapus, Greek god of the phallus, distinguished by his oversized member and a permanent erection. The Romans became enamoured with him, his engorged penis finding its way onto frescoes and canvases, and even a book of short verses, often attributed to the pens of Virgil and Ovid, spoke of his vigour—'

'For real?' She spluttered into guffaws, pinching her thigh hard in an effort to gain control.

He nodded sagely. 'Saw a fresco of him in Pompeii years ago. You know of all the things I learnt in med school, I remember the bit about priapism most clearly of all.'

'Priapism?'

'Refers to a long-lasting erection without any obvious stimulation. Can get painful, apparently. The prof almost brought the house down until he started on the case studies. That sobered us blokes up quick smart.'

'No women?'

'None in my year. The condition's also called angel lust. Rather romantic, don't you think? I'd think that's more of what we're seeing here rather than priapism.' He kneeled on the carpet, closely examined a plastic bag, possibly a bin liner, lying on the floor. 'You asked about probable cause before we got onto loftier matters. Most likely asphyxiation,' he said, gingerly prodding what looked like a white shoelace with a gloved finger.

'You mean—?'

'Anything's possible Ange. Be easier if he'd been wearing that watch,' he said, pointing to the bedside table. 'If I'm not mistaken, it's one of the latest models and will be able to give us all sorts of information. Up until he took it off, that is. But I'm a bit concerned about those marks. See?' Thin red lines wound part way round the man's wrists, like fine bracelets.

Her phone, tucked into her pants pocket, vibrated. Turning towards the wall, she checked the caller ID. 'You have to do something, Ange. And you have to do it now,' Rosie blurted out when she answered. 'He's just not ready for this. And neither am I. It's terrible. You have to do something.'

'I'm at work—'

'I DON'T GIVE A FUCK WHERE YOU ARE!' She was screaming. Micelli pressed the phone hard against her ear. 'We're hurting here and you can do something. So do it!' She was now sobbing.

'Rosie, I love you. I love Nick...'

'Ah, thought that might be the case.' Sutcliffe was crouched down, pointing out a pair of handcuffs jammed between the night table and the bed. 'What do you think, Ange?'

Thrusting her phone back into her pocket, she fished around for some words. 'Wouldn't it be hard to get those on by yourself?'

'Even harder to remove a bag from your head, as well as unlock the cuffs.' She bit her lip. 'After the event, that is.'

Micelli stomped back to the hulking building on the corner of Spencer and La Trobe Streets where Homicide had their offices. She jabbed at the lift buttons. Emerging onto the grey-carpeted floor of level six, she knocked lightly on Goddings's door.

'Yes?' He peered over rimless spectacles. 'Oh, come on in, DSC Micelli. Coffee perhaps, before we start?'

'Two scenarios, Sir.' She sipped the mug of scalding Nescafe handed to her by Doris, grey hair clipped in a tight bun, calf-length grey skirt, matching blouse. Goddings referred to Doris as his right-hand woman, but Micelli felt more uneasy about her than she did about Goddings. Micelli noted the shadow of a moustache marching across her upper lip when she offered the sugar bowl. Deep breath in. Too bad if the hovering Doris raised her Frida Kahlo eyebrows in disgust, she just needed to spit it out. 'Sex gone wrong, other person gets scared and flees. Or scenario two, the whole thing was staged, ending in murder.' She described the scene as best she could, aware that Doris had already placed print-outs of crime scene photographs onto Goddings's desk.

'Umm,' said Goddings slowly, examining each of the pictures. 'You don't think it could be self-inflicted?' He pointed to the picture showing the handcuffs and plastic bag. Micelli felt her face colour, recalling her naïve conversation with Sutcliffe. 'You're probably too young to recall the Geraldton case. British politician. Found in his hotel room, similar circumstances. No one convicted as the investigation team concluded, rightly so according to the director of Scotland Yard, that the victim had done it to himself.'

'Was Geraldton handcuffed?'

'I don't believe so. Tied to a chair, if my memory serves me right. Same effect though as handcuffs, wouldn't you say?'

She nodded. 'In any event, Sir, I'll need some assistance.'

Goddings beckoned to Doris. 'Who's free at the moment?' She brought up a screen on her computer, hit the print button, handed the sheet to Goddings. He scanned the list, tapping the end of a pen against his teeth. 'Umm.' He crossed a few names, ticked another couple, before handing the page to Micelli. 'Get these officers together in your team. I expect a briefing tomorrow at twelve.'

She took the stairs down to the third-floor office she shared with O'Leary and Nguyen, pushed open the door. Her paperwork was as she'd left it before getting the call to go to the hotel, files strewn over the conference table, laptop humming away. She opened the fridge, poured herself a glass of chilled water, bit into a peach. Didn't take the taste of Doris's awful coffee out of her mouth. She swiped the screen on her phone. No connection available. Remembered the new number he'd given her that morning. Punched it in. 'Got a minute?'

O'Leary answered on the second ring. 'How's it going?'

'I've got Rory Harris. Pleased about that one. And Barry Pritchard. Again.' She groaned.

'Ange, he's a good detective, just hard to control, that's all. You'll have to put your foot down right from the start, let him know who's boss.'

She winced at the memory of the last investigation they had

worked on together when Pritchard had practically run his own show, haring off round Ballarat, stumbling onto a murder scene, almost getting killed. Still, she had to concede, he'd done a good job in getting information out of slimy Phillip Sinclair. Probably slimier still since becoming police minister, but he was no longer her concern. 'Know anything about a Mick Skelton?'

It was O'Leary's turn to groan. 'You haven't drawn him, have you? What the bloody hell is Goddings thinking? Shit Ange.'

'Why? What's the matter with him?'

'One of the force's finest survivors, shall I say. I'll leave it at that for now.'

Micelli wheeled the whiteboard into the conference space and waited for her new team to arrive. First in was Rory Harris, sun-tanned and beaming. 'G'day DSC Micelli. How's it going?' Blue shirt, jeans, brown leather lace-ups, looking like he'd just stepped out of an RM Williams catalogue, suit bag over his arm. 'Brought you a coffee.'

'Hey, just what I need.' She prised off the lid and swallowed a mouthful. 'That's good. Any goss?'

'Not that I know of,' he said, pulling out a chair. 'Been on holidays since mid-December. Tell you the truth, feeling a bit rusty. Hope this is going to be an open and shut case.'

'So far no wife, no girlfriend, no enemies.' Before she could add more, the door opened and a slim man whose bald patch was overtaking his number two entered, gunmetal grey suit, pale pink shirt, a pink-and-grey striped tie. Micelli was struck by the choice of galah colours. 'Mick Skelton?'

'Haven't forgotten me so soon, I hope,' said Barry Pritchard extending a hand.

'My god.' She looked at him more closely. 'What's happened to you?'

He smiled broadly, same yellowing teeth, same exposed gums. 'Weight Watchers.'

Harris began to chuckle, remembering the slob Pritchard had been last time they worked together. 'Bloody hell, Pritchard. I love it.'

Pritchard pulled out a chair and sat beside Harris. 'Anyway, what's the go and who's doing what?'

'We're still waiting for a Mick Skelton,' Micelli said. 'Either of you two know him?' They shook their heads. She checked her watch. 'Think we're going to have to start without him. Lot to get done. First up, victim's a tennis manager from Estonia here for the Open. We're assuming the circumstances are suspicious, but until the autopsy occurs no one's able to confirm cause of death. We need some intel. Fast. Family if there is any, who he knows in Melbourne, what his Estonian life was like. That sort of thing.'

'Vision?' asked Pritchard.

'Start at the hotel.' She tapped the marker against the board. 'Exact arrival, movements to and from the tennis. Anyone he's met,' she said, adding more items to the whiteboard. 'Obviously Markus Kross and his entourage, if he's got one.'

Harris nodded. 'Others? Maybe drivers, racquet stringers, media.'

'Add that to your list, Harris?'

'Which bit?'

'The bit about drivers, racquet stringers, the media. I know someone who might be able to shed some light on what tennis managers do, sponsorship deals and that sort of stuff.'

Harris grinned. 'How well would that be?'

The door pushed open and a man about the same age but taller and skinnier than O'Leary strode into the room, pulled out a chair and plonked down onto it. He rocked back, balancing the chair on two legs, clasped his hands behind his head. His elbows were scaly and red. Old sweat had stained the underarms of his short-sleeved white shirt a dirty yellow. 'Mick Skelton?' asked Micelli.

'Yeah,' he sneered, rocked back even further before lunging forward to snatch a mint from a bowl in the middle of the table.

Her phone began to vibrate. Rosie's picture danced into frame. *RING NOW!* She scowled. 'Come on, get a move on you two,' she said, and nodding to Skelton, 'I'll be with you in a tick.' He strode over to the kitchenette and disappeared behind the partition. Hitting the dial function, she walked to the window and waited.

'Are you family or what?' Rosie's voice bellowed into her ear. 'He needs YOU,' she screamed, 'TO FUCKING DO

SOMETHING!'

'Rosie, I can't intervene. It's already a charge. There's nothing I can do to make it go away.' She hoped the anger she felt wasn't coded in her voice.

'You're as weak as piss, Ange.' In the background was a dull sound like a punching bag being repeatedly thumped. 'That fucking cricketer. His evidence mysteriously disappeared. One of your mates could do that and he wasn't even family. Weak as—'

Micelli ended the call. Stared out the window. Turned to see Skelton seated at the table, a mug of something in front of him. 'What's with all the fuckin' fruit? What happened to Arnott's Family Assorted?'

She ignored his questions, instead formally introducing herself and telling him she expected punctuality and good manners from people on her team. He raised his eyebrows and grinned like a kid in a lolly shop when she got to the bit about manners.

'Got it,' he said loudly. 'I'll be all pleases and thank yous from now on. Nothing I like better than good manners.' He clasped his hands as if eager to please. 'Is it the right time now for wham bam, thank you M'am?' He smirked. 'For the lesson, that is.' Micelli grimaced.

Before she could react, another text flashed in. *MUM SAYS SHE HATES YOU!!!!*

'Okay, let's get one thing straight. I'm running this investigation. You're part of a team. My team. You treat me and the other team members with respect. And cut the foul language.'

'Yes, Mum!' He dropped his bottom lip, looked at her with dog eyes. Except his were a yellowish green.

She grasped the edges of the table. 'Read the whiteboard. Note any questions you might have. Report to me in ten.' She stalked out of the room, banged the door behind her.

In the lift to the ground floor, she resisted an urge to bash a wall with her fists. Or text Rosie back. Instead, she called David. 'Hi, got a minute?' Walked across the foyer and took the steps down to the street.

'Sure, always for you, Ange. But first, say you'll come with me to cocktails tomorrow evening prior to the night session.'

'Love to.'

'Great. Now what can I help you with?'

'What makes you think I want help?'

'Could tell by the business-like tone. Still gorgeous, just different.' Practically purring down the phone.

'God David.' She was practically spluttering. 'I wanted to ask you—'

'Something to do with a certain tennis player? And his now dead manager, perhaps?'

She tried to wipe the smile off her face. 'Yes, as a matter of fact. Like, who a manager might come into contact with, that sort of thing.' She listened while he explained the role as best he knew it. 'What qualifications would you need for the job?'

'Nothing formal, but good networks and business acumen helps. Managers need to be able to decide where the best opportunities are to maximise prizemoney, keep any sponsors happy and seek out offers, perhaps manage social media if the player has a high profile.'

'Like a PR job with extra bits about money?'

'If you're wondering how Markus Kross will be faring minus manager, I can ask around, get back to you. I heard from a colleague that Azarov was a high-flying businessman in Estonia and had secured a good sponsor deal for Kross. TransferWise, I think. Unusual to catch such a big fish, given that Kross hasn't won any majors yet.'

Smoke the colour of an old man's singlet filled the Glenlyon air. Farmland on fire east of Daylesford, bush burning somewhere off Green Gully Road. O'Leary nursing a mug of tea outside HQ watched three eastern greys hop frantically across the clearing. Pity about the slow-moving koalas. They had no hope once a fire took hold. Bastards who deliberately lit fires mustn't care for animals any more than they did for people, although it was more than likely that lightning strikes were the culprits for these fires after last night's dry thunderstorm.

Nguyen swung open the flywire door. 'Want a refill, Boss?'

'Nah. Coming in now to look over the stuff you've been working on.' He threw the dregs from his mug on the dirt, watched the rivulet of liquid run off the parched ground. 'Got my message about Ange?' He clambered into the van.

'Yep, and I've messaged her and followed up with an email. Haven't heard back, though.'

'Yeah. Not surprised. Goddings has assigned her to a case involving a murdered bloke that's got something to do with the tennis.'

'Right.' Nguyen chewed on his bottom lip. 'Have we got anyone else who can do some chasing up?'

'What about your friend? Whatshername? Worked with us last August on the Dangerfield case.'

Nguyen cleared his throat. 'You mean Elsa Janzen. Used to be in Drugs but moved to Homicide?'

'I'll see if Goddings'll let us commandeer her for a few days.' O'Leary picked up his phone, lumbered out of the caravan. After a few moments, he opened the flywire, gave the thumbs up sign, let the door slap back on its catch. Changed his mind, climbed back into the van. 'That lawyer Elise Lanigan. She's connected to Valentino.'

Nguyen raised his eyebrows. 'Through Anson?'

O'Leary sat down in front of a laptop. 'Adriana implied her husband could have been having an affair with her.'

'Lanigan and Valentino? Wouldn't that be crossing lines?'

'Not everyone in the legal profession behaves legally, you know. Kickbacks. Power. Sex. Even love, so I've heard. All powerful motivators in the right conditions.'

'You mean like that woman solicitor who married Carlos the Jackal?'

'Huh?' O'Leary was skimming the laptop screen.

'That terrorist. Married his French lawyer. Anyway, Curiouser and curiouser, as Alice might say.'

O'Leary turned to Nguyen. 'It was interestinger and interestinger, wasn't it?'

'How much you want to bet?'

O'Leary dragged out his wallet, extracted a fifty-dollar note.

'This in red wine, winner gets to select.'

'You're on,' said Nguyen, laughing.

They were silenced by a knock on the side of the caravan. 'Yes, mate?' Nguyen was first to the door.

A man dressed in navy blue overalls and heavy work boots who'd be hard to see if he stood sideways, waited in the shade of the caravan awning. 'Boss said you might want to come down. We're ready to start digging.' Turning, he walked quickly towards a small group of similarly blue-overalled officers who were listening intently to Rod Jones. A unit experienced in the art of careful digging, a bit like archaeologists.

O'Leary and Nguyen followed the group along the recently worn trail, dry grass crunching underfoot. 'Hope those fires don't decide to come our way,' said O'Leary, sniffing at the air. 'Lots of fuel down in the gully. Wonder the local shire wasn't onto Krakauer. Get him to clear his land a bit.'

Nguyen stopped, held up a wet forefinger. 'Wind's coming from the south-east. Should protect us from the fire in the bush. Think the Daylesford outbreak might be under control, according to the latest from the CFA.'

'Well, at least that's something.' O'Leary surveyed the area where the dig was about to begin. Wooden stakes had been hammered into the ground. A single strand of tape marked out the area of possible excavation. Two officers, wielding short-handled shovels, had begun work on the first site, digging a perimeter line an arm's length from where the mounds were. Trowels, forks, a couple of plastic garden sieves, a tape measure, other bits and pieces spread out on a piece of blue tarp beside a pile of evidence bags. A bit like a garage sale, O'Leary thought. Then he noticed the body bags neatly stacked to the side.

'Slowly does it,' called Jones, who was standing to one side, trying not to block a third officer recording the operation on camera. Deliberately, the pair worked their way closer to the mounds, their trench now knee-deep. Eight, maybe ten shovel's full later, one of the diggers jerked his head back, motioned to Jones. O'Leary craned his neck. 'Better start with the small stuff now,' said Jones. Down on their hands and knees, they used the trowels. Before long, a pair of feet in faded red sneakers had been uncovered. Kid size. No doubt about that.

After viewing CCTV tapes covering the last twelve hours, Pritchard returned to the main lobby at the Condor Hotel. A receptionist showed him into a room, offered him coffee. 'The security manager will be with you shortly, Sir. In the meantime, is there anything I can help you with?'

'Some water'd be good.' He settled into a plump armchair, placing his notebook on a slab of oiled redgum to his side. 'No ice, thanks.' But the heavy door had already closed. He looked around. A large gilt-framed mirror, wall lights shining on dot paintings and a decorated didgeridoo, a concoction of kangaroo paws rising from a rough-glazed pottery urn. A long leather couch adorned with cushions, two more redgum occasional tables, a stack of magazines. He was about to pick up the latest edition of *Australian Geographic* when the door swept open.

'Ah, Detective Pritchard.' Almost needed to duck under the doorjamb. Black stilettos, fire-engine red skirt, cream silk blouse tied in a loose bow at the neck. White-blonde hair pulled back. Makeup perfectly applied to a perfect face showing a hint of leftover adolescent plumpness. 'I hear there's been a problem with some of our footage?'

He rose from his chair.

'Helen Kapp,' she said, advancing on him with an outstretched hand. Firm grasp. Soft skin.

'Yeah,' he said, sitting down again. 'The system seemed to be working okay until 23.08 Monday when the transmission from Azarov's floor cuts out.'

'Remind me.' Her voice was as smooth as her face. She sat carefully on the edge of a chair, patting down the skirt. 'What floor was that?'

'Nine.'

'Ah yes.' Sweetness turned on. 'I know it doesn't help you, but I am terribly sorry about that.'

Pritchard noted how she emphasised certain words like *know* and *am*. He wondered how you got to be security manager of a major city hotel when you were barely weaned from your mother's breast.

'You see, we had an issue with our system yesterday. Seems a whole floor was disabled, so to speak.' She smiled as if he should be delighted to hear the news.

'How could that happen?' He scratched his head, frowned. 'I mean, was it only one floor, or was there a general outage? So to speak.'

She threw back her head and laughed a full-throated laugh, open mouth revealing two rows of perfect white teeth, not a filling in sight. 'You see, we just don't know. I've asked the technicians, well, not asked so much as commanded them, to get to the bottom of it. Poste-haste. Not that—'

'I see,' said Pritchard. 'But you do have footage of the lobby and all the other floors?'

She blinked rapidly, glanced at her wristwatch, a giant of a thing carved out of some ancient pink mineral deposit.

'Don't you?' he prompted.

'I believe so, Detective. Would you like to see the footage?'

'Could you courier it over to our office, Ms Kapp?'

'Certainly can.' She walked over to where he was sitting. 'Here.' She held out a tawny-brown card edged in gold. 'Do call if you think I can help further.' She strode out of the room without a backwards glance.

Removing his sunglasses, Harris took a moment to let his eyes adjust to the restaurant's inside lighting. A woman with short grey hair, silver-framed spectacles, event polo shirt over beige shorts was sitting alone. Harris did a quick scan. She was the only customer. 'Glenda Williams? Courtesy car driver?' She nodded. He pulled out a chair and sat down.

'I took Mr Azarov to his hotel on Monday,' she said, after he had ordered their coffees. 'Didn't say much. Not many of them do, especially if they don't have a lot of English. Polite enough, though.'

'Can you be more precise?'

She took off her glasses, polished the lens with a handkerchief. 'I took a call round five forty-five to pick him up. Took about ten minutes to his hotel. Traffic was lightish. I can get the exact time the call came through from the records guys, if you like.'

He shook his head. 'Was there anything about him? Something that may have stood out?'

'He did seem a bit shaken. When I pulled up, I saw two men coming my way. They didn't seem to be on friendly terms.'

'How did you work that out?'

'Judging by their body language, they were arguing. The back one, a burly type, grabbed Mr Azarov by the sleeve, gave him a shove. Course at the time I didn't realise it was Mr Azarov until he showed me his lanyard. He was in a hurry to get into my car, that's for sure.'

Harris, who had been taking notes, looked up as their coffees arrived. 'What did the man following Azarov look like?'

She tore the end off a stick of sugar. 'Sort of like a rugby player, only older. Didn't really get a good look at him, but I'd say somewhere close to sixty. Standout was probably his hat. One of those huge-crowned white hats that cowboys wear in the movies. Couldn't really see his face under the brim. Definitely a ten-gallon model. No one wears those for real, do they?'

He asked a few more questions, but Glenda couldn't tell him anything further. Thanking her, he paid the bill and asked for directions to Security.

Waiting his turn at the counter, Harris showed his badge, explained that he needed to look at some of yesterday's CCTV footage from five until seven pm. 'Courtesy car park. Area where drivers pick up their clients from.'

The man got up from his chair, SECURITY in yellow letters emblazoned on the back of his black shirt. Certainly burly. And close to fifty. Harris looked for a ten-gallon white hat, but none was in evidence. 'Check with the boss,' the man said gruffly, before disappearing through a security door that clicked shut behind him. Harris glanced at his phone. No messages. Flipped through his notebook. Struck a line through *driver*, tapped his pen on *vision*. The man reappeared. 'Come through here.' He lifted a section of the desktop and ushering him through the locked door. 'Take a seat,' he said, pointing to a stool tucked under a bench holding three large screens. 'Vision's on its way.'

Micelli walked into the lobby of Hotel City Edge, a converted former factory in North Melbourne. Dwarfed by a fake floral arrangement made for a much bigger space, the receptionist was seated behind a timber bench running the width of the room. Bronze makeup layered over what was probably good skin, dyed black hair pulled so tightly in its ponytail that Micelli winced as if her own eyelids were being stretched. After introducing herself, Micelli enquired about Markus Kross.

'Just a minute.' Lacquered pink nail scrolling on a mouse, eyes darting from side to side. 'Yes,' she said, both hands now resting on the desktop, 'he's staying with us. Shall I call him?'

'Please. Could we talk in here?' Micelli asked, gesturing to a room furnished with several sets of easy chairs overlooking the street. 'And I'd appreciate it if you could put a do not disturb sign on the door.'

A few minutes later, the man whose picture was featured in Sunday's sports pages emerged from the single lift. He was taller than she had imagined, mint green checked shirt overhanging beige chinos, tan-coloured leather loafers, no socks. When he smiled, his teeth gleamed straight and white in a face the colour of honey. His hand outstretched, he strode over to where she was standing beside the water cooler. 'Hello. I am Markus. I am very interested in why a police wants to see me.'

Micelli guided him into the room, indicated a chair, and shut the door. After taking down his details in her notebook, she leant forward and said, 'I'm afraid I don't have very good news, Mr Kross.' As briefly as she could, she told him that his manager had died. 'We are not one hundred percent sure as yet, we are still conducting investigations, but we think a person or persons may be responsible for Mr Azarov's death.'

'Uh?'

Searched around for words that a layman would understand. 'There may be someone who caused Mr Avarov's death.'

'You mean he is murdered?' Kross's face was now almost as white as his teeth. 'I see him yesterday at my game. And after. He alright then.'

Micelli nodded, noted his words in her notebook. 'And when was that Mr Kross?'

He glanced at his watch. 'I play on outside court at midday and finish before two. I see Alexei in players' room after match. He say I am good.'

Micelli chose not to mention that she had seen his match against the young Australian, instead asking if there was anyone she could notify on his behalf.

He shook his head. 'No. Yes. Artur and Kristo. They upstairs. I will tell them now.' He jumped out of his chair and was marching towards the door when Micelli stopped him.

'Please sit down, Mr Kross. I have some more things to ask you. For one, who are Artur and Kristo? Are they part of your crew?' She scribbled down their full names and occupations. 'The receptionist will phone their rooms, ask them to come downstairs.' She poured a water and handed it to Kross. His colour had returned but judging by his incessant leg jiggling, he was clearly unsettled.

A knock on the door and Artur, Kross's coach, and Kristo, his nutritionist-cum-masseur, appeared. Almost carbon copies of Markus. Micelli repeated what she had told Kross, who kept his eyes fixed on the floor during the retelling. His leg was still jiggling rapidly, and when he stood up to pour another water, Micelli could see sweat stains under his arms.

When she finished explaining the situation Artur immediately leant back and clasped his hands behind his head. 'Ah shit.' He exhaled audibly. 'We do everything now, I guess.' He fixed his gaze on Kristo. 'Not just the ninety-nine per cent we already doing.'

'Yes, what will be the difference? Hey, Markus?'

Kross looked up, a frown creasing his brow. 'But he dead. He manage funds. We not know how to do any of that.'

Artur scoffed. 'Oh, we can manage. What's happened before is good for Mr Alexei and not so good for us, no?'

Kristo chimed in. 'You won forty thousand last week in Sydney. Where is money? Why we not in the same hotel in this city? How come we travel back class and Mr Alexei sit up front of plane? Huh?'

'He made this happen for me. For us. He not bad man.'

Both Artur and Kristo groaned in unison. Kross resumed his examination of the carpet.

Micelli fumbled for her vibrating phone. Rosie again. She hit the red button. 'Look Artur, Kristo, this is a potential murder enquiry. I'm going to have to get a full statement from each of you.'

'How? When?' asked Artur, his voice raised. 'No trouble. We drop everything for you. Markus play tomorrow. But no, we give statement instead of going to courts for hit-up now.' He broke off, half laughing. 'And he win? I don't think so with no practice.'

'And me? I give statement too?' asked Kross.

Ignoring him, she said, 'DS Skelton will take your statements. This afternoon. Do not leave the hotel.'

After searching his colleagues' faces, Kross turned to Micelli, a smile that could have been a grimace displaying his white teeth to perfection. 'I win, I win. I lose, I win.'

Micelli frowned. 'Pardon?'

Pritchard meandered along Southbank Promenade, stopping to watch a rowing scull that had drifted too far south on the Yarra, its rowers frantically thrashing oars trying to turn the craft around. He was prepared to bet that if Helen Kapp was in charge, it would glide silently by, oars perfectly synchronised, course as straight as the Stuart Highway. Through habit he wandered into the food court. Left the spring rolls and potato cakes to dry out under bain-marie lamps. Instead chose a fresh juice combo of beetroot, carrot and ginger. Across the bridge and onto Queen Street, he strolled past bodies still huddled beneath sleeping bags, donated donuts and 7-Eleven sandwiches left under the nose of a curled up Staffy as comatose as its owners. When he stopped to read a message from Micelli, he noted that it was already thirty-four degrees. But what he saw next took him by surprise. On the Bourke Street corner traffic and pedestrians had come to a standstill. Naked people pedalling bicycles streamed through the intersection. 'Save our bike lanes!' they chanted. Followed by 'Bet you can see us now!' Some had slogans painted on their backs; some had signs calling for an end to climate change attached to their bikes. Pritchard watched in awe, waited while the banked up traffic cleared the intersection. Checked his watch and saw that if he hurried he still had enough time to get some lunch from the canteen before the one o'clock meeting.

As usual, Mavis was behind the counter, a broad smile on her face. 'That'll do you good, Barry,' she said, spooning chickpea and roast pumpkin salad into a takeaway container. 'I'll pop in a fork just in case.'

'You wouldn't believe it, Mavis. About 200 people, stark naked, riding up Bourke Street just now.'

'Get on with you.' She took the twenty-dollar note, handed him change. 'Hope they were wearing sunscreen on a day like today. You weren't tempted to join them now you've lost all that weight? You look ten years younger, you know.'

He smiled warmly. 'Mavis, you're not too bad yourself. What is it you're celebrating next week? Your fiftieth? Hope you're not thinking of retiring. We wouldn't be able to cope.'

'Ah, you'd be alright,' she said laughing, before someone else caught her eye. 'Next.' Her voice had lost all its friendliness. Pritchard looked to his left. Skelton was towering over the counter, ropey arms crossed over his chest, shoulders stretching the seams of his white shirt.

'Pie 'n chips,' Skelton barked. 'Make that two serves of chips. Don't forget the sauce, either.'

Pritchard gripped his salad, walked to the stairwell.

'Such a change,' said Micelli, when he sat down at the conference table. 'I'm used to great big brown bags full of dim sims. You're making the rest of us look like slobs.'

Harris was busy mouthing a salad roll, dripping shreds of carrot and lettuce onto the tabletop. 'Yeah,' he said, patting a chocolate and coconut covered slab of cake sitting in front of him. 'It's nice to know my lamington's safe.'

'Okay,' said Pritchard, 'that's enough.'

'Anyone seen Skelton?' Micelli was leaning against the kitchenette doorframe, waiting for the kettle to boil.

'He rang,' said Harris between mouthfuls. 'Said he's been held up.'

'Bullshit,' said Pritchard. 'Just saw him in the canteen. Ordering Mavis round like she was his personal slave.'

Micelli took a deep breath. 'OK. Enough. We've got a murder enquiry to concentrate on, so why don't you kick us off, Harris, tell us where you're up to. Start with the personal stuff on Azarov.' She gestured towards the whiteboard. 'Then we'll go onto other matters.'

Harris began. 'Family migrated from Moscow to Estonia in 1983 when Azarov was a kid, although authorities said the date might not be quite accurate. Apparently, a lot of Russians were forced to migrate, up until the USSR broke up in 1990. They wanted to Russify the country—'

She raised an eyebrow.

'You know, disempower the local culture—'

She tapped a marker against the whiteboard. 'No one likes a bit of history more than me, but that hardly helps us with who he is now. Birth details?'

He referred to his notes. 'Passport states first of April 1964 but that could be wrong as a lot of records were lost or tampered with, as far as anyone knows. Born at the City Hospital, Leningrad.'

Micelli raised her eyebrows. 'Leningrad?'.

'Called St Petersburg now. Travels as an Estonian citizen. Passport's in order, checked with immigration. Bag was selected for random inspection. Nothing showed up. No alerts according to the embassy in Canberra.'

'Is he Russian or Estonian?' asked Micelli. Her awareness of dual citizenship issues was limited to recent calls to strip dual citizens convicted of serious crimes of their Australian citizenship and deport them.

'Estonian. His father applied for citizenship for him after

Estonia became independent in 1991. Apparently there's still a lot of Russians with Grey Passports—'

She rapped the marker she was holding on the whiteboard. 'Did you get his next of kin?'

'Wife. And two kids. Parents both dead. May have a sister. Embassy couldn't be sure if she's still alive, or even if she's still in Estonia. Embassy said they'd handle the notification and body repatriation. If he gets sent back, that is.'

'Okay. He's married, a father, and either sixty or close to it,' Micelli announced triumphantly. 'That took a while.' She noted the details on the whiteboard.

'And just like a lot of sixty-year-olds,' began Pritchard, 'can't help himself when it comes to a pretty girl.'

'Tell us more, Pritchard,' said Harris

'Ah, let me see—' He licked his finger and leafed back through his notebook. 'Here we are. F1.'

'F1?' enquired Micelli.

'Female. Description?'

She sighed. 'Yes please.'

'F1.' Pritchard straightened up, tucked in his stomach. 'Approximately a hundred and eighty-five centimetres, wearing high heels. Black, or dark-haired at any rate. Feasibly, size 10.'

'And how would you know that?' Harris grinned. 'New girlfriend about size 10 is she?'

Pritchard rolled his eyes.

'Guess no one's got an ID? No hotel sign-in?'

'None.' Casting his eyes back to his notebook, he said, 'she approached AA in the lobby at 20.07, sat down, back to the camera, they had a drink, then she accompanied AA to south lift well at 20.30.' He handed Micelli a floor plan of the hotel lobby, the south lift highlighted in yellow, and a map of the ninth floor, showing the lift in relation to Azarov's room. She Blu-Tacked both pages to the whiteboard. 'They emerged on floor nine at 20.37.'

'Seven minutes in a lift to go up nine floors?' asked Harris incredulously. 'Is it pulled by little old men with ropes or something?'

'Why, what's the typical speed?' asked Micelli.

'A standard lift'd go at a hundred and fifty metres a minute. Nine floors is about three hundred metres. Two minutes tops. All it should've taken.'

'Good point, Harris,' said Pritchard solemnly. 'That's why I looked at the lift CCTV as well.'

'And?' said Micelli expectantly.

He grinned. 'Not a lot. But I can confirm that AA and F1 were in the lift for the duration. And that it did not stop at any other floor.' He looked up from his notes. 'Hard to see what was going on though.'

'Why?'

'Someone unfurled an umbrella.'

Harris began to chuckle. 'Dirty bastard.'

Journalists were scattered around the media room. Micelli walked to the lectern. Muffled talk, giggling from the back corner. Kelly Georgiou from Channel 7 slipped into a front row seat, fixed Micelli with her bottomless blue eyes. Coiffed bottle-blonde hair draped artfully over one shoulder, slender fake-tanned legs crossed demurely. Not a lot had changed since Micelli had last seen her, except for a huge diamond ring that she was absently turning full circle. Micelli scowled. 'Good afternoon, ladies and gentlemen. Thanks for your attendance today. We have confirmed the identity of a deceased man found by a room attendant in the Condor Hotel early this morning. The man was Alexei Azarov, an Estonian citizen who was born in Russia. Mr Azarov was visiting Melbourne in his capacity as the tennis manager of Estonian tennis player, Markus Kross, who is contesting the men's singles title. Mr Azarov's family members, who live in Estonia have been informed of his death, as has Markus Kross and his player entourage. We are treating the death as suspicious. There is no obvious motive at this point in our investigation and we do not as yet have access to the results from forensic data collected at the crime scene earlier today. However, we do have some footage of Mr Azarov at Melbourne Park. We want to speak to a man seen with Mr Azarov yesterday afternoon. Please take a moment to read the brief my officer DC Harris will be handing out.' She glanced over her shoulder as footage of Azarov and the man they wished to identify was beamed onto the screen behind her. Weightlifter build, definitely athletic judging by the way he bounced on the balls of his feet. Face hidden by a large western-style hat. They did not show the part where he gripped Azarov by the arm, turned him round and yelled into his face. Harris moved down the centre aisle distributing leaflets which contained a description and a still image copied from the CCTV tape, as well as basic information about Azarov and his business for being in Melbourne.

A finger went up in the front row, far left corner. 'Susan Watson, *The Gazette*.' She smiled widely revealing apricot lipstick marks on her teeth. 'Will Markus Kross continue to play at the Open?'

'Questions when I've finished, please Susan,' Micelli said amiably, not wanting to offend her as she had proved to be useful in the past, unlike a lot of her colleagues, too busy climbing corporate ladders to be of much use when it came to police matters. 'Returning to the brief, if members of the public can assist us identify the man, it would help move the investigation forward. I want to stress that at this stage we are only seeking this man's cooperation. Further, Mr Azarov was seen in the lobby of the Hotel Condor around eight pm yesterday evening in the company of a woman. Her image, and I apologise for its lack of clarity, appears on the reverse side of the brief just handed to you.' Thirty-five fliers were turned over. 'Again, if through you or Crime Stoppers this woman can come forward, we'll be able to pinpoint more accurately Mr Azarov's movements between eight o'clock last night and when his body was discovered at seven this morning.'

Another hand, this time from a woman seated down the back, holding a phone out in front of her. Micelli could just make out an image. 'Sorry,' the woman blurted, 'but social media sites all over this already. Saying stuff about prostitution.'

Micelli drew in a breath. 'As we know, users of Facebook and so on can jump the gun sometimes, and our officers are monitoring all social media as I speak. I'm sure you all understand, this is a sensitive enquiry due to its international ramifications and we have the full support of all relevant authorities. I urge anyone with information as to Mr Azarov's movements on Monday evening to contact Crime Stoppers. Important to stress that all information will be treated with the utmost confidentiality.' She threw what she hoped was an apologetic smile in Susan Watson's direction. 'Susan, your sports journalists would be better placed to handle your query as to the tennis.' A man, also in the front row, raised his hand. 'Yes?'

'Steve Burns, *Times*. How was the victim killed?' Lank hair was falling over his forehead. And judging by his grubby and wrinkled shirt, he obviously hadn't taken a new year's resolution to improve on personal hygiene.

She licked the edges of her teeth. 'Thank you, Mr Burns. We are still waiting for the autopsy results, but early indications suggest the victim may have suffocated.'

'Truth in the rumour that he worked for the Russian Mafia?'

'As I said before, we're examining all possible motives. If you hear any more, don't hesitate to give Crime Stoppers a call. Force needs all the help it can get on Russian criminal activity. Okay, all for now. Thank you for your attendance.'

Kelly Georgiou was still twirling the ring when her colleagues filed out of the room. 'Could I have a word,' she said, rising to her feet.

'Sorry, press conference is over,' Micelli said, nodding to Harris that it was time to leave.

'I didn't want to say anything in front of the others,' she babbled, face reddening under the metallic blusher, 'but I heard that you were involved in an upskirting incident at the tennis last night.'

Micelli stopped in her tracks, turned swiftly, jabbed a finger at the reporter. 'If I ever hear you say anything like that again. Or if I hear you peddle this nonsense on your pretend current affairs show, I will personally guarantee you will never, and I mean never, set foot in a police press conference again.' She turned on her heels and stalked out of the room.

'What was that all about?' Harris had practically broken into a run to keep up.

'None of your fucking business.' She disappeared into the Ladies.

Flicking on the radio in the caravan, O'Leary listened for CFA warnings. No mention of the Daylesford area. Followed by the three o'clock headlines. Tropical Cyclone Anna intensifies off northern NSW coast; second seed in the Open knocked out by wildcard entrant; Police Minister Phillip Sinclair announces a review of the police integrity commission, possible inquiry on the way. 'You hear that? Just what we fucking need.'

Nguyen jerked his head in O'Leary's direction, caught by the vitriolic tone. 'You okay, Boss?'

'That fucker Sinclair. Wouldn't want to dig too deep. Might uncover things best left under the mat.'

Nguyen looked puzzled. 'What's best left under the mat?'

'Doesn't matter,' he said, turning off the radio. 'Going down to the diggings if anyone wants me.' He needed another look. Might be something. Perhaps their spacing? Direction? Some sign that might correlate with other burials of murdered victims populating the crime database. Anything was worth following up if it could give them a clue as to who might have buried these children.

By mid-afternoon Rod Jones and his team had packed up and left the site. The remains of two small bodies had been excavated, placed in bags, and were on their way to Melbourne. The clothing found in the burial location matched the description of the twins' clothing given by their parents when the children were last seen at Beaumaris. Thank god for synthetics. Cotton and wool would have rotted, maybe vanished altogether, depending on how long the garments had been underground. O'Leary hoped that whoever had killed the twins, had done so not long after they were abducted. Perhaps the kindest thing, given what he'd briefly seen on the uploaded videos. Not that their parents were going to see it like that. And that was his job now, go door knocking, break the news to Gina and Paul Mascord.

O'Leary pulled his cap low over his eyes and trudged back to the caravan, picked two bottles of water out of an Esky and guzzled one down. Mechanically, he waved a hand, disturbing a small mob of lethargic bushflies that had settled on a plate of lunchtime sandwiches delivered by an SES volunteer. No one was going to eat them now. It wasn't only the heat that had sapped appetites. He clambered into the van, threw his hat on the bench and twisted the top off the other bottle. 'You be right here if I go back to Melbourne?' Sweat dripped from O'Leary's forehead.

'Sure thing,' Nguyen said, looking up from a laptop screen. 'Might come with you. Do the driving.'

O'Leary wet a towel in the sink, wiped his face and neck. 'Yeah. Maybe.' Pressed a couple of painkillers out of foil, swallowed them down with the last of the water.

'Plenty I can do in the city now we've got bodies.'

'Let's get on the road, then.'

Nguyen checked that the van door was locked before following O'Leary out to the car. Down the driveway and onto Green Gully Road, the smoke hazing the road ahead. A kangaroo dragged itself across in front of them. Singed on one side. 'Could've been hit by a falling branch,' Nguyen said, coming to a stop. 'Should call it in.'

'Who to?'

'Wildlife rescue people.'

'What would they do?'

'They help a lot of animals. You must've seen the picture of that koala taken after Black Saturday?'

O'Leary recalled an image of a firefighter dripping water into a koala's mouth from a plastic water bottle. Was on all the front pages. 'It died, though.'

'But not from the fires,' said Nguyen. 'She died during an operation to remove cysts caused by chlamydia.'

O'Leary eyed his colleague. 'Really?'

'She's in the museum now.'

'How come you know so much about a koala? I thought chlamydia was a sexually transmitted human disease.'

'It is, but it's also a disease koalas get. Makes them blind and infertile. That's why there's not many koalas left in Queensland and New South.'

'You're wasted in the force, DC Nguyen.' O'Leary shook his head from side to side and smiled. 'No doubt about it. All this information.'

Nguyen made a call and pulled back onto the road. 'Wildlife rescue said someone'd be here in under half an hour.'

'That's good.' O'Leary yawned. Before they turned onto the main road, he was snoring softly.

'I've just spoken to Sutcliffe,' Micelli said to Harris when she returned to the office after the press conference. 'Autopsy on Azarov booked for later this arvo. Meet you in five outside on the front steps. Just got to do a couple of things first.' The couple of things included assigning Skelton to take statements from Markus Kross, Artur and Kristo, before checking to see if Rosie had sent further messages. She hadn't, but there was one from David Romano. *Looking forward to tmr xxx.* Reading it made the colour rise and warm her cheeks, same as when she had a crush on an English teacher in Year 10 and every time he'd said her name, she'd felt her olive complexion turn a dull red. She thought about sending a few emoticons in reply like the adolescent she felt but decided on *Me too* instead.

Harris was waiting on the steps for her, jacket slung over one shoulder, tie pulled askew. 'Are we seriously going to walk to the VIFM in this heat?' he asked, offering her one of the water bottles he was holding.

'Less than 30 minutes. Do us good. Bit of fresh air and all.'

He scoffed. 'Hardly call walking along Spencer Street a chance for fresh air.'

'We'll go via William and over Queensbridge, then. That make you happy?'

'Sure thing,' he said, sidestepping to avoid a large pram crammed full of kids.

As they walked past the law courts, the streets erupted with swirling black gowns and wheelie cases. 'Looks like we've hit peak hour,' Micelli said, dodging around a bevy of legals crossing the road. 'By the way, you been to an autopsy before?'

'House fire last year. Didn't see much of the procedure. Bodies weren't in much of a—well they weren't all there, if you know what I mean. Also went to a course. Mainly on protocols for grieving relatives. And remember the body parts retrieved from the Maribyrnong River? That was kind of interesting as there was only an arm and a leg on the table. This one'll be a bit different I expect. Intact and all, isn't he?'

'You know they use power saws, don't you?'

He hesitated. 'I thought it was all done with CT scanners now?'

'Not always. Depends on whether they can tell enough from a scan. Hey, want to grab something to eat first?' They walked across Queensbridge towards Southbank. 'Food court's just along a bit. We've practically got to go through it anyway.'

He looked at her sideways. 'You're kidding, aren't you?'

Once at the VIFM, they settled themselves behind the glass wall of Room 1, dubbed the homicide room. An array of instruments was laid out on stainless steel trolleys covered with green surgical towels. Sutcliffe was leaning against a bench, eyes on a computer screen, scribbling something into a notebook. 'Hello, Ange,' he called, looking over the top of his gold-rimmed spectacles, 'just checking the CT scan report. Evidence for asphyxiation isn't easy to pick up unfortunately. Oh, and who's that you've got with you?'

'DC Rory Harris. Joined the team yesterday,' she said, glancing at her pinging phone. Rosie again. *YOUR FAMILY NEEDS YOU!!!* She sighed, shoved it back into her pocket.

An assistant wheeled in a gurney bearing a body and positioned it under the overhead lights. She removed the covering, revealing the body of Alexei Azarov.

'What's that on his knee?' whispered Harris.

'A star. I looked it up on Google after I saw it at the Condor. Some Russian thing, apparently.'

'Meaning?'

'Google said that whoever has it, doesn't kneel for anyone. Probably shows that he's a tough character. Or at least has been somewhere along the line.'

'But he isn't Russian.'

'Yeah?' she said. 'Thought you said he was before he moved to Estonia. Anyway, probably got it when he was still a Russian.'

Before they could discuss the issue of Azarov's genealogy further, Sutcliffe walked over to the gurney, pulled on gloves, positioned himself adjacent to the dead man's head. 'Ready to start, Ange? Rory?'

Starting with the face Sutcliffe pushed and pinched skin as if he was inspecting an animal skin, sizing it up for its quality of leather. He lifted strands of hair, looked into ears and up nostrils. Paying particular attention to the eyes and eyelids, he scrutinised them for several minutes, shining a high beam light into first one eye then the other, propping open each in turn with a speculum. He ran a finger round the mouth cavity, peered in, laid the tongue out and attached a clamp on the end. All the while he spoke into the microphone, describing each mark on the dead man's body. An assistant standing nearby was taking photographs, and in addition the whole procedure was being videoed.

After the examination of the victim's face, Sutcliffe moved down the body, continuing to map the skin. He moved to the victim's wrists, used a magnifier to enlarge reddened marks. After reaching the feet, the body was rolled onto its front, and the examination continued.

'How long does this go for?' hissed Harris, pointing to his watch.

'As long as it needs to,' replied Micelli, taking a quick look at her phone that had been vibrating in her pocket. Five messages since the autopsy had begun. All from Rosie. She was about to toss her phone into her bag when Sutcliffe announced the next step. 'As you can see, we've examined the entire body from the outside. We're going to open him up now. Any questions up to this point?' An assistant wheeled over one of the instrument trolleys and plugged in a small saw.

Harris slid out from the seat. 'Need the Men's. Too much coffee.'

Micelli grinned. 'I'll keep your seat warm.'

Just as the city was emptying out office workers, O'Leary and Nguyen pulled into the car park under the Spencer Street offices. 'Did Ange have a chance to look at any of those files?' asked Nguyen, opening the door into the stairwell for his boss.

'Texted that she'd had a quick look, but she's got her hands full now. That murdered Russian I told you about.'

'Russian or Estonian?' asked Nguyen, climbing the stairs two-by-two. 'Or is it just the tennis player who's Estonian?'

'Not sure.' O'Leary was wheezing. Once he used to climb three flights in under 30 seconds.

Four heads turned when they walked in. 'Hi,' called Micelli, who was standing in front of a whiteboard at the window-end of the office.

'G'day,' said Nguyen, moving quickly to shake hands with Harris. 'Long time no see. And this is?'

Pritchard laughed. He stood up, offered his hand to Nguyen. 'Changed that much, have I?'

Nguyen gasped. 'My god. Is that really you Pritchard?' Last time they'd met, Pritchard's stomach was hanging over his waistband and every shirt and tie sported food stains.

'Amazing what a few months at the gym can do for a bloke,' he said, 'and a new sweetheart.' He did a little twirl, showing off his slender new self.

'Before we get too carried away in the self-improvement movement, this is DSC Skelton, the other member of our team for this investigation.' Micelli indicated the man sitting at the end of the table, hooded eyes fixed on her face, shirt sleeves rolled to the elbows displaying muscled forearms.

O'Leary nodded curtly, shut himself in his office.

'What's up with him?' muttered Harris.

Nguyen walked towards Skelton, hand outstretched.

Skelton flicked a strand of greying hair off his forehead. 'You must be Sum Ting Wong,?' He cackled. Yellowed teeth. Grey tongue.

Nguyen stopped short, raised an eyebrow. 'Oh, I get it,' he said, nodding his head. 'Keep an ear open for the funny lines, do you?'

Skelton pushed back his chair. 'Yeah. Don't you? Anyway, need a fag.' The door banged behind him.

A few seconds passed before Nguyen reacted. 'And lovely to meet you, too.'

'Don't worry,' said Pritchard, 'I was on a case with him once and he called me Lard the whole time.'

Micelli shook her head, handed a note to Nguyen. 'Here's a quick update re that email you sent. You know the phone that was found in Krakauer's house? Valentino's number comes up. Last time on August 31 last year. All I had time for.'

'Yeah, but we don't know whose phone it is yet,' said O'Leary wearily, who had emerged from his office as soon as Skelton had left. 'Krakauer's denying it's his.'

'Where's his phone, anyway?'

'Said it was lost.'

Micelli snorted. 'Likely story. More like flushed down a toilet somewhere.'

'It wasn't on him when he was arrested in Sydney, according to the notes,' said O'Leary.

'Maybe someone disappeared it after the event.'

'What're you suggesting, Ange?' O'Leary's hackles were up now.

'Just needs to be properly investigated, that's all.' She turned to face the whiteboard. 'Want to know where we're up to with Alexei Azarov?'

'Only if it's relevant to Krakaeur.' He walked towards the door. 'Need to see the boss.'

Goddings was sitting with his back to the open door of his office in one of two regulation black leather easy chairs, feet up on a regulation marble-look laminex coffee table. Splinters of white leg flesh showed in the gap between navy blue sock and navy blue trouser. O'Leary knocked lightly on the doorframe. 'Got a minute, Sir?' Goddings stood up abruptly, waved him in. O'Leary sniffed the air. Doris had undoubtedly clocked off, as the room lacked the bouquet of her trademark perfume.

'Ah, Brendan. News from Glenlyon?' He whipped round behind his desk and sat, spectacles pushed down his nose, pen tapping against a writing pad.

O'Leary took a deep breath, looked around the room, last year's calendar showcasing a snow-capped peak still hung on the wall. 'Officially, we've found the remains of two children,' he said, easing himself into a chair, 'identities unconfirmed. Parts of a body, skeletal, probably belonging to a child, also unidentified. And Vincent Valentino's wife has positively identified the clothing and personal effects found on the body in the mineshaft. After our meeting I intend to contact the parents of the missing Beaumaris twins, ask them to formally identify some clothing found on the remains unearthed today. Then I want to charge Krakauer.'

'Is there any evidence linking Krakauer to the bodies?'

'They're on his property. There's those videos on that dark web site I was shown. Pretty sure the twins are in them.'

'And Valentino?'

'Nothing yet,' O'Leary said. 'But there's a phone linked to both. Him and Krakaeur.'

'How so?'

O'Leary fumbled through an explanation. He wasn't surprised when Goddings came up with the same objections he'd already considered.

'Any ID yet on the men in those videos?'

O'Leary looked down at the floor. 'We're working on it. Theory is that Krakauer was the lynchpin, arranged the production and so on. Careful to keep himself out of the camera's range.'

'Not going to fly, Brendan,' he said, rolling his lips inwards, wiping a hand across his mouth. 'Get me some forensics. Or a witness that puts him at the scene with the smoking gun in his hand, so to speak. Otherwise, he can say it's all a nasty coincidence. All for now?'

O'Leary hesitated. 'I wanted to talk to you about Skelton.'

'What about him?'

'I don't want him in our office.'

Goddings blinked twice in rapid succession. 'And?'

'He's racist. That's just for starters. You should have heard what he just said to DC Nguyen. And to put him in a team headed by a woman, after his last—'

'Enough,' said Goddings, his top lip curled. 'I assign officers in this squad. Understood?' He rose from his chair and walked O'Leary to the door. 'Get on over to Beaumaris. You've wasted good time here interfering in something that's none of your concern.'

O'Leary drove out to Beaumaris, followed his nose to a street where the council had decided one streetlight was enough. He parked outside the Mascord's house and walked through an open gate swinging on its hinges. He knocked on the front door of a triple-fronted brick veneer built sometime during the seventies, now owned by Paul and Gina Mascord. On the way over from the city he'd had to pull over, get out and loosen his tie. Take a few minutes to breathe, try and stop his heart from thumping in his chest. He'd been talking with the Mascords for a bit over ten years, pretty much since Zoe and Jack were new borns, but the news he was about to deliver would bring an end to any hope they may be still hanging onto. If he had been trained to break the news of a death to a relative, he couldn't recall a single thing he'd learnt. In his time in the force he'd had to notify dozens of people that a loved one had died. Didn't matter how that death had occurred, could be suicide or a road accident or a death at work or a homicide. People acted pretty much the same. He could still picture the husbands and wives, the mothers and fathers, staring at him as he stood at their front doors asking to come in. For some, the penny dropping instantly. They'd stand aside, wait for him to enter, point him to a lounge or a kitchen. Sometimes the keening had already begun before he made his announcement. Call it sixth sense. Clairvoyance. Whatever. They were the hardest to tell. It was like they straight away morphed into a primal state. Eyes neither looking nor seeing. Faces pale as a sick person's. Deaf to any further talk. Even if the news came as a complete shock, he knew that nothing he could say would ever be enough.

The Mascords had had years of thinking about their twins, pivoting between knowing they were dead, just wanting to know where their remains were, yet always dreaming that they'd come waltzing up the front path, say hi, check the fridge then face-plant with their phones like normal eighteen year-olds. Fact and fiction intermingled for the Mascords, and they were not alone in that awful world walked through by grief-sodden parents. O'Leary had recognised the signs during his many visits with Paul and Gina. Banners in the kitchen on the twins' birthdays. The bedrooms left the same as the day they'd disappeared, except beds were made, toys were neatly stacked on shelves, books were lined up in a row. On one visit he'd noticed a row of ultrasounds held to the fridge door by magnets. When he'd taken a closer look, he realised these were foetal shots of the twins from eight weeks to near birth. The images had since disappeared from the fridge, but he still wondered about the implications of the display. Had they been there all along or were they recent additions to the fridge, dredged out of some memory box or the like.

O'Leary took a seat at the kitchen table directly in the path of an ancient split system that was chugging away trying to cool down the air in the stuffy room. Watched as Gina paced the floor, her body rocking to and fro as if she was soothing a fractious baby, tight black t-shirt moulding over her bony shoulder blades. Paul sagged down opposite O'Leary and leaned forward, kneading his forehead with the fingers of both hands. Grey hair hung over his shirt collar, still dressed in the suit he would have worn to work in his suburban accountancy firm. Finally, Gina sat down, stared at O'Leary. 'Can't be good news that brings you out here at this time of night?'

After showing them pictures of the unearthed clothing, it had been easy to persuade them to allow a visit from forensics to collect DNA, something they had refused when the twins first went missing. He couldn't remember their reasoning. Could it have been religion? Or were they in denial? He wasn't sure now. No longer mattered.

'It should never have happened.' Gina wailed, eyes ringed black as if she hadn't slept for the last ten years. 'We were only a minute behind them. Weren't we Paul?' Her husband said nothing, head bowed, hands now shoved into pants pockets. O'Leary nodded, sat and listened to their stories, wondered how many times they'd repeated them to police, to family, to the media. Later on, a cup of teabag tea made with UHT milk. No biscuits. He'd said goodnight, told them to expect a couple of investigators in the morning.

WEDNESDAY

ANOTHER WARM morning. Micelli embraced the battle with a strong northerly as she rode into the city. Once in the office, she texted her team, *Meeting 8.30*. A quick shower and enough time to print the crime scene files sent over from Macleod yesterday. Taking a seat at the meeting table, she flicked through the photos. Couldn't see anything that she hadn't seen yesterday.

First in was Skelton, navy blue suit, tie draped round the collar of his shirt, phone to his ear. Without glancing in her direction, he headed straight to the kitchenette which made it impossible for her to hear his conversation. Emerging with a steaming mug, phone no longer in evidence, he hunched down at the table and picked up a copy of *The Gazette*. Micelli considered how to break the silence when Harris strolled in, crisp in pale blue and black, carrying two take-away coffees. 'Here,' he said, setting one down before her. 'I got you a double shot.'

'And,' said Pritchard, still in his grey suit but with a green shirt and tie today, 'I've got a fruit salad to share.' He put a domed plastic container brimming with pineapple chunks and watermelon cubes on the table, along with plastic forks and paper napkins, before sitting down. More like a grass parrot today, Micelli thought, placing the pile of photos onto the table near the whiteboard.

'A veritable fucking feast.' Skelton scowled, pushing the fruit away. 'As I said before, what the fuck happened to the biscuits?' He pushed his chair back and headed towards the door.

Micelli frowned. 'Where are you going this time, Skelton? Another fag?'

Without turning, he raised his right hand, the middle finger extended. The door closed behind him.

Micelli breathed in and out slowly. Noted Harris and Pritchard exchanging glances. 'Give me a minute.' She followed Skelton out the door. Returning a few minutes later, she said, 'Okay. Time to get going. Let's go over what we already know starting with the scene. Can you put these up? We need names and connections.' She slid three markers held together with a rubber band towards Harris, indicated the photos. He Blu-Tacked them to the board.

'Do we know if any other Estonians came to Australia at the same time?' asked Pritchard. 'Or Russians, for that matter?'

'You chase that up,' she said, 'and there must be an Estonian community somewhere that might be happy to chat.'

The office door swung open. Skelton swaggered towards the table. He pulled out a chair and extracted several creased sheets of paper from the back of his notebook. He began to iron them with his knuckles, using his thumb on the middle folds.

'And Harris, you find out about Azarov's business interests.' Turning to Skelton, she said, 'How'd you go yesterday afternoon with the boys?'

'That big piece of wog shit you wanted me to interrogate?'

Frowning, she said slowly, 'It's inappropriate for you to refer to anyone in that manner. And I asked you to take their statements. Not interrogate them.'

'I'll rephrase then. You know that fancy-pants hot-shot you wanted me to talk to? And his mates? Well, I have. Hard to understand, but I've done the interviews with the cunts.'

Rising to her full height, she eye-balled him, neck at forty-five degrees. 'No more warnings, Skelton. You abide by our team's culture, or I'll speak to Goddings.'

He laughed, deep throaty stuff that morphed into a cough. 'Here.' He slid the pages across the table towards Micelli. 'Nothing more to report.'

She picked them up, suppressed the urge to dash out and wash her hands. She scanned the creased notes. 'All you got are their details. We already know their details. What did I ask you to do?' He pushed back from the table. 'Skelton, this is a team meeting,' she yelled, as he walked towards the kitchenette. Her heart thumped against her breastbone.

'I'll investigate the brothels.' He sneered over his shoulder. Pritchard stifled a giggle, straightened the pages of the newspaper still lying opened on the table.

'What brothels?' demanded Micelli.

'The ones that wog cu—chaps like them frequent.' That laugh again.

'You two,' Jerking her head towards Harris and Pritchard, she said, 'be back here at midday. Phone or text if I need to know anything.' She waited until they left the office before following Skelton into the kitchenette. 'I'm going up to see Goddings.'

'Yeah?' He was spooning sugar over a bowl of cereal, phone in hand.

'Ask him to reconsider your position on my team.' She was interrupted by the sound of a barking dog.

'Hey, Phil?' Skelton said. Teeth bared, he began to pick at something in his mouth with his little finger, phone pressed tight to his ear. Micelli turned on her heel but not before she heard him say, 'Yeah. And pigs might fuckin' fly.'

'That a new bike in the car park?' O'Leary asked when he blundered into the office, well after nine-thirty.

Micelli looked up from the papers she was shuffling. 'You like it? Mum and Dad gave it to me for Christmas. Always wanted a white bike.'

'Go faster than your red one?'

'Goes like a cut cat.'

He chuckled. 'Haven't heard that expression for a while. Dad used to say it about every new car he bought. None of them actually did go like cut cats, more like lumbering elephants. Sleek and five kids never did go together.' He dropped into a chair next to her desk.

She eyed him carefully. 'You look tired, Brendan.' Now wasn't the time to vent about Skelton.

'Glenlyon's going nowhere fast. The Mascords want answers. Not that I blame them after all these years.'

She fingered a gold hoop earring. 'Any ideas yet about who's in those videos?'

He shook his head. 'Special Victims are working on it. Pretty doubtful we'll get anywhere. No face shots. Obviously. In the meantime, Krakauer can't be charged with anything more than possession of child abuse materials.'

'And drugs. That's on this week, isn't it?'

He leaned forward, angled himself out of the chair. 'Yeah, Friday. That'll keep him behind bars for at least eighteen months.' Shambling towards the sink, he filled a glass with water, snapped two more painkillers out of a blister pack and swallowed them.

'You're not taking too many of them?' Before he had time to reply, her phone buzzed. 'Micelli,' she said, swinging her chair round to face her desk. 'You sure?' She scribbled a name and address into her notebook. 'Who said press conferences didn't work?' O'Leary had already shuffled off, closing his office door behind him. She finished what she was doing then sent a text to her team. *ID for tennis man. Sergey Serchanov. I'm going there now*.

Before she left, she peered into O'Leary's office. He was leaning back in his chair, eyes closed.

O'Leary, hollow-eyed and racked by pain in his thigh, was sitting in Goddings's office going over the events that had occurred since he'd been on the Krakauer case. Doris had made him a coffee which remained untouched on the table between them. 'I can see you're worried, O'Leary, but let's take the first incident. Your phone could have dropped out of your pocket when you were walking round the Glenlyon site. You were right to have it cancelled and sent to Macleod for testing.' He crossed his legs at the ankles, revealing navy socks and white flesh. 'Doris?' She appeared in the doorway, a headset angled like a rock star might wear a mike at a concert. 'Get onto Macleod for me, will you? I want a full report on O'Leary's phone.' She nodded, returned to her desk, hid herself behind a large computer screen. 'Now the twins and Claire. That's more serious. And I agree with you that if someone did take your phone, they could have used some software to obtain addresses and so on. But a simpler explanation is that you could have been followed to Claire's house. How often do you go again?'

O'Leary explained that he picked the kids up midweek for an overnight stay, Wednesdays ideally, but this could change depending on his work commitments, as well as going over on the weekend. He and Claire had flexible arrangements, happy to change things when one or the other couldn't make it.

'So, twice during the week and twice at the weekends, assuming you also drop the kids back to their mother's? Wouldn't be hard for someone bearing a grudge to follow you.'

O'Leary nodded. No use arguing with Goddings who seemed determined to knock down the list of irregular goings-on, as if they were no more than a house built of cards. 'Remember though, whoever is behind this sent guns to the twins. So real looking that they scared the wits out of everyone.'

'But they were still toys. No real harm done. Wouldn't you agree?'

O'Leary didn't agree. Never would. He'd seen enough damaged souls when he was in uniform. A memory flashed into his brain. A woman who'd been a university lecturer confined to a two-bedroom unit, sleeping in the bath as that was the only place left where she could move in a house full of paper. Workplace bullying had tipped her over the edge.

'I think we'd be better off looking at people who might have a grudge. Don't you?' Without waiting for a reply, he called to Doris again. 'Forensics at Macleod?'

She stood up, this time without headphones. She glanced at a note in her hand. 'Apparently the team who've worked on the phone said the report's completed and they'll send it to you, Sir, but said to say there were no fingerprints.'

'See what I mean?' erupted O'Leary. 'If the phone had dropped out of my pocket it would have been covered in prints. You know yourself how many times a day you swipe the bloody thing.'

'Ah, but the SES chap who picked it up might have been less careful than you. Could have accidentally wiped it on his pants. Who's to know?'

O'Leary picked up the coffee cup and out of habit took a swig. His face creased as if he'd tasted one of the twins' concoctions, they liked to make with stuff they found in the pantry. He gasped, pushed the cup out of arm's reach. 'Okay, I get what you're saying. And I get that we can't just mount surveillance whenever someone gets a fright. But.' He took a deep breath. He knew what he wanted to say, that two little kids, his ex-wife and her partner, and himself, come to that, were scared of what was going on and wanted to know who was behind it all. But what to say to Goddings to convince him this case was altogether different. In the end, he tried to make a deal. 'One more thing and we act. Can we agree to that?'

Goddings pursed his lips, uncrossed and re-crossed his ankles. 'That seems reasonable, I suppose. By the way, I want you to get another check-up from the medico. See how your leg's progressing.' He hesitated, eyeballed O'Leary over his spectacles. 'And everything else too, while you're there.'

O'Leary felt the blood rising in his cheeks. What did *and everything else* mean, exactly? Was Goddings trying to make out that his health was to blame, or at least was partially responsible, and he was doing little more than imagining all this stuff? It had happened before to other colleagues. Go on sick leave because of a physical incident and then the top brass might try to make out you were sick in the head as well. If they wanted to get back at you for something. Or get rid of you altogether. Of course, the ones who really were sick in the head—and he could name a few, perhaps starting with Skelton, but including his old boss when he was a uniform at Glen Waverley—were ignored. What was the thing with psychopaths in the workplace he'd heard about in the training course they'd sent him to after he got promoted last time? Psychopaths frequently rise to the top of an organisation because they actively seek advancement through any means available, including via some methods that most sensible people wouldn't consider. Then when they become the boss, they blame and shame their team, not afraid to lie when the heat is turned up. Perhaps Goddings was a mild psychopath, if such a condition existed, looking to blame O'Leary for what was going on. Probably easier than ordering an investigation into the irregular happenings.

Goddings interrupted his train of thought. 'Bring me a report by Thursday. Let's hope it's nothing more than a storm in a teacup.' He raised himself from his chair and offered O'Leary his hand, opening the door for him. O'Leary was left wondering what report he was to bring. Was it to be one about his health or one about the goings on?

O'Leary looked up from his huddle with Nguyen when Elsa Janzen knocked softly on the door. The desk was awash with mugs of half-drunk tea, a bottle of water pinning down a stack of papers. 'Hi,' she said brightly, smiling at Nguyen, 'Inspector Goddings said I might find you here. Tried to call before, but—'

'Went flat,' O'Leary growled. He fumbled in a drawer, found a charger which he plugged in and attached the phone lying on his desk. Remembered to smile too late. Tried to make up for it, gestured to Nguyen to move a stack of files from the other chair.

'I've gone over a few things,' she said, removing black-rimmed glasses and wedging them into curly blonde hair that had slipped out of its bun, now cascading onto her left shoulder. 'First, confirming there's no reports of Gregory Anson being dead. More than a kilogram of Ecstasy turned up on the Gold Coast last week. Had his trademark, blue and red, a dog etched into the pill press. Not the bulldog imprint we found last year, but a dog nevertheless.'

'Might be a copycat. Can't jump to conclusions. Need substantiation.'

She tugged at her navy pencil skirt that had ridden up well over her knees. 'You're right. Of course. Without direct evidence linking him to the stuff, could be anyone's.' She placed a folder on the desk and opened it to reveal neatly typed pages encased in plastic document protectors. 'Probably best if I give you a copy of my summary of the Anson material.' She pushed the folder, labelled with a complete file note, across the desk. 'By the way, did you know his legal rep is Elise Lanigan? Think her success rate stands at 97 per cent. Amazing mind.'

O'Leary snorted, recalling his last encounter with the flame-haired lawyer on a trip to Sydney last year, the beginning of the Krakauer case. 'If she *has* got a good mind, and I'm not saying she hasn't, why waste it on lowlife is my question.'

'Plenty like that,' said Nguyen. 'But back to Anson. What stood out for you in all the data?'

Janzen sat back in her chair, pushed more runaway curls behind an ear. 'That Anson's smart. And getting smarter. And he's got connections. Probably in high places. He's a bit like a ghost. You could swear you can see him just there in front of you, but when you move, not a trace.'

'We've got his DNA, haven't we?'

She bit her bottom lip. 'We haven't, you know.'

O'Leary glared at her. 'Well bloody well get it!' Voice hard-edged, eyebrows raised to their limits. 'And don't forget to let that scumbag lawyer of his know that we want it and we're prepared to get a court order if necessary.'

'Sir.' Janzen raised her chin. 'But wouldn't it be hard to enforce such an order if we don't know where Anson is?'

O'Leary stood up, pointed to the door. 'All for now. Got a few things to do.'

Nguyen followed Janzen out to the main office, suggested they grab a coffee. 'Here? Or takeaway?'

Nguyen led the way to the door and out to the lift. 'You arced up a bit in there.'

'Don't like being yelled at.'

'Who does?'

She scowled. 'Ah, Mr Empathetic, I see. Anyway, what's up with him? Last time he was okay. Very calm. Easy-going even.'

Over coffee Nguyen filled her in on where O'Leary was at, including his injury. 'He's on edge. Weird things happening at

Glenlyon. It's as if we're being shadowed, but no traces. Although I think we'll have some intel soon. Last time someone made a visit to the site, they weren't as careful as they should have been.'

Pritchard hitched up the knees of his new suit pants—charcoal with a faint stripe—as he wriggled onto one of the stools positioned at a stand-up desk. Logging in, he opened the AQUIS site listing arrivals at Melbourne Airport and set a date search from New Year's Day. A spreadsheet opened. He positioned the mouse on the drop-down box marked Nationality and hit E: Ecuador, Egypt, El Salvador, Equatorial Guinea, Eritrea, Estonia. One arrival from Estonia. A woman called Ludmilla Bagrova. Cleared immigration at 8pm on the eleventh of January. No incoming travellers with the name Alexei Azarov. Searching this time for Sydney arrivals, he learned that Azarov entered on the fifth of January along with Markus Kross. Two other men carrying Estonian passports on the same flight, Artur the coach, and Kristo the masseur. A search of all international arrival locations across the nation yielded Russian arrivals in every capital city, a total of one hundred and eighty-seven men and sixty-four women. Some of the Russian names he recognised from the sports pages. January was certainly international tennis stars-and-wannabes-month in Australia.

Ludmilla Bagrova had given an address in North Melbourne as her intended residence while in Australia. He checked Google maps, wheeled the mouse to view up and down the street, examined the front of the house. Just another terrace, two storeys, painted dark blue. A nineteen minute walk. He took his jacket from its peg near the kitchenette and set off northwards along Spencer Street, past the Remand Centre, crossing the street to benefit from the shade.

The house was no longer blue, now sleek white with a black trim. He opened the wrought iron gate, crossed two metres of tessellated tiling to a front door hung with a brass knocker. A small doorbell with intercom was attached to the doorjamb. He chose the bell. Seconds later a woman's voice, heavily accented, said,

'Yes?'

Pritchard identified himself and asked to see Ms Bagrova. 'I her,' came the reply.

'Police. Please open the door. I need to speak with you.'

Almost immediately the door opened, but only a crack, a thick security chain in place. A woman's face, eyes shielded by a hand. 'I see your papers?'

He held up his badge. She reached for it. 'No, you can't hold it,' he said, introducing himself. 'I need to talk to you.'

'Okay.' She unhooked the chain and moved back, almost hidden behind the door. Up close, he realised how tall she was, legs like a ballerina's on full display in tight denim shorts. High cheekbones, green eyes heavily outlined in black, a swathe of blue-black hair tumbling down her back towards a narrow waist. She led him into a small sitting room furnished with cream leather sofas and a massive television screen above a fireplace. 'Sit. I get you drink.' He noted a lamp and several glass objects arranged on the central coffee table, sharing space with maps of Melbourne and a folder, open at a page proclaiming *Welcome to our Airbnb*. An ashtray held three butts, all smoked less than halfway down, stubbed and broken. He couldn't see a cigarette packet or lighter. 'Here,' she said, returning to the room. 'It is water. Good, no?'

He took a sip, 'Good. As I said at the door, I need to ask you some questions. Do you need an interpreter?'

She screwed up her nose, 'Interpreter? All my work at home is English.'

He opened his notebook, laid it on the coffee table amid the maps. 'Could we start with what you do and what brings you to Melbourne, Miss Bagrova?'

Folding herself into an armchair, she kicked off silver sandals and reached for the ashtray. 'I smoke. Okay.' She fished out cigarettes and a lighter from somewhere inside her shirt and lit up. A wisp of smoke circled above her lips before it was whisked away by the air conditioning unit on the wall. 'I come for holiday. Not crime. What makes you talk with me?'

Pritchard began to explain, describing that a man travelling with an Estonian passport had been found dead in a Melbourne hotel room. She leapt to her feet, smashed the cigarette into the ashtray. 'What you say? Who this dead man?'

He raised one eyebrow. 'Do you know Mr Alexei Azarov?'

Her big green eyes filled with tears before she ran from the room, screeching in a language he didn't recognise. Following her down the hallway, he found her bent over a dining table, fists pounding the tabletop. 'Miss Bagrova—'

'Get away!' she shouted. 'He not dead. You lie.' She fixed him with her eyes, now red from crying. 'I see him. He alive.'

Pritchard pulled out one of the dining chairs and manoeuvred her into it. 'Is there someone I can call for you?'

'I tell him be careful. He not listen.' Further sobbing broke out.

Taking a glass from a shelf, he filled it with water, placed it on the table. He sat down next to her, offered her a tissue from a box he had picked up from the kitchen bench. She grabbed a handful, her shoulders shaking with the effort of controlling her crying. He asked her again if there was anyone he could call, this time suggesting Markus Kross and his two sidekicks, but she shook her head.

'I not know no one. Just Alex.' A further gale of tears, to the point where her breath jagged, choking as if the air was thick. He felt inclined to put an arm round her shoulder, pat her on the back like his mother used to do when he was a kid. Instead, he slipped up to the sitting area, brought back his notebook and water glass, waited until she rubbed more tissues into her eyes and blew her nose.

For the next half an hour Pritchard listened and tried to take notes as she told him about her affair with Alexei Azarov that had begun in Tallinn five years ago. She had been working for international financiers trying to secure funds for a Russian oil company keen to expand into the Baltic Sea, north of Estonia. Azarov had been introduced by one of the executives at a monthly dinner held in Tallinn's old town. 'When I see Alex I know. We have chemistry.'

'Is that why you're here? Your job?'

'Of course not!' She almost spat the words at him. 'I here to have holiday with Alex, away from Tallinn, away from wife. We plan this. After tennis, we go to Barrier Reef.' She got up, splashed running water on her face and dried it on a tea towel. 'I want to see him.'

Driving north along Nicholson Street, Micelli was reminded of her childhood visits to a North Carlton shop where her mother stocked up on the family's supply of *salame finocchiona*, a garlic and fennel salami that her father loved. No longer available in that location though, she noted. Instead, a café called *smallgoods*. Plastic kindergarten stools dotted the footpath. The usual array of coffee drinkers chatting away the morning. Two doors up, Sergey Serchanov was waiting for Micelli, sitting in a deck chair on his front verandah, smoking a cigarette. The small garden was overgrown, weeds and straggly orange marigolds competing for dominance. Even though he was partially obscured by a grapevine struggling to gain purchase on a rickety trellis, she could not miss his flinty stare. She prised open the front gate, rusty hinges resisting her force and marched towards him. 'I know who you are. Come in' He turned on his heel and preceded her through the front door and down a narrow passageway hung with jackets, coats, hats, including the white hat described by Glenda Davis, the volunteer driver from the tennis centre. Once in the kitchen, he pointed to one of two chairs. 'Sit. You vant tea?'

Doing as she was instructed, she looked around for somewhere to place her notebook and phone, reluctant to add to the clutter on the tabletop. She thought the pile of newspapers listing to the left might topple if she pushed back a stack of books, a world globe, or a plate adorned with a pair of rimless spectacles despite the egg and bacon leftovers crusted onto it. 'Black. Not too strong, please.' He was already busy with a large silver pot steaming away on a wood stove. 'Is that a samovar?'

'Of course. How is tea made vithout?'

She absorbed the room, eyes wandering up and down walls covered in brightly painted shelves holding a profusion of photographs and trinkets. One shelf was given over to sporting trophies; another, bowed in the middle, was stacked tightly with papers bulging from a ratty collection of manila folders. 'Mr Serchanov, how well did you know Alexei Azarov?'

He shoved aside the dirty plate and placed two cups in its place. 'Not vell,' he said, sitting down in the other chair. She could see his thighs straining against the light summer fabric of his trousers. 'He not a good man. I don't vant to know him, but I do.' He slurped a mouthful of tea.

Micelli shifted in her chair trying to relieve the pressure of the hard wooden seat. 'Okay, you didn't know him well, but you decided to meet him at the tennis?'

'Of course.' Another slurp from the teacup.

She took a sip, her stomach immediately protesting the sudden intake of tannin. 'Can you tell me why that was?'

'Of course.'

She waited.

He emptied his cup in one swallow and put it on the plate, nudging aside the spectacles. 'Ven I discover he in town, naturally I go to meet him. He need to pay for vat he did to my mother. He rob her. In Estonia. She die, how you say, a porpoise.'

'A porpoise?' Micelli stifled a giggle.

His eyes blazed. 'Vat you call that in this crazy language, then?'

'Ah,' she said slowly, catching his meaning. 'A pauper. But how does your mother dying with no money relate to Mr Azarov?' She noticed that Serchanov's brow was beaded with sweat.

'I tell you how.'

Micelli listened and jotted notes as best she could as a story of dubious financial practices unfolded. She did not fully understand the complexities of what he was recounting, but it appeared that Serchanov's mother, a Russian national living in Estonia since the time of the breakup of the Soviet Union, had placed her life savings in an investment scheme managed and owned by Alexei Azarov. 'He take her money, tell her she get twenty, thirty, percent.' He waved his hands around, voice getting louder, accent more clipped. 'It all lies. In one year, no interest. None. And ven she ask, he tell her no money left.' He thumped the tabletop, face flushed, breathing harshly. The pile of newspapers began to slip forwards. Micelli tried to hold them back, but they cascaded onto the table and knocked her teacup to the floor. Serchanov grabbed the pile and shoved them onto a spare space next to the sink. He bent to pick up her cup, which had not broken, and filled it with more tea. 'Here,' he said, wheezing from the effort of bending down, 'drink more. Vere vas I? Oh, I know.' He positioned himself back in the chair, resumed his tale. 'He say father firm in Austria go bankrupt and he have to give money to them.'

'Azarov said that?' He looked at her as a teacher might regard a particularly stupid pupil. She faltered only slightly. 'Why wasn't he charged with fraud?'

'In Estonia we have the Obtshak. Like Mafia. Russian and Estonia join in this together. They look after Azarov.' Serchanov described a recent Obtshak crime, fully supported, according to him, by the Estonian police minister and several high-ranking police officers. This she could fathom, given what she knew and could readily imagine about her own minister for police.

She thanked him for the tea, explained she would return with a statement for him to sign. Showing her to the door, he said, 'I glad he dead. I kill him myself.'

She stopped, turned to face him. 'Did you kill him, Mr Serchanov?'

He scoffed, a smile flitting across his lined face. 'Not so lucky. But I shake hand of man who did.'

The twins were having a lazy morning in front of TV, breakfast dishes sprawled everywhere from a big pancake cook-up. When they heard the knock on the door, they jumped up. 'I'll go, Mum,' yelled Jack. Claire shook her head, shrugged on a dressing gown and shuffled down the passageway. 'Who is it?' She strained to see the time on her watch without her glasses.

'Delivery, ma'm.' Crisp, manly. But why the ma'm? The word irked her. She peered through the peephole. Her vision was obscured by a giant floral display, white gladioli towering above blush-pink roses, lilies and carnations vying for space, bluegum tips providing a contrast. 'Interflora,' the disembodied voice said.

'Any ID?' A card was slid under the door announcing A.J

Brownings, Floral Arrangements with Care. She picked it up, glanced at the address. 'I can leave this here, if you like.' She opened the door, squinted at a man silhouetted against the morning sun, his tightly wrapped red turban coming into focus as he bent forward and offered her the bouquet.

'Wow!' chorused the twins who'd followed her down to the front door.

She shooed them back. 'Thanks, just wasn't expecting anything, that's all.' She closed the door in his face, hoping he wouldn't misinterpret her shortness. Tied to a piece of raffia circling the bunch was a card. She pulled it from its envelope and tried to read it on her way back to the kitchen. 'Happy birthday! In deep gratitude.' No signature. Karen, perhaps, but that didn't make a lot of sense as she'd already received Karen's gift brought to her bedside, along with an early morning coffee. Her mother? Unlikely. Especially the deep gratitude bit. No, definitely no one in the family, as none of them had ever thanked her for anything that she could recollect. Someone at work? No way. HR might know her birthdate, but as far as she knew, no one else did. Brendan. Perhaps. He did know when her birthday was, and he had been grateful for her help when he was in hospital and during his convalescence. Maybe. She found her phone on the table, searched for his new number. 'G'day, Brendan. Lovely flowers. Thank you very much.' She reached up to a high shelf for the cut crystal vase an aunt had given them on their wedding day.

'What're you talking about, Claire?' He sounded jumpy.

'I didn't expect you to remember my birthday,' she said, snipping raffia and unwrapping pink tissue. 'They're gorgeous.' Already the kitchen was awash with the clove-like scent of the carnations.

A sharp intake of breath. 'Claire, happy birthday, but I didn't give you any flowers.'

'Oh, okay then. Can't think of who else might have sent them.' She placed the bunch into the vase, careful not to disturb the arrangement. 'I'll let you go, then. Sorry to disturb. Enjoy the rest of the day.'

'Hang on, Claire. You say flowers were delivered and you don't know who they're from?'

She could hear something else in his voice as she straightened a gladiolus, her least favourite stem in the whole arrangement. 'Yep, that's the story.'

'Everything else alright?'

She assured him that the twins were fine, excited about going to the beach after lunch, that nothing had happened out of the ordinary at home apart from Jack talking about going to see his grandparents on the weekend.

'I'll see you later, then, when I pick up the kids.'

'Absolutely,' she said, carrying the vase to the centre of the kitchen table. 'I'll make sure they're ready to go.'

Doris peered over black-rimmed spectacles, arose from her desk and showed Micelli to Godding's office. 'Coffee?' she asked.

'Just had one, thanks,' Micelli lied. 'Maybe water?'

'Ah,' said Goddings looking up from a newspaper, 'it's always instructive to see what our fellows in the press come up with. Just reading that Steve Burns thinks we should check out Russian Mafia links to Azarov.' He chuckled. 'But I suppose you're already on to it.'

She smiled. 'No, but we do have preliminary autopsy results, the team are following the investigation plan, and the police department in Tallinn, Estonia, where the victim was living up until he came to Australia, have cooperated.' She passed across a folder containing the findings to date.

He put on his glasses and read. 'Good work,' he said, looking up. 'I see you've been careful to observe the rules of an evidence brief. Saves time later.'

'Thought that was a good way to proceed, Sir.'

'It is, DSC Micelli. But, on another note, I hear you recently waded into a matter that was none of your concern.' He closed the folder and leaned forwards in his chair.

Shutting her eyes, she pinched the bridge of her nose between thumb and forefinger. Now was not going to be the time to complain about Skelton. 'I know I made a grave mistake, Sir. My sister was beside herself. I just didn't think.'

'No doubt you're aware of Minister Sinclair's announcement. This is the sort of thing that we must stamp out in the force. Relatives or no relatives. Pulling rank is part of a culture that has seen its day.'

Mouth desperately dry but too nervous to pick up the glass of water Doris had brought in, she waited for him to go on.

'You are to apologise to the officer. Immediately. If she accepts your apology that will be the end of the matter.' He placed his glasses in their case and moved it aside. 'Now, get on with this Azarov investigation and don't let emotion sway you. You're a good officer, DSC Micelli. Maybe even one with a bright future.'

Suit jacket over the back of his chair, Harris's eyes were fixed on a computer screen, his index finger gently controlling the cursor's movement through a densely printed list. 'Got it! Players International is the registered name of Azarov's business, according to the Department of Justice in Tallinn.'

'Sounds like a cigarette company,' said Micelli. 'What exactly does Players International do?'

'Represents sportspeople who are good enough to compete internationally,' he said, easing the knot of his tie slightly. 'And that should be past tense. Doesn't seem to be any other directors or shareholders.'

'Many represented?' She looked up from her notebook where she'd been checking her notes from yesterday's autopsy.

'Estonia's not big. About 1.3 mil, quarter of them born in Russia like Azarov. Reckon the number of sports stars must be pretty low.'

'Haven't heard of too many.' She scratched a mosquito bite on her ankle, courtesy of outside dining with David Romano. 'But enough apparently to keep him in a job?'

Harris paused. 'According to his tax returns, small pickings.'

'Then how did he afford to fly halfway round the world and stay in a luxury hotel?'

'Dunno. But I'll find out.'

She nodded, returned to her notes. Although Sutcliffe had performed an extensive investigation, he still wasn't entirely satisfied that homicidal asphyxiation was the cause of death. 'This is a difficult one, Ange,' he'd said while the assistant was clearing the bench and sewing up the body. 'You see, it takes around three minutes for someone to die of oxygen deprivation—there's signs of that in the trachea and organs—unless of course a cardiac arrest is triggered. For a man of his age, his heart's in reasonable shape, maybe a bit too much fatty tissue surrounding the organ, but no signs that led to his death. So, back to the suffocation. You'd think our victim would have kicked up a fuss, not remained peacefully on a bed while someone held a plastic bag over his head. Which leads me to consider autoeroticism. Yet the handcuffs don't tally with this interpretation.'

'What about the fact they'd been removed? I know we sort of talked about this on yesterday at the scene, but don't they suggest the involvement of at least one other?'

He had taken off his gold-rimmed spectacles and cleaned them with a surgical swab. 'I tend to agree. I had a look for some obvious toxicity, thinking maybe our chap had been put to sleep before the suffocation. And this is where it gets a bit trickier. We'll have to wait for the lab results, I'm afraid. Can't help more than this at present, sorry to say Ange.'

Pritchard boarded a Number 55 tram to Coburg. He had an appointment to meet with the secretary of the Estonian Society at eleven. As the tram passed through the revegetated park near the Children's Hospital a kid dressed as Superman, with his mother and grandmother on guard duty, stood on the seat and began pointing at trees. 'Koala! I saw a koala!' He repeated his claim several times. His mother wrestled him onto her lap, bent close to his ear and said something Pritchard couldn't catch. The kid started to giggle, jumped out of her grasp and balanced in the aisle. 'We're all going to the zoo, tomorrow,' he sang at top volume, 'zoo, tomorrow'. Before he could complete the verse, his mother scooped him into her arms, held him tighter this time. Pritchard was glad when they all got out, trailing baskets and strollers and enough spare clothing to see them safely through a Melbourne day.

He got off a few stops later and checked the address on his phone. Turning left, he sauntered down the leafy side of the street, looking for the correct house number. A grey weatherboard, white trim, red petunias in need of water drooping listlessly from pots lining the fence. In the front window an A4 piece of paper confirmed this to be the home of the Estonian society. He opened the fly screen and knocked once on the solid wooden door painted egg-yolk yellow. 'Hello.' A plump-faced woman whose grey hair was mostly concealed by a red and green floral scarf, stood on the threshold. 'You are the policeman, no?'

He was shown into a front room furnished with mismatched armchairs, most draped with knitted rugs. 'I am Mrs Olesk. I get you a coffee then we talk.' She pointed to a chair and disappeared from the room. He could hear dishes rattling from the back of the house, a man's voice, a radio tuned to music he did not recognise. Bustling back in, she placed a small tray on a table next to his chair. A plate covered with a lace doily held six or seven biscuits. 'These walnut and ginger. I make yesterday.'

Cautiously picking one off the plate, careful not to disturb Mrs Olesk's arrangement, he placed it on the saucer of his coffee cup. When she hovered over him with a sugar bowl, he shook his head. 'I'm sweet enough, Mrs Olesk. Or at least, that's what my girlfriend says.'

She patted his arm, smiling to show a row of perfectly white teeth. 'You good looking man with good job. Your girlfriend a lucky woman. Now, what do you want?' she asked, putting the sugar bowl down and settling into a chair opposite him.

Setting out the situation as briefly as he could without telling her that Azarov was dead, he asked whether any of her members might know of him.

'Azarov!' she yelled, jerking forward. Spittle had collected at the corners of her mouth. A man tall enough to be a basketballer came into the room, slid onto the arm of her chair, put his hand on her back. 'He hurt many of us. We come to Australia but before we go he take our money and make these vows and we never see our money again.' She began to sniffle, wiping at her eyes with a lace-trimmed handkerchief. 'My husband tell you more.'

The man kept patting his wife's back, thick locks of white hair falling over his forehead that he pushed aside with a forefinger. 'We lose many kroons. Some of our members must go back to work here, sweeping floors, cleaning offices. Like the poor Valk family. Both at work and over seventy years old, now. And Mr Kapp.' He looked at his wife who nodded for him to go on. 'Mr Kapp is no longer with us. He kill himself, he so upset and ashamed.'

Pritchard frowned. 'Mr Kapp?' He flicked through pages in his notebook. 'Can you tell me more about Mr Kapp, please?'

Mr Olesk described how Bruno Kapp had migrated to Australia with his young daughter in 1996 soon after his wife had passed away with breast cancer. 'We neighbours in Tallinn. We catch plane together to Australia. He very upset when he get letter from bank telling him he has no money left. All the money from when he sold his house. All his wife's money.' He swept his hand in a long arc. 'Gone, like a deer in the forest.'

'When was this?'

He furrowed his brows. 'I think in 2006,' he said slowly, 'or maybe 2007.'

'No, 2006, *kallike,*' said his wife, shaking her head vigorously. 'Remember, we have ticket for Commonwealth Games, and we miss event to go to funeral. And then young Helen stay with us for a week after.'

'Who?' Pritchard picked up his cup, took a sip. 'Sorry, could you repeat that? Did you say Helen as in Helen Kapp?'

'Yes,' Mr Olesk said, nodding his head, 'you are correct. Bruno die in March 2006. We have Helen for a week. Poor girl. She found him, you know.'

For the next half an hour Pritchard asked questions and noted the answers he was given. Helen Kapp, daughter of the dead Bruno, and Helen Kapp, security manager at the Condor Hotel, were one and the same person. A bright student, her school had provided a boarding scholarship for her when she became an orphan, a decision that paid off well when at the end of the following year she was offered a place at a prestigious hospitality school west of Sydney. According to the Olesks, she had advanced up the corporate ladder quickly, and was on the verge of accepting a job offer in Switzerland.

'Always she come to Day of Restoration of Independence and Christmas celebrations if she not working. Soon we will be back under Russia's thumb,' said Mrs Olesk. 'That President. First Crimea. Then Ukraine. Soon it will be us. Thank God we are here in this country now.' Pritchard could hear fear mixed with disgust in her voice.

He took his leave, thanking them for their help. He galloped back along their street, dashing across the road just in time to board a city-bound tram. He half fell into a seat when the tram rounded the corner into Dawson Street, one hand swiping a Myki card, the other reaching into a shirt pocket for his phone. 'Guess what?'

'What?' said Micelli.

'Helen Kapp has a story.'

Straggling in through the front gate, the twins dragged boogie boards and towels along the path. 'Hey, how did you go?' Karen was leaning on the front door jamb, mug of tea in her hand. 'Bet you rode those waves like Mick Fanning.'

'Who's he?' Jack was first in the door.

'He got eaten by a great white shark,' said Zoe, pushing up behind him.

Jack stopped in his tracks. 'Is he dead?'

'Course not. He was on TV when it happened. I saw it last year at school.' Zoe started to fill Jack in on the details when Karen interrupted.

'Go on you two,' said Karen, choosing to wait for Claire to finish unloading. 'There's icy poles in the freezer. The ones with pineapple.'

They bolted off down the passage and bounded into the kitchen.

Claire slung their backpacks over her shoulder, gathered up the

Esky and beach shelter and locked the car. 'Bugger the icy poles. I need a wine,' she said, kissing Karen lightly on the mouth. 'Too hot for tea.' Karen took the Esky and followed her through to the kitchen. 'What's this?' asked Claire, spying a padded post bag on the bench addressed to the twins. She picked it up, turned it over, gave it a shake. Jack and Zoe raced over, icy poles in hand. 'You haven't been ordering things from that booklet you get at school again, have you?'

'Course not!' said Zoe. 'I only ever did that once.' She jumped up to reach the parcel that Claire was holding over her head.

Claire took the glass of wine offered to her by Karen. 'You have to tell me the truth before I let you open it.'

The twins looked at each other then turned to their mother and began to profess their innocence.

'Okay, I believe you. So, who's going to open it?'

'Me!' they both yelled together.

She put the package on the table and stood aside. Jack ripped open a tab to reveal shiny gift wrap. 'Wow! Look at this Mum. Do you think it's real gold?'

'Course not, silly!' said Zoe, grabbing the edges of the post bag and pulling it apart. Two identical parcels lay inside, each wrapped in gold foil and tied with black velvet. Small gift tags with hand-written messages: *To Jack—aim high Dad XXX* and *To Zoe—shoot for the stars Dad XXX*. Both twins stared with open mouths. 'It's your birthday, Mum. Not ours. Do you think Dad's got the dates mixed up?'

Claire moved closer to the table, her brow creased. 'Where did the parcel come from, Karen?'

'A bloke in a post office van handed it to me. I'd just got home after work and hadn't even unlocked the front door.'

'Well, go on, then,' Claire said, 'open them.'

Careful not to tear the paper, Zoe had her gift unwrapped first. A black box. She prised off the lid. Snuggled in black velvet was a gold-coloured pistol, pink grip, pearlescent pink slide, no bigger than the palm of an adult's hand. She screamed, pushed the box away, clutched at Claire and began to sob. Before Karen could get to Jack, he had his box open, an identical pistol inside, this one all black.

Nguyen knocked on O'Leary's open door. Leaning against the doorframe, he said, 'Hey, Vincent Valentino's dental records perfectly match the body found in the mineshaft. You going to inform Adriana, or you want me to?'

'What?' O'Leary jerked his head up. 'Sorry, mind on the Mascord twins.'

'Do you want me to go and see her,' Nguyen said more slowly this time, 'confirm it's her husband whose body we found?'

'Yeah, why not?'

'Will I need a warrant?'

'Not to talk to her.'

'But wouldn't we want to look around while we're there. See if there's computers and that sort of stuff?'

O'Leary reached for his ringing phone. He could hear the acid in Claire's voice, feel the heat down the phone. 'What's going on?' He checked the clock on the wall. Still a good hour before he needed to leave to pick up the twins for the night. 'What do you mean, Claire?'

'Guns is what I mean, Brendan. When did it seem okay to you to send the twins guns?' She was yelling loud enough for Nguyen to hear, who darted off and returned with a glass of water.

'Claire, I did not send anything to the twins. Not guns. Not anything,' O'Leary said slowly.

'Real guns?' mouthed Nguyen, standing stock still.

'Real guns?' he asked Claire, listening intently while she described what she had seen.

'Don't touch them. I'll get them picked up straight away and sent for testing. Call you back soon as I know when.' He rang off, staring at the phone he was holding as if it might leap up and bite him. 'And that's not all. Claire got flowers this morning. Thought they were from me.'

'And?'

'It's her birthday, but no, not me. I didn't even remember the date, that's how lousy I am. Nah, the flowers were from someone who didn't skimp on quality and size according to Claire. And didn't sign the card thingo that came with them.'

Nguyen sat down on a chair that for once was not covered in paperwork. 'Do you think someone's putting the frighteners on?'

'Too many things happening for that not to be the case. Phone missing at Glenlyon, now flowers and guns. Yeah, and I'm absolutely sure someone came into the caravan on Sunday night, the night my phone mysteriously disappeared, and that SES bloke found it next morning over near Krakauer's house. That smell. Found it I reckon last night in the bathroom cabinet.'

He frowned. 'Found what smell?'

'I smelt it in the caravan. Could swear to it. Then last night I was lying in bed when it struck me that I'd smelt it before. It's fucking aftershave. Brut 33. Got it for Christmas years ago. Still in the bathroom at home. Put it on once. Claire said I smelt like I was off to a knock shop, so I didn't wear it again. Stupid stuff aftershave anyway, if you ask me.'

'Do you want me to get the parcels sent for testing? And what about asking for surveillance on Claire's place?'

'Yeah,' he said, 'and there's about as much chance of that happening if I know Goddings as there is of proverbial pigs flying. But I'll give it a go. Trouble is, he's never had kids so wouldn't know what it's like.' He opened a drawer and took out his keys and sunglasses. 'I'm going to call it a day and head over to Claire's. Kids are meant to be with me tonight. Wonder if that'll happen. But before I do, I'll organise that warrant you need.' He picked up the desk phone. 'Inspector Goddings? Alright if I send up DC Nguyen to get authorisation for a search warrant of Vincent Valentino's home?' Goddings bellowed something about a meeting. 'Yep, I'll tell him to be quick, don't want to hold you up, Sir.' Hand over the mouthpiece he said, 'Get it sworn straight away. You know where she lives don't you? Take Janzen.'

'You didn't ask him about surveillance.'

O'Leary grunted and waved him out. 'It'd be a waste of breath on the phone. The kid's will be okay tonight. I'll see him tomorrow.'

Nguyen nodded, picked up his phone and notebook and together they walked out of the office.

Scrolling through endless online tennis articles was not a job Micelli relished. Same words, different people saying them, same ardour for the top seeds who in the eyes of the media didn't seem to put a foot wrong. Endless details about hamstrings, elbows, shoulders. How knees were holding up, or not, as was the case for most it seemed. And which players had a meeting with the knife, as one colourful report about various joint reconstructions was titled.

Tennis bad boys consumed more than a few column inches as well. Fast cars, leopard skins in Hollywood bedrooms, casino visits where thousands were dumped on a roulette table in a single spin. These stories were sometimes tied to tales about fathers and how they caused psychological trauma and tennis court meltdowns in their attempts to make a champion tennis player out of a daughter or son.

And then there were the on-court antics to read about. One article listed the ten worst men, the American John McEnroe topping the list followed by Ilie Nastase from Romania, both of whom she'd seen providing special remarks for a commentary team. But not so lucky to be on the TV was the Russian, Marat Safin, winner of the 2005 Australian Open, who came in at number six and was now a member of the Russian parliament. Pausing over press photos from the time, she concluded that it must have been the three pouting blondes in his player's box, one with her nipple exposed, that gave him the extra oomph to beat Lleyton Hewitt, the hometown favourite.

Wearied by all the tennis trivia, she wandered off to the kitchenette and made a coffee. Returning to her desk she picked up a preliminary report from Macleod, detailing some of the Condor Hotel room findings to date. Scanning headings, she flipped to the section describing fingerprints. Those on the champagne glass matched the victim's. A different set on the platter, as yet unidentified. The plastic bag bore only the victim's prints. But there was nothing on the bottle. Or the handcuffs, either. As far as she knew, no one had actually been asked to provide prints, or DNA for that matter, so no wonder the report was thin on detail.

The data from the smart watch was much more interesting, even though the Macleod team had been unable to link it to a phone. But along with the number of steps Azarov had walked and how many calories he had expended on the day he died, it also detailed his heart rate. She studied the graphs and saw a rapid rise of four minutes in duration on Monday afternoon that would have coincided with his run in at Melbourne Park with Serchanov. The heart rate went up significantly again at 18.30. She noted it stayed highly elevated for seven minutes. That was the time it took for Azarov to get from the lobby to his ninth-floor room at the Condor, according to Pritchard's review of the Condor's CCTV tapes. Pritchard had implied that sexual activity had occurred in the lift with the mystery woman, hence the unfurled umbrella designed to block the in-lift cameras. The elevated heart rate was not conclusive confirmation that sex of some description had taken place, but it certainly supported Pritchard's assumption. Then normal heart rate again until nine o'clock when there was another elevation, not so dramatic this time, which she attributed to Helen Kapp's sushi delivery and possibly the champagne. Then nothing from 21.56 onwards. That must have been when he removed the watch. Or someone removed it for him.

Stretching both arms above her head, she walked to the window, looked down on La Trobe Street through the scragged branches of prematurely moulting plane trees. A woman and kid waiting for a tram; a jogger in acid green runners pelting along the far side; a fat businessman in suit and tie talking into a phone. She eyed her watch, half past four. Returning to her desk she read on.

Fresh semen stains on the bed linen. Matched to the victim. Semen in condom also the victim's. How do you get semen stains on the sheets if your condom is still intact? More than one encounter, only explanation she could think of. And why not a condom the first time? Didn't make sense.

She already knew the wallet contained very little. A couple of credit cards that had checked out and several hundreds of dollars in Australian notes plus two hundred Euros. Phone's SIM purchased on arrival in Sydney, according to a notation that also included the phone records. Only one outbound call. Number unknown. No texts. It struck her as odd that there'd be no texts between Azarov and Bagrova. Or calls. They were lovers who'd planned a holiday post-tennis away from the prying eyes in Tallinn. Wouldn't they be calling or texting to arrange hook-ups? Bagrova had flown into Melbourne so there must have been some way she was going to communicate with Azarov, otherwise how would either of them know where and when to meet? Was there another phone? Perhaps a laptop somewhere? Surely not an internet café. Did they exist even?

She swung her legs up on a chair, kicked off her shoes. Sat staring at the whiteboard. She got up and in thick red marker added two phrases: *how did A contact B?* and *why only one glass*, underlining the words twice.

A flood of western sun poured through a gap in clouds that promised rain but failed to deliver. Just like they had all January so far. And most of December last year. Jack and Zoe for once hadn't argued about who would sit in the front having claimed the sun was making the windscreen too hot for next-to-dad travelling. O'Leary considered the aircon more than made up for the heat generated through the windscreen. Nevertheless, they were occupied and seemed happy enough, colouring in and drawing in their books as if nothing had happened. He wondered how much longer he could enjoy their simple naivety before they morphed into modern Australian teenagers, draped in cords and earbuds, phones turned to silent grasped tightly, so even the most vigilant of parents didn't know what was going on in backseats and bedrooms.

It hadn't been an easy pick-up this time. Claire was on edge and although he'd tried to console her, there wasn't much he could say without making the situation worse. 'The guns are at Macleod. They'll be thoroughly checked along with the packaging and so on. I expect to hear back on Thursday, Friday at the latest.'

'And what if there's nothing? Just Karen's and mine and the kids' traces? What do we do then? Course, if there was foreign DNA it'd only be useful if it matches something already collected. Isn't that right?' He'd rubbed her forearm, only to have her lurch away.

'It's only going to make it worse if we have a fight about it.'

'I'm not fighting,' she'd said, then burst into tears. The twins spilled out onto the verandah and demanded to know what was going on.

He'd bent down and wrapped them both up in his arms, wishing he had the courage to do the same with Claire. 'Mum's upset, that's all.'

'Duh,' said Zoe. 'Tell us something we don't know.' Then she'd burst into tears. 'I don't want any more scary presents.' In between sobs she said, 'And Jack doesn't either. You have to stop them coming, Daddy.' He couldn't remember the last time she'd called him Daddy. Maybe when she was three or four. Since then, it had been Dad, even Brendan on occasions when he'd overheard her talking on the phone to her friends. 'Stop them doing this to us and to Mummy!' She'd stamped up and down a couple of times, let out a final wail then threw herself at her mother's hips and clutched on tight.

At that point Karen had appeared in the doorway. 'What about everyone comes back in and we'll have a cool drink and a talk.' They followed her to the kitchen and sat down at the table. She had already made a big jug of iced water with lemon cordial, chocked full of fresh mint leaves and ice blocks, which she poured into five glasses. 'It's been a tough day. We've all had a bit of a shock. You agree Jack? Zoe?' They'd nodded their agreement. 'And tonight, you're off to Dad's for a slap-up dinner and a good night's sleep. Maggie'll be there too—'

'And the chooks,' Jack burst in. 'There might be eggs and everything. Bags I go first to the chook house! Let's go, Zoe.' He'd jumped down from the chair and grabbed his sister by the hand and led her up the passageway.

O'Leary thanked Karen and followed the twins to the front door where they were piling more stuff to take in the car.

'I'm gutted by all this,' Claire had said.

He'd wanted to tell her that everything was going to be okay. Instead he'd said, something he instantly regretted. 'You don't think it could have anything to do with your work, do you Claire? You haven't made any enemies or crossed people who'd want to get back at you?'

She gave him a withering look. 'Yes. I've made enemies, shall we say. But I've never heard of anyone who's given birth wanting to scare the shit out of their midwife. Have you? Piss off Brendan. I'll see you tomorrow.' She'd practically pushed him out the door before slamming it shut.

Nguyen clicked on the radio, something to dull the edge of driving west through the early evening peak hour. He nosed the vehicle onto the Westgate, chose an inside lane away from the barriers hastily erected after a bloke threw his kid off the bridge. Air brakes hissing as B-doubles edged into lanes, diesel fumes filtering through the aircon. He switched to internal air. Someone's stale perfume instead. Elsa Janzen sat beside him, tendrils of curly hair escaping from a bun, wholly focused on her phone. He wondered if she knew she smiled a lot when she did this.

Paperwork on the back seat. Adriana Valentino hopefully at home. He placed both hands on top of the steering wheel, tried to focus on a story about money laundering in Russia, gave up and switched channels. Heavy bass, barrage of guitars. AC DC. Turned the radio off. 'Hey, Elsa, wanna grab something to eat after we do the search?'

'Where are we going again?' she asked, looking up from her phone. 'Sanctuary Lakes or something?'

'Yep.'

'Maybe Footscray on the way back?' Returned to her phone.

'Deal,' he said, taking the Princes Highway exit. 'You done this before?'

She nodded. 'Sure. Only with Drugs though. Is it other stuff this time?' She wriggled round to face him. 'Do you want me to make a list?' Fingers poised ready to enter data into her phone. 'Oh, and do we have gear with us?'

'It's not a forensics search. If we find anything that needs photographing professionally, we'll call it in, just like if we find other stuff that needs expert assessment.' He pulled off at Exit 14, drove south along Point Cook Road. Kept an eye on the GPS. Houses the size of small palaces. Out onto an island, ducks skimming across the surface of a man-made lake. Brought the car to a stop outside the Valentino family home. No fence, broad pathway leading to a portico big enough to shelter a football team, heavy-looking door decorated with a sweep of glass.

Janzen pressed the intercom. 'It's one of those ones where you can see who's at the door on a screen inside,' she whispered, stepping back.

'Who is it?' A woman's voice rattled through the grille.

Janzen introduced herself and Nguyen. Said they'd only take a few minutes of her time.

The door opened onto a wide hallway, burnished ash-coloured tiles picking out a path in thick ash-coloured carpet through to whatever rooms lay beyond. Adriana, hair pulled back, no makeup, dressed in grey yoga pants, hot pink halter top. Nguyen explained the reason for their visit, gave her the warrant to inspect. 'Anyone else at home, Mrs Valentino?'

'My sister. She's upstairs. Do you need to see her?'

He shook his head. 'Did your husband have an office?'

They followed her along the tiled walkway, turned into a room as utilitarian as an operating theatre except for the floor-to-ceiling mirrors on the back wall reflecting a metallic desk. A row of cupboards at bench height stood opposite a picture window shrouded by filmy curtains. Not an object anywhere. 'I'll leave you to it,' she said. 'I'll be in the kitchen if you need me.' She pointed to a door on the left.

'Wow,' said Janzen, checking out their dual reflections. 'Some home office.' Moving towards the back wall, she pressed fingers to one of the mirrored panels. It slid away to the left. Nine folders, three each in purple, red and black. A printer, reams of paper, framed pictures of racehorses. One propped against the wall contained three photos. A grey pushing its nose over the finishing line, a purple and gold horseshoe-shaped Pegasus in the background. A bevy of well-dressed racegoers flanking a gold cup. A close-up of Adriana and Vincent holding the same cup aloft. *Grey Prince 1ˢᵗ at Caulfield, Australia Day* read the caption. She picked it up to get a better look at the Valentinos. 'Check this out. Happier days by the looks of it.' She carried it over to Nguyen who was on his knees taking things out of the bottom drawer of the desk and placing them on the floor. Boxes of stationery supplies including staples and paperclips, unopened packets of document protectors, pencils, pens. Underneath the pile was an exercise book, the type that school students use. 'That's weird,' she said, 'why would he have a kid's exercise book?' He flicked it open. Appeared to be unused.

'Beats me. Anything of interest in the cabinets?'

'Not so far, but I'll keep looking.' She propped the photo on the desk and returned to the wall of cabinets. Taking a purple folder, she flipped it open, flicked through pages of monthly balance sheets, profit and loss statements, arranged in chronological order beginning with the most recent dated July last year. *First Holdings* was the header in each document. Another purple folder, this one full of accounts, arranged in both alphabetical and chronological order. The third purple folder held company returns and assessment notices from the tax office. She removed a red folder. Same as before except the business was called *Second Holdings*. No surprise then that the black folders contained papers related to *Third Holdings*. 'What sort of business did Valentino run?' she asked, flicking through the last folder. A piece of paper fell out and floated to the floor. Nguyen had his head buried in a stack of old newspapers he'd removed from another of the desk's drawers. 'Had something to do with betting.'

She picked up the slip of paper. 'So why would he have a list of names? Like politicians and that?'

He frowned. 'Give us a look.' He ran his finger down the list. The premier, several ministers including Phillip Sinclair and Olivia Owen-Spencer, minister for health, Elise Lanigan the lawyer, several high-profile businessmen. He straightened up, checked his watch. 'No idea. You seen enough for now? Let's take a copy then grab dinner.'

'Just a tick. Only one more to go,' she said, sliding the final panel door open. 'Hey—look what I just found.'

Joining her in front of the cabinet, he said slowly, 'So is unlocking combination safes one of your specialities?'

She grinned. 'I'll put it on the list for the Macleod mob.'

She collected her jacket and followed him into the hallway. They located Adriana in the kitchen, gleaming stainless-steel surfaces reflecting the screen of a wall-mounted TV tuned to the tennis. Perched on a stool, she was stirring a swizzle stick round and round a glass filled with ice and something else. She turned to face them. 'Like a drink?'

Nguyen shook his head. 'We'll need to take another look tomorrow.'

'Sure,' she said, turning back to the tennis. 'Kross is going well. Considering.' A newspaper was lying on the bench, open at a story about Alexei Azarov's death.

Fifty-five minutes to get ready. Micelli laid out her things. Underwear, black wedge sandals, new dress—chocolate and white, stripes increasing in width on their descent towards the hemline. Twisting her hair into a knot, she turned the shower on full-blast and stepped in. As she soaped up, she revised the day's achievements. Some footage from the Condor and the tennis. Harris and Pritchard on target. But then there was Skelton. Couldn't really talk over the situation with O'Leary. He had enough on his plate with the Glenlyon investigation. Towelled off, she massaged moisturiser into legs, arms, pulled on knickers, fastened her bra. Squirt of Chanel, slipped into the dress, tied on the wedges. Leaning in close to the mirror, she examined teeth, eyebrows, applied lip-gloss.

David Romano was waiting for her at the front entrance to Melbourne Park. Aware he had watched her climb each of the steps up to the forecourt, she was already flushed when he put his hands lightly on her shoulders and kissed both cheeks. 'Going to be fine and hot tomorrow by the looks of it.' She pointed to the broad streaks of purple and orange already colouring the sky to the west.

'You look magnifico,' he said admiring her from head to toe, adroitly placing one hand on her linen-clad back and steering her towards a bar. 'Drinks first, then some tennis if you're up for it.'

'Sounds good,' she said, letting herself be propelled through a crowd anxious to take their seats before the start of the evening program. 'Who's playing?'

He rattled off the names of two women and two men, only one of whom she recognised. 'Who are you tipping?'

'Think I'll go for the Czechs both times.' He led her by the hand into a room staffed by young men and women in black and white circling with trays of canapés and drinks. Her mind immediately turned to Nick who should have been among them, dispensing cheeky humour with each glass. 'Sparkling?' Romano removed a flute effervescing with pale amber wine and handed it to her, before taking another for himself. 'Saluté, Angela. Here's to a fabulous evening.' He grinned. 'Suppose it's too much to ask whether your phone is turned off?'

Before she could answer, a woman wearing a sleeveless black lace dress cut dangerously low over pushed up breasts, blonde-streaked hair falling over tanned shoulders, said, 'Hey, David. Haven't seen you all day. Been hiding from me?'

He air-kissed both cheeks. 'Bella, I would never avoid a gorgeous creature like you! Join us, please.' Resting his free hand on the small of Micelli's back, he gently pushed her forward. 'This is my friend, Angela Micelli. Angela's a newcomer to tennis, more of a cycling buff, aren't you Angela? I'd like you to meet Bree Hansen, marketing department for Head.'

'Sounds very intellectual,' Micelli said, raising an eyebrow.

Romano burst into laughter. 'Not that head, Angela. Head is a tennis racquet manufacturer.'

'Oh,' said Micelli. 'Kind of like me talking Surly.'

They both looked at her blankly. Romano coughed, pointed to Micelli's glass, 'You're empty, Angela. I'll hunt and gather while you two get to know one another.' He turned on his heel and was swallowed by a gaggle of tennis-groupies, teeth bared in face-aching smiles, reminding Micelli of the school sharks she had seen when fishing with her dad, darting in and out, gorging on the carcass of a dead seal. She was thankful when her phone began to vibrate.

'Excuse me, Bree, for a tic,' she said, taking the phone out of her bag.

WHAT SORT OF A FUCKIN SISTER ARE YOU???!!!

Micelli heard her stomach rumble, snuck a quick look at Bree to see if she'd heard too. No sign that she had, white teeth gleaming behind glossed lips the colour of ripe apricots stretched into what was probably a permanent smile. Bree seemed to be waiting for her to say something, judging by the keen-puppy look on her face. 'Work. You know,' Micelli said, that eyebrow rising again, 'or maybe you don't?' She stuffed the phone back in her bag, determined not to look at it again until she arrived home. If Harris or Pritchard had news, it'd have to wait. She couldn't deal with any more messages from Rosie. Especially this evening.

'Oh my god, there's Asher. Prince you know,' gushed Bree, downing her half-full glass in one swallow, obviously as keen to remove herself from Micelli as Micelli was to get away from her. She looked in the direction that Bree was straining towards, her free hand waving frantically at the so-called prince. Dark hair swept back, open necked blue shirt with maybe a faint stripe, white linen jacket and pants. He certainly looked like a Middle Eastern prince. 'It's lovely to meet you but I really must catch him.' Bree winked conspiratorially. 'We might be announcing something really big tomorrow.'

Left on her own, Micelli scanned faces in the crowd. 'Where's Bree? asked Romano, whisking in beside her with a fresh glass of wine.

'She had to meet a prince. Something about letting down her hair and tall towers.'

He blinked, frowned. 'Pardon?'

Micelli nudged him in the direction of Bree, sipping on another glass of sparkling and laughing up into the face of the picture-perfect prince.

'Oh. I get it.' He laughed as he took a red, white and green titbit that looked like a mini Tower of Pisa from a passing waiter's tray. 'Prince is another brand, Angela. You Aussies are very funny people, you know. Very funny.'

'Is that right, David? I thought New York was renowned for—' She stopped mid-sentence, her glass slipped sideways, spilling onto the floor.

'Is something the matter? You look like you've seen a ghost.'

She sneered. 'Not a ghost, exactly. But certainly a presence.' She jerked her head in the direction of the Honourable Phillip Sinclair, Minister for Police, arm around a blonde she could swear was the Channel 7 reporter Kelly Georgiou, holding the floor while his adoring group hung on every word. 'More like a ghoul, I'd say.'

Romano glanced towards Sinclair, framed in a tight circle of laughing heads. 'Would you like to go?' he asked gently.

She glanced at her wristwatch 'Match must be about to start anyway.'

THURSDAY

SEAGULLS SCREECHED overhead on their way to the southern end of the beach. Micelli gave the chain a wipe before pumping both tyres to maximum. Sunrise was scheduled for 6.13am, yet the sky was already light, pink and orange-tinged clouds framing the city skyline as she set off down the street to the beach. Wheeling left onto the Esplanade, she clicked into the big chain ring and accelerated. Warm air rushed past, the bike almost silent as she pushed it to more than 35kph. She couldn't help grinning. All those poor bastards stuck in their cars snaking along Geelong Road, over the Westgate, into the city snarl. Footscray Road was its usual mess of construction and truck brakes screeching to a stop, on past Docklands, up La Trobe and into the underground car park. Time enough for a leisurely shower and breakfast before the others arrived.

Flicking through the sports pages before the briefing, she noted that Kross was through to the third round in four sets. Ousted a Ukrainian national by the name of Denys Kravets, who, according to the article, was also Kross's doubles partner. Before she had time to read more, Pritchard strolled in followed by Harris.

'Want a coffee?' Harris called as he disappeared into the kitchenette.

'Didn't get takeaways this morning?' she called after him.

'Nah. Too many people in the queue. Didn't want to be late.'

She busied herself at the table. Checked notes. Glanced at her phone. Harris emerged carrying two frothy cappuccinos, placed one in front of her.

Skelton was last in, the usual once-white shirt half untucked, brown suit jacket slung over one shoulder. He flopped into a chair and slurped noisily through the lid of a take-away cup. She felt her top lip curl, refrained from rolling her eyes when she caught Harris glancing her way. 'Okay, time to start,' she said instead.

She motioned Pritchard to join her at the whiteboard, listened while he recapped his meeting with Ludmilla Bagrova, Alexei Azarov's mistress. 'Do you think we can get anything else from her?'

'Probably. Think she knows more about our victim's business than she's letting on. The Estonians are interesting, too.'

'In what way?'

'Well, they're tight-knit in that everyone seems to know everyone, as well as what's gone wrong in their lives. Probably similar to most migrant groups. Stick together a bit, especially the first generations to arrive.'

'Is that why you texted me about Helen Kapp and her backstory? Maybe you could fill everyone in.'

Pritchard cleared his throat. 'Helen Kapp came with her father as a youngster after the mother died. The father thought it'd be best for a fresh start, had some money put away, lost it all. He committed suicide. The couple I talked to at the Estonian Society think it was because of a scheme run by our recently departed.'

'You mean Azarov?'

'Might be good to talk to her again, don't you think?' Micelli added an asterisk beside Kapp's name. 'And I've spoken to a Mr Sergey Serchanov. He's the man in the CCTV footage from the tennis centre that I texted you lot about. Says Azarov is a crook. In cahoots with the Russians, something called the Estonian Obtshak.'

'Obtshak?' Harris's eyebrows were raised.

'Look, not sure. A mafia type thing is what I gathered, but finding out more would be good. Ask your contacts in Tallinn when you speak to them next.' She turned to face the whiteboard.

'So, we've got Estonians and or Russians in abundance, all tied up somehow together. A dead man, his mistress, and a burly Russian emigre.' Micelli eyed Skelton. 'What about the Kross team? Any news there?'

Skelton shook his head. 'Boys watched Kross last night.'

'What about Monday night? That's what you were asked to find out about.' He remained silent. 'Did you or did you not speak to them?' Her voice had taken on the tone of a headmistress investigating sexting. She caught herself, tried to smile, but too late to head him off.

'Course I fuckin' talked to them.' He sneered. 'No brothels. No casinos. Only a pizza shop. The physio one, Kristo, gave Kross a massage, and the other one oversaw the pizza topping.' He closed his notebook, clasped his hands behind his head and leaned back in the chair. Shirt straining across his chest, a hint of ink on his right forearm, grey tie loose round his collar.

She smiled again. 'Thanks for that, Skelton. Great report. So now I want you to visit them again. I want statements this time. Bring the three of them in if you have to. We want to know money, movements, contacts. Ask about the mistress. Take Pritchard with you. Text when you're finished.' Both Pritchard and Skelton remained seated. 'Go on. Now,' she said.

Pritchard slipped into his suit jacket and followed Skelton out the door. She waited until the lift sounded in the hallway. Breathing out, she collapsed into a chair.

'Good job,' said Harris. 'He didn't know where to go when you smiled at him.'

'Yeah. Thought I'd try a different tack.' She screwed up her face, slurped some coffee. 'Hurt me though. Do you know how hard it is to smile at someone you'd really like to see dead?'

He laughed. 'Don't let him hear you say that. He'll have you charged.'

'Probably. Anyway, we've got work to do. Pritchard's laid the groundwork with the mistress, so I'll let him keep beavering away with that, find out more about the international financiers she works for and Azarov's interest in them. In the meantime, I think we should pay Helen Kapp a visit. See if we can't get her to tell us her life story.'

Last night's dishes unwashed on the sink, grainy red wine crystals in the bottom of a glass. O'Leary turned on the tap and filled a mug with water. Downed it in one go. The guns had scared O'Leary. Scared him badly. Let alone their effect on the twins. He had tossed and turned all night chewing over who might be behind the mystery gifts. Could there be a connection between the temporary disappearance of his phone, the flowers and now the guns? He crept down the hallway and peered into the room where the twins were asleep. Arms flung over their heads, breathing gentle. Turning, he almost tripped over Maggie who had padded up behind him. 'C'mon, old girl, we can get a walk in if you're quick.'

When he opened the back gate, Maggie bolted for the bridge and coursed along the creek before disappearing into what the twins used to called Bear Woods, a copse of she-oaks and spindly black wattles on the north bank of the creek. He tried to recall exactly when they'd become too grown up to imagine that bears might hide in this thin plantation. A strong wind was bending the tops of the eucalypts near the bluestone bridge. With a neighbour's help, he'd planted these trees years ago. Leftovers from a community planting. Seemed like a good idea to screen the bridge. But the trees had grown tall and rangy, leaving the bridge's architectural problems clearly on display. Four cockatoos delighted in swooping low over the handrail and gliding to a stop on one or other of the rough-barked limbs. Nothing he liked better than to pull up a chair on the back deck where he could watch them leaning in close, heads together, scratching each other's cheek feathers with their beaks. Reminded him of lovesick teenagers hidden away from their parents' gaze. How many years to go before his kids were hiding away? Surely. They wouldn't turn out like him? He pushed that thought out of his mind. Recalling Deborah Dangerfield, his first love, was no longer pleasurable after her murder last year. Much better to focus on the future. But what future? Just thinking about how he'd played around with that dating app while he was on sick leave caused him to redden from the neck up. What had he been thinking? Uploading a selfie, scripting a profile that was more a job ad for Ms Perfect than a rundown on what mattered most to him. As if he could fail to mention he was the father of twins. And that the twins and he spent time together each week, and nothing was ever going to get in the way of that. Or that he had a dog who gave him so much and needed so little. And a family he loved and cared for, even if they were not always front-of-mind. Thank god the phone had been lost. No chance to check if there'd been any replies seeing he'd forgotten the password.

Walk finished, he unlocked the back door. Zoe was calling for him from the bedroom. He checked the clock above the stove. Six forty-eight. He'd have to get a move on, get the kids back to Claire's before eight. 'Time to get up,' he answered. 'What do you want for breakfast?'

Zoe scuffed into the kitchen, the cuffs on her too-long pyjama trousers hiding her bare feet. 'I feel sick, Dad.' She coughed hoarsely. 'In my throat.'

He sighed. 'Okay, hop up here and I'll take your temp.' While she clambered onto the kitchen bench, he located a thermometer in the odds-and-sods drawer.

She looked at him with disgust. 'Yuk! You're not going to use that old thing, are you? Mum'd kill you.'

He ran it under cold water and shook down the mercury. Before she could protest further, he jammed it in her mouth, told her to keep it shut for sixty seconds. He got out bowls, a large packet of cereal and bananas from the fruit bowl, placed spoons on the bench and turned to open the fridge.

'Mdaaa.'

Turning, he could see Zoe pointing at the clock above the stove, face flushed. She'd probably thought she had to hold her breath, too. He stifled a laugh, whipped the instrument out and held it up to the window. 'Umm, looks like you've got a slight temp.' Wishing he could remember whether normal was thirty-seven or thirty-eight degrees. Or was it thirty-six? 'Go back to bed, and I'll call Claire.' He lifted her down from the bench, ruffling her hair.

'Oh, and wake that brother of yours up and tell him to get down here lickety split.'

Jack soon wandered into the kitchen rubbing sleep from his eyes. O'Leary watched as he hoisted himself onto a stool, pyjama top on back-to-front, and pulled the cereal packet towards him. Before he poured a serve into the bowl, he read the back of the packet. 'Dad, it says you can win a red car if you go online.' He grinned at his father. 'Can we enter? It'd be cool to have a red car.' He put his hands on an imaginary wheel, vroomed around a corner at a speed almost enough to dislodge him from his seat.

O'Leary tucked in his shirt, adjusted his belt. 'Sure, Jack, but we have to get a move on. Eat up and get dressed. Your clothes are over there.' He pointed to a rumple of blue jeans and a red and white striped rugby top. Jack glanced at the outfit and frowned. A red and white beanie sat on top. 'It is *Where's Wally Day*, isn't it?' asked O'Leary.

Jack moaned. 'I'll look like a Swan, Dad.'

It took O'Leary a moment to register. 'Yeah, but Wally only wears red and white. You've got blue jeans.'

Jack sighed and began to pull the top over his head. 'Do you think Zoe'll be able to go to holiday program today?'

'Dunno. We'll get Mum to take a look at her when we get over there.'

Claire's front yard was ablaze in the morning sun with kangaroo paws, a few bottlebrushes still in bloom. The front door was open. 'C'mon in.' Claire's voice carried up the passage to the front door. Already dressed for work in pink shirt emblazoned with a stork logo and white canvas pants, she kissed Jack's cheek, lifted Zoe onto the bench. 'Open up and say ahhh for me.' She shone a torch onto Zoe's throat. 'A touch of strep, I think. You'll need lots of lemon and honey drinks after we go to the doctor to get you some antibiotics.' Zoe screwed up her nose.

'I'll take her,' Karen said, still in her dressing gown, munching on a piece of Vegemite toast. 'You need to get to work. Okay with you, sweetie?' She took her plate to the sink and lifted Zoe down from the bench. 'Unless you want to?' she said quickly, aware of O'Leary's eyes on her.

He cleared his throat, put his unfinished coffee onto the bench top. 'Go with Karen, Zoe.' 'I'll call later and see how you are,' he said, struggling to be heard over Jack's giggles wo was grasped in a bear hug. 'And don't forget. We need to enter that red car comp, mate, when you're over on the weekend.'

'Hang on a mo,' said Claire, following him outside. 'You know those flowers and the guns?'

'I probably shouldn't have said anything last night to the kids. But I asked them how they were feeling. Think Zoe's pretty worried by it all. Jack—' He stopped, trying to find the right words. 'Seems like it's water off a duck's back for him.'

Claire fingered the chain around her neck. 'I don't feel good about this, Brendan. If you think we're being targeted, can't we have surveillance or something?' Her voice was trembling.

He wanted nothing more than to wrap his arms around her, assure her that nothing bad would happen, keep holding her. But he couldn't. Instead, he folded his lips inwards, chewed the side of his mouth, uttered the obvious. 'Claire, I want you to ring me straight away should anything like that happen again. Or anything else, for that matter.' He drew in a deep breath. 'I can't stress that strongly enough.'

'What's the union say about police's families put at risk? And what about OH&S?' A flush spread up her neck and suffused her cheeks with pink. 'Even at the hospital we've got security guards. Terrible to think we need them in a maternity ward of all places, but they make us feel safer. Specially after that attack last year.'

'I'm asking Goddings today. Don't think it's going to be the answer you want, though,' he said, turning towards the gate. His voice became husky. 'Just call any time, Claire. No matter how stupid you might think you are.' Her eyes narrowed. 'Just that we hear so many people say they didn't do anything because they felt stupid. Then this bad thing happens.'

She let out a deep breath. 'You have a good day at work. I'll let you know if there's anything more about Zoe. See you Saturday.'

O'Leary waited outside Goddings' office. 'I know you're busy, but this'll only take a minute,' he said, sticking his head round the doorway.

Goddings waved him in, gestured to a chair. O'Leary remained standing. 'There's stuff going on at home with the twins. Someone's sent them guns. And Claire got a bunch of flowers from an anonymous source.'

'Maybe someone likes her, wants to get in before St Valentine's Day.' He sniggered, gestured to the chair again.

'Don't think so, Sir.'

'What do you want me to do about it?'

'I want some surveillance at their place.'

Goddings glanced at his watch. 'Look, I've got a meeting in fifteen minutes.'

'Will you agree to it?'

'No chance. Is that all?'

O'Leary held up his right hand. 'I swear that if anything happens to my kids, or to my ex-wife, it'll be on you.'

Goddings rapped the pen he was holding on his desktop. 'Is that a threat, O'Leary? Because if it is, you're treading a dangerous line. There are sanctions for officers who threaten their superiors.' He narrowed his eyes. 'I'm not afraid to go there if that's what the situation requires.'

Doris thrust open the door from her office, marched in and set a cup of her foul-smelling coffee on Goddings's desk. 'Anything for you?' she asked O'Leary.

He didn't move a muscle. 'Sounds like you're threatening me,' he snarled, staring straight at Goddings.

'Did you want a coffee or not?' asked Doris who was hovering in the doorway. 'It'd be no trouble.'

'No, I don't want a bloody coffee! I want some fucking sense out of this idiot,' he said, pointing at Goddings forehead.

'Get out. 'Goddings's voice was low and quiet.

O'Leary turned on his heel and walked out the door.

Driving through the Sanctuary Lakes estate was like driving on an old country road: no vehicles clogging the road for school drop offs, all the workers gone hours ago to join the barely moving traffic along Geelong Road and the Westgate. A flotilla of red-shielded moorhens sailed on the lake as Janzen and Nguyen drove towards the Valentino house. 'Still annoyed at how O'Leary spoke to me. But my god, fancy sending kids guns,' said Janzen.

'Getting back at a cop is one thing. Not through his kids, though. Even for the scum we deal with. Pretty sinister. The kids aren't that old.'

'Is he worried about tracking?'

Nguyen frowned. 'Tracking?'

'Yeah. You can put tracking devices into anything. Even voice recorders and cameras are that small now. Lot of those creep DV perps put them in their kids' toys, wife's car. Makes stalking that much easier.'

Nguyen braked, pulled the car up on the shoulder. 'Could they be in flowers?'

'Can be in anything.'

Nguyen pulled into the Valentino driveway, grabbed his phone from the console, dialled O'Leary's number. Rang out. 'Shit. Bet he hasn't even thought of that.'

'I'll put him on speed dial.'

A forensics team were getting organised, donning overalls and lugging equipment out from the backs of vans. A man built like a bunch of leeks approached Nguyen. 'Tom Hudson,' he said, shaking Nguyen's hand. 'We worked together before?'

'No. Don't think so. To date, haven't needed a safe cracker.' They exchanged a few words and flipped through paperwork on a clipboard, before Nguyen and Janzen approached the front door. Adriana was there to greet them. More fitness gear, this time a combination of mint and apricot, hair tied loosely, full lips painted with matching apricot lip-gloss.

'You're early. And you've brought friends?'

Nguyen explained that forensics would spend some time in the office area, open the safe, remove files to take back to the labs.

'Fine with me,' she said, patting at her hair, 'I'll be in the kitchen if you want me.'

Janzen showed Hudson where the safe was, indicated the

coloured folders to another team member who began to take them off shelves, sticking a bar-coded label to the front of each one, before stacking them into a box. Desk drawers were emptied and examined for false compartments. Shelves in the mirrored panel unit were given the same treatment. Hudson meanwhile was fiddling with the combination dial on the safe, listening intently to the mechanism, every now and then entering figures into a keyboard housed in an aluminium case. 'I think we know the safe combination,' said Janzen. 'I've got it in my notes if you can hang on a minute.'

He shook his head. 'Bet I can find it quicker than you,' he said, turning the dial slowly, ear pressed to the metal front of the safe. One more turn and the door clicked open.

'Good one,' she said. 'Beat me to it by milliseconds.' She peered over his shoulder. Several sheets of paper. Something wrapped in chamois. Hudson removed it as carefully as if it was a newborn baby, laid it on a plastic sheet, unrolled the chamois. A small black pistol. Beretta logo followed by the name in capital letters engraved on the barrel.

'Hey, that's a little beauty,' said Janzen.

'Papers? Want them?' Hudson removed two sheets. This time he slid them into plastic envelopes. Called over the photographers. Lists of names. Same as the ones on the list she'd found last night. Only these names had columns with ticks beside them. And phone numbers.

Harris followed Micelli downstairs to the carpark. 'I'll drive to Helen Kapp's. You can finish your brekkie.' He pointed to the plastic container Micelli was carrying. Looked like frog's eggs, black dots swirling through greyish stuff, blueberries on top. 'What is that, by the way?'

'Chia and yoghurt.'

'Event coming up?'

She settled herself into the passenger seat. 'Only a couple of weekends until Cadel's ride.'

'You competing?'

'Nup. Too old. I'll go down to Geelong, see the race, ride back. The food's just part of my new year's resolutions.'

'What's Kapp's street number again?' He keyed it into the GPS, fifty minutes to drive to Thornbury on one route; thirty-five the other. He chose the shorter, reversed out of the park, turned right into La Trobe Street. 'I didn't make any.'

'Any what?' Micelli was looking at the forty-strong protest group marching down Swanston Street, banners aloft demanding *LET THEM STAY* and *Say NO to Racism*. Headscarves, lots of purple, flowing skirts. A few bearded men, one or two pushing bikes. More than twenty uniformed cops sauntered along the footpath beside the protesters. Made her glad she was no longer a beginning cop, slogging it out in the CBD.

'Resolutions. Stupid if you ask me.'

'Probably why you don't achieve anything,' she said sharply. 'We all need goals. Otherwise we're no more than mice on a treadmill. Same thing day in day out. Just a slow road to the cemetery.'

'That right?' He jerked the wheel to the left to avoid a delivery truck that had pulled out into the traffic. The driver stuck a finger up, mouthed an obscenity. 'Might just pull him over. Let him ponder the good sense of doing a U-turn across tramlines.'

She checked her watch. 'Forget it. No time. I've got to be back by 12.30.'

He glanced over. 'Anyone special?'

Eyes bored into him. 'Yes. Very special. My dad if you must know.'

He grinned. 'You need to get out more, Acting DSC Micelli. Any others?'

'Any other whats?' Her voice couldn't hide her irritation.

'Resolutions. Goals. Whatever you want to call them.'

She turned to look out the passenger-side window, Smith Street awash with coffee-carrying hipsters, bargain shoppers milling round the factory outlet stores. 'None I want to share with you.'

Harris focused on the tram he was following along Alexander Parade, turned behind it up High Street. Last year He and Micelli had out for drinks a few times, chewed the fat about all sorts of things. It had seemed to him like she'd had a bit of a crush, judging by the way she'd dressed for their dates. Careful. Not flashy. Not trying to be sexy. Just careful. Best way he could think to put it. But given her olive skin, dark eyes, thick dark hair, it was hard not to be sexy in that plain unfrilly sort of a way that a lot of Italian women have. Maybe he should ask her out again. After work drinks. There was that new place in Footscray his mate had told him about. This wasn't the time to test the waters, however. 'Shit!' He was facing a No Right-hand Turn sign. Could see on the GPS there was another street that ran into Kapp's. He drove to the next intersection and turned right.

Micelli was first out of the car, smoothed her hair, stood looking at the house. Single-fronted weatherboard, green front door, small verandah with iron lace. Three rose bushes in full bloom scented the footpath. She opened the squat gate, waited for Harris, knocked on the front door. Footsteps. Then nothing. 'Who is it?' A woman's voice.

'Police officers. We want to have a chat to Miss Helen Kapp.'

A lock clicked, the door opened ten centimetres, security chain still in place. 'May I see your ID?' Her face was silhouetted in the gloom.

Micelli showed her warrant card. 'Is Miss Kapp at home?'

Security chain removed, she opened the door wider, stepped onto the verandah. 'I am Helen,' she said. She was dressed in grey track pants, a grey t-shirt, blonde hair pulled into a loose ponytail. 'What can I help you with?'

Micelli extended her hand. 'I'm Detective Senior Constable Micelli and this is Detective Constable Harris. Homicide Squad. We need to ask you some questions in relation to Mr Alexei Azarov. I believe you've already spoken to our colleague DC Pritchard.' She shifted forward. 'Could we come in, Miss Kapp?'

'I've been for a run, sorry. Not really expecting anyone.' She looked down at her runners, hot pink brandished with a black swirl along each side. 'Will it take long?'

Micelli shook her head. 'Just some background. Shouldn't be more than ten minutes.' She smiled brightly, edged forward again.

Kapp stepped aside, opened her arms in a gesture of welcome.

'Coffee?'

They followed her down a narrow hallway to a large room comprising kitchen, dining and lounging. A pot was bubbling away on the stovetop, filling the room with coffee smells. She pointed to the dining table. 'Take a seat while I pour. Sugar? Milk?'

'Black's fine,' said Micelli, choosing a seat facing a floor-to-ceiling window overlooking a courtyard teeming with greenery. Ferns, palms, vines. Even a potted fir tree. Harris eased himself into a seat beside his boss, adjusted his tie, yawned. 'You right,' hissed Micelli, not loud enough for Helen Kapp to hear.

The coffees were brought to the table. Harris beamed warmly. 'Some garden you've got, Miss Kapp.'

'Yes,' she said, sliding onto a bench opposite the two detectives. Micelli cursed inwardly. With Kapp's back to the window, it was hard to make out her facial expression. 'Is this a formal interview?'

'No,' said Micelli slowly. 'I know you may have already provided some answers to DC Pritchard, but if you don't mind, we want to go over some things.'

'Okay then.' She picked up her coffee mug in two hands and held it to her mouth. 'I am happy to help, but this needs to be quick. Work starts at midday and I still have so much to do to get ready.' She swallowed noisily, put the mug back down on the table.

'We'll be out of your hair in no time,' said Micelli. 'Just need some background to help our investigations. You came to Australia when?' She left the question hanging in the air.

'My father Bruno migrated here from Tallinn when I was six. He came to Melbourne and found us somewhere to live. My mother had died, and he wanted a better place for us, a new start. He did not like the Russians.'

'I'm sorry to hear that,' murmured Micelli. 'I suppose you don't remember much about your life in Estonia?'

'That is where you are wrong. I was six when we came here. I remember the flat we lived in. It was five storeys tall, four flats per floor, and we were on the top. On one end of the building written in different coloured bricks was *Khrushchev 1957*. There was no lift. When my mother got sick, it was very hard for her to go out. I did most of the shopping at our cooperative. I could go back to our home tomorrow and know my way round. I went to school around the corner, and I can still remember the names of the three neighbours on our floor.' She wiped imaginary crumbs from the tabletop. Sniffed. 'I miss my country.'

'And you see people from Estonia now?'

'Yes. Although not so often now I am working.'

Harris cleared his throat. 'You know Mr and Mrs Olesk?'

She held both palms out to him. 'Of course. When my father died, I was in Year 11. I stayed with them until I finished school.'

Micelli checked her watch. 'I know you don't have a lot of time, so perhaps I can ask you some questions about what happened at the Condor Hotel on Monday evening. Were you on duty?'

'Yes.' Voice stony.

'And did you know Mr Azarov was a guest?'

'Yes. I did.'

'You would normally welcome someone from Tallinn?' asked Harris, pen poised over a clean page in his notebook.

'No one from Tallinn has stayed in the Condor before, so there is no normal.'

'But you welcomed Mr Azarov,' said Harris.

'I suppose you could call it that.' She stood up, gathered the mugs in one hand, took them to the sink. 'I ordered some complimentary champagne for his room.'

Harris followed her over to the bench dividing the kitchen from the sitting area. 'He liked that?'

'I'm not sure. It was delivered by room service.' She ran the tap, rinsed out the mugs with a dishcloth, stood them on the draining board. 'Now I'm sorry, but I really do have to get ready.' She marched up the hallway and held the front door open. 'I'm very happy to assist with your enquiries, but if you need to speak to me again, please call first.'

'What's news in your world, Mick?' Pritchard asked Skelton as they walked out onto Spencer Street and headed for the North Melbourne hotel to see Markus Kross and his two associates.

'Don't think we've worked together for more than ten years.' The wind was picking up from the north, blowing Pritchard's tie over his shoulder. 'That bloke thumping his girlfriend in Little Collins, wasn't it, then opening fire on the good Samaritan who came to help.'

Skelton pulled out a pack of cigarettes, tried to light one. Turned the lighter upside down, tried again. Gave it a bash against his knuckles, scarred from more than thirty years in the force and goodness knows what else, threw it into the gutter along with the cigarette. Pritchard snuck a look sideways. Skelton's head was down, beating into the wind.

'Know anything about tennis?' Pritchard asked. 'It's a rest day for Kross today. He's into the third round. Next match is against the world's number one.' He stopped to tie a shoelace. 'I'll say one thing,' he said, running to catchup with Skelton, 'since losing weight, tying shoelaces has been much easier.'

'Give it a fucking break,' growled Skelton, quickening his pace.

Arriving at the hotel, Pritchard pulled a pressed handkerchief from his trouser pocket and wiped his brow before approaching reception. Reading the name tag pinned to the man's pink shirt, Pritchard said, 'Good morning, Ron.' Ron looked up from whatever had been holding his attention on the desktop. Eyes ringed with black eyeliner applied perfectly symmetrically, arc-shaped eyebrows, a diamond stud positioned in his left nostril.

'How can I help?'

Pritchard produced his ID for Ron to examine, gestured towards Skelton who was facing the window, hands in pockets. 'My colleague and I would like to see Markus Kross and his roommates. Can you ask them to come to the foyer, please?'

Ron nodded. Picked up a handset, punched in several numbers, purred down the line. 'There's two gentlemen to see you all in the foyer. Can I tell them you'll be down straight away?' He inclined his head to the side, raised his eyebrows and began to giggle. 'Certainly.' He returned his attention to Pritchard. 'The boys'll be down shortly. Very late night, apparently.' Ron winked, held Pritchard's gaze a moment longer than necessary. 'Can I get you men anything?'

Settling in the room to the side, Pritchard took a chair near the window, sipped on a cafe latte with a love heart etched into the froth and studied his messages. *Got tix c u at 8 xxx k*. Before he had time to reply, Kross walked in carrying a bulging racquet bag. 'I already talk to police,' he blurted. 'I go to training now.' Pritchard jumped up, explained the need for a formal statement, assured him it would not take long. 'What new things can I say? I tell you everything already.' He slouched against the wall, dropped the bag on the floor.

'Will Artur and Kristo be down soon?' asked Pritchard.

'Maybe. You want me call?' he asked, phone in hand. But there was no need. Artur and Kristo entered the room, dropping the bags they were carrying onto the floor next to Kross's. A few quick words in a language foreign to Pritchard. 'Okay. We ready.'

'Right,' Pritchard said brightly. 'We will need to take a statement from each of you. Separately, though.' Kross cocked his head, eyebrows furrowed. 'One at a time.' Pritchard held up one finger.

Skelton, until now slurping a cappuccino while flicking through a motoring magazine, got up from his easy chair and pointed at Artur. 'We'll do you first. Go on you two.' He waved them towards the doorway. 'Wait in the foyer.' He sat down at the table in the corner, moved aside a potted plant and laid his notebook on the surface. Pritchard shut the door and pulled a chair over for Artur.

'Let's start with your full name and home address,' said Pritchard.

Artur rolled his eyes. 'I already told police that.'

'I know, but it doesn't hurt to do it again to make sure we have everything correct, does it?'

Preliminaries out of the way, Artur described arriving in Australia the week before and attending the Sydney International warm-up tournament in his capacity as Markus Kross's coach. 'It is small tournament. Only 32 players. Markus make it to quarters.'

'Did he win anything?' asked Skelton.

'He win four thousands.'

Writing down a figure in his notebook, Skelton remarked,

'Doesn't sound like much.'

'It okay for now. In Melbourne we already win with twenty thousands, and if Markus win tomorrow, that grow another eighteen thousands.'

'Can you write those figures down for me?' asked Pritchard, ripping out a page from his notebook and passing it across the table.

Artur took the pen offered and wrote 40 000, 200 000 and 180 000.

'Ah,' said Pritchard, pushing the page across to Skelton.

Skelton snorted.

'How much does Azarov take of the winnings?' asked Pritchard.

Artur ran his tongue over the edges of his teeth. 'I say too much. Markus and I fight about this.'

'Yeah, but how much?'

'He take twenty-five points of sponsor money and winning money but he say out of winning money Markus has to pay me and Kristo and hotel and travel and everything. It not leave enough for Markus to get really good. He need top coach. Me. I just his friend from school. I know some things. But not like top coach does.'

Pritchard frowned. 'To be clear then, Kross holds all the money he wins minus a percentage? Therefore, he has the cash from last week's matches?'

'No,' spluttered Artur, whose face had turned a shade of beetroot red. 'That is why Markus and me argue. Azarov keep it. Say it safe with him. Now he dead.' He threw his hands in the air. 'How Markus getting money from dead man?'

Their interview with Kristo confirmed what Artur had said about their activities since arriving in Melbourne, adding that he went to the zoo on Sunday afternoon to see kangaroos and koalas. 'Did the others go with you?' asked Pritchard.

'Only me and Artur go. Markus see them last time he in Australia. Then we go to St Kilda to beach. It's okay.'

'And what about nights?' growled Skelton. 'Don't tell me young bucks like you aren't out on the tear.'

Kristo screwed up his face. 'Out on tear? I not understand.'

'Clubs, bars, that sort of thing,' said Pritchard.

Kristo nodded. 'Ah. Yes. We go on Sunday to casino. It's okay. Monday we go to pub here in North Melbourne. Very good bar.'

'And Markus?'

'He have to have early nights. No beers.'

'So you and Artur left Markus at the hotel on Monday night? What time did you leave and return?'

He screwed up his face again. 'I think we go out at seven and come home at ten. Some time like that.'

'Can Markus verify that? You know, say it is right?'

'I think so,' said Kristo slowly. 'He will have call from me when we get back because outside door locked and we forgot passcode, so he give it to us then we come in.'

By the time it was Kross's turn to be interviewed, he had worked himself into a lather. 'I tell you. I need to practice. Tomorrow it is a big game. How long will this take?' he demanded, fingers drumming the tabletop.

'As long as it takes.' Skelton grinned. 'Hold your horses and keep calm. We need to find out what you've been up to. Can you show us your phone?' Kross reached down to his racquet bag, extracted a phone from a zippered section and passed it across. Skelton slid it back across the table. 'Unlocked'd be good.' Kross did what he was asked and handed it back. 'You took a call from your mate Kristo on Monday? That right?' Kross nodded. Skelton flicked his thumb along the screen. 'Can you tell us his number?' Kross gave the number, Skelton stopped scrolling. 'Call came in at 22.34.'

'Okay,' said Pritchard. 'That gives us something to work on.' Turning to Kross he asked, 'Did you visit Mr Azarov on Monday?'

'After the game he went his way and we came back here. Got here maybe at four. A driver bring us.'

'And did you leave again? Go out for a meal?'

'Yes. We ate just here.' He gestured towards the left. 'After, Artur and Kristo say they going to win money at casino. I come back. Watch some tennis. Have shower.'

'Can anyone verify that?'

He shook his head. 'I use passcode to get in.'

Pritchard raised one eyebrow, leaned forward in his chair. 'You see we've already taken a look at that. There's certainly footage of you and the others leaving the hotel a bit after seven. But the funny thing is it doesn't show you getting home until a few minutes before the others. Can you tell us where you were after leaving the café?'

'I leave now!' he shouted. Kross thumped his fist on the table. 'This stupid. I watch tennis in bar at café. Then come back.' He gathered up his bag and strode out of the room.

Pritchard was first to his feet. 'Think we'd better visit that café and see what their facilities are like.' Skelton pulled out a packet of cigarettes and stalked down the street, leaving Pritchard staring after him. Two doors up from the hotel and right beside the café where Kross said he'd been watching tennis, a pharmacy had its sandwich board on the footpath. A few minutes later, with a wide grin on his face and a USB in his pocket, Pritchard exited the pharmacy. Kross may have been in the café watching tennis on Tuesday evening, as he said he was, but that didn't stop him from ducking out to conduct a conversation with someone in a hoodie, back carefully turned away from the prying lens of a CCTV camera set up by the pharmacist to catch anyone thinking bad thoughts about acquiring prescription medicines or Ray-Ban sunglasses for free. Not so careful though, Kross, his face full on to the camera, hands gesticulating wildly every few seconds. Under three minutes, then back into the café. Had to be prearranged. Next question, who was wearing the hoodie? Shorter than Kross by a good head, dark pants, white shoes, possibly runners. No clue as to sex. Not a lot to go on. He might have to rely on putting further questions to Kross to find out more.

Slouched in his chair staring at the wall, O'Leary decided to call Macleod, find out if there was any data ready about the further forensic scan of Krakauer's house at Glenlyon that he'd ordered on Monday. He listened intently, asking a question here and there, noting down what the duty officer was saying. 'You sending this over by courier?'

'Still not documented. But I'll email it to the officer who put in the request when it's ready. Will that do?'

'Guess it'll have to,' said O'Leary, thanking him and ringing off. No use getting the techies at Macleod offside. He got up from his chair, rolled his shoulders and walked into the kitchenette. He selected a green coffee capsule and placed it in one of the machines lined up on the bench top and watched his mug fill with hot liquid. One sugar, a dash of milk, a peach from the fruit bowl. Back to the office. More staring at the wall.

'G'day, Boss,' said Nguyen, knocking on O'Leary's open door. Elsa Janzen stood behind him, notebook in hand. 'Good time?'

'Good a time as any,' O'Leary said. Cleared a space on his desk.

'Everything okay, Boss?'

'Just on the phone with Macleod about Krakauer's house. Human traces that weren't detected when they first went over the joint. A strand of hair in the shower drain. Footprints near the back door they reckon are new.'

Nguyen glanced at Janzen, sat down across from O'Leary. 'Least it's a positive.'

'Yeah,' O'Leary conceded, 'but it doesn't get us anywhere right now. And by the way, they'll be emailing you the report, so let me know the second it arrives. Anyway, any progress on Valentino's joint?'

Janzen smiled. 'He's got this office you wouldn't believe. As big as a ballroom almost with hardly anything in it. Folders that the accountancy team are working over, a safe that's now been opened. Not much in it. But there was this very interesting list of names.' She opened a folder and turned it so O'Leary could see.

He whistled softly. 'Our Police Minister, the one and only Honourable Phillip Sinclair, I see.'

'There's got to be link between Valentino and him. I could ask Pritchard if he knows anything,' said Nguyen when O'Leary finished scanning the list of names. 'He got some pretty good info from and about him last year.'

O'Leary scratched his chin. 'Wasn't there some stuff about horse trainers?'

Nguyen recounted what he knew about Phillip Sinclair's interest in horses and the fact that he had been Minister for Racing before ascending to the Police portfolio. He'd been at the forefront fending off threats to the running of the Melbourne Cup, on account of a quick-moving horse virus, but in the end the Cup had gone ahead as planned, no horses or trainers dying except for the inevitable broken-down horse that had to be shot on course.

'Valentino's definitely got a connection to horses if his wife's to be believed. Adriana told me herself she'd met Sinclair at some cocktail do at Flemington.'

Nguyen rubbed his chin. 'Isn't Anson a bagman for a bookie?'

Interrupted by the landline ringing, Harris put aside a half-read report and ambled over to the phone desk. 'Homicide.' After a few moments, he pulled open a drawer, found a sheet of paper, began to make notes. Brow furrowed, he pressed the handset closer to his ear. 'Are you able to fax through this information to Melbourne HQ?' He waited. Tried again. 'Fax. Can-you-fax-this-to-me?' Slow this time. 'Email?' Another pause. 'Fax is good.' Reading aloud a number from the pinboard behind the phone, he thanked the caller and hung up. Back at his desk he called Micelli. 'Just heard from the boys in Tallinn.'

'Be at the office in five,' she said, voice echoing on the line.

He hung up, wandered over to the kitchenette and switched on the jug. He dangled a silken teabag into a mug. At least they'd upscaled, brought in something resembling tea, rather than the dyed-black sawdust they used to supply at St Kilda Road. Loaded up the coffee machine with a generous slug of grounds and left it to do its magic. Opening the fridge, he noted a full fruit bowl side-by-side with tubs of yoghurt, skim and full fat milk as well as almond and soy. Not like the old days. He selected skim for his tea and waited for Micelli's coffee to finish, the machine dribbling strong black liquid into a cup.

'Hey,' Micelli said, bursting through the door and dumping her stuff onto the central table. 'That was quick. Usually the internationals take their time giving us intelligence.'

He carried over the drinks, grabbed his notes and sat down. 'Alexei Azarov is more complex than first impressions indicate. He's got a wife and two kids. Lives in an apartment with them in Tallinn. He doesn't spend much time at home. Business takes him away most of the time, including nights.'

'And the wife is?'

He spelled out the name Ingrid Ilves. 'Think that's right, lots of crackling on the line. Kids' names? Don't know. But one's a boy and the other's a girl.'

She sipped her coffee. 'Do you know if they're legally married, by the way?'

He shook his head, wisps of streaked blond hair falling over his forehead.

'She doesn't know much about her man?'

'Seems not. Says he hardly sees the kids and deposits funds into her bank account each fortnight. Tells her he does business in Russia and Latvia. She's not sure what, exactly. Knows about the tennis management stuff but thinks he could have some finance business as well.'

'We know he scored TransferWise as Kross's sponsors.' She got up, walked to the whiteboard, noted the new info. 'But they're not a finance business. Find out what she means by finance businesses.'

'Do we want to request a search of the apartment?'

She considered his question. 'Nah. By the way, how did Ingrid take the news of his death?'

'Calmly, apparently. If I understood the bloke I spoke to correctly, she doesn't want his body repatriated. Just the ashes. She's Estonian and she says he's not despite what's on his passport, so she thinks there's no need for a traditional funeral. We're getting official documents faxed over from Tallinn with her permission to cremate the body and arrange for it to be forwarded to her.'

'Do we definitely know there's no one else? No other living relatives still in Russia? Or anywhere for that matter?'

He shook his head. 'Don't know.'

'Better find out.'

Hi phone rang. The search of Azarov's office was complete and the team were now busy compiling a report that would be emailed soon. 'When can I expect it?' Harris spoke slowly, choosing words carefully. 'The report?' Wondered why they didn't use Skype seeing it was their country's major achievement. Although there had been Kazaa, too. But who'd remember that now? Free music had been good. Spotify was okay. You could still get stuff free. Had to put up with the ads, though. But Skype'd made it easier to communicate, being able to see the person on the other end. 'Will I get the report today?'

'Yes, yes. We finish now and put on server. Many files, you understand. Will take some time.'

'I understand. What type of files?'

'Money records. Other records. Photographs.'

Harris thanked the caller and hung up, made a quick note before pushing his chair back. Micelli was staring intently at a computer screen, right hand nudging a mouse up and down. 'We're going to get the stuff from Tallinn today.' She looked across at him, brows creased. 'From Azarov's office,' he explained.

'Right,' she said, focus still on the screen.

'What do you want me to do now?' Silence. He returned to his desk. A ping on his computer. Emails from Tallinn already. He pivoted his chair towards the screen. Another ping. Opening the first email, he read the subject line. *Contents of Buro.* An attachment listed equipment and machinery. Nothing that piqued his interest—IT hardware, printer, stationery and so on. Even down to *plants x 2 in pots* and *photo x 1, children.* Several picture files including the plants and the kids. A shot of the whole office showing the desk, a filing cabinet, two chairs. Minimal. Nothing to indicate wealth, either legitimate or ill-gotten.

The second email was more interesting. Scans of documents he recognised as financial transactions. He hit print and stuffed the pages into a folder. Picking up his phone he scrolled down until he found what he was looking for. 'G'day, Elena. Wondering if you've got a minute?' Aware that Micelli's fingers were no longer tapping her keyboard, he got up from his desk and walked towards the kitchenette, drank a glass of water. Returning to his desk, he picked his jacket off the back of the chair. 'Just ducking down to see Elena Kamborova. Might be able to help with understanding this stuff. Can't read Russian.' He waved the folder in her direction and disappeared out the door.

On a whim, Micelli picked up her phone, dialled Serchanov. 'Yes?' he bellowed, forcing her to hold the phone at arm's length. 'Why you call me, police lady?' Obviously remembered her number then. She scrolled through the images she had found online. Adopting what she hoped was an inviting yet professional tone, she said. 'Mr Serchanov, I would like your opinion about some tattoos.'

'You mad?'

'The first one is a star on the knee. Can you tell me what that represents?'

He must have turned on the radio as the strains of an orchestral piece reached her ears.

'Defiance,' he said finally. This she already knew having researched the image after seeing Azarov's body at the Condor.

'And what about a knife running through a dollar sign?' This tiny image had been etched onto Azarov's left buttock, a drop of blood in faded red dripping from the knife's point. So far it had not shown up in any of her searches.

She could hear him wheezing on the other end. 'Might be money washer. Now leave me alone. I talk yesterday.' The line went dead.

Slumping forward, she kneaded her forehead with the fingers of both hands. Was the tattoo important? She sat back, zoomed in on the image of the knife and dollar sign. Black ink blurred on the borders of the image. A few patches of faded red ink. Didn't look like a professional job. She searched the internet again for tattoo meanings, couldn't find anything relating to money laundering tattoos, but reading how the dye is made in prison made her cringe: a mix of burnt rubber and urine. No red bits though on any of the heavily tattooed Russians online, so probably not a prison job. But if it did indicate money laundering, why have a blatant advertisement that you were into shady deals written on your backside for anyone to see? Surely Azarov's wife must have seen it. She texted Harris: *ask Tallinn if wife knew or suspected AA was a money launderer*. And then there was his mistress. After all, lovers examined every square millimetre of each other's bodies. 'Oh god.' She smiled as heat flooded her body, images of her recent dalliances with David Romano flicking through her mind like a late-night SBS movie. She brushed a tissue over the moisture that had formed on her upper lip before taking herself off to the bathroom. Examining her reflection in the fluoro-lit mirror did nothing to reassure her, neck blotchy and cheeks resembling a teething baby's. She groaned. Checked her phone for messages.

YOULL NEVER BE ABLE TO SHOW YOUR FACE AT MY DOOR AGAIN!!!!

She wished that Rosie had gone as quiet as David Romano has since their evening at the tennis.

Tucked into a laneway off Lonsdale Street was an Italian restaurant Micelli's family had patronised for years. When she turned the corner into the laneway, she could see her father sheltering from the full blast of the sun under the red and white striped awning that protected the restaurant's front door. He was wearing a short-sleeved blue and white checked shirt that complemented his tanned face and greying hair to perfection. A pair of beige chinos and tan leather sandals completed his outfit, no doubt put together for him by his wife, a woman who deemed good grooming to be almost as important as religion. 'G'day, Dad.' She held him lightly by the shoulders, kissing both cheeks. 'Sorry I'm a bit late. Caught up at work and then had to battle through the milling crowds to get here. Shouldn't be surprised. It's Melbourne and it's summer. Anyway, how are you?'

'You know me, Angela. Always good.' He opened the door for her, walked her to the table he had reserved for them at the back of the restaurant, open to a courtyard draped with grapevines. A few sparrows were busying themselves, darting in and out of the vines, which were heavily laden with acid-green bunches of grapes. Fairy lights were woven here and there, and several tables were pushed together to make a table for ten or more. Red-and-white-gingham tablecloths adorned each table, held in place with special clips.

'And Mama?' She settled herself into the chair her father had pulled out.

'You know her, Angela. If there's a drama, she wants to star.' He sighed deeply.

Micelli laughed, reached over and poured water into their glasses. A waiter brought a basket of bread and recited the day's dishes. Her father listened intently before deciding on the fish and *caprese* to share.

'Everything will work out,' he assured his youngest daughter.

'Aren't there any dramas going on with the other grandkids? Surely someone else is in trouble. Impossible that nine grandkids could all be toeing the line at the same time.'

'All are good.' He grinned and helped himself to a slice of bread which he dipped into a bowl of oil, the colour of an unfurling fern frond. 'Rosie and your mamma need time to cool off. You know us Italians. We yell first, think second.' He beamed one of his best smiles at her. 'Or at least that's what we do in the movies.' They both laughed.

Micelli loved everything about her father. Hair no longer black but still rakishly styled, brown eyes flecked with gold, and an almost permanent smile. For him, the world was a good place where very occasionally bad things happened. But not to him. And not to his family. When she was a kid being scolded for some misdemeanour or other, he would tell her that she could have saved herself the trouble of travelling halfway round the world to find a new home, by staying put where the Devil wouldn't have had any trouble finding her. It didn't seem to matter how many times she reminded him that she'd been born in Australia, he'd still trot out the same warning. 'Dad,' she said reaching over to stroke his sun-speckled hand, 'what's happened is terrible. You must be very disappointed. With all of us.'

He rubbed a thumb over her knuckles. 'Ah, worse things always possible. Most important, how are you *mia cara*?'

'You know, Dad,' she said scooping oil onto bread. 'Wish none of this had happened. But what's done is done. Can't change it now.'

He tapped a finger on the tabletop. 'You not answer my question, Angela.' A plate of sliced tomatoes interspersed with basil leaves and fresh mozzarella drizzled with olive oil, along with a platter of white fish fillets dribbled with melted butter, was placed on their table.

'What happened, and is still happening for that matter, isn't the best. I've cried, I've been angry. I'm still angry, actually. How dare Rosie treat everyone like she has?' Her hand trembled slightly when she picked up her glass. 'Getting Mama riled. No excuse for that. None at all.' The glass landed back on the table with a thud. 'And I'm sad. I just hope that things will settle down soon and Rosie'll go back to being Rosie and Mama will forgive and forget and—' She squeezed her eyes shut.

'Here.' He handed her a crisply ironed handkerchief.

'Oh Dad, I'm so sorry.' She rose from the table. 'Be back in a tick. You start. We don't want the fish to get cold.'

When she returned her plate was piled with fish, lemon wedges placed on the side. 'Now we eat. Okay?' her father instructed.

Cramming a forkful of fish into her mouth, she said, 'Haven't had flathead for ages. Remember when we used to catch these off the pier at St Kilda? Mum'd crumb them with polenta and parsley and we thought we were in heaven. Bet no one catches flathead there now.'

They ate in silence, savouring every last morsel of the fish before wiping their plates with bread. Another platter of fish arrived, this time butterflied sardines doused with *salsa verde*. 'Do you think I should try and see Rosie? Tell her that I can't do anything? That it's against rules?'

He shook his head. 'When she's ready, she'll talk.'

'I've already been told off by my boss for what happened.' She grabbed up her napkin, held it to her mouth as if to stop further words escaping.

Putting his fork down, he shook his head slowly from side to side. 'You must not let this interfere with your work, Angela. As head of this family, I tell you two things. Nick needs to learn a lesson and his mother needs to let him be a man.'

DC Elena Kamborova was waiting when the lift doors opened. 'Need a ciggie when we're outside,' she announced. 'Don't mind, do you?' She joined Harris in the lift, red-dyed hair pulled into a chignon, cheekbones accentuated with blusher. High-heeled black boots, despite it being thirty degrees outside.

'Thought you would have given up by now. Joined the movement.' He was referring to the campaign being waged by HR designed to encourage healthy habits and a fitter force. Posters in shared spaces, reminders at staff meetings, little pop ups attached to emails. *Eat Healthy–Exercise Daily–Quit Smoking*. Fruit bowls everywhere you looked, recipe leaflets, notices in the lift exhorting passengers to walk the stairs instead. Sometimes he felt like he was working with a weight loss corporation rather than the cops.

Once outside she took a pack of cigarettes and a lighter from her handbag, lit up, inhaled deeply. 'Can't read Estonian,' she said, eyeballing him through her sunglasses. 'Let's hope they're in Russian.'

They walked down Spencer Street to the mall. 'Want to grab a coffee?' she asked. She stubbed her cigarette on the heel of her boot, followed him in through double glass doors. 'What'll you have?'

'Cappuccino. Large. No chocolate on top.' He selected a bench to the side of the entrance, scattered with the day's newspapers. An almost-full-page picture of a grinning Julia Kneebone, headlined *Love Two* filled the back page. Skimming the article, he learnt that Kneebone had made a clean sweep of her two tennis opponents so far, beating each hapless woman 6–0, 6–0. The reporter was predicting a fifth championship for Kneebone, confidently stating that her only real opposition in the coming matches would be Svetlana Novotny, the Czech wunderkind. He turned the paper over. Big picture of a music festival covered the entire front page. Written across it, *Drug Bender. Lives Claimed*. No brainer to have drug testing at events, but the Right wasn't going to have a bar of it, despite members of the force saying it would save lives. Couldn't even get the right amount of safe injecting rooms in Melbourne, despite overdoses continuing unabated.

When she returned from ordering their coffees, Harris handed her the folder 'Here's the material.' She frowned as she flicked through the print-outs. 'Bank statements. Several accounts. This one,' she said pointing to something titled банк народов, 'has the most credit transactions. Large amounts.'

'Whose name is the account held in?'

'Players International. It's a business account.' Taking a pen from her shirt pocket, she asked, 'May I?' He nodded. She wrote credit and debit over the words кредит and дебет.

A bearded man who would have looked more at home chopping wood in the Depression era slid two coffees between them. 'Sugar's in the jar. Enjoy.' Harris picked up the small oval-shaped biscuit that had been placed on his saucer and bit into it. Waited for Kamborova to finish her trawl through the pages.

Putting her pen down, she said, 'You need to take these to forensics. Lot of info here. Not clear to me. But at a guess I'd say he transferred incoming money from the business account into other accounts, and just as quickly it went out again. But I can't see where to.' She picked up her cup and drained it in one go. 'Think I've translated all the key terms for you.' She swivelled off her stool, straightened her skirt, 'Your shout?'

Harris nodded, waited at the counter to pay. Kamborova went outside, lit up another cigarette. When he joined her to walk back to the office, he swore he could detect a slight wheeze.

The sun had almost set when O'Leary pulled up outside Micelli's apartment in Altona. Seagulls were whirling over the sand where beachgoers were soaking up the last of the day, the smell of fish and chips scenting the air. 'Seems like ages since we had a catch-up, Brendan,' she said, standing aside as he walked in. He put a bottle of shiraz on the bench and offered to open it. She got out glasses and filled a bowl with mixed nuts that she took over to the coffee table before dropping into one of the two armchairs flanking the couch. She tucked a leg under her, a gesture Marbles understood as an invitation to jump onto her lap. 'You've been doing it tough, with the stuff going on at Claire's.'

He nudged the other chair closer to Micelli's, flopped into it, sprawled his legs out. 'Had better weeks.'

'Possible that your mum could take the twins for a few days? Give you and Claire a breather?'

O'Leary pursed his lips. 'Not a bad idea. I'll think about it. And you? How's the upskirting nephew going? You coping?'

'Yeah,' she said, before contradicting herself. 'Actually, no.'

Frowning, he asked, 'Anything I can do?'

She shook her head, waved away his offer. 'It's not so much Nick. It's his bloody mother.' She threw some nuts into her mouth, ground them noisily on her molars. 'And my bloody mother, too, if it comes down to it. Anyone'd think I was to blame for what he's done, the way they're treating me.'

O'Leary sighed, swallowed a mouthful of wine. 'Families can be difficult. Probably your best bet is to wait it out. Let them run their course with the blame game and just be supportive when you can. Don't do anything that might put your career in jeopardy.'

She grimaced. 'Think I came close to that the other night when I showed up at his interview. Don't know what came over me, telling that policewoman off.'

'No harm done, though.'

'How can you be so sure?' she said.

'Goddings hasn't hauled you in, so reckon you're pretty safe.'

'Oh yes he has. I'll tell you about that later. But first, I've got a question.' She picked up the bowl of nuts and offered them to O'Leary. 'It's about Skelton. Saw him in deep conversation today with Goddings. They were like kids plotting something, heads together, finished with a high five. You said you'd fill me in. Reckon now's the time.'

'What's that?' He jumped out of his chair, went to the window, peered out into the gloaming.

'You're jumpy. It's a branch screeching against the window. Must get round to trimming it off. Always makes that noise when the wind's up.'

He sighed, twisted his glass round and round in his hand. 'Skelton. Where do I start?'

'Try the beginning. That way I won't get lost.' Motioning for the nuts, she popped a couple more in her mouth before plumping a cushion and wedging it behind her back. 'I'm all ears.'

'Worked with him when I first started. Pretty matey back then. You know, young blokes. Think you're invincible.'

'And irresistible. If I know anything about young blokes, that is.'

He grinned. 'That too. Had some wild times, that's for sure and sort of because of the fun, I pretended I didn't notice at first. Wanted to keep on going out with Mr Party Animal. He could attract anyone he wanted.'

'Sounds like he did, but not in a good way?'

'No, not good at all.' O'Leary began to describe how they would be out and someone would sidle up to Skelton, then together they would slip off to some place where they couldn't be seen. A few minutes later Skelton would return and drag his mates onto the next party spot. 'Reckoned it happened one or two times a month at first. Then it got more regular. And he got more careless. Seemed like towards the end, he didn't care that he was in full view handing over a package then counting a wad of notes and stuffing it inside his jacket.'

'Drugs?'

'Had to be. Back in those days, the property lock-up wasn't always locked. Possible for anyone to go in and help themselves to whatever had been confiscated the previous shift—dope, hash, heroin, LSD. You name it, we had it. No shortage of the stuff. In the end, I requested a transfer out.'

Micelli suddenly sat forward, tipping the cat off in the process. 'You mean you didn't report him?'

He could hear the indignation in her voice. He explained that back then whistle blowers were not the most popular members of the force. 'Still aren't, actually. Look what happened to that bloke from Northern who reported his colleagues for fraud. Now on permanent sick leave. Think I read somewhere he's got PTSD because of the things they did to him. Poor bugger.'

She shook her hair out of its ponytail, wound the elastic round her wrist. 'Yeah, sorry for jumping down your throat, Brendan.

Dunno what I'd do in the same situation. Bad enough what I did the other night.'

'Stop blaming yourself, Ange. No wonder your family thinks you're guilty of something.'

Smiling, she got up and put the kettle on. 'Coffee?'

'No way. If I had one of yours I'd still be awake this time tomorrow.'

'You know, you're not leaving until you've explained why Skelton hates you so much now, given that you didn't dob him in way back then.'

'Ah, yeah. See, I did dob him in. But that was much later.' He broke off, attention turned to his phone. 'Claire? What's up?'

Micelli busied herself in the kitchen making a coffee for herself. The cat rubbed itself up against her, miaowing plaintively, taking short trips to the fridge as if to say, 'I know there's cold chicken in there. It couldn't hurt to share a piece with me.' When she opened the fridge door to get out some milk, the miaowing became even more sorrowful. 'Okay, Marbles, you win.' She took out a container and selected a piece of breast flesh. 'Into the laundry. Now.' The cat bolted past her, skidding to a stop on the tiled floor right in front of its bowl. The chicken had scarcely landed before the cat began to rip it to shreds, gulping greedily. 'God, Marbles, anyone'd think you hadn't been fed for a week.' Micelli returned to the kitchen, poured herself a coffee. 'Sure you don't want one, Brendan?'

'Stay right there!' He was shouting into the phone. 'I'm leaving now.'

'What's up?' she asked, taking in his white face and shaking hands as he fumbled the phone into a pocket and fished round for car keys. She grabbed them off the bench and thrust them at him. 'Has something happened to the twins?' An unsteadiness had infected her voice. 'I'm coming with you.' She followed him outside, the front door banging shut from the force of the wind. Racing to the car, she swung herself into the passenger seat, no time to fasten the seatbelt before O'Leary roared off down the street, surely only two wheels on the tarmac as they rounded the corner into the Esplanade. 'Brendan, what the fuck's happened?'

'I read Jack a story,' wailed Claire, 'then when I went to check on them before Karen and I went to bed, they weren't there.' She paced between the sink and the table, bare feet slapping the floorboards. Karen was hunched over in a chair, one hand rubbing her face from forehead to chin, over and over. O'Leary's breath came in short bursts as if he'd run all the way to Claire's. Micelli took his arm, tried to sit him down. He shook her off, went to say something but no words came, just something low, hoarse. He went to the sink, filled a glass with water, swallowed it in one gulp. All eyes turned as a police officer entered the kitchen from the hallway, walking through the room and out the back door.

'What was she holding?' O'Leary said, slamming the glass onto the draining board.

Karen stopped her rubbing, looked up at Micelli, eyes squinted as if she had a migraine.

'Have you given them clothes? They'll need it for the dogs.'

Claire's sniffing and nose blowing filled the otherwise silent room. An old mantle clock sitting on a shelf above the sink that he remembered used to adorn his mother-in-law's sitting room chimed the hour. Everyone looked up. Eleven pm. He checked his watch as if to verify its accuracy. 'How long is it now?'

'About an hour.' Claire gulped.

'Since you checked, or since they went to bed?' His voice like a sergeant major's. Micelli tried again to manoeuvre him towards a chair. 'Stop it,' he barked.

Karen pleaded with him. 'Sit down. Please Brendan.'

He glared at her. 'When I catch who's done this—'

'Mr and Mrs O'Leary, can you come with me, please?' The policewoman had returned to the room, this time a torch the size of a small umbrella swinging from her left hand. Claire grabbed O'Leary's arm as they followed the policewoman through the playroom and onto the deck.

'What's going on? Why are we going out here?' O'Leary's questions went unanswered. Hastily arranged spotlights lit up the yard, beach towels still on the line, a set of red plastic cricket wickets awry on the lawn. Claire began to sob. He put his arm round her waist, felt her ribs heaving.

Shining her torch into the apple tree, the policewoman asked them to follow the beam. Like watching a strobe light as leaves blown almost horizontal by the wind first revealed then blanketed four skinny legs dangling over the edge of a makeshift treehouse. O'Leary took a moment to focus, then rushed at the tree. 'Get down here this minute,' he bellowed. 'Both of you! Now!' Claire pulled on his arm, tried to get him to back away. 'Do you know what you've done?'

'Brendan! Shut up, for God's sake,' yelled Claire. 'They're here, that's all that matters.' Up above them a thin wailing began. 'You're frightening them,' she said, pushing wind-blown hair off her face. 'They need to get down and go to bed, not be yelled at.'

'Trouble is,' said the policewoman, 'they're stuck. Have been for ages according to your daughter. She said they shouted but couldn't make themselves heard over the wind. But don't worry, we'll have them down in a jiffy. Fire brigade's on its way.' She winked at Claire. 'And you're right. No shouting. Lots of cuddles is what they'll need after this.'

FRIDAY

A THUMP on the roof awakened O'Leary. Wide-eyed, he strained towards the open window, listening for more. Another thump, this time sounding as if it was coming from directly above his head. Maggie began to growl, throaty and low. He peered over the edge of the bed. In the moonlight, he could pick out her head, ears pointing forward, snout twitching. 'What is it,' he whispered, reaching over to stroke the back of her neck. His voice sounded hoarse even to himself, every muscle in his body tensed. Maggie stood erect, lips twitching to reveal bared teeth. 'Shhh,' he murmured, carefully peeling back the sheet, dropping his feet to the floor. Then a sound like drumbeats reverberated overhead. Rubbing a hand over a worn and tired face, O'Leary slid back into bed. 'Possums,' he said, stroking Maggie's muzzle, 'three of the bastards by the sound of it. Go back to sleep, old girl.' He rolled over. Within moments, he was breathing evenly, oblivious to the world.

'Morning all,' said Micelli, hair loose on her shoulders, dark-ringed eyes fixed on her team as she stood at the whiteboard. After the twins' escapade, O'Leary had been keen to unwind. She didn't get back to her place until after one, and by then she was overtired, the wind banging its way through the neighbourhood keeping her on edge. Skelton began to snigger. 'Problem?' she asked, her cheeks flushing.

'Had a late one, did you?' He pointed in the direction of her crotch. She looked down. Her pants' zipper was undone. She drew in breath, pulled the zip up.

'So nice of you to be concerned for my social life, DSC Skelton. Let's catch up over coffee later so I can tell all.' She smiled like a hungry lion facing an injured wildebeest. Skelton averted his gaze, turned his chair to face the window, a fly-by of seagulls fighting the wind on their way down to the harbour. 'If we're all ready, we'll get on with today's program, shall we?' She narrowed her eyes, looked into the middle distance, mumbled something to herself.

'And that is?' asked Harris hesitantly, dressed this morning in a blue checked shirt she hadn't seen him wear before. Tapered charcoal pants, black lace-ups, aqua and mint diagonally striped tie.

'I'll remind you it's now three days since we discovered Alexei Azarov's body. And we're no closer to locating any person of interest than we were then. We need to move forward. And quickly. Does anyone have anything to report?'

She eyeballed the team. Pritchard was examining his phone. Skelton was still glaring through the window. Only Harris met her gaze. 'I'll start then,' he said. 'Sent some financials they found in Azarov's Tallinn office over to forensics. Awaiting results but looks like money comes into his business account and he moves it out as soon as it arrives. Unclear as to where. Can't locate pay-outs to any specific accounts as yet.'

'Must be why those snivellers who hang round with Kross aren't happy,' said Skelton, swivelling round to face the whiteboard.

'Skelton.' Pritchard looked up, raised a finger as if talking to a naughty puppy. 'The boys told us they're all together in the same room in that two-star hotel, eating takeaways, or when they can, at the players' canteen, while Azarov booked himself into five-star. Not exactly the high life for them, and if anyone's going to be making money, it's Kross. If he wins his way through to where the real prize money is, that is. He has reason to be disgruntled.'

'Disgruntled enough to kill?' asked Micelli, brushing a strand of hair behind her ear.

Pritchard exhaled audibly. 'If it's a money motive, then yes, he has it in spades. They all do, I reckon. Their conditions must be some of the weirdest and worst on the circuit.'

'Know a bit about the international sporting scene then, do you? Only tennis, or are you over a bigger range? Say soccer, boxing, cycling?' Skelton's tone could have been mistaken for genuine interest.

Before he got any further, Micelli snapped her fingers. 'We don't have time to waste in idle chatter. Skelton, do some work on their backgrounds. Hot day today, good desk job. Course, you could go and see them, have a chat, but you've already done that so I hear. Pity you didn't report anything.' Skelton snorted. 'What about the mistress, Pritchard? Is she worth another probe?' asked Micelli, eyeing off Pritchard who was scratching his neck, finger snaking under his collar. His eyes were glued to his screen again.

Looking up, he mumbled, 'I'll see if she's remembered anything else that might help.'

'Do you think she was with him in the hotel, or just that other woman? And have we got any leads on the other woman as yet?'

Pritchard slipped his phone into his breast pocket, gave his full attention to Micelli. 'I can ask Helen Kapp about her again if you like. My guess is she regularly prowls the Condor, looking for easy money.'

'Speaking of the Condor, only one glass was found in Azarov's hotel room, as we know.' She pointed to where that was underlined on the whiteboard. 'Anyone got any ideas?'

'Doesn't make much sense that someone'd open a bottle of bubbly, put on a condom, then die from asphyxiation,' said Harris.

'Michael Hutchence,' said Skelton. 'Or are you lot too young to remember?'

Micelli took in a deep breath. 'I think we all know that case well enough, DSC Skelton, but thank you for reminding us. Though apparently it wasn't as clear-cut as it may have seemed at the time. Saw a doco about him just the other day, in fact. Former girlfriend—'

'Yeah,' interrupted Harris, 'I saw that too. Kylie wasn't it? Claimed he was a broken man when they split?'

'Yep, then he got a belting in Copenhagen,' said Pritchard. 'Left him brain-damaged which led to serious depression, so not accidental. The coroner actually ruled it as a suicide.'

Skelton rolled his eyes, turned his chair to face the window. She flipped him the bird, causing Harris and Pritchard to guffaw. He spun round. 'What the fuck?' he growled.

Raising her eyebrows and opening her eyes wide to keep herself from bursting out laughing, she said, 'Oh, didn't you see Harris do the locomotion? Pity, it was rather good.' Skelton spun back to face the window. 'Time to recap,' she said. 'Pritchard, you're reviewing the mistress. Skelton, you're on background checks for the tennis lads. Harris, you and I are going through forensics again to see what we might have missed. If stuff comes through re Azarov's financials, then you get onto that as a priority. Everyone understand their jobs? Good. See you for another round at four this arvo, unless someone finds out something critical before then.' She turned on her heel and headed towards the kitchenette, stopping halfway to pull her phone out of her pants pocket. She gripped it so tightly her knuckles turned pale. Enough. Family or no family.

Ludmilla Bagrova was still in her dressing gown when she opened the door to Pritchard. 'You again. You want coffee?' She flounced down the hallway, her long legs silhouetted by the sunlight streaming in through a doorway at the rear of the property. 'It ready in kitchen.' He followed her and took a seat at the table.

'Good of you to see me so early, Miss Bagrova.'

She plonked a cup of oily black liquid in front of him and pushed across a sugar bowl. 'So, what we talk about today?' She sat down opposite him and lit a cigarette. The blue smoke curled from her nostrils as she took a sip of coffee.

Pritchard explained that he needed her to go over a few things with him to help with the case, her movements and so on since arriving in Melbourne. 'Did you see Mr Azarov last Monday?' He stirred a teaspoon of sugar into the cup in the hope that some sweetness would make it drinkable. 'Perhaps you went to the tennis? Or met up with Mr Azarov after the Kross match finished?' No harm in fishing. So far there was no intelligence about where Azarov went after the CCTV footage showed him and Serchanov at Melbourne Park in some sort of altercation. He had disappeared until the hotel footage captured him in the Condor foyer with a woman. Three and a half hours. Azarov must have been somewhere. Done something. Hooking up with his mistress seemed a likely scenario.

She stubbed her half-smoked cigarette into the ashtray. Took a long swallow of coffee. 'Okay. I tell you. I meet Alexei and we have drinks.'

'Where was that Miss Bagrova?'

'Here.' She lit another cigarette.

Pritchard hesitated, wondering how he could get more than a one-word response from her. 'Talk me through it. Mr Azarov comes here to North Melbourne and you have a few drinks. You haven't seen each other for a little while. It's fun catching up, then what?'

She flared her nostrils. 'What you think?'

'Dinner? Plans to go to the casino, perhaps?' He let the unspoken sex hang in the air.

'No. He say he have to go for meeting and leave me. He say we have dinner later. But I never get call from him.'

'You stayed here all evening waiting for his call? No going out to get something to eat? More drinks, for instance?'

'No. I not hungry.'

'And he'd called you before? He had your number?'

She blinked, half shook her head. 'Of course.'

'Because you see there were no outgoing calls registered on his phone. Or at least the phone we found with his belongings. Do you know if he had more than one?' She stood up and put her cup on the sink where many other dishes had accumulated since his last visit. No evidence of food, he noted, but there were several wine glasses lined up. He wondered if one had been used by Azarov.

'You go now?' She took his half-drunk cup and poured the remains into the sink.

O'Leary stormed into the office, cheeks on fire, hair falling over his forehead. Janzen and Nguyen had been waiting for him to arrive for their scheduled nine o'clock meeting. He mumbled an apology, dragged a chair out from behind his desk and threw himself into it. The other two exchanged glances. 'If anything happens to those kids,' he began, thumping the desktop with his fist, 'fucking Goddings'll be the first in the firing line.' He lurched forward, both hands massaging his forehead.

Nguyen closed his notebook. He slipped silently out of the office, leaving Janzen nervously fiddling with strands of hair, vainly attempting to push them back in place while she tried to work out whether the noises coming from O'Leary were sobs or curses. 'Here,' Nguyen said, returning to the office with a steaming mug of tea that he set down in front of O'Leary. 'There's muffins out in the kitchen, too. Want one?'

O'Leary gave his face a final rub, looked up, elbows still resting on the desktop. 'Let's just get going. Sooner we make progress, sooner I'll feel better.' He slurped a mouthful of tea. Exhaled. 'Follow up from Macleod arrived?'

Janzen nodded. 'Not enough to go on with most of the bio samples. Footprints, on the other hand, do get us somewhere—'

'Do you need to get that phone?' asked O'Leary, pointing to where it was jumping around on the desk.

'Ah, no,' she said, quickly checking the caller ID before shoving the phone into her jacket. She opened her notebook to a page she'd marked with a hot-pink sticky note. 'Size nine Nike Air Max sneaker. Wearer about ninety kilograms, they reckon.'

'And where were the footprints picked up from?' asked O'Leary.

'Kitchen and bathroom, both of which have vinyl-clad floor coverings.'

'Can they tell how long the prints had been in the house?'

'Not according to the officer I spoke to. Soil attached to the soles matched surrounding soil where the house is located. Evidence of dried couch grass in crevices.' She looked at O'Leary across the desk. 'Which he said would be the lawn in the yard. Hard heel strike indicated by wear patterns, more pronounced on right side. Could be a right-handed person with a weaker left side, or someone with either a current or previous injury to some part of their left leg. Wear indicates that the person walks with their toes pointing outwards approximately fifteen degrees.'

Nguyen, who had been doodling in his notebook while Janzen gave her report, looked up. 'Therefore, we're looking for someone with small to medium-sized feet, probably on the short side, probably male. Suffered a sports injury when young. And wouldn't trip over the pointy toes on his proper shoes as his feet would be out to the side.' He waddled two fingers across his notebook to illustrate. Janzen looked down at her notes hoping her grin wouldn't be seen.

'How'd you work that out?' O'Leary took another slurp from his mug. 'Could be a tall slim woman for all we know. You know what assumptions do, don't you?'

'Make an ass out of u and me,' parroted Nguyen, who'd heard O'Leary say these words more times than he could recall.

'What else?'

Janzen continued with details about the towel in the bathroom, confirming it had been used to wipe a male body according to the vestiges of DNA.

'London to a brick that it'd be Anson's on that towel. Although surprising that the dirty scumbag would—'

Nguyen interrupted. 'What makes you think it'd be his, Boss? Last seen in New South somewhere, wasn't he?'

Janzen nodded. 'Maybe. Pills like his trademark ones were found at the Gold Coast.'

'Have we got Anson's DNA yet?' demanded O'Leary. Several things, for once, added up. There was last year's visitation to brother Stephen O'Leary at their Ballarat pub, the Golddiggers Arms, followed by the shoot-out at the farm where O'Leary had been shot in the leg. Still not clear what the shoot-out had been about, but O'Leary was sure that it had been an announcement by

Anson that he had it in for the O'Learys and was going to get them one way or the other. The lost then found phone, the flowers for Claire, the guns for the kids. Someone with evil intentions had to be behind all that. And right now he couldn't think of anyone much more evil than Anson, probably the man who'd murdered Charles de Havilland in hospital, probably shot Simon Thomson-Paton and dumped his body at the Organ Pipes, and if ballistics were to be relied upon, and he couldn't think of why they wouldn't be, the same weapon had been used to shoot Vincent Valentino before he'd ended up in the mine on Krakauer's Glenlyon property. No doubt in O'Leary's mind that it was Anson who was up close and personal.

'Even if he's behind it, and I'm not saying he isn't,' said Nguyen, 'wouldn't he get someone else to do his dirty work? Can't see him sleeping on a floor. And for what? To keep an eye on what we're doing?'

'He's bad news,' was all O'Leary could offer. 'I want him found and locked away for good. And the first step is to start getting the evidence we need to do that. I thought I told you to get his DNA the last time we met?'

'You did, Sir, but we haven't been able to get his DNA,' Janzen said. 'I've been in touch with his lawyer, Elise Lanigan. She claims she doesn't know where he is. I contacted forensics at Macleod. They haven't got him on their database.'

Slurping down the remainder of his tea, O'Leary said, 'What about his daughter? You know, that little girl who caught the plane to Sydney with her mother? What was the mother's name again? Christina? Couldn't a test on the girl give us the data we need?'

Nguyen sighed. 'But we don't know for sure that it is his daughter. We speculated that she was most likely his daughter, but no one ever checked for sure.'

'Well, what are you waiting for? Get onto Births, Deaths and Marriages now and fucking find out.'

Janzen shifted in her chair.

Nguyen picked his notebook up from O'Leary's desk. 'See what we can do, Boss. Let you know soon as we know. But don't forget we're going to the County Court this morning for Krakauer's appearance.'

O'Leary rubbed his forehead. 'Yeah. Forgot about that. Look, just do some searching after you come back. Okay?'

'Sure, Boss,' said Nguyen.

Janzen followed Nguyen to the kitchenette. He ran water from the filter tap into two glasses. 'Here,' he said, proffering a glass, 'good to keep up your fluids on a day like today.'

She nodded towards O'Leary's door. 'Bear with a sore head?'

'Mmm,' sighed Nguyen. 'Think it's more than that. Something's not right, that's for sure. Could be his leg, but reckon it's more likely that the weird stuff going down's got him spooked. I've never seen him like this.'

'He wants to watch it. Last week's memo was all about bullying in the workplace.'

Nguyen narrowed his eyes. 'O'Leary's a good cop. He's been under a lot of pressure. Work and home, as well as health. Think we need to give him the benefit of the doubt before doing anything stupid like dobbing him in.'

She reddened, lowered her head. 'Didn't mean I was going to do anything,' she said quietly. 'Just saying that there's a bit of a blitz on.'

'Yeah, well—If we get that inquiry that's rumoured into police integrity, time enough for all the dirty linen to be aired then. And speaking of airing stuff, we'd better find out after our visit to court this morning everything that O'Leary wants to know about Anson before he pumps air up our arses for not second-guessing him.'

Back in the office, Micelli was aware that Pritchard was waiting on her to finish a call. As soon as she hung up, he launched into a retelling of his conversation with Ludmilla Bagrova. 'Do we know how Azarov travelled to meet Bagrova in North Melbourne?' she asked.

'Nup. Maybe taxi?'

'But not an Uber, as there's no record of that on his phone.'

'Maybe a courtesy car from the tennis?'

'Good one. All drivers would have to log their trips, so that'd be easy to check. Anyway, go on about Bagrova.'

Pritchard nodded. 'And there's a whole lot of glasses and stuff on her sink. Possible we could get them tested? If Azarov had been there, that'd be one way to prove it.'

'Not going to fly. We'd need a warrant, and at this stage Bagrova's not even a person of interest. What I'd like to see is any neighbourhood CCTV, check out if she's telling us the truth when she said she didn't leave the place after Azarov departed. That's if he was even there.' She dabbed her forehead with a scrunched-up tissue. 'We're treading through treacle. Least that's what it feels like. Wish we knew the ID of that woman in the Condor lift.'

'What about forecourt CCTV? We haven't looked at that yet.'

'We're going to be known as the CCTV crew the way we're going,' said Micelli, pausing to make a note. 'But you're right. It could give us a sighting. I'll give that job and the tennis courtesy car stuff to Harris. That is if he ever emerges from yet another meeting with the forensic accountants' She checked the time on her phone. 'You heard from him? Or Skelton? Not that he's any use.'

Pritchard shook his head. 'Nothing from either of them.'

'And if it was a taxi that Azarov caught to Bagrova's North Melbourne place, we'd be trying to find a needle in a haystack. Could give it a go though. An extra job for Harris.'

'Another curious thing,' Pritchard said. 'There's the matter of alleged phone calls. Bagrova said Azarov had called her to let her know he was on his way, that of course he had her number as he'd called her before. But as we know there were no outgoing calls on Azarov's phone. He either used a different phone or he never did call her. And, we've only got her word for it that they were lovers, by the way.'

'Do you think that smart watch on Azarov's bedside table was connected to some other phone that we haven't traced?'

Pritchard pushed up his left shirt sleeve. 'In my experience most people using a smart watch like this one do connect it to their other devices. More convenient that way. Mine's connected to my phone and the home laptop. It's easy to download the data into a spreadsheet and use it to track what's going on. It's a recommended weight management tool. Surprised you haven't got one.'

'Do you think I'm fat?'

'No, not at all,' he said, quickly. 'What I meant is that you're very physically active and it could be useful to see how your body's going. Like monitoring your sleep, for instance.'

'Why would I want to do that?'

'Because sleep quality is a key health indicator. Anyhow, back to the case. We've made assumptions, or at least I have and passed them on as if they were fact. There's no proof she was Azarov's lover. Just because she said she was, I believed her.'

Micelli's face lit up with a smile. She slapped his palm in a quick high five on her way to the whiteboard. 'You're good, Pritchard. So good!'

'Lucky she's blind,' said Nguyen pointing upwards to the Lady of Justice hanging on the Lonsdale Street side of the County Court. He and Janzen were standing on the opposite corner in William Street waiting for the lights to change. 'Course she wouldn't be able to see much of the city with that huge thing overhanging her.'

'At least it's not one of those angled verandah things,' she said. 'This one'd keep you dry if it rained.'

They crossed the street in the company of three robed and wigged barristers deep in conversation, their minions towing wheelie suitcases the size of small wardrobes. 'Wanna grab a coffee first? It's only five to ten.'

They joined the queue at the coffee cart. 'I'll have a skinny latte. And a muffin.' She smiled. 'Ran out of time this morning.'

'Skinny milk?' Nguyen frowned.

'Know it's counter-indicative or intuitive or whatever, but I don't like the fatty taste of real milk.' She handed him a ten dollar note which he refused to take. 'Go on. Don't be an idiot.'

'Nuh. You buy the next one.'

Once through security they checked the day's lists, caught the lift to level nine. 'Judge Brewin. Know anything about him?' asked Nguyen.

'He's a she. Inga Brewin. Been in her court before. She's tough.'

'O'Leary'll be happy then. If she's tough on Krakaeur, that is.'

They slid into seats in the back row. Only two other people in the public gallery: a man Nguyen guessed would be sixty-odd, lank hair falling onto the collar of his Hawaiian shirt, doing a crossword in a folded-up newspaper. Along from him, a chubby-faced teenager with tightly curled red hair tied up with a floral scarf, was sprawled across two seats, thumbs working frantically on the screen of a mobile. 'Wow. She's so fast,' whispered Nguyen, nodding his head sideways to indicate the girl.

Janzen grinned. 'At least they don't have to hide in the broom cupboard with the landline cord snaking along the hallway like I had to do. Much more civilised.'

'What about cyber bullying, though? Got a friend who's a psych nurse. Says they're being admitted into hospital with breakdowns at the ages of thirteen and fourteen.'

She scoffed. 'No worse now than when I was at school. We had this gross fat kid in our class. Boy, did she cop it. Teachers didn't seem to, or didn't want to, know what was going on. In the end she had a massive blow-up and got herself expelled.'

'And what's become of her now, I wonder. Imagine if you were that fat girl. I got bullied so I know what it's like. They called me slope head and slanty eyes and stuff like that. I punched a kid out one lunchtime. Got hauled into the office, suspended for five days. Like it was my fault.'

Two more teenagers squeezed past Janzen and Nguyen, sat in the middle of the row, pulled notebooks and pens from their backpacks.

'School excursion?'

'Wouldn't their teachers vet them going to a case like this?' said Janzen. She looked round her and up at the clock: 10.23. 'Doesn't look to be any media here yet.'

Nguyen rolled his shoulders, arched his neck, found a more comfortable position on the seat. He pointed towards the front row of the gallery. 'That's whatshername, isn't it? The woman from *The Gazette*?'

She twisted sideways, directing her gaze to a woman with well-coiffed caramel-coloured hair, head bent low, probably reading from a phone. 'Susan Watson,' she murmured. 'Covers politics mainly. Wonder why she's here?'

A tipstaff dressed in black robes entered the courtroom from behind the judge's bench. 'All stand!' he demanded, which roused the legal teams to their feet and general shuffling in the gallery, prior to the same door opening and a slight woman in judge's wig and gown walking towards the high-backed chair behind the bench.

'You okay?' asked Harris, eyeballing Micelli across the conference table where they were trawling through the forensic lab reports about Azarov. 'You seemed a bit shaken at the end of our meeting.'

'Yeah,' she said, 'not pleasant dealing with someone who's as rank as Skelton. But anyway, whingeing isn't going to change anything.' She lowered her eyes and read out loud from Sutcliffe's preliminary autopsy report. *Despite the presence of a plastic bin liner and white cord directly adjacent to the body, it does not appear that either were the cause of death.*

'Someone must have put it there, though,' Harris said, doodling on a notepad. '

'What?'

'Bin bag. It doesn't find its own way onto a floor.'

'Gloves.'

He frowned. 'What do you mean, gloves?'

'The person who placed the bag was wearing gloves.' A slight grin.

'But gloves would leave traces of glove powder, wouldn't they?'

'Maybe it was there before he even entered the room. Fell off housekeeping's trolley

or something.'

'They don't take trolleys into the rooms. They leave them in the corridors. Least that's what I've always witnessed.'

'Look, I dunno how the bag got there,' she said, jaw clenched, 'but it's there, and there's no other info about it as far as I can see. Do you think it's important?'

Harris scratched his left ear. 'Dunno. Maybe we make a note and follow up?' He reached for his notebook and opened to a new page. 'What about the condom results, then?'

She skimmed some more. 'Semen, Azarov's, found on the inside. Saliva on the outside.'

'Mustn't have had enough fun in the lift,' he chuckled. Micelli shot him a look that could have frozen a penguin. He swallowed hard, straightened his tie. 'Does it say whether the saliva belonged to a male or female?'

'Female. Definitely a failure to get sufficient air, so the report says. And fine bruising on both wrists from handcuffs. No marks on neck.'

Harris frowned. 'What's that mean, then? How can you be strangled and there be no marks?'

'Maybe he wasn't strangled. Says here he had an empty heart. Whatever that is.' She traced a finger to the bottom of the page she was on, flicked to the next. 'Ah ha. Means reduced flow of used blood returning to the heart. Causes low blood pressure.'

'Can you die from low blood pressure?'

She used a highlighter to underline a section. 'Listen to this.' Her voice took on the tone of a news reader's. *This condition, in conjunction with a swelling of the larynx, is often seen when the cause of death is anaphylaxis.* She hesitated. 'And Azarov's larynx was also swollen. You don't think he could have been poisoned, do you?'

'No idea. But if cause of death is anaphylaxis, it isn't caused by poison. It's caused by an allergy of some sort. Like a bee bite or eating lavender or something.'

'Yeah. But that's poison. Even peanut butter's poison to someone who's allergic. Remember that kid who died on a school camp?'

He shook his head. 'Anyway, we'd better go through the forensics report again.' She got up and went over to her desk where she took a wad of papers from the top shelf, returned to the table and plonked them down. Riffling through, she pulled out a folder. Her phone rumbled on the tabletop. How long since he'd texted? Heart racing, she picked it up. *You are dead to ALL MY FAMILY. DON'T EVER SPEAK TO US again!!!!*

'And fuck you too,' she muttered, slamming the phone down.

'Did you say something?' Harris was standing up, stretching his back.

'Nothing. Just family. You got family?'

'Yeah. But they're all in New South so hardly see them since I moved down here. Miss them, though.'

'Probably lucky they're not close by. Not if they're like mine. Where were we?'

'Forensics report.' He took a seat next to her. They skimmed through the pages, searching for anything that might explain anaphylaxis. 'Sushi,' he said, pointing to a reference in the report. 'Might have had prawns in it. People can be allergic to shellfish.'

'Wouldn't he have seen prawns sticking out the end?'

'Maybe he didn't know he was allergic. Or it could have been that cheap sushi where you can't distinguish anything much.'

She screwed up her nose. 'Can't stand the things, personally. Only taste okay if you slather them with soy and wasabi. Then, what's the point of the so-called delicate flavours?'

'You wouldn't say that if you'd had proper ones. Ever see that doco about an eighty-five-year-old Japanese chef who's spent his whole life perfecting sushi? Reckon his'd be alright. Apparently, he spent the first fourteen years chucking away everything that he made.'

She rolled her eyes, tugged her laptop over in front of her and began tapping away on her keyboard. 'Mr Google has quite a lot to say about sushi and allergies, including an article about dead things.'

'Dead things?' He leaned close and peered at her screen. The article described a study showing that dead microscopic nematodes still had the power to cause a reaction in a person who may have consumed them previously in raw fish.

'What's a nematode? I thought they were things in the garden that stopped you planting tomatoes in the same spot.'

He raised an eyebrow. 'Do you grow tomatoes?'

Ignoring him, she scrolled down.

'Hang on. Says here they're parasites,' he said, pointing to a sidebar on her screen. Several pictures of coiled and slimy snake-like organisms appeared beneath the text. 'Ugly bloody things.'

'They're in raw fish.' Micelli stabbed a finger at the screen. She turned to face him. 'Don't all Russians eat raw herring?' She pushed the laptop to the side. 'Reckon we're onto something here?'

'Maybe. When I was there, the supermarkets only sold pickled fish and vodka. Or at least that's what it looked like. Oh, and beer too. Only got to be classed as alcohol about ten years ago. Drink of choice at breakfast time for many. Probably still is.'

'Didn't know you'd been to Russia. Any good?'

'Tell you some other time. Maybe over a drink after we've cracked this case. What else is in Sutcliffe's report?'

Micelli put the autopsy report back in front of her and flipped to the back page. 'His conclusion's inconclusive, for want of a better word. He's saying there's anaphylactic symptoms, but until the toxicology reports come in, he's holding fire. Anyway, if it's just anaphylaxis then it's not murder, is it?'

Harris ran fingers through his hair. 'Dunno. If you knew that the person was allergic to say shellfish, and you disguised it in a sushi roll, and you poured enough grog into someone, it could be murder, couldn't it?'

She pushed back her chair and stood up. 'Want to get some fresh air? I need a break. Get my thoughts in order.'

He picked his jacket off the back of his chair and followed her towards the lifts.

Harris was trying to juggle lunch at his desk and a phone call from a police officer stationed in Tallinn. 'Yep—yep—yeah, will do.' He brushed imaginary crumbs from his pants, thighs rippling under the thin woollen fabric. 'Yes—I'll wait for your email. And thanks a heap for following up.' He clicked his email program open. Ran a thumb along his calf muscle that had tightened up after last night's soccer training, raised his foot onto a neighbouring chair, eyes all the time on the screen. Two emails popped up, neither from Tallinn. And then another. This was the one he was waiting for. Jumping straight to the attached document he began to read.

The Estonian Government is monitoring an island off the north-east coast of the country in the Gulf of Finland. The permanent population numbers under two hundred, adults involved in either fishing or administration, and younger children attending a small school on the island. When they reach secondary school age, they must make their way to the mainland. The 22.5- kilometre crossing by ferry takes approximately one hour.

So much for the Wikipedia-type info, Harris thought, quickly scrolling through the remainder of the document. Nothing caught his eye that couldn't wait for a more thorough read after he'd sifted the key information.

He opened another file attachment. A picture of a man standing on barren rocks staring out to sea followed by an article originally published in a Finnish national newspaper, the headline proclaiming *Search results in arrests, cash hauls.*

A joint Finnish and Estonian operation raided a private compound on Prangli Island on September 21 this year. Police and military troops entered the island's main harbour and headed to the north-east coastline where a fenced compound stands that has been out-of-bounds for locals for several years. Locals reported several helicopters in the area on the morning of the raid.

When our reporter talked to local islander, Svend Orcistrata, he described his long-held suspicions. "Why did they come here at night and put up this fence? We used to fish off those rocks and then no more, big signs everywhere, barbed wire like an internment camp. And no fishing, even from a boat. They have buoys stopping us getting closer than a kilometre."

Locals suspect that the property is used for criminal purposes, but no one can confirm this. "What is all the secrecy about? Are they making drugs?" asked one islander. Another said that helicopters would fly in, always at night, then take off again before dawn. "What can they do in the dark? I tried to see once but they had dogs on the fence line that sniffed me' out so I got back in my car and made a run for it."

Officials confirmed that the compound is owned by a Russian, Dmitry Orlov, from St Petersburg, a close friend so it is rumoured of the Russian President. The property is equipped with a proliferation of satellite dishes, five piers and a helipad. And at least five large buildings, presumably for accommodation.

Three men were arrested and taken into custody by Estonian officers after the raids. It is believed that two men are from Estonia, but of Russian descent, and the other is a Russian national. There is no confirmation that the Russian man is Dmitry Orlov. Seized during the raid were large sums of cash including 3.5 million euros. Computers and files were also removed, and are being examined by Estonian and Finnish intelligence and forensic officers.

Parliamentary discussions are taking place regarding the strengthening of property laws in Estonia. The largest group of property owners in Estonia are from Russia, and Estonia wants to change the law to prohibit those outside the European Union from owning land in the nation. The Prime Minister said the proposed legislation would strengthen the country's ties with the EU as well as ensure better national security.

He re-read the paragraph about the cash. A stash of more than the 3.5 million in euros. The balance was in other currencies waiting to be laundered. Or was that merely an assumption on his behalf, sparked because he knew that Azarov had been involved in dirty dealings with money. Until he could get a handle on Dmitry Orlov and what role he might have played in Azarov's affairs, he'd have to ditch that as a fact and merely note it as a possibility. Intriguing though, given Orlov's seemingly high profile indicated by his friendship with the president. Who in Australia would have such cosy relations, he wondered. But not for long as Micelli burst into the room looking like thunder.

'Have you seen Skelton since our meeting?' Hands on hips, bottom lip trembling. She swore loudly.

'You alright? Sounds like you've got Tourette's or something.'

'I asked him to follow up and get more info on the Kross team.

Not a hard job, I wouldn't have thought. Few databases, some phone calls here and there. So what happens? I get a text.' She fumbled in her pants pocket and pulled out her phone. 'Here,' she said, thrusting the phone towards Harris, 'read this crap!'

At tennis. No info yet on Kross & boys. MS

'What the fuck does he think he's up to?' She grabbed her phone from Harris's hand. 'I've had it with him. I'm going to see Goddings again.' She turned on her heel and stormed out of the office.

Harris followed her out hoping to catch her at the lift. Try to persuade her to calm down before confronting Goddings, as any fool could see that a meeting with the boss when she was so worked up would be counterproductive. But the arrow was showing the lift ascending, no doubt to Godding's floor with Micelli on board, steaming up the mirror. He returned to the office and sat back at the table. Tried to focus again on the recent information he'd read. Three questions for his colleagues in Tallinn: what were the results after the computer gear had been to forensics; was anything known that could link Azarov and Orlov; and if there was a link, what was its significance?

Whenever O'Leary had felt under pressure in the past, he'd gone for a run. True, he'd slowed down over the years, but the act of throwing on an old t-shirt, shorts and lacing up his runners, had always been the best method to calm his mind. Running, or jogging he supposed more accurately described his style these days, was presently denied to him. Rubbing at his right thigh, he breathed deeply, used his thumb to knead the ridge of scar tissue that ran down his leg from the groin to the knee. If he still believed, he would have sent a prayer to St Luke asking for a quick mend. His mother was doing that for him, though, he reasoned, so no need to overburden the saint whose work was in all likelihood cut out for him. Thinking about his mother brought a smile to his face. Kathleen was a good woman, no doubt about that. Raising five unruly O'Leary kids and putting up with her husband would surely get her into heaven. He and the twins had planned to go to the farm tomorrow, and without doubt there'd be cold roast meat, with tomatoes and beetroot from her garden, lettuce piled high in a bowl and a jug of condensed milk mayonnaise to go with it. Addicted to that mayonnaise as a kid, he loved scooping spoonfuls out of the jar in the fridge when no one was looking. Appeared that Zoe and Jack were following in his footsteps, pouring the creamy sweet stuff over their lettuce in abundance and coming back for seconds and thirds of lettuce, just so they could pour on more mayo.

He looked at his watch. Twenty past two. Nguyen and Janzen should be back from the court soon. Meanwhile, he needed to tidy up his morning's work, let them know what had come across his desk, which was a forwarded Interpol report confirming that a global child porn ring had been successfully infiltrated, and police had arrested and charged more than two thousand people living in over eighty countries. The strike had been made after a server host worker noted suspicious activity related to hits on a particular site. Further investigation revealed videos showing the sexual abuse of children. Although not clear as yet, it appeared from the footage that some of the videos available for download had been made in the Asia Pacific region featuring Anglo kids. The report from VIC JACET, the joint ADF and Vicpol unit dealing with child exploitation, was inconclusive regarding the Mascord twins, but he'd been promised information regarding sources if anything came to light.

His rumbling stomach reminded him that breakfast had been a cup of tea and a muffin. In the café downstairs, Mavis was tidying up the display case after the lunchtime rush. 'Afternoon Brendan, you're a bit late today. Anything take your fancy?' He selected a Buddha bowl of mixed veggies and grains, a splotch of orange dressing on top. 'You heard about the new integrity inquiry?' she asked. 'It was on the eleven o'clock news. Due to start on Monday.'

'This coming Monday?'

'That's what they said. Surprised you're not in the know. Lot of them been down here gossiping about it, heads down, all hush hush like butter wouldn't melt in their mouths. Wouldn't think you'd have a lot to worry about though. Not like some others I could name.' She winked, passed the bowl, a napkin and bamboo cutlery across the counter. 'Have a good one, Brendan.'

After his meeting with O'Leary to report on Krakauer's case, Nguyen settled down to write a report of the morning's court case. He'd almost completed it when the phone rang. The voice on the other end announced himself as DSC Hargreaves, Sydney CID. 'Boss thought Melbourne might be interested in some news to hand. Christina Rosa Gallo has been admitted to St Vincent's Hospital. Severe facial lacerations, bruising, some teeth missing, suspected broken ribs and a collarbone, broken right arm. She's not talking.'

It took Nguyen a moment to process this news. 'Gregory Anson's girlfriend?'

'That's right, mate. Hasn't been interviewed as yet.'

Nguyen recalled photos of a tubby little blonde that he'd seen dotted around Anson's apartment last year. 'Is her daughter okay?'

'Hang on a minute, can you?' He could hear Hargreaves talking to someone else in the background. 'Apparently the girl wasn't at home when the attack occurred. Gallo provided the name of a family where she was staying. Community Liaison's making arrangements for the girl's care. Want their number?'

Nguyen's thoughts went in all directions. Had the place where Christina lived been sealed off? Was it being forensically examined? Should he go to Sydney and interview her? What if she wouldn't talk, like she wasn't talking apparently to the New South Wales detectives? What about the girl? Would she know anything? What were the rules about interviewing kids in New South? 'Yep, give me the number,' he said. 'You the best person to liaise with about this?'

Hargreaves said he was before rattling off some other names and numbers that Nguyen might find useful to contact. After spelling out both the first name and surname of the first officer, Hargreaves made an offer. 'What's your email there? I'll send it all through. There's three all up, two for the assault, and a female officer from community liaison.'

'And are forensics on the job?'

Hargreaves hesitated. 'Look, to tell you the truth, I don't know. Call one of the two whose names and numbers I'm sending you. Okay then? Look out for my email.' He rang off.

Better talk to O'Leary. Knocking lightly on his office door that was slightly ajar, Nguyen found O'Leary with his feet on the desk, head against the wall, softly snoring. A half-full glass of water was in danger of spilling if his right foot moved a millimetre sideways. A blister pack of tablets lay next to the water.

Returning to his desk, Nguyen opened the promised email from Sydney and printed off the names of the contacts. Hargreaves had attached a short note. *Forensics are on the scene.* At least that was one piece of good news. He picked up the phone and dialled the number of a DSS Paul Gunn stationed at Surry Hills. After the necessary formalities, Gunn told him what was known to date about Christina. 'Not sure who called it in, but ambos attended not long before lunch. 11:23 to be exact. Brought her straight to hospital. She's very scared. Let slip to one of the ambos that next time she's facing death. They asked her what she meant by next time, but she didn't answer, just said something like, they'll be back. Very possible there's more than one person involved in the assault. The girl, Tanah, was having a sleepover at the time. Makes you wonder if someone pre-planned the attack on Gallo and didn't want the girl to witness anything. By the way, she's playing up apparently, demanding to see mummy and daddy.'

'Hasn't said who daddy is?' asked Nguyen.

'Nup. Said everything else, evidently. Right little spitfire.'

'And the people she was staying with for the night? Any possible link between whoever did the assault and where the girl was?'

'You mean has anyone from that address been reported before?' Nguyen could hear paper rustling before Gunn answered. 'Haven't got any data on the residents as yet. Possible, I spose. Early days though. We've only just found out about the assault.'

'Yeah,' said Nguyen in a tone he hoped was sympathetic, although if it'd been him in charge, he would have had the whole force crashing down. Still, New South didn't understand what Anson was capable of like he did. 'Anyone at your end have any ideas about why Christina was targeted?'

'Hospital's confirmed she's tested negative for drugs and alcohol, so not a lot to go on until forensics have finished in the apartment. According to paperwork filed with us by Vicpol from October last year, she had been living with Gregory Anson, a suspected drug manufacturer and dealer. Then she fled up here with the girl and Anson disappeared into thin air. That still the case?'

Describing the details of Christina's relationship with Gregory Anson, including that he was probably Tanah's father, the little girl who was now giving her carers hell, and the fact that Anson had not been sighted since he disappeared from Tullamarine airport last September, took a few minutes. 'Haven't got a DNA sample for Anson as yet. If anything turns up in Sydney, can you let us know? By the way, does Christina have a phone with her?'

Gunn rustled more paperwork. 'Can't see any reference to it. Want me to check the number that called in the assault?'

'That'd be good,' said Nguyen. 'Suppose you can't ask for her phone? I know she's the victim here, but if we could get a lead on Anson then more than a few of our problems might be solved.'

'Like?'

'We think he's involved in multiple homicides.' Nguyen decided not to detail O'Leary's unfounded suspicions about the terror campaign being waged against his family. He wasn't as yet convinced that Anson was the man behind it all. Seemed too personal, somehow. He was sure Anson had bigger fish to fry than scaring O'Leary.

The city was closing down for the weekend, La Trobe Street ribboned with bikes whizzing across the Spencer Street intersection and down the hill towards Docklands. Micelli, scanning traffic from the office window, estimated six out of ten riders were wearing high-vis jackets. Most yellow, some orange. Wondered how many had been involved in what had happened earlier today. A few riders dressed in black. At this time of the year it didn't matter as much as it did in winter. She'd had a discussion—she didn't know what else to call it when one person asserts something improbable, cites no evidence, then challenges the listener to disagree—with a mechanic in a bike shop once. He'd claimed that wearing black made drivers more aware than if the rider was in high-vis. He even said that not having bike lights was good, too. Because he was doing her a favour, she hadn't put up much of an argument, but to her it was signalling a death wish to ride a bike in black. Let alone no lights. Not that there was any shortage of idiots in the world. Her phone distracted her from further thoughts on the matter. 'DSC Micelli,' she said, wedging her phone between shoulder and cheek, returning to her desk for a pen and riffling through her notebook to the next spare page. 'Sorry. Steve Burns was it? From?' She wrote down the journalist's name and phone number. 'You have information about the Russian Mafia in Australia, you say?' Sizing up the distance from her office to his, she said, 'What about downstairs at yours in fifteen?' She grabbed her gear and headed out onto the street.

Waiting at the Bourke Street corner for the lights to change, she looked north. No sign of the chaos that had occurred in the city earlier. Estimated that more than two thousand naked bike riders had gathered at Parliament House, entering the city from all directions, before riding up and down Bourke Street to the mall and back, blocking traffic for more than an hour. Trams were backed up. Office workers skurried out to get a good look and got caught up with pedestrians in the crush. Ambulances couldn't gain access. Police had no idea what to do. Melbourne had seen nothing like it.

Burns was already seated when she arrived, coffee in front of him. Seemed he'd washed his hair since he'd been at Tuesday's press conference. And put on a clean shirt. White with a navy blue and green stripe, open at the neck. Tufts of chest hair just visible. She sat down opposite. 'What'll you have? Long black?'

She nodded, watched him chat to the barista, pocket the change. Grubby beige-coloured chinos, though. 'I know very little about politics, Steve, so appreciate you keeping it simple if that's possible.'

He grinned. Same yellowed teeth. 'Not my forté either, but something clicked the other day. When you said Estonia, I'd been doing a bit of research about the credit card scammers who got picked up in the city last week. Estonian passports, but couldn't speak a word of the language.'

She cocked her head. 'Ah, don't get it.'

'Russians, you see. One of the journos who's into Russia in a big way told me it's common for Russian crooks to operate in former USSR countries like Estonia. Trafficking, drugs, money scams. You name it, it's been done. And that's what Azarov was offering, wasn't he? Some investment opportunity that went bust. Like a Ponzi scheme. Know about them?'

'Not a lot.' She sipped her coffee, adding half a stick of sugar, stirring it in.

He opened his notebook. Lines connected to a couple of stick figures, words she couldn't read upside down. 'It's like this,' he said, turning the book around, using his pen to point out the starting point. 'A person—let's call him Mr X—sets up an investment account, calls it something fancy, seeks funds from bunnies who believe what he tells them, that they'll get a ridiculous return on their money, like fifteen or twenty percent. More than twenty percent sometimes.' He stopped, pushed a lock of hair from his eyes. 'People give Mr X the money, wait for the three months, and he pays up. Trouble is, he uses the money that the last lot of people into the investment scheme gave him, to pay the first ones in.' He slurped up a mouthful of coffee. 'Okay so far?'

'So far so good,' she said, recalling her conversation with Sergey Serchanov whose mother, so he'd said, had been promised up to thirty percent by Azarov.

'Then those first people with their fifteen or twenty percent are so pleased they tell all their friends. So more money flows in for Mr X. Soon he's raking it in, always using recent funds to pay original investors. If he's smart, he might offer less return to later investors, but still substantial enough, say ten percent. Heard of Bernie Madoff?'

'Was he that bloke in the US?'

'Biggest fraudster in American history. Owed over sixty billion dollars to investors.' He drew breath. 'Sixty billion,' he said again. 'Considering that Australia spends less than four billion a year on foreign aid, puts it into perspective a bit.' She raised her eyebrows. 'His Ponzi scheme had been running for almost twenty years, they think.'

'Heard of Sergey Serchanov? Now in Australia?'

'Burns squeezed his eyes shut. 'Yeah.' Eyes open again. 'He's ex-KGB if I remember correctly. Is he in on all this as well?'

She ignored his question. 'Okay, I think I get the Ponzi scheme stuff now. Or at least enough to work with. But how have you connected Azarov to the Russian Mafia?'

'Ah.' He swivelled his notebook back towards him. 'Heard of the Obtshak?'

'I have.' She gave herself an imaginary high-five for having at least heard about something. 'And?'

He leaned forward again. 'Because it was the Obtshak who got Azarov off, paid his legal expenses, set him up as a sports agent.'

'Why's that significant?'

'Because he must have known someone in a gang that was a member of the Obtshak. A single operator like Azarov isn't likely to be a member in his own right.'

Stirring her coffee once more, she asked, 'And any ideas about who that gang might have been?'

He bit his bottom lip. 'Some. Still working on it.'

She got up from her chair. 'Thanks for the coffee, Steve. Keep in touch if anything else comes up.'

Another bloody idiot, she mused, trying to flag down a taxi to take her home. Deep in the weeds, but not so deep in the real world. Eventually a car stopped abruptly on the corner of Bourke and Collins, indicating she should get in. She gave directions to her apartment in Altona and settled back to think some more. But the taxi driver was on for a big chat. Apparently, the situation in Punjab, where it seemed to Micelli that all of Melbourne's taxi drivers hailed from, was not so good. But his tales of woe were interspersed with his need to educate her about his homeland.

'You know what Punjab means?' She could hear the pride in his voice.

'Seven rivers?'

He giggled. 'Very good, lady. Very good. But not seven. Five.' He was rocking in his seat like one of those Elvis dolls people put on their dashboards. 'We have five waters in the Punjab.' His hands gripped the steering wheel, his voice went down a decibel. 'But now we only have two. Two,' he said, turning to look sternly in her direction. 'That's what Partition did. You know Partition? Terrible thing. We still don't have real borders, you know.'

She tried to think of what he meant by partition. A memory of modern history at school with Miss Hazelwood flitted across her consciousness. 'After the war, something about India and Pakistan?' It was more of a question than a statement.

'Ah, you good.' His smile returned like a lost dog. 'But not the war. The British, lady. It happen when British leave India. 1947. They carve things up. Now Pakistanis have three rivers and Punjabis only have two.' He snorted. Returned to the current mess. 'They have bad economy, can't play cricket—'

Her mind began to wander. A weekend. A murder enquiry. Trouble in the family. No call from David. O'Leary's kids. Indeed, O'Leary himself. His brother last year and now his stories about him and Skelton in his younger days. She was reminded of the stuff she'd had to deal with on the beat in St Kilda, later Footscray. People ravaged by abuse, alcohol, drugs. Same story over and over. Men whose body weight would hardly be that of a thirteen-year-old scratching sores on their faces, botting fags from passers-by. When they smiled you could see only red gums and yellowed stumps that were once teeth. That is if there were any dental remnants at all. All the street walkers she'd tried to help, some as young as fifteen, runaways from abuse in their families. Easy to be angry with the street people. But she knew that their perpetrators before them had too often been victims before they became abusers. And the church. The church she was brought up in. The church her mother and sisters still frequented. What about its contribution to those poor specimens of washed-up humanity on the streets that cops and social workers and all manner of do-gooders work with on a daily basis? Suffer the little children. Yeah.

The taxi swerved to avoid an overtaking delivery van listing menacingly to the left, which jolted her back to the present. '— and then I go to Australia. I send money back to my family. Soon my youngest brother will come and start school. He very bright boy. Start business at Swinburne College. You know Swinburne College?'

'You missed the turn-off,' she yelped. 'You'll have to take the next left.'

He humphed. 'Okay, lady. I turn now.' He swung the vehicle into a wide arc, just missing the kerb on the opposite side of the narrow street but failing to avoid two wheelie bins standing in the road where they'd been left after the morning's garbage run. He brought the car to a screeching stop out the front of her apartment. She fumbled in her bag, swiped her phone on the Cabcharge reader and scrambled out, practically running up the pathway to her front door. Marbles, reclining on the windowsill, lifted its head and watched as Micelli turned the key in the lock. 'Okay, dinner for you, shower for me.' The cat had jumped off the sill and was now miaowing at her feet. 'God, what a day, Marbles.' She opened the pantry, took out a can of cat food and an already opened bottle of red. She held it to her nose then poured a glass larger than a 185ml standard drink and downed it in one go. 'And fuck you too, David Romano.' She poured the remains of the bottle into her glass, took a large gulp then headed for the shower.

Hair still wet, she donned an old pair of yoga pants and a white t-shirt. Scribbled a list on the back of an envelope and hoped she wouldn't see anyone she knew in the supermarket. First, the bottle shop. She wandered along the rows and rows of wines arranged by variety before choosing a bottle of shiraz from Coonawarra. 'How's your day been, darl?' asked the grinning salesman, acne reddening his neck.

Feeling herself bristle, she forced a wide grin onto her face. 'Actually, it's been a blast. Drugs, money laundering, murder. Oh, and a bit of sex, too.' The red flush spread from his neck upwards over his prominent chin where it met chubby cheeks that couldn't be a day over eighteen. She kept beaming, screwed up her nose a little bit like she'd seen Nicole Kidman do. Hoped it looked impish. 'You know. That sort of thing.' She tapped her card, picked up the bottle and stuffed it into her backpack. Giving him a wink, she said, 'See you next time, dude,' and danced out of the store as if she really was Nicole Kidman in that wellbeing ad, but minus the scuffed boots and sunflowers.

She turned on the news when she got home. Footage of the naked bike riders in Bourke Street, drivers yelling abuse, people looking on smiling and laughing. Police under attack from the media for gross incompetence for not controlling the situation. She got up from the couch and sculled the rest of the wine she'd poured earlier. Turned to see what the newsreader described as a brilliant game, smashing his opponent out of the park. Kross's blonde hair plastered with sweat, white teeth on show as he raised his arms in a victory wave at the Court 3 spectators, most on their feet, clapping enthusiastically. A group of five or six in front row seats waved the Estonian tricolour: blue, black and white. A new kid on the block, the newsreader opined. Micelli paused the TV, examined the faces. No one she recognised. But then, they'd only just begun to scratch the surface of the Estonian community in Melbourne.

She struggled to a sitting position on the couch when she heard a knock on the front door. She muted the tennis. She peered through the peephole in the front door. 'Who's there?'

'It's Nick.' Voice low. 'I need to talk.'

She opened the door to her nephew who looked as if he'd slept in his clothes for the last week. 'You alone?' He assured her he was, having made the trek to Altona by train, walking from the station to her place. 'Look at you!' She shook her head when she saw him up close in the light of the living room.

He began to sob. She wrapped him in her arms, marvelling that he was no longer the little kid she used to pick up and dust off after a fall from a bike, but a muscled and well-built young man. 'Nick. Nick.' She patted his back, held him tight. 'You'll get a good behaviour bond, that's all. It's not the end of the world.'

'It's not me I'm worried about—' He wailed even louder, tears and snot comingling. 'It's you, Aunty Ange.' He pushed his way out of her hold and stumbled into the bathroom where she could hear loud nose-blowing prior to the tap running. When he emerged, she sat him on the couch, having already turned off the television despite wanting to know the result of a tight tie break in the third set between Kross and his opponent. 'Does your mother know you're here?'

'I don't care if I never see her again.' His voice came out somewhere between a wail and a bellow. 'What she's done to you. And what Nonna's done to you, because of her—' He stopped, taking in gulping breaths.

'Take a drink and slow down, Nick.' She passed him a glass of water. 'Can I get you a coffee? Don't have any beer, sorry.'

He swallowed half the water. 'I don't know what I did. Or what I'm doing for that matter. It's like a monster inhabited me or something. I didn't mean to take photos. It's just that my phone dropped, just like I said. And when I bent down to pick it up, I saw the possibilities. I just did it. Because I could.' He fiddled with the piping on a cushion, finished the remainder of the water. She sat down beside him, put her arm round his shoulder. Immediately a purring Marbles jumped up and settled on Nick's lap. He grinned, patting the cat in long strokes from her ears to her tail. 'You still love me, don't you.'

'We all still love you, Nick. Me. Your grandmother. Especially your mother.'

He screwed up his face. 'Don't think so. I'm not even allowed in the house. Don't you darken my door until you repent. That's what she said. Can you believe it? Repent! What the hell does she mean by that?' Tears slid down his cheeks again. Micelli got up and fetched a fresh box of tissues from the bathroom. She waited until he was calmer before asking him where he had been staying since Monday night. 'In the bungalow. She said I could live there seeing I was a degenerate and she didn't want any reprobates darkening her door. I don't even know what those words mean.'

A giggle escaped. 'Think she's been reading too many novels.'

'It's not funny,' he said, looking accusingly at Micelli, who was now having a lot of trouble stifling her laughter. When Nick let out a loud guffaw before doubling over and howling in glee, it was too much for the cat who took off as if shot from a cannon. 'If she'd called me a pervert I could have understood,' he said between gales of laughter, 'but reprobate. Who's ever been called that?'

Recovering slightly, Micelli got up and opened the pantry. 'Glass of shiraz do you?' She poured two glasses and brought them to the coffee table. 'It's Friday night, so officially you've been in the doghouse for five nights, counting tonight. What do you think might change your mother's mind about the situation?'

He took a sip. Put the glass back on the table. 'Dunno. She seems pretty determined.'

'What about your dad?' Micelli had wondered about the relationship between Rosie and husband Frank many times over the years, especially when it came to their kids. On the outside they seemed like traditional Italian parents, Rosie doing all the house stuff while Frank went to work and brought home the money. But never once had she seen him so much as raise his voice to their kids. Not like the family she'd grown up in. And when Rosie did try to be consistent and insist on some rules, Frank would sabotage them as soon as she wasn't looking. Like the time she said Nick couldn't have his Nintendo for a week because he'd not cleaned up his room despite a deal they'd made. Next day Frank came home with a brand-new Xbox.

'Nothing. He hasn't spoken to me.' Nick leaned forward and took his wine off the table.

'Do you think he's confused about what to do?'

Nick shook his head. 'Scared of Mum, more like it. I heard her shouting at him when we got home on Monday night. Said he wasn't to interfere like he always does. Let things run their course. But it's gunna take ages before anything happens. Even the cop told me that. I haven't even been formally charged.'

Micelli frowned. 'Thought that happened on Monday at the tennis centre?'

'Nup. Cop said she needed to find out what the girl wanted to do.'

'But didn't they take your computer and find other images on your phone?'

He stared at her as if she was an alien who'd just entered the conversation. 'No. What are you talking about? She just looked at my phone that night. There were five photos. And no one's been to the house, far as I know.'

Jack's chooks fed and locked away for the night, O'Leary climbed the steps onto the back deck and sank into a deckchair. Maggie padded after him, sniffed what was left in her bowl, flopped down by his side. Darkness had fallen but he could still hear people out in the park, calling to their dogs, greeting one another. It had been another stinker of a day, the thermometer reaching thirty-four degrees by mid-afternoon. A slight cool change had brought some relief, but nothing seemed to be relieving the aching in his leg. Probably too much red wine and not enough sleep over the last twenty-four hours.

After a while he went inside, turned on the TV. Vision from Bourke Street. Apparently more than thirty treated for minor injuries caused by the crush of onlookers. He wondered what Ange would make of the protest. She often complained about rude drivers who thought they had a monopoly on the roads.

Three raps on the front door. Loud enough to rouse Maggie who ran in from the deck and up the hall, barking as she went. O'Leary lumbered after her. 'Who is it?'

'Police.'

Heart racing faster than feet, he loped the rest of the way, threw the door open. Recognisable anywhere as cops, dour faced under the light. 'Are the twins alright?' His voice a pitch higher than usual.

'Detective Senior Sergeant O'Leary?' asked one, tall as a beanpole, voice clipped.

'The twins? Are they okay?'

'We're not here about children, DSS O'Leary,' said the other one, holding out her badge, stubby fingers, hard-bitten nails. 'Can we come in, please?'

He opened the door wider, followed them into the kitchen.

Beanpole's suit pants barely covered a rumpled pair of black socks. Had he seen him before? Maybe, but couldn't place him. Was certain he'd never seen the woman before.

'What's this about, then?' Flicking off the television, he took his papers and books off the kitchen stools, indicated they should sit. Beanpole remained standing, head about the same height as the pendant lights suspended over the kitchen island. O'Leary stood on the other side of the bench, resisting the urge to lean forward to ease the pain in his leg.

Over the course of the next few minutes the detectives explained that O'Leary was going to be investigated over his involvement in an incident at his brother Stephen's place last year. Stephen had been living in a cottage at the family's farm fixing up the pub that he and O'Leary had bought. Stephen was in with the wrong crowd. Absolutely the wrong crowd. One of them had ended up dead— Charles de Havilland—and the other, Gregory Anson, still on the run. He listened as they outlined the situation he was facing.

'Further, our intelligence indicates that you also,' the female detective said, hesitating then eyeballing him, 'have a connection with drug trafficking.'

O'Leary reeled forward, lunged at the bench top. 'What!' He exploded. 'What the fuck?'

Beanpole folded both lips inwards, swayed back and forth on his heels, started off in a voice that grandparents use with unreasonable children. 'I think, Mr O'Leary, if you'll come with me, we might locate something in your laundry.'

O'Leary's eyes bulged in his head. 'Get out!' He was shouting. 'There are no fucking drugs in this house. Never were. Never will be.' Snarling now.

The two detectives exchanged glances. 'If you show us where your laundry is,' said Beanpole.

'What'd you say your name was?' O'Leary asked.

He produced his badge again. DSC Liam Moriarty. Weren't one of the Goons called Moriarty?

'And you?' pointing at the female officer.

'DSC Sandra Milligan.'

O'Leary collapsed onto the bench. 'Shut up, Eccles. Shut up.'

He splurted a spray of spittle between guffaws, 'I say, you're cutting it rather fine.'

Another exchange of glances.

'C'mon,' said O'Leary, straightening up and wiping his eyes with the back of a hand. 'This way to the laundry.' He marched towards the back of the house and threw open a door on the right. 'Don't suppose you can put a load on while you're here?' He gestured towards a basket overflowing with clothing. 'Haven't had a chance myself since last weekend.'

Moriarty and Milligan followed him in. Milligan opened the broom cupboard, Moriarty reached to the top shelf and pulled down a small cardboard box about the size toothpaste comes in. 'You recognise this?' he asked.

Hadn't Jack been mucking around with old boxes and packets a few weeks back? Making a space station? He couldn't recall the details, but there'd been a lot of glue and cardboard involved.

'Our intelligence indicates it contains ecstasy tablets. Packaged into three pill lots ready for the street. Twenty grand's worth or more.'

O'Leary grabbed for the box. 'Let me see.'

'Steady on, Mr O'Leary,' said Moriarty, holding the box in the air out of O'Leary's reach like a big kid in the school ground playing keepings-off. 'We'll go back to the kitchen, shall we?'

'When did you plant this?' Lip curling. Not moving. 'Of course, it wasn't you directly, was it? One of your hired hands would have done the job.' He glared at each of them in turn. Milligan reddened under his gaze. 'Did I hit the nail on the head, Spike?'

Moriarty stepped forwards. 'Back to the kitchen. Let's just get this finished.'

'Is now when I'm supposed to pull a wad of notes out of my back pocket? Unless you're going to take me in for questioning, you can get the bloody hell out of here right now.' Grabbing for the box again, this time he made contact, but didn't manage to get it. 'Arseholes!' He stormed up the hallway and threw open the front door. 'Out! Now!'

It wasn't until he'd calmed down somewhat that he realised he should have asked for a receipt and to see what was in the box.

The so-called evidence to suggest he was a drug trafficker was now in other hands. It was anyone's guess as to what might happen next.

SATURDAY

AN INCOMING text woke Micelli from what had been a fitful night's sleep. *Had a chance to read the docs?* Steve Burns had been busy since their late afternoon coffee. Wedging herself on one elbow, she scrolled through her emails. No less than five, the first arriving in her inbox at 23.03 and the last at 23.56 yesterday. Before she opened them, she slipped out of bed, padded to the living room. Nick was still curled up on the sofa, right forearm flung over his face, left hand dragging on the carpet. She tiptoed to the kitchen and filled the cafetiere, flicked on the gas. He didn't stir. She had almost forgotten what it was like to be an adolescent, capable of sleeping hours and hours at the weekend, worn out by school and part-time jobs. Marbles was curled up at his feet. She retrieved half a can of cat food from the fridge and ladled it into a bowl, which she set down on the laundry floor. Waiting for the coffee to begin perking, she opened the first of the incoming emails headed *Russian Mafia and the KGB* and began to read.

Russia is a virtual mafia state, as are many of the former Eastern European member states of the USSR. Organised crime and government are almost indistinguishable. Represented by high-level law firms, the influence of organised crime is concentrated in the top echelons of government, where criminals can do what government cannot do, as instanced by selling arms that ultimately destabilise countries such as Turkey.

She minimised the window, opened the second email titled *Azarov and Money Laundering.* More like it.

Privatisation which began in Russia in earnest in 1991-92 made way for enormous profits to go the way of organised crime. Organised crime began as early as 1917, and under Stalin's rule criminal gangs in the Gulags formed the thieves in law or vory v zakone. Often distinguished by their distinctive tattoos, members—not murderers themselves—mafia states—interests in Spain, USA, Canada—

What was it about this case that attracted blokes to delve into Russian history and politics? She skipped down to the last paragraph.

Sergey Serchanov, who came to Australia in 1991, was an official in the Department of the Interior until the breakup of the USSR. His life was threatened when he refused to cooperate, that is accept bribes from organised crime figures who wanted part of the oil industry.

Serchanov? Micelli's heart thumped. What was it he'd said when they met on Wednesday? I glad he dead. And when she'd asked him if he had killed Azarov, he'd replied, not so lucky, but I shake hand of man who did.

'Hey. Coffee smells good. Any left for me?' Nick raised himself on one elbow, grinned at Micelli. 'Hardly got a wink of sleep. Like that cat doesn't know *anything* about sharing space.'

Giving her nephew a friendly punch on the arm on the way to the kitchen, she asked, 'Would his lordship desire bacon and eggs, too? Or perhaps something fancier? Say smashed avo on toast?'

'Don't go to any trouble on my account,' he drawled. She rolled her eyes to the heavens. 'Just bacon and eggs'll be like fine.' He threw off the doona she'd laid over him last night and stumbled towards the bathroom, where judging by the sound of water hitting glass, he'd turned the shower on full blast.

She took a pan from the cupboard and opened the fridge. No bacon. Shrugging, she heated oil, cracked in three eggs, stuffed slices of bread into the toaster. Deciding she needed to call Burns, she poured a coffee and waited for him to pick up. She explained that she needed more detail about Serchanov. Did he come on a refugee visa? Did someone sponsor him?

Burns ruminated. 'Haven't found out that much about him, to tell you the truth,' he said. There was something about that phrase *to tell you the truth* that made Micelli's blood boil. People deliberately telling lies as a matter of course, then having to let you know when it was truth time? 'Came here as a migrant. Fifth wave—'

'Fifth wave?'

'You know, the fifth major intake of Russians into Australia. After World War Two was probably the biggest, but post-USSR was pretty big, too.'

She put the phone on speaker while she buttered toast, flipped the eggs. 'Would he still be pursued by Russian criminals after arriving here?'

'Hard to tell. Maybe. Maybe not.'

God, how did journalists ever get anything in writing given their tendency for verbal procrastination. 'So?'

'Pretty sure he came here as a refugee, so he'd be risking his permanent residency if he was to get caught up in anything illegal. Could be deported. And if that happened, he'd be back where he started, only with no protection and at the mercy of the organised crime gangs. Not something he'd like I wouldn't think.'

'For me?'

She held a finger to her lips and pointed to the phone.

'What was that?' asked Burns.

'I've got someone here, that's all.'

Nick scooped all three eggs onto his plate already lined with toast. 'Mmm,' he whispered, grinding on pepper and salt. 'Better than Mum's breakfast.' He angled his lean frame onto a stool and tucked in.

She poured herself another coffee. 'Do you know if Serchanov has been squeaky clean since he came to Australia?'

'No records of anything untoward. Want me to dig?'

'Much appreciated Steve.'

Nick was scraping his knife on the plate trying to get the last morsels of egg. 'Like, you wouldn't be able to do more, Ange?' Big cow eyes pleading his case.

Laughing, she fired up the stove, cracked more eggs into the pan, put four slices of bread in the toaster this time. 'What's on for today that you need to be so carbed up?'

'Not a lot. Might ring mum. See if we can talk offline.'

'Offline?'

'You know. At a café or something. Where she can't get loud.'

'Good luck with that.' She lifted the freshly cooked eggs onto a clean plate. 'I've never seen her quiet in the thirty years I've known her.'

He attacked the eggs with gusto.

Micelli was flat out keeping up the supply of buttered toast. 'Want me to walk with you to the station?'

He grinned. 'That'd be ace, Ange.'

The traffic coming into the city on the Tullamarine Freeway was barely moving. Nguyen's taxi on the other hand was travelling at a fast clip, only slowing to take the Airport Road turnoff. 'You said Qantas domestic, didn't you, mate?' The taxi driver joined the queue for the drop-off lane. Slowly up the rise and on to the end terminal. Nguyen tapped his phone, grabbed his laptop bag. He could see Elsa Janzen waiting near the middle doors, navy skirt suit, white shirt, black shoes. Looked like she was still in uniform. She fluttered a hand in his direction as he got out of the cab.

'Hey, let's get through security and get brekkie. I could eat the crotch out of a low flying duck I'm that hungry.'

'What did you just say? If it's what I think you said, then you sure as hell deserve this.' She balled her fist and punched him hard on the upper arm.

He sprang back. 'What's wrong with what I said? Kids at school used to say it all the time.'

'Do you even know what it means?' She was spluttering.

'Ah, not really. Never thought about it.' He removed a laptop from his bag and placed it in a tray, added wallet, house keys, belt. 'Didn't think, that's all,' he said, eyes trained on her like a dog caught in the act of digging a hole in the garden.

She met his gaze. 'Hope your pants fall down!' She pointed to his belt that was flapping over the side of the tray, a security officer trying to pack it down safely before the tray entered the scanner.

Once through the body scanner, they walked towards the Qantas Lounge. Standing just behind her on the escalator, he could smell her soap, see each of the blonde curls that were not quite reined into her ponytail. 'Look, I'm sorry. Okay?'

'S'okay. I'm hungry too.'

Once inside they peeled off to separate areas of the lounge, Nguyen choosing scrambled eggs, bacon, grilled tomatoes, hash browns, a mini tower of toast teetering on a side plate. He positioned his plates onto a tabletop, arranged cutlery, looked around for Janzen. She was staggering towards him with two coffees and two bowls. Must have been a waitress in another life. 'Look at this Bircher muesli. Fabulous.' She slid him over one of the cappuccinos. 'Full of almonds and all sorts of goodies. Do you think we'll get another brekkie on the plane?'

'Probably, but to change the subject, our main focus has to be a plan of what we want out of Christina, so best chow down now.'

She mumbled a reply, mouth full, jaws working hard. 'Asking her about Anson'd be the main game wouldn't it?'

After walking Nick to the train station, Micelli jumped into the shower, ignoring the water pooled on the floor where he'd forgotten to put down a bathmat. Seven forty-five. She'd let the morning run away, too busy being the good aunt, forgetting that Prichard would be waiting for her at the office. She looked up at the wall clock, counted off the minutes. Just time to ride in. She grabbed a change of clothes and stuffed them into a backpack. Tugged on bike pants, slipped an old shirt over her head and checked that all the doors were locked.

It was already warm, a northerly breeze gusting every few minutes. She sped off down the Esplanade, through the leafy streets of Willamstown, crossed into Spotswood where she picked up the bike path near Scienceworks before going under the Westgate. Normally she'd use the road the whole way, but she wasn't going to fight the congo line of trucks banked up waiting to turn onto the freeway. Tunnel digging had reduced Saturday morning traffic to one lane at the on ramp. The air was heavy with diesel fumes as trucks inched forwards, brakes squealing in the morning thrum.

She sped through Footscray and Docklands, pulled into the carpark under police headquarters and chained up her bike. Funny that. You'd think parking under Victoria's largest police station would be the safest place in the world to leave a bike, but not so. Theft was rife, same as any other carpark. So far she'd lost a set of lights, front and back, and an old rain jacket she'd left strapped to the top bar. Climbing the stairs to the office, she checked her phone. Not bad. Forty-seven minutes, 18.7 kilometres. Good to blow out the fuddle of the last couple of days.

Pritchard, sleeves rolled to his elbows and tie as yet unknotted, was sitting at the conference table reading the *Gazette,* a teaspoon sticking out of a tub of fruit yoghurt. Full-colour pics of yesterday's protest adorned the newspaper's front page. 'That was quite something,' she said, bustling into the kitchenette for a much-needed glass of water. 'What's the man on the street saying?'

Pritchard chuckled. 'You can imagine the puns.'

Her attention was drawn to her pinging phone. 'Oh my god. Guess what?' Before Pritchard could answer, she told him that the message she was looking at had come from Goddings. Skelton had been pulled from the team as he was needed for a special operation. 'Special operation my arse! And no, before you ask, there is no replacement, so it's just you, me and Harris from now on.'

'Probably easier without him.' Pritchard flicked to another page. 'Won't have to put up with his snide comments.'

Her phone began to shrill. 'Sorry, should have put it on silent after that message.' She fumbled for the volume control. Pritchard kept reading, but not for long. Her screeching filled the room. 'What? They looked for drugs at your house? Who? Shit, shit, shit.' She was storming around the table, raking fingers through her hair, every now and then bending over as if about to be sick.

She finished the call and sank into a chair. 'The bastards have tried to set him up.' She groaned. Put her head in her hands. 'Came looking for a box, knew exactly where to go. Someone put it there. For sure.'

'What bastards? Set who up?'

'Bloody drug squad, cops. O'Leary's place. Last night.'

Pritchard jumped up and reappeared a few moments later carrying a steaming mug of black tea from the kitchenette. 'A bit of sugar won't hurt.' He handed her a teaspoon and two sugar sachets.

She gulped a mouthful. Pulled a face. Her mouth had been expecting coffee.

He sat down opposite her at the table. 'What did they find?'

'Nothing. Meant to be drugs, supposedly. But they haven't given up. O'Leary's now waiting for a team to turn up with a search warrant. Go through the entire house.' Her face looked as if she'd been slapped, red blotches covering both cheeks.

'Has he got a lawyer?'

'Shit. Forgot to ask. Who's the best for this sort of crap?'

Pritchard stood, tucked in his shirt that had come adrift, and began searching in various pockets for his phone.

'What about Katherine Cronin? She represented that politician last year. You know, the one that had been set up with child porn. She's tough. And as sharp as a woodchopper's axe. You want me to call her?'

'I'll call O'Leary first and ask what he wants to do. I'll tell him you've got a good contact.'

'I wouldn't say she's a contact, exactly—' But the phone was already in her hand.

'Brendan, Barry Pritchard says to call Kathy Cronin,' she blurted.

'Katherine,' Pritchard corrected.

'Katherine, so I've just been told. Do you want her number?' She gestured towards Pritchard, thumbs texting on an imaginary phone. 'He'll message you now. They turned up yet with the warrant?' She held the phone to her ear, sliding an amber medallion dangling from a gold neck chain back and forth in her fingers. 'Sure. Speak soon.' She put her phone back down on the table. 'Says they haven't been round.'

'It'd take a while to get a warrant sworn, though,' Pritchard said, 'unless they'd lined it up already. Do you think Goddings knows?'

'Spose I should phone him.'

'He'd have to know,' he said, taking a thin silver clip out of his breast pocket. He began to knot his tie, slipping the clip into place when he'd finished. 'He's mates with that head of Drugs, isn't he? Whatshisname?'

She caught a whiff of aftershave wafting across from Pritchard, reminding her that she needed a shower and a change of clothing. Pronto.

Straightening the knot in his tie, Pritchard asked, 'Is Nguyen in? He'd be the best one to talk to I reckon about how O'Leary might be feeling. They've been working pretty closely together this week, haven't they?'

'I'll give him a call. Probably not doing much on a Saturday. Not like Glenlyon's a red-hot case.'

Pritchard checked his phone, smiled to himself, opened his notebook. 'By the way, when you've got a minute, can I have a word about that job you assigned me yesterday? I've got an idea I want to run past you.'

Downing the rest of her tea in one gulp, she said, 'Soon as I've spoken to Nguyen. And had a shower. Any point asking Skelton for his notes about our case?'

Pritchard shook his head.

'Yeah. Figured as much.' She took her backpack off the chair where she'd left it and headed out the door.

Yesterday Pritchard had re-visited Ms Ludmilla Bagrova at the North Melbourne pied-à-terre where she was staying. After searching online and a few discreet conversations with those who have access to certain data, he'd concluded that although he'd already seen an awful lot of Ms Bagrova in her too-short shorts and skimpy halter top on Wednesday, there could be even more to see in a subsequent visit. Things she hadn't mentioned during his first visit, perhaps things she didn't want on display during any visit.

It had not taken long to find out that she had entered Australia with an Estonian-issued passport which was in fact a grey passport of the type issued by Estonia to aliens. Was that a coincidence, given that Alexei Azarov had also entered on a grey passport? Not according to the Estonian Consulate who confirmed that most Russians preferred the grey passport to their own national document, as it gave them better access to countries with less questions asked when travelling. However, the consulate also confirmed that Bagrova was currently resident in Vienna, Austria, where she was listed as an employee of TALfund Investments.

TALfund Investments was a company registered in Georgetown, the principal city of the Cayman Islands, a hub for the world's financial giants. And possible, no probable from what Pritchard had read, a hub for companies who wanted to avoid too much financial scrutiny.

Regarding her career as a TALfund representative, Pritchard discovered that her sole role was to entertain potential investors. Nothing about translating, although he suspected that a good grasp of English would be necessary for some who might be visiting the firm's fund-raising headquarters. A little more digging revealed her most recent job involved a group of Russian oil company executives in need of a hostess to assist them with entertainment options during a three-day visit. It wasn't clear if they were in Vienna to raise money or to invest it, but judging by the description Bagrova had provided, nothing had been spared as the trio enjoyed lavish dining, the best in luxury accommodation and even a private box at a Vienna State Opera performance.

On the question of how she and Azarov hooked up, she repeated her earlier version of events, insisting that he phoned her, that no she hadn't seen him on the day he died, and that they were going to Queensland after the tennis.

On his return to the office, what Prichard searched for and couldn't find was a possible link between TALfund and Azarov's business dealings. He looked up from his laptop when Micelli came in, flicking damp hair in her fingers.

'You know that Steve Burns from the *Times*?' Micelli said. 'The one with the greasy hair and unwashed clothes? Well, he's been doing some digging into Azarov and Russian Mafia stuff and reckons that Azarov went in big time for a Ponzi scheme. You know what that is?'

'It's when someone acquires investors and the first lot are paid the promised high returns by the next lot of suckers, isn't it?'

She nodded and sat down at the table. 'Why don't you read the emails he's sent me? See what you think he's on about.' After entering a password, she slid her laptop over to Pritchard, open at Burns's email thread.

Pritchard scrolled through the messages, making a few notes as he went. 'You've spoken to Serchanov? He say anything else about Azarov apart from wanting him dead and that he's a protected species by that mafia outfit, the Obtshak, or whatever it is?'

'Yeah. You know that Serchanov's ex-KGB. That'd make him knowledgeable about all sorts of ways to kill someone, wouldn't it?'

Pritchard rubbed his chin. 'Depends on whether he was mainly military or mainly intelligence. If he's been able to emigrate to Australia, I'd be thinking it was more on the army side of things. Not a lot of secret intelligence officers got to leave Russia after the KGB coup that led to the breakdown of the USSR I don't think. Unless they defected.'

Micelli rolled her eyes. 'More bloody history lessons. What is it about you blokes? How come you know so much about all this stuff?'

'Big deal when I was at school,' he said. 'We had this teacher, Miss Evans. She loved Russian intrigue.' Smiling now. 'Long red hair that looked like a champion horse's mane—'

'Okay.' She held up both hands. 'Enough of the nostalgia. I'll repeat. If Serchanov's ex-KGB, he might be a dab hand at getting rid of people. Right?'

'Yes,' he said, eyes squinting into the distance. 'But I think you might be able to say that about any number of Russians, ex-KGB or not. They're right up there in the murder stats.'

'Give me the Russians again.' She moved to the whiteboard.

'Ludmilla Bagrova, involved with some dodgy investment firm. What did you say its name was again?' She wrote TALfund and connected it with an arrow to Bagrova. 'And Sergey Serchanov, a Russian-turned-Australian who hates the dead man.' She turned to face Pritchard. 'Who else?'

'The Estonians. Helen Kapp and Markus Kross, along with his sidekicks Artur and Kristo.'

'Sure all of them are Estonians?' she asked, eyebrows arched, underlining Kapp and Kross. 'No one else?'

Pritchard shook his head.

She capped the marker and sat back down. 'What are we missing?'

Scuttling cloud threw shadows over the mountain and into the kitchen where Kathleen O'Leary was putting the finishing touches to the lunch she was preparing for her number one son Brendan and the twins. Getting out the beaters to whip up some cream for the pavlova, she stopped short, listened to the end of a radio news bulletin. Another bomb exploded in central London followed by a wild rampage through Hammersmith, several deaths occurring when passersby were pushed from the bridge into the Thames, swollen with a winter downpour. She felt she knew exactly where this had happened, as her daughter Deirdre had taken her to a Hammersmith pub on the banks of the Thames one summer's evening where they'd sat outside until closing time, watching the world go by.

She missed Deirdre terribly. Still, if Deirdre was taking care of her brother, Stephen, Kathleen and Kevin's youngest son, and keeping him out of trouble, she had Kathleen's blessing. There wasn't much else to bless these days, the local paper focusing again on the inquiry into child abuse and recent claims of sexual abuse made against George Pell, even though he was dead and buried. The Catholic Church had not fared well. Kathleen wondered, not for the first time, if any of her brood had been subject to some priest's perverted attention, as Ballarat certainly seemed to have harboured more than a few paedophile priests in its schools. Maybe going to the local primary school had saved the boys when they were young, and none of them had served as altar boys or in the choir. But Brendan spent time at the big school, and the big school was definitely a place where boys were abused. Still, she reasoned, he didn't go there until his last two years, so maybe he was too old by that time, priests preferring younger boys. Besides, Brendan was over six foot in his final year, a runner and a footballer. Would have given any man who'd tried to molest him a run for his money. She finished whipping the cream and slathered it over the pavlova, before adding a topping of strawberries. She could imagine Jack's grin when he found out there'd be pav for dessert. Great kids, those twins. Brendan was lucky to have them. And lucky that Claire believed—Her thoughts were interrupted by the phone. She popped the pav into the fridge and walked up the hallway to where the phone sat on its table made by Brendan before he went to the big school. 'Hello,' she said, settling onto the padded seat that formed part of the piece of furniture, 'Kathleen O'Leary speaking.'

'G'day Mum.' O'Leary cleared his throat, eased down onto a stool at the kitchen bench. 'Got some bad news, I'm afraid.'

She sat up straighter, picked up the notepad she always kept by the phone and fanned her face. 'Is everything all right, Bren?'

'We can't make it up today, Mum. Sorry for the late notice. Something's come up,' he said, taking a deep breath. He got up and went over to the sink. 'Needs immediate seeing to.'

'Not the twins?'

He exhaled. 'They're fine. Pretty miffed at me, though, for not picking them up this morning.'

'I bet they are. And I've got lunch ready and all.' She checked her watch. It was 10.09. 'Would tomorrow work for you? Everything'll keep until then, I imagine.'

'Dunno, Mum. Can we take a rain check?' he asked, straightening up paperwork that was strewn over the kitchen bench.

'Look, I don't want to pry or anything, but last time we spoke, Wednesday evening wasn't it, you said you were going well now that you're back at work and that the case you're working on is important but not urgent. That's what you said, didn't you?'

'Yeah.'

'I'm no rocket scientist, Brendan,' she said, her voice gaining in volume as she spoke, 'but ever since you could first talk, I've been able to tell when something isn't quite right. And now's one of those times. Your voice is all funny. You're hesitating and carrying on like your father when I ask you a direct question. You going to tell me what's going on, or just let me worry myself to death?'

Despite himself he began to chuckle. 'Oh, Mum, don't worry yourself to death on my account. Plenty of other things that could be worse. But you're right,' he said, reaching over to grab the dishcloth and wiping the cleared-off bench, 'as usual.'

'Well?'

'Okay then. There's a few odd things happening. Dunno why and dunno who's behind them. First I couldn't find my phone and then it mysteriously reappeared. I reckon someone broke into the caravan I was staying in up at Glenlyon where the job's at and took it, found the stuff they needed then dumped it.'

'What would they need on your phone, for goodness sakes?'

'Numbers, Mum. Like Claire's for example.' He got up from the kitchen stool and straightened out his leg. It was as if just talking about Glenlyon brought on pain. 'Maybe even yours. Or Stephen's. And addresses if I've put them in there.'

'What else?'

'Someone sent the twins guns—'

'Jesus, Mary and Joseph!'

'And Claire blasted me. Then the twins disappeared, but we found them again and they were okay. And last night two detectives from Drugs came round and said I had drugs on the premises and that they'd execute a search warrant and that I'd have to face the new integrity inquiry that that bastard Sinclair has announced, and the pain in my leg isn't—' He felt tears coursing down his cheeks well before his chest began to heave.

'Are you telling me that all this has happened in the last two days?' she asked, the tone she used the same as when he and his brothers had been up to no good and told her a story that was never going to hold water.

'Yep,' he said, his sobs subsiding. 'It's been a helluva time.'

In a voice that seemed to quiver down the line, she asked, 'And did they find any drugs at your place, Bren?'

Micelli announced that she needed to interview Serchanov again. 'I want to know more about some of that stuff Burns sent me. You read it, didn't you?' she asked, looking at Pritchard.

'Agreed. Want me to come with you?'

She shook here head. 'I'll phone him first. Put him on speaker. You can take notes.'

During the call Serchanov told them what he knew about Azarov double dealing his investors and how he wasn't surprised that he'd eventually been killed.

'I serve in London for time as USSR officer in diplomatics. Then after 1989 I already back in Russia and things happen. I have to relocate. Your friends there help me get to Australia.' He'd arrived in Australia as a refugee on some special deal arranged by Canberra involving the British government. Micelli had already checked to see if he had a police record. There was nothing on file. He reiterated that he didn't kill Azarov and happily agreed to a DNA test if she wanted to come to his house. 'Anytime. I always have samovar on.'

Almost as a parting comment he recounted his refusal to accept bribes which is what got him into trouble immediately after the breakup of the USSR. 'Everyone want to get rich quick when the command economy finally blow up and countries go back to own states. Much money to be made and some ruthless Russian people get in on ground floor. There is oil for one. Rigged auctions. People buy companies from government and in return give money from profits to rotten officials. Always protected from the law by the law. They rich men now. Own soccer clubs, big boats, big houses. Live the high life in London, Vienna, Zurich. How you say, all trimmings, nothing spared. Rotten government, rotten businesses, rotten men. And scum like Azarov, he is a little man. Thinks he can be rich like the big boys. But he only a little bit rich because he take money from little people then leave them for dead. Worse than oligarchs. They leave little people alone. Only go for big business and governments.' After delivering his opinions, his breathing was laboured as if he'd been on a run round the block. The speech also left the detectives a bit breathless, barely knowing whether to clap or just hang up. Micelli decided on the latter. 'Thank you, Mr Serchanov. You've been very helpful. I'm looking forward to our next cup of tea.'

'Interesting what he said about people like Azarov, not playing in the big time,' said Pritchard. 'Wonder what it takes to change up a gear, get where there's serious money.'

'For all Serchanov knows, and us for that matter, he may have already tried to climb the league ladder. Maybe he annoyed someone enough to come looking for him. I'll ask Harris when he comes back in. He can ask his Tallinn counterparts. They'd know more about what's going on with money laundering and organised crime in their region than we would.'

The ride from Sydney airport to St Vincent's had taken less time than expected. Nguyen had phoned Hargreaves at Surry Hills to make sure they could still question Christina as arranged yesterday, and that nothing had changed. 'Any more info about her condition?' Nguyen had asked.

'Nah, same as yesterday, except she's been moved from ICU to her own private room. Last time I got word she was off the critical list, so probably feeling better than she was yesterday when we tried to talk to her.'

Nguyen followed Janzen into the foyer of Sydney's St Vincent's Hospital. 'Can I help you?' An older bloke dressed in a waistcoat and tie. Name badge indicated he was the concierge. Nguyen explained who they wanted to see. 'The front desk team'll be able to assist you with that,' he said, pointing towards a long bench bookended with white floral arrangements of roses, gladioli and gardenia stems that looked more suitable for a society wedding than a hospital foyer. 'And there's also our volunteers who'd be happy to go with you so you can easily locate the room you're after.' He pointed to a table next to the front desk where six or seven men and women were sitting in easy chairs, some plying knitting needles, everyone engaged in chatter.

Janzen nudged Nguyen as they stood in line. 'Since when did hospitals employ concierges? We'll be having one at headquarters next.'

Before Nguyen could reply, he was called forward. He kept his voice low, showed his badge. 'DC Sean Nguyen and DC Elsa Janzen, Victoria Police. We're here to interview Christina Gallo.'

'Ms Gallo?' The woman peered at a computer screen. 'Ah, yes.' She picked up a phone, tapped a pencil on the desktop. Spoke quietly. Smiled. Nodded. 'Okay then.' Motioning towards a man sitting at the end of the table, she called him over. 'Our volunteer Joe will take you to her now. And Joe, show them where the hand sanitiser is, please.'

As they made their way up to where Christina was on the third floor, Joe prattled on about what the weather was like in Melbourne and how it'd been sodden lately in Sydney. Silver cross pinned to the lapel of his open-necked shirt. Slight stutter and a face that bore the remains of a fearsome adolescent acne attack, or conceivably, a raging heroin habit. If it was the latter, he was probably now paying back to those who had saved him.

'She's in there.' Joe stopped in front of a closed door guarded by hospital security. 'Show him your badges and you'll be allowed in.'

Christina's bed was in the middle of the room. Several chairs were dotted around, one of which was occupied by a recent recruit to the force who looked nervous. Trollies, machines, a small, barred window high up on the wall above the bed. Banks of flouro lights. A gas cylinder and oxygen mask behind the bed. A door to the left, padlocked, with a sign indicating it was a bathroom.

Dressed in a white hospital gown, Christina was propped up on pillows, a line pumping a colourless liquid from three separate IV bags running into a cannula inserted into her left hand, right arm plastered up to the elbow and strapped to her body with a gauze sling. Stitches above her right eye, more underneath her nose. Her eyes, reduced to small slits, were open. Nguyen and Janzen approached her bed, stood on opposite sides. 'Hello Christina, do you remember me?' Nguyen's voice was soft as a mouse.

She slowly inched her head to the left, looked directly at him. 'Yes. Last year. My place.'

Nguyen held up his ID. 'This is DC Elsa Janzen.' He nodded in Janzen's direction. Christina slowly moved her head to the right, then moved back to face Nguyen.

'Tanah?' A tear rolled down her cheek.

Nguyen swallowed. 'Tanah's with a lovely family, being cared for very well. She's got two other kids her age to play with.' He grinned. 'Apparently, she's asking about ice-cream all the time.'

A smile? Hard to tell on a face so disfigured by swelling and bruising.

'She's able to stay with the family as long as it takes for you to get well. Now, I'm wondering if you can tell us how you came to be here in the first place.'

The silence was punctuated by electronic beeps emanating from a screen monitoring one or more of Christina's vital functions. Several coloured lines danced across from left to right in time with the sounds.

'Who did this to you, Christina?' He pointed to her right arm.

More beeping.

'Was it Gregory Anson?'

She held up her left hand, indicated the bedside drawer unit. Nguyen opened the top drawer. A ring in a ziplock bag, large and studded with what he guessed to be diamonds.

'Engaged?'

She nodded. Another tear rolled down her cheek.

Janzen scribbled something in her notebook. 'It will help you a lot, and us,' she said, 'if you tell us who the person was who injured you.'

The machine began to utter loud staccato beeps, a red line dashed up and down like a mad skier. Christina's eyes shut.

A nurse threw open the door, checked the screen, opened Christina's left eye with his fingers and held a penlight to it. 'You'll have to leave,' he commanded, pushing the call button. The police officer stood, Nguyen and Janzen moved towards the doorway. Two more nurses bustled in, one pushing a small trolley loaded with several dishes and syringes. 'Blood pressure's gone through the roof.'

Janzen gulped as she was pushed out of the room as more medical staff ran in. 'Do you think she's alright?'

O'Leary paced up and down, turned the TV on then off again, consoled Maggie who'd missed out on her run in the park this morning. He'd been up half the night, going through every cupboard in the house looking for something that might resemble a stash of drugs. Nothing. He racked his brain. Stephen hadn't been to the house since late last August, almost five months ago, unlikely that he'd hide anything anyway, and as far as O'Leary could recall, no one else had been over the threshold except for the twins, Bonnie from over the road, and Angela Micelli. There had to be another explanation. Like the phone at Glenlyon. It hadn't simply been lost, like Nguyen had tried to imply. Someone had taken it, copied what they wanted, then dumped it where they were sure it would be found. The guns for the twins. Flowers for Claire. And now this. In his own house. He fucking hated drugs. He plonked onto the couch. Maggie jumped up beside him, rested her head on his knee. Stroking her ears between his thumb and forefinger he went through a checklist of enemies. Or at least a list of people evil enough to deliberately want to do him harm.

Gregory Anson. He put him at number one. Krakauer could be in top spot but was limited in scope. Might have a contact on the outside, though. Work colleagues? He'd had a run in with that prick Borodoni from Drugs over a house fire incident in West Footscray last year, been roundly told off by Goddings for his attitude. There was the woman whom he'd beaten for promotion a couple of years back. She did eventually make it to senior sergeant, but still couldn't talk to him, walked the other way when she saw him. What was her name again? Couldn't remember. Who else? He trawled through his career. There was of course Mick Skelton, but they hadn't had any contact in recent years. Coincidence he'd been assigned to Micelli's team? The matter

Skelton might want to seek revenge for was so long in the past, surely even he would have buried the hatchet by now. That dickhead constable who'd tried to punch him in the pub. Stupid bastard had been so drunk he didn't compute that O'Leary had simply asked for a fag, not called him a fag. That was years ago. Maryborough. The Golden Triangle. O'Leary's second posting. Jack Ryan. That was his name. Fiery red-headed bogan from the north somewhere. Boort? Birchip? Something starting with B. Bealiba. That was it. The Ryan boys from Bealiba. Renowned for their bluster. He remembered playing footy against a few of the Ryan clan. Rough bastards. Squeeze your balls, throw an elbow out when you were running past, a leg too, for that matter. He'd loved playing with the Rovers, wearing the Collingwood strip, running out onto Jubilee oval on game days. Seemed a long time ago all of a sudden. As if on cue, his right thigh cramped, sent pain running from his groin to his foot. 'Fuck.' He straightened his leg in an attempt to ease the pain. Maggie leapt off the couch, sat on the floor looking up at him, brown eyes almost liquid. 'It's alright, old girl,' he said, patting the couch where she'd been lying. 'You can get up again.' The dog settled herself down, this time curling into a ball at the other end of the couch.

Someone wanted to get at him. Of this he was sure. What about people he'd put away? Their families, perhaps? And why wait years to seek revenge? Didn't make sense. Before he could think about more enemies, Maggie was up and running to the front door in response to heavy-handed knocking.

A fleet of officers stood behind Moriarty and Milligan, who was holding a warrant in her hand. Perhaps it was the breeze, light this morning compared to yesterday, that was making the paper shake. 'Good morning, Mr O'Leary,' she said, 'following up from last night.' He snatched the warrant, stood with his back to the door and waited while ten officers trooped in behind the detectives. 'Make yourself comfortable in the lounge room, would you please, Sir,' said Milligan. *Sir*, he noted. Not *mister*. Both had called him mister last night. Anything to glean from this? Paranoia, is what he told himself. Giving Maggie a pat, he eased himself back onto the couch. She curled up on the rug in front of the fireplace as if a winter fire was warming her. He'd have to take her for a run after they'd finished. He checked his watch. Couldn't be more than an hour in a small house like his.

The team peeled off in pairs: three bedrooms, kitchen, laundry. O'Leary watched the kitchen pair take out all the opened goods from the pantry, shake jars, plunge their gloved hands into containers, finger the contents. At least they weren't emptying everything onto the bench. Examined the motley collection of past-their-use-by-date spice jars. Held Bonnie's half-eaten apricot jam and a jar of honey up to the light. Who'd stash drugs in honey? Next the junk drawer. This time everything was heaved out onto the bench. Rubber bands, old receipts, leftover bottle tops from his beer-brewing experiments, the celadon spoon snapped at the handle that he'd been meaning to glue together. Tea towels and foil, lunch bags, the bottle opener that he'd lost years ago. Everything on display. They fished around in the cutlery drawer, piled dishes and plates on the countertop, and poked their noses into every saucepan, frying pan and baking dish that he owned. When they'd satisfied themselves there was nothing to find, they motioned him onto a stool at the kitchen bench and set to work on the lounge room. Books, magazines, the kids' toy box, CDs, DVDs, the inside of the vase on the mantlepiece that hadn't held flowers since Claire left. His attention was diverted when he felt his phone vibrating in his pocket. Nguyen. *Call when you can.*

Milligan emerged from his bedroom, was about to scuttle out the front door with one of the officers who was carrying a paper bag, sealed at the top. 'What's in that?' O'Leary launched himself off the stool and lumbered up the hallway.

'Something of interest,' replied Milligan, smiling like those customer service geeks in mobile phone shops.

'Show me!'

Her smile widened. 'Sorry, Sir, no can do.' She shielded the officer who disappeared out the door.

Micelli was in the kitchenette putting the finishing touches to a bowl of salad and boiled eggs when her phone pinged. Nick. A thumbs up emoji. Another ping. *Mum & me talked all good :-) call u later xx n*. She carried her phone and the bowl into the conference room and placed them on the table.

'Good news?' asked Harris. 'Haven't seen you smile for a while.'

'Yeah,' she replied, tucking into her lunch, 'family stuff. Not much to smile about otherwise. We're not getting very far with this investigation.'

'It's tough. Penny for your theories so far?'

'O'Leary always says if you can pin down a motive then you're halfway there. We seem to have several clear motives, as well as a whole lot of other crap. Serchanov wanted Azarov dead because of how his mother suffered at Azarov's hands. Same with Helen Kapp, her family suffered too. The tennis guys aren't overly pleased with Azarov. They say he was withholding money that was rightly theirs, or at least rightly Kross's. Azarov's wife is living a simple enough life, no outward trappings of ill-gotten money, used to her husband's absence and probably knows nothing of his affair with Bagrova. But we don't know for sure. She could be the typical revenge-seeking wife who's been wronged by her man. And Bagrova has been telling you she'll practically die now that the absolute love of her life is dead. Yet she works as some type of hostess for an oil company, so that doesn't really add up.'

'You're right. She could be pulling the wool over our eyes and has really come out to Australia to do him in rather than do him,' said Pritchard, looking up from his plate of chicken salad.

'Enough! You're sounding as coarse as you know who.' She continued with her train of thought. 'If what Burns says about the Obtschak is right, it's entirely possible someone could have organised a hit, someone we don't even know about. Maybe I should ask Serchanov what sort of people the Obtschak employ to kill foreign nationals when they're overseas.'

'Apparently there's been a spate of weird suicides. Actually suspected assassinations, according to Tallinn, by the way,' said Harris. 'They're saying Russia is fed up with petty crooks muscling on territory.'

'Kind of discredits what Serchanov said on the phone then,' said Micelli.

'Yeah.' Pritchard stroked his chin, eyes turned to the whiteboard. 'Anyone could be responsible for Azarov's demise, and as we don't have a definite cause of death which might give us a clue as to who's done the job, beyond anaphylaxis that is, then we're fishing in a big ocean for a little minnow.'

She raised her eyebrows. 'Pure poetry, Pritchard. Didn't know you had it in you. But you're right. Anaphylaxis is all well and good. But we can't discount the plastic bag, the handcuffs, the female saliva on the condom.'

'Female saliva on a condom. Could have been the woman who got into the lift with him at the Condor.'

'What? After whatever happened in the lift, he goes up to his room, condom still in place, eats sushi, drinks champagne then strips off, jumps into the bed, puts a plastic bag over his head, puts on handcuffs and dies? I don't think so. Besides, didn't Helen Kapp go up and deliver champagne after the lift incident?'

Pritchard flicked through his notebook. 'Yep. That's what she said.'

'So now we've got someone answering the door with a used condom still on their member?' She burst into laughter. 'Really? That is not going to fly. Ever!' She swivelled her chair towards the window, dropped her arms to the side and lifted her shoulders up and down. 'You know, Helen Kapp's got motive and she's got opportunity. At present we don't have any other leads that are more likely than her, and we've got a few who are almost as likely as her, so I reckon we go through them one by one. Bring them in for an interview. See how they stack up.'

'And ask them to give us a DNA sample?'

'Definitely, and if they don't agree, we take one. I can be the authorising officer. Just need to make sure we caution them prior to the interview.' Marker in hand she rose and walked over to the white board and wrote *Interview 1* beside Kapp's name, got as far as *Interv* beside Kross's name when her phone pinged again. *6pm outside Rod Laver. Drinks then dinner. Suit you? Xxx D*. Stopping short, fingers hovering over her phone, she mumbled something about logistics then headed towards the kitchenette, phone in hand. Less than a minute later, she rushed back out. 'You're not going to believe this. Serchanov is dead. We were only talking to him an hour ago.'

Travelling in a tram along St Kilda Road reminded O'Leary of the time before his injury, before all the current shit began to swirl round him. He'd begun his detective days at number 412, overlooking the wide boulevard full of all-day rumbling trams and school kids, mornings and afternoons. Regular enough to set your watch by. When he ducked out for a coffee he could catch the announcements from the grammar school over the road if there was an easterly. But the trams no longer rattled and rumbled like they used to. Now trams were smooth quiet capsules. Except when the driver stopped. Then people and bags lurched forwards or were thrown backwards like untethered dogs on the back of a ute.

The 1980s brown-brick building where Katherine Cronin practised was wedged next to an Art Deco apartment block, set back from the footpath. A summer garden of large ornamental trees surrounded the lawn, the colour of unripe bananas. Some mirrored glass monstrosity had been plonked in the middle of it, appearing to sway and buckle as clouds skimmed by. He checked the street number on his phone before entering the foyer, feeling the full blast of aircon set too low. Explained why the workers strolled along outside with jackets and cardigans flung over their shoulders. NO doubt at the ready to throw them back on when returning to their offices.

In small plastic lettering housed in a glass-fronted directory beside the lift well was Dr K. G. Cronin, PhD, LLB 8:23. O'Leary scanned the other names, none he recognised, pressed the up button. Her office was the last one along the corridor. The door was open, but he knocked anyway. She squinted up at him, a pair of tortoiseshell spectacles more than half-way down her nose, hair the colour of weak tea falling in bangs round her cheeks. 'Come in,' she mouthed, pointing to a phone lying on her desktop. She gestured towards three chairs that were grouped round a coffee table in the corner of the room. O'Leary lowered himself down, adjusted a cushion to his liking, sat back to admire the view of the back end of the Alfred Hospital. Gesturing again, this time to help himself from the carafe on the table, she said in a tone that would make small children run and hide behind their mother's skirts, 'Ignore my advice at your own peril. I may have mentioned that my fees rise considerably if I'm required to visit clients in prison.' Realising she wasn't speaking to him, he poured himself water, fished a couple of painkillers from his shirt pocket, swallowed them down. 'Very well, then,' she said, 'I'll see you in court tomorrow.' Pushing her chair back towards the wall, she stood up with the grace of a ballet dancer. O'Leary was surprised to see that she was nearly six foot, yet as thin as a sheet of rice paper. Striding over to him she gave the door a swift kick to shut it. 'Don't bother to get up. I saw the trouble you had sitting down in the first place. Katherine Cronin.' She shook his hand firmly. 'Pleased to meet you Detective Senior Sergeant Brendan O'Leary. May I call you Brendan?'

Folding herself onto a chair beside him she removed the spectacles and rubbed the bridge of her nose. 'Honestly. Why do people bother to seek me out, pay my not inconsiderable fees then decide at the last minute that they know best and career ahead to certain criminal suicide.' She reached under the tabletop, pulled out a pad and pencil. 'Guess there's no immunisations for stupid.' She broke into a giggle that sounded a lot like Zoe when she beat her brother at Snap. 'Now what brings you here, Brendan? Not trouble with our new Minister of Police, I hope.' She placed her phone on the tabletop and hit record.

O'Leary shuddered. Phillip fucking Sinclair. He hoped he'd never have to deal with that man ever again. 'No, or at least not yet.' He recalled that Milligan and Moriarty had both said last night that he'd be fronting Minister Sinclair's inquiry into police integrity. 'Much more personal at this point.'

Over the next thirty minutes he told her about Stephen's escapades with drugs last year, the shooting at the farm, the discovery of a small box in his laundry, then this morning's search while she peppered him with questions, writing down every detail, her pencil skimming over the paper like a hovercraft. He started to tell her about his lost phone and the stuff that was going on with Claire and the twins when she held up a hand.

'Stop. Please stop,' she said gently. 'I've got cramp in my hand, the phone's running low on battery and I've got to dash out and see my boy play football at three, then I'll be back. I think we need to get a few things straight before complicating the picture with all the other things going on. Not saying they're not relevant. Or unimportant. But the main game here as I see it is the last eighteen hours. Did they give you a receipt for what they took from your house? And have you got it with you?'

He pulled his wallet out of his back pocket and produced the receipt: *Short-sleeved polo shirt, colour blue; Box of laundry powder, opened, Surf brand; iPad and cover; Apple laptop computer.*

'Is that all? Did they list the IT stuff on the warrant? You still got that?'

O'Leary pulled out the warrant.

She scanned it quickly. 'Bastards! No IT stuff on the warrant. They're meant to itemise that separately. Suppose they asked you for your phone, did they?'

He shook his head. 'Probably already knew I had a new one.'

'Look,' she said, checking the time on her watch, 'let me have a think about this and I'll call you back round four this arvo. Does that work for you?'

'I've got to attend a meeting with my boss at 3.30, so if it's later than four, that'd work.'

'See what I can do.' She waited while he took a final slug of water before shaking his hand and seeing him out the door. 'Lovely to meet you, Brendan. Be in touch soon.'

The Care Café was located in the hospital foyer. Subway tiles, glass display cases, two coffee machines. Nguyen and Janzen took their lunches to a small table near the entrance. 'How long do you think it'll be before we can go back and see Christina?' asked Janzen, taking a bite from a vegetarian wrap.

217

'No idea. Let's finish lunch then I'll ask again at reception. Dunno much about hospitals and how they work. Do you? Guessing if it was a full-on emergency, then we'd have to wait a couple of hours at least.'

A young woman brought over two coffees, removed the number from their table. Janzen checked her phone. 'Reckon we'd better contact Qantas and cancel. No way we'll make it by four. It's already two. Book for later?'

'Let's leave it until we find out what's going on with Christina,' said Nguyen, brushing a stray crumb off the tabletop. 'I'll call O'Leary, ask him what he wants us to do. You be right here for a while?' He rose from the table and wandered over to the florist shop, phone to his ear.

People were everywhere in the foyer. Saturday afternoons would have to be a prime time for visitors. Janzen watched the constant parade come in through the doors, most going straight to the elevators. The few who needed directions were dealt with promptly by the front desk staff, the small army of volunteers on standby ready to assist. One vollie took the arm of an older man and led him towards the bathrooms; another relieved a woman of a bunch of flowers and gift-wrapped box she was carrying, allowing her to focus on a little boy who was carrying a Buzz Lightyear, almost as tall as he was. He was refusing to hold his mother's hand, but relented when a woman who could have been his grandmother bent down towards him. He started to giggle, put Buzz on the floor and together they watched as Buzz strode across the foyer floor. 'C'mon,' said his mum after she'd found out where to go, 'Aunty Bree's waiting for us upstairs. Do you think her new baby will like Buzz?' All three, plus Buzz, trooped off towards the elevators.

Janzen was so engrossed in watching that she didn't immediately notice Nguyen striding across the foyer towards her, mouth open, phone in hand. 'Boss's place's been searched. Suspected drugs cache.' He was gabbling, shallow breathing.

'Pardon? What'd you say?'

'The boss. O'Leary. Just spoke to him. He's got to go to a meeting with Goddings this afternoon. Apparently two Drug Ds came round last night. Executed a search warrant for his place this morning. Took away stuff. Reckon's he's going to be suspended from duty.'

'Who's in charge, then?'

A ping from Nguyen's phone. He bent his head, scrolled down. 'Shit, shit and more shit!'

She shushed him, pointing to a priest entering the café. 'What's up?'

'They're going to put me in charge.' He thrust his phone towards her. 'See?'

She read the text. Noted Goddings's name. 'That's okay then. About you that is. Not about O'Leary, but.'

He glared at her. 'No it's not okay. I don't like being in charge of anything, let alone all the crap involved in this case. Anson, Krakaeur, Valentino.' He drew breath. 'Kids buried on a farm. It's horrendous. And what about O'Leary. What's he ever done to deserve this? Bet it's his stupid brother. The one involved with drugs last year. That's how come O'Leary got shot, you know.'

She put her hand on his forearm. 'Want another coffee?'

He flopped onto a chair. 'Orange juice if they've got it. And a water.'

Janzen got up from the table, leaving Nguyen bent over his phone. When she returned with the drinks, he was still engrossed. 'Anything new?' He shook his head, gulped down the water and unscrewed the lid from the juice.

'Better go up and see how Christina's faring,' he said between swigs. 'What is it, half an hour since we were kicked out of her room?'

'Do we need an escort again?'

Joe was happy to accompany them to level three and left them to walk the length of the corridor to Christina's room. 'What's that smell?' asked Nguyen as they approached Christina's door.

Janzen rolled her shoulders. 'Some el cheapo aftershave applied too liberally, I'd say, unless the cleaning staff have got a contract with Lynx.' This time there was no guard and the door was open. They peered in. 'That's a body bag,' hissed Janzen, pointing to a gurney being wheeled across to the bed where Christina was lying.

'What?'

'There. On the gurney.' Nurses were busy disconnecting equipment and rolling up cords while two orderlies were raising the gurney to the height of the bed. 'She's being disconnected from everything.' One of the nurses shooed them away when she saw them standing in the doorway. Nguyen and Janzen turned and walked back down the corridor to the elevators.

'It's going to be a long night, fellas,' said Micelli, setting up a new board to go through what had already come to light about Serchanov's death. She'd been in touch with Frank Sutcliffe who'd confirmed that the body was now at the morgue and he would be conducting an autopsy later that evening.

Straight after Goddings's call she and Pritchard had rushed to Serchanov's North Carlton terrace and battled their way into the kitchen past members of the forensic investigating team and their equipment. 'No struggle, I don't think Ange,' Sutcliffe had said, 'as there's no visible signs of him fighting off someone. But he could have struggled in his death throes, hence the collapse of the kitchen shelving.' Serchanov was prone on the kitchen floor, books, newspapers, dirty dishes strewn around him. His beloved samovar had been knocked off the stove and was now on its side leaking tea and water everywhere.

'Break in?' Pritchard had asked a team member.

One of the officers had pointed to a wallet on the table and a phone beside the body on the right side.

Harris fiddled with his tie clip. Pritchard chewed the inside of his cheek. Micelli looked at the board. 'We've got nothing,' said Micelli. 'Sutcliffe said there wasn't any obvious sign of what he'd died from. Pretty sure it's not natural causes, though. All we've got is a dead body and some intel that he was once a KGB agent. Question is, do I mention this death at the media conference later on?' O'Leary pushed open the door. 'Hey. Brendan. You okay?' She hurried over, gave him a quick hug. 'Thought they'd suspended you?'

'Not quite.' He checked his watch. 'Got a meeting with

Goddings in a couple of minutes when that'll become official.' He looked jowlier than she remembered from two nights ago, like his cheeks had dropped with the weight of the blackness underscoring his eyes. 'It's shit, Ange. Just make sure you do everything by the book.' He disappeared into his office where she could hear him opening drawers, flicking through papers. 'And watch out for that prick, Skelton,' he said as he walked out the door.

O'Leary was referring to Skelton's history as a bully and a serial abuser. Anytime a new woman cop was assigned to a team Skelton was on, it would take about a week before she was found crying in the Ladies' but silent when it came to making a formal complaint against him. O'Leary didn't blame these women— young, often their first post, but not always, and in the male-dominated hierarchy of the force twenty-five years ago, there was no real way to complain despite what was written in the policies. And no one to complain to, either. He wondered if it was any better now, thinking back to how Goddings had snapped at him when he said it was inappropriate for Skelton to be on Micelli's team. He wasn't sure how it was going with Skelton, too much on his plate to enquire, but he knew that if things got bad enough Micelli wouldn't hesitate in making a complaint. Whether it would go anywhere with Goddings was another matter, as in O'Leary's opinion he was firmly rooted in the past.

When the lift opened, O'Leary took a moment to straighten his tie, pull his jacket down at the back. Knocked lightly on Goddings's door. 'Sit down, O'Leary. I realise it's Saturday and you've had to rearrange personal matters but matters such as these can't be put off.' Goddings was sitting squarely behind his desk, turning the pages of a stapled document. 'Serious matter, O'Leary. Serious matter all round. For you. And for the force. I'll begin by asking you if there's any matters you wish to put on the table before I go through the allegations that, as I'm sure you understand, will lead me to formally stand you down as soon as this meeting is concluded.'

O'Leary breathed in and out slowly. Tried to recall the points he intended to make in the order he wanted to make them. Couldn't. Began with Claire and the twins. Attempted to tie together the threats to his family to Friday night's raid, but lost track of the connection. His mouth didn't have enough saliva in it to stop his words smacking together at the ends, so he gave up trying to explain that and launched into a new theme. 'Whatever was found at my place was not mine and was planted there by someone who wishes to discredit me, and as a matter of fact, Sir, seeing we're concerned with all sorts of matters, I don't even know what exactly was removed.' He pulled the search team's receipt out of his wallet. 'This is what it says. Short-sleeved polo shirt, colour blue; Box of laundry powder, opened, Surf; iPad and cover; Apple Laptop computer.' He was aware that his voice was getting louder, less quavery as he read the list out loud. 'No details here that lead me to believe there's anything untoward. What is it, Sir, exactly that I'm missing?'

'What you're missing is respect, O'Leary, for one thing,' thundered Goddings. 'And secondly, you know as well as I do that a small cache of drugs was removed from your house on Friday evening by two of our Drug Squad detectives who reminded you that given your association with a known drug dealer several months ago, last August wasn't it, I'm gobsmacked that you can sit across from me like this and display such insolence.'

'You mean my brother, Stephen? It's a bit hard not to be associated with your own family, don't you think, Sir?' The last bit came out between teeth clamped so hard he could feel his jaw muscles twitching.

Goddings cleared his throat. 'You're not making this any easier for yourself, O'Leary, or me. You are doubtless aware of the Inquiry into Police Integrity that has been called by Minister Sinclair, due to begin on Monday. I understand retired Supreme Court Judge, Justice Beauchamp-Barr has been appointed to chair it, and—'

'It was only announced on Tuesday. What's the fucking rush?'

'I'll choose to ignore that remark. As I was saying, you will be one of the officers called to front the Inquiry on account of your association with drug dealers and a shooting that left you injured. Added to that will be the recent evidence collected from your house.' He smoothed the dog ears on the stapled document and placed it to the side. 'Now, I've got a few things to do to make your suspension formal, so that will be all. You will be met in the foyer to execute the handover and sign the paperwork before being escorted from the building.' He rose from behind his desk and opened the door. 'You'll be notified of the time and place for the hearing in due course.'

Waiting in the foyer were two PSOs. One carried a clipboard and the other a small cardboard evidence box labelled with O'Leary's name and number.

Helen Kapp surveyed the interview room, smile tight, back straight like an army officer. White-blonde hair pulled into a sleek ponytail, expertly applied makeup enhanced her high cheekbones and wide blue eyes. She checked her watch, sighed heavily. Could have been waiting for a lover who was running late, or running a meeting with hapless staff members. Jock Willoughby, her lawyer, had eased his two-plus metre frame into a chair, and was drumming a black and silver fountain pen on a notebook. 'My client is keen to move this interview along.' Voice sharp as an axe.

Pritchard entered the room, settled himself down next to Micelli. She looked up from her notes. 'Mr Willoughby. We're ready to begin now.' Smiling broadly in his direction.

Willoughby opened his notebook and unscrewed the cap from his pen. Micelli watched as he wrote the time and date in black ink onto the top of a clean page.

'Miss Kapp. You see, there's a few things about Mr Azarov's demise that has us puzzled and we're hoping you can shed more light on what happened.' At the mention of Azarov, Kapp's eyes narrowed. Micelli continued. 'We need to get a very clear picture of what went on in Mr Azarov's hotel room for starters. Can you take us through again what exactly happened in the Condor hotel room, starting from when you knocked on his door.' Micelli was leaning forward slightly like an encouraging teacher.

Kapp sighed, looked at her watch again. 'I was pushing a cart with glasses, a bottle of champagne and a platter when I knocked on his door. He opened up almost immediately. Looked me up and down like a man does who wants more than a drink and something to eat. I introduced myself. He said to come in.'

'Had you seen CCTV of Azarov going to his room?' asked Pritchard, head bowed as he scribbled a note.

She sucked in her stomach and sat up even straighter. 'It is my job to oversee that the CCTV is monitored at all times when I'm on duty, check if any incidents are reported when I am not there and take whatever action is indicated.'

Looking up, Pritchard said, 'Well, in that case you would have clearly seen the woman who met Azarov in the foyer. And you would have seen them get into the lift together.'

She tossed her head back. 'Of course I saw them. I thought you meant something else.'

'What else could I mean?' he asked, frowning slightly as if puzzled. 'We're not talking about the lift footage. Are we?'

Willoughby's pen began to drum again. Colour rose in Kapp's cheeks. She dropped her head, examined her slender fingers, a tiny band of gold decorated with five or six very small red stones on her middle finger. 'Yes.'

Pritchard's eyes were firmly fixed on Kapp's face. 'Yes, what?'

'I was,' she said finally. 'I hope this unfortunate event will not be subject to media scrutiny. At the Condor we try to ensure those things do not happen.'

Pritchard nodded as if he perfectly understood her embarrassment. 'No need for the media to know, unless of course it's revealed in court proceedings.'

Kapp wriggled in her seat, lost the military poise for a moment. 'Can we get this over and done with,' she said as if giving orders, 'I have a job to go to.' Willoughby drummed insistently, glared at Pritchard who was now shuffling through pages of hotel floor plans, A4 prints taken from the CCTV footage, some annotated with yellow sticky notes.

'Let's get back to when you were knocking on Mr Azarov's door and he asked you to come in,' said Micelli calmly.

'Very well.' Kapp swallowed hard. 'I set the platter on the coffee table, explained I was born in Estonia, that I wanted to personally welcome him to our hotel as we don't receive many guests from my home country.' She stopped, glanced sideways at her solicitor. He motioned her to continue. 'He said he was very pleased to be personally welcomed, then he started speaking in Estonian to me.'

'What did you do?' asked Micelli.

She swallowed again. 'I explained that I didn't really speak the language as we had left Estonia when I was only six. He switched to English. Not very good English, but good enough.'

Micelli's voice even. 'You poured champagne, sat on the easy chairs and talked about the old country?'

'No.' Kapp began to redden again.

'So what did happen?'

'He sat on a chair, I poured the wine and he asked me to pass the board to him. Said he was hungry, had missed lunch in the players' dining room. I said I thought it went all day, food service, that is. He said he'd had a meeting and that's why he didn't get round to eating.'

'Did he say who the meeting was with?'

Kapp shook her head. 'Said it was to do with sponsorship.'

Willoughby cleared his throat. 'Look. What has anything about sponsorship got to do with my client?'

Micelli beamed at him again. 'I wouldn't think very much at all, Mr Willoughby. Just trying to understand fully what happened when your client went to the victim's room. Bear with us please. Won't be much longer.' Turning back to Kapp, she said in a voice sweet-natured aunts use with their favourite nieces, 'One or two glasses of bubbles?'

'Two. Of course.' Kapp screwed up her nose as if explaining the simplest arithmetic to a dullard.

Micelli adopted Kapp's tone. 'But there was only one champagne glass in the room when it was examined.' Stopped. Eyes on Kapp's face. 'Can you explain why one glass would have disappeared without trace?'

'How would I know?'

Pritchard placed a CCTV print uppermost on his pile of papers. 'What time did you go up to Mr Azarov's room? Can you recall exactly?'

'It was a little after nine. I had finished my shift, organised the wine, chatted to the chef on duty. Possibly ten minutes or so.'

Pritchard pushed a piece of paper forward on the desk. It showed Helen Kapp pushing a small room service trolley along a corridor. It was time-marked 21.11.

'Sorry to go over this again, Miss Kapp. But I don't want to miss even the smallest detail,' said Pritchard, measuring a few millimetres between his thumb and forefinger. 'What exactly was on the trolley? I can see a bottle and two glasses. And a cloche. Can I ask what was under the cloche?'

'That's a charcuterie plate.'

'Did you say charcuterie, Miss Kapp? Not sushi?' asked Micelli.

Kapp frowned. 'No, not sushi. Charcuterie. Only a small board, cheese, a few muscatels, a few slices of various meats, some olives. Oh, and biscuits. Think that was all.' Micelli and Pritchard exchanged glances. 'I can check what usually goes on a board if you like. Maybe I've missed something.'

By the time Katherine Cronin called O'Leary he was home making arrangements with Claire to pick up the twins. They had complained that the trip to Dunnstown to see their grandmother and ride one of their grandfather's horses had been put off, but still happy enough to spend the evening with their father, Maggie and the chooks. 'Could Ange come over for dinner?' Jack had asked on the phone. 'You always cook really good when she comes.' For the first time in a day, more like the first time in two days, O'Leary had laughed. 'I can ask,' he'd said, 'but it's Saturday night and Ange is probably going somewhere with friends. But I can still cook really good,' he assured his son, listening while Jack reeled off his idea of what a really good cooked dinner would comprise. When Katherine asked him to hold for a minute, O'Leary wrote a list of things to pick up at the supermarket.

'Sorry about that, Brendan,' she said, 'small person needed a hug after a not so good match result. You know how it is. But as I was saying, not a lot we can do. The receipt they gave you this morning isn't up to par but it's not so bad that we can bring a challenge. The warrant was properly sworn, so nothing there either. You say that the drugs, or whatever they found in the box on Friday night, were not receipted, yet it formed the basis of why a warrant was sought and granted to search your house. Correct?'

O'Leary confirmed that was the case. 'Milligan and Moriarty said it contained seventy one-gram packets of crystal meth with a street value of twenty-thousand. I didn't see what was inside the box so only their word to go on. Could be full of anything by now. And then there's the stuff she took with her this morning, not on the receipt, but in a sealed evidence bag.'

'And you'd no idea there would be anything to find?'

'None whatsoever. Even with my brother staying with me last year, I don't think he would have hidden anything in the house.'

'But he could have. Is there a way to check?'

'Suppose I could give him a call. See what he says.'

'Do that and as soon as you know, get straight back to me.'

O'Leary checked what the time would be in London. Either eight or nine in the morning as far as he could work out. Decent enough time to call. He hit S in his contacts before cursing that of course he no longer had any under S, or many other letters either, because of the new phone. He hadn't synced it as yet with his laptop, and now he couldn't, because that had gone with the cops as well. ICloud? He fiddled in Settings but couldn't find anything helpful. Nothing for it but to call his mother and get Stephen's number that way.

'Are you alright, Brendan?' Not even a hello first when Kathleen answered. She must be worried.

'Yes, Mum, I'm good,' he said as cheerfully as he could muster. 'But I need a favour. Can you give me Stephen's phone number?'

'His London one? Hang on a minute, will you love.' He heard her walking down the hallway to the ancient telephone table where all the family's conversations were once conducted. No privacy for anyone. Made it tricky asking a girl out. He had to time it just right and keep his voice down if he didn't want his three brothers dancing down the hallway screeching the latest love song from the radio, or worse, loud fart noises. 'Here it is love, got a pen handy?'

'Stephen? Brendan here.'

'Hey, Brendan. How are you? You got a new number? Your name didn't come up.'

'Yeah, long story. But that's not why I rang. Had a visit from the cops. Drug Squad. They found a couple of things. Anything you might've left in my house last year?'

A faint echo on the line. 'God no. Why'd you think I'd do that?'

'Because I know Jack saw drugs in your duffel bag once.'

'No Brendan. I've never left anything incriminating at your place. I know that time you're talking about, and I never brought a duffel bag into your house again. Jack seeing the stuff scared the shit out of me, as a matter of fact.'

O'Leary's hackles rose. He could clearly recall Stephen arriving at his place one evening unannounced. They'd drunk a few beers, had pizzas and then by the time O'Leary woke in the morning, Stephen had vanished. Hard doing this over the phone. If he could see his brother, he'd know for sure if he was lying about stashing stuff. 'Maybe you left something and forgot about it?'

'No, Brendan. I did not. What's happened to get you on the phone asking these questions?'

O'Leary briefly explained the situation, how a small cardboard box had been found in the laundry cupboard with a stash and then this morning, something else had been discovered.

'You haven't had any other dodgy guests? No other visitors?' Stephen asked.

'Nup. No one.'

'The love life hasn't improved then?' Stephen chuckled. 'Should come over here, brother. Aussie blokes are popular. Especially ones like us, good looking, good players, good—'

'You're right, I have no love life! But I do have two kids remember and a job that's as frustrating as all hell so I don't need you of all people giving me a hard time. I'm about to be dragged before this new police integrity inquiry that's been called, and as from today, I'm officially suspended. So stuff your fucking Aussie blokes crap. I just want a straight answer.' He would have landed a punch on Stephen's jaw if he'd been in the same room, despite his hand shaking like an old man's.

'Sorry for your troubles, Brendan, but it wasn't me.'

Pritchard was fiddling around in the kitchen making coffees and toasted sandwiches after the Helen Kapp interview, waiting for Harris to return with Kross and the boys. 'What did you make of the charcuterie board? I'm not mistaken am I in thinking there was a plate of sushi in Azarov's room?' he called to Micelli.

She wandered in, buttered both sides of the sandwiches just out of the press. 'I'm confused, too. We don't have any evidence of a charcuterie board or a second champagne glass, but we do have evidence of a champagne bottle and one glass, prints wiped off, and a plate that's obviously held sushi, probably eight or nine given the size of the plate, with two left over.'

Taking their snacks to the table, they sat looking at the whiteboard. 'Kapp was certain it was charcuterie. Even offered to check the exact ingredients with the chef. She wouldn't do that if she wasn't sure.'

Pritchard took a mouthful of sandwich, a trickle of melted butter running down his chin. Micelli began to laugh. 'What's so funny?' he asked.

'Nothing. It's just a bit like old times, you with food on your chin.' He glared at her. 'Look out, there's a glob of melted cheese heading for your shirt!' He tossed the sandwich onto his plate and pushed back from the table. 'Sorry,' she brayed, laughter barely under control, 'that was rude.' He sat back down and took a sip of coffee. 'Seriously, I'm sorry. Feeling a tadge hysterical. Nothing's making sense in this case and I'm worried about O'Leary.' She didn't add that the prospect of further threats from her sister didn't help to improve matters. 'Anyway, we better finish this and get back to the job in hand.'

None of the tennis contingent had asked for a lawyer to be present, but Micelli wanted to make sure they had representation, so when there was no response from the Consulate, she organised a solicitor from legal aid. Hoped she wasn't breaking any international protocols. Tomas Hader, a pimply-faced lawyer with slicked black hair wearing an ill-fitting suit, was already seated in the interview room when she entered, followed by Harris and Kross. After the introductions, Harris switched on the tape and began to run through a set list of questions. Kross offered mostly monosyllabic replies, his hands clasped on the table that was between them. 'You okay, Mr Kross?' Harris asked, when he noticed that sweat had broken out on the tennis player's forehead. He assured them that he was, and continued by telling them that he didn't know his manager very well at all. And that it was news to him about questionable financial practices, and no, he didn't know Azarov had a mistress.

'No mistress. I am sure.'

'Why are you so sure?' asked Micelli.

'Because he say he never going to give woman anything. Tell me do the same. Women too much trouble, he says. Focus on tennis. Make money.'

There was a knock on the door and Pritchard entered, pulled a chair up next to Harris. 'Markus,' he began, 'you don't mind if I call you Markus?' Kross nodded. 'Mind saying yes for the tape please?' Kross complied. 'I want to take you back to Sunday night. Artur and Kristo went to the casino. You didn't go with them because you had a first-round match on Monday. That right?'

'Yes.'

'And then on Tuesday they went out again, you stayed back, but you only got into the hotel a few minutes before they returned because you'd been watching tennis in a café next door to where you're staying.'

'Yes. That is right. I play on Wednesday, so no going out for me.'

'What I'm interested in, Markus, is who you met outside the café that night.'

Kross blinked rapidly. 'I not understand. I meet no one.'

Pritchard opened his laptop and turned on the room's data screen. Showed Kross the CCTV footage from outside the chemist shop. Kross was now breathing hard.

'That is you talking to someone, correct?' Kross nodded, glanced at Tomas Hader who was writing furiously on a yellow legal pad. 'Please say yes,' prodded Pritchard.

'Yes. He a fan. He want me to get him a ticket.'

Pritchard leaned back in his chair. 'Right. I guess you often get asked for favours. But what's puzzling me is how this fan knew you were in that particular café, and how did you know to go outside to meet him?'

Kross remained silent.

'Do you know who this fan is?'

No response. Tomas Hader, focused on his legal pad, was offering no direction to Kross.

'Did you phone, or did the fan phone you?'

'No call. Not me. Or him.'

Pritchard scratched his head. 'You know, that doesn't really make sense, does it Markus?' He slid a clean sheet of paper towards Kross. 'Write your phone number here, please.' This time Tomas Hader nodded when Kross looked at him, indicated he should do as requested. 'We're going to need to look at your call records.'

Kross took the pen that was offered and wrote a number on the page. 'But no calls. You check.'

'Will that be all?' asked Tomas Hader, removing his spectacles and wiping them with a handkerchief. He straightened his tie and put the pen he'd been using in his breast pocket.

'No. Not all,' said Kross, dipping his head into his hands. 'You keep it quiet. Please.' Tomas Hader swung round to face his client. Micelli, Harris and Pritchard leaned forward in their chairs, everyone's attention focused on Kross. 'I tell now what really happen, but it horrible. I ashamed.'

Over the next five minutes Kross told his listeners a rambling story about how he was going to be paid a bribe to lose his next round match against a low-ranked Russian. Azarov had set this up saying they would all win millions on betting, much more than if he was to keep winning and even win the entire tournament.

'And you believed Azarov?' asked Micelli.

'No. I not believe him. I not take orders they give me on

Tuesday. That's who you see at the café. He order that I go out and lose against wildcard on Wednesday. I don't know if there is bet or not because Azarov dead. No one say anything to me. Yet. But maybe it still be said sometime. I don't know. I now scared. In case there was bets and bad people lose money.' He slumped forward onto the table. It was if all the air in his body had been expelled and he was left like one of those inflatable tube men advertising a tyre outlet that had been slashed by louts out for a bit of fun on a Saturday night.

Nguyen phoned Hargreaves at Sydney CID and requested full cooperation after explaining that Christina Gallo was dead. Hargreaves assured them that he would talk to his boss and get all the necessary paperwork assembled and signed off. 'It'll take a couple of hours, so do you want to come over to the station? I can show you the file we've got on her.'

'Any chance we could ask to see the hospital CCTV from her floor before we go across?'

'Hold on a minute, will you.'

Nguyen put his phone on speaker and was immediately assailed by music from Smooth FM. 'Hate this MOR crap', he snapped, turning the volume down.

Janzen cocked her head. 'MOR?'

'Middle of the road, like the stuff you hear in elevators and shopping malls. Pap and crap, all rolled together. I hate it when they take a classic and philharmonic it somehow. Prefer to listen to the Chipmunks chitter their way through Rolling Stones classics.'

Janzen began to sing a high-pitched version of *I Can't Get No Satisfaction*, but stopped instantly when Hargreaves came back on the line. 'Boss is calling the hospital, asking for access to the tapes. Sending me over in a taxi. If I pray to the Saturday traffic gods should see you in the foyer in less than 10.'

Hargreaves was a big man, tall and wide. He had a grin to match. 'G'day,' he said, extending his hand to both detectives in turn. 'Sorry she's dead. Any intelligence we might have had a chance of scoring's gone. But mostly, feel sorry for the kid. Met her this morning. Only a little girl and now she's completely on her own. Cruel world, isn't it? Anyway, better get on with the matter in hand.' He marched over to reception and after a few quick words motioned for them to follow. A door opened and the three officers were swallowed up into the inner sanctums of hospital operations. 'Monitoring occurs in the basement. Said they'd be able to accommodate us with separate screens. Not too bad. There's twelve or more hours of tape, so if we spilt it, we'll make it more efficient don't you reckon?'

Once they were seated the technician started the tapes, Janzen's screen set from Christina's admission yesterday at two in the afternoon until midnight, Hargreaves from midnight to eight and Nguyen had the remainder up until four this afternoon, after Christina had been pronounced dead and her body wheeled down to the mortuary. 'We looking for anything in particular?' asked Hargreaves.

'Anything or anyone that doesn't look quite right is my guess,' said Nguyen.

'I've got a picture on my phone if that's any good.' He scrolled through a few screens and brought up a photo showing a heavy-set man, on the short side, balding, leaning against a wall, ice cream in hand, a dazzlingly blue ocean in the background. Nguyen studied the shot before passing it to Janzen. 'Handsome, isn't he?'

At least eight hours of tapes each to skim through. Luckily they didn't have to watch in real time, having a choice of doubling or quadrupling the speed. Hargreaves was racing through his tape quickly, stopping it every now and then to write a couple of notes. 'Bastard! He's disappeared,' he spluttered. The other two stopped their machines, leaned over to see what Hargreaves was seeing. 'Here he is walking down the corridor. It's the security guard, not Anson,' he said, aware that the others were bewildered. 'Into the Gents. Three minutes forty-nine seconds. That's how long the visit took. He would've been given a clear instruction to stay at the doorway, not leave his post, and he takes himself off to the bloody dunny. Only been on duty for less than an hour.' Hargreaves was still muttering when they turned back to their machines and restarted the tapes.

Janzen stopped her machine and got up to walk the perimeter of the room, windmilling her arms to the front then the back. 'Anyone else need a break? I'm going to have a look around. See what I can find.' One of the techies sitting by the door smiled at her. Told her there was a toilet and couple of vending machines along the corridor to the left. When she returned, she was carrying bottles of water, and a round of sandwiches encased in plastic. 'There's all sorts of stuff in the first vending machine. If anyone's hungry, that is.' She resumed her seat, prised open the sandwich box and began to munch on ham, cheese and tomato encased in white bread.

The rolling tape showed a lot of activity in the corridor on Christina's floor, nursing staff and the occasional doctor coming and going. Every fifteen minutes someone went in and out of Christina's room, presumably checking her vitals. In addition, a machine got wheeled in as regular as clockwork every hour and wheeled out again five minutes later. Janzen was about to ask one of the techies if he knew what it was for when Nguyen leapt out of his chair. 'It's him! He's heading towards Christina's room!' He pressed stop, catching in freeze frame Anson removing what looked to be a sizeable amount of cash from his wallet. The next few frames showed the security guard holding out his hand and shoving whatever Anson gave him into the inside of his jacket. 'Time is 13.06,' said Nguyen, 'about half an hour after we left her.' He returned to watching the tape which showed Anson leaving the room at 13.11, closing the door behind him. From 13.16 until 13.18 there was a flurry of activity in the corridor as medicos and nurses rushed to Christina's room. There was no sign of the security guard.

Artur was next into the interview room and confirmed Kross's story that it was unlikely that Azarov had a mistress. He had begun to laugh when Micelli asked him the question. 'Azarov too tight to pay for anyone else. Azarov greedy man. Want to keep everything for himself.' She followed up with a question about match-fixing. 'Some Russians, Egyptians have done it. I know because I am on the circuit and you hear things. Maybe a man from Brazil, too, but not sure.'

'Not heard any rumours about this tournament?'

He shook his head. 'Too many medias. And we have integrity now. Besides, only best of best at this tournament.'

'Kross ever been approached?' asked Harris.

Artur scrunched up his face. 'Never. Not that I know. He tell me for sure if he asked, he know what happens if you fix matches. All players know that now. It is part of what you read when you sign up for a tournament. Azarov would show him the paperwork. Get him to sign.'

'Even if he stood to win millions as a result of bets being placed on a match?'

'He good player. He has long career in front. Like Djokovic, like Alcaraz. Markus would not risk career for bets.'

Harris thanked him and showed him the door, ushering Kristo in and indicating where he should sit. Kristo's eyes darted about the room and his breathing was shallow and fast. 'Here's a water for you,' said Harris, sliding a bottle across the table. 'Take a minute. Keep calm. We just need to see if you can help us out with a few details, that's all.' Kristo, like both Artur and Kross, said he'd not heard talk of a mistress, nor seen any evidence that there was one. And, like Artur, he'd not encountered anything that might lead him to think Kross was engaged in match fixing.

'Markus not even visit casino when we go,' he said, swigging down the last of the water. 'He not play cards with us. Nothing. Yes, I like to bet. But not Markus. He say it waste of his time and money.'

'And did you have a bet on the tennis this week?' enquired Micelli. 'You know, just for fun. On Kross. Or anyone?'

'No way!' he rasped. 'We not allowed to bet on tennis. Against rules everywhere. I never bet on tennis.'

'You know we can check that, Kristo, so are you sure you didn't bet?'

He looked pleadingly at Tomas Hader. 'I not bet on tennis. I tell you truth. I only go to casino and play blackjack and some tables.

No bets. Never.'

'Okay, thank you Kristo. Oh, and before you go, care to provide us with a sample for DNA purposes? Just a quick swab.' As he had done when Kross and Artur were in the room, Tomas Hader warned his client that he didn't have to participate.

'I okay. I nothing to hide.' He opened his mouth while Harris rubbed a swab on the inside of his cheek, inserted it into a vial and wrote Kristo's name and the time and date on it. Passed over a statement for him to sign saying he'd willingly provided a sample. Tomas Hader countersigned as his witness.

After Kristo and Tomas Hader were shown out, the three detectives picked up their notes and files and trooped back upstairs. Micelli looked at her watch, ten past seven. Despite Pritchard's toasted sandwich earlier, her stomach was rumbling. 'Anyone for a takeaway?' She dumped assorted menus on the table. 'If we can all agree on the one place, it'll be quicker. I fancy something Asian. What about you blokes?'

'Fine with me,' said Harris.

'Happy for you to order on my behalf,' said Pritchard, disappearing into the kitchenette, phone in hand.

'Nobody allergic to nuts?' Micelli was looking at Mr Minh's offerings. Harris didn't object, so she ordered Vietnamese duck salad, a serve of chicken salad and a mix of spring and rice paper rolls for starters. Wondering if that was enough, she phoned back and added a beef salad. 'May as well be healthy if we're going to be doing a long night.' Harris groaned. Pritchard was still in the kitchenette murmuring into his phone. 'Forty minutes, they reckon for delivery. Time enough to organise Miss Ludmilla Bagrova. Probably another job for Tomas Hader, I'd say, unless she's got contacts in high places.'

'Hader's probably having himself a jolly Saturday night. Can only envy the poor blighter if he is.'

'Hey, we're on a roll here. We've got a mistress who isn't by all accounts and we need to sort it out.'

'What opportunity did she have to kill Azarov?'

Micelli glanced at her pinging phone, another message from Rosie, and shoved it back in her pocket. 'That we don't know as yet, but I intend to find out.' She checked her watch. 'Hey, look on the bright side. We'll be finished by at least midnight. Plenty of time left for you to party into the wee small hours.' Walking towards the door she announced, 'I'm going to get some fresh air and wait for the food delivery in case some other hungry cop snaffles it.'

Micelli walked to the corner of Spencer Street and halfway across the La Trobe Street bridge. Hundreds of seagulls wheeling above the Bolte Bridge were silhouetted against the western sky. She leaned over the railing and re-read the message she'd only glanced at in the office. Rosie. No longer steaming with aggression. Charge against Nick was dropped. No explanation as to why. And apparently no apologies forthcoming from Vic Pol either. Rosie hadn't been able to resist adding a couple of sentences that made Micelli's blood boil. *All of this no thanks to you. I'll try to be civil when you come for dinner on Sunday.* Micelli suppressed the urge to text her sister, tell her that cops had better things to do other than apologise to the likes of her. And that she had better things to do than accept a back handed invitation to dinner. Instead, she opted for a conciliatory *Great news Rosie. A.* She even added a couple of heart emojis. Just for fun.

'We'd better call a press conference before we speak to Bagrova,' said Micelli, when she returned laden with steaming plastic bags. 'They're milling on the steps wanting to know what all the action's about. Can you organise that, please?' She pointed to Harris.

'Sure thing. Not much to tell them, but,' said Harris.

'Never underestimate the power of the media. Burns came good with information that although, not exactly fingering a suspect, has nevertheless assisted us understand a bit of background. Susan Watson from the *Gazette* is always a good stick. Did I show you the pic she sent me on Friday morning?' Harris and Pritchard leaned over her shoulder as she located a photo showing a jubilant young Australian tennis player holding up her hands in victory.

'So?' asked Harris. 'How's that helpful?'

'Umm,' said Pritchard. 'I'd say it could be very helpful, even if not in this case. Let's say it's good background material.'

Harris peered more closely. 'Fuck!' He gestured for the phone which she handed to him. Used his thumb and forefinger to enlarge the image. 'Well, well, well. Our ever-ready Mick Skelton with our favourite minister of police having an amiable chat at the tennis. This must have been on Thursday afternoon. That's when she won that match.'

'Good thinking, Harris. I can see your detective skills are as sharp as ever. But let's eat. I'm ravenous.'

After binning the leftovers, Micelli retrieved her phone, picked up her notebook and files. 'Everybody ready? Media conference then Bagrova. Don't want to keep her waiting. She was snaky as it was, being asked to come in on a Saturday evening. And no Tomas Hader this time either. Adamant she didn't want a lawyer. Said they were petty fogs or something. Didn't make sense.'

Pritchard began to chuckle.

Although half past nine in the evening was late for a media conference, the room was filling up with journalists from all the main outlets. Harris was hovering on the dais, tie straight and hair combed. Micelli wished she'd taken more care during her brief visit to the Ladies, maybe some lip gloss for the cameras, take the emphasis away from the rings under her eyes. But looking around, she saw she wasn't the only one. She nodded as Steve Burns took a seat in the front. 'Been a long day?'

'Without a doubt. Hoping what you're about to tell us might give me some more specifics for a feature I'm working on. Don't mind a long day if it pays off.'

'We'll see how we go.' In a louder tone she called the room to attention. 'Thank you for coming in at this late hour. I know you've all got much better things to do on a Saturday evening in summer. But unfortunately, the criminal class aren't always considerate.' She stopped until the titters of laughter had died away. 'As you know Mr Alexei Azarov was found deceased in his room at the Condor Hotel on Tuesday morning. He was in Melbourne in his capacity as tennis manager for Markus Kross from Estonia who is an entrant in the men's singles of the

Australian Open.'

'And the men's and mixed doubles,' came a voice from the back.

'Thank you for that correction, but we're here this evening to appeal to you and your audiences for any information that people may have about this untimely death. We're hoping to get some answers so the case can be concluded, and Mr Azarov returned to Estonia where he has a wife and two children. We're specifically seeking anyone who saw Mr Azarov on Monday after five o'clock when he was last seen at Melbourne Park. We have no further information about his whereabouts until later that evening when he was captured on the hotel's security cameras catching the lift up to his room on the ninth floor. That gives us a window of four hours unaccounted for. In the lift with him was a woman whom he met in the hotel lobby. She is described as tall and slim but as we have no facial shots, we have little information to go on.' She motioned to Harris. 'DC Harris will hand out a screen shot, and we'd appreciate your cooperation in making this public.' She reached behind her to grab a bottle of water from the table and took a swig while the handout was being distributed. 'Questions?'

First hand up was Susan Watson from the *Gazette*. 'Did Mr Azarov appear to know this woman?'

'As far as we can deduce from examining the footage, no. But we have no proof either way. That's something we're hoping the public can assist with. Maybe someone saw Mr Azarov dining perhaps at Federation Square or at Southbank somewhere. Monday afternoon and early evening was quite warm as you may recall. Sitting outside would have been ideal.' She reflected for a moment on her Monday evening with David Romano, eating oysters and drinking Prosecco from a first-floor restaurant at Southbank. She'd much rather be doing that right now than briefing journos with news feeds to fill.

'Steve Burns from *The Times*. Can you tell us who you've brought in for questioning?'

'As you may be aware we've asked a number of people to come into headquarters for a chat, purely on a voluntary basis. Indeed, we have not formally questioned anyone at this stage. Everyone has cooperated and we have some further informal interviews to conduct after this media conference. We have not charged anyone with anything as yet. All our interviewees have volunteered their time.'

'What *is* new then, or why else call a press conference at this hour? Sorry, Kelly Georgiou, Channel 7.'

'Ah, Kelly, not at the tennis this evening?' She smiled beatifically at Georgiou who was dressed more like a WAG on Brownlow night than a serious news hound. She took another mouthful of water. 'But in answer to your question, there are some details that have emerged—no,' she said holding up her hand to stop Georgiou's interruption, 'before you ask I'm not at liberty to reveal them. Let's just say they are of a forensic nature that has led us in the direction of wanting to find out more about Mr Azarov's movements on Monday from five in the afternoon when he was seen with a man at the tennis, who thanks to everyone's good work after our last briefing, has been identified and was happy to provide us with valuable information.' She looked sideways at Harris then around the room. Obviously news of Serchanov's death hadn't filtered through as yet as no one jumped up to fire off a question about this latest death. 'The gap we're looking at is from five until nine or thereabouts when Mr Azarov was seen on the hotel's cameras, and you all have a time-stamped print in front of you, showing the as yet unidentified woman with Mr Azarov.'

'I'm wondering if the authorities in Estonia have been notified of Mr Azarov's death given the growing tensions between Russia and that country as evidenced by the build-up of Russian navy vessels in the Baltic Sea, where there is also a heavy NATO presence?' Carefully enunciated from the back by a well-coiffed young woman.

'Sorry I missed your name.'

'Annabel Fisher, cadet journalist on the Foreign Affairs and Crime desks at *The Gazette*.'

'Thank you, Ms Fisher. Yes, we have notified all the relevant authorities. But at this stage the Defence Force is not involved. Any further questions?' A hand shot up to enquire about the murder weapon. 'There is no murder weapon to be found,' she replied, 'as I said on Tuesday. This was not a savage attack leading to death, more a death by—how can I explain it, more a death by stealth. The victim was asphyxiated but we are still investigating how that occurred and if there were any other issues at play. That's all for now ladies and gentlemen. Thank you again for coming out at this late hour and I reiterate that we need the public's assistance with locating the woman seen with the victim as depicted in the handout you all have.' She gathered together her things and followed Harris out the door leading back into the restricted area. She pressed the button on the lift. 'How'd that go, do you reckon?'

He laughed. 'Thought you were going to put in a call to the head of the defence forces there and then when that Fisher woman asked her question. Talk about up herself.'

'Yeah, not like they used to be, straight out of school to learn on the job. Now fully trained in degree programs before they're recruited. And don't they like to show it when given the chance. Anyway,' she said as they pushed open the door to the office, 'time for a quick break then back to the interview room where Miss Bagrova will be awaiting the pleasure of our company.'

SUNDAY

THE SUN was well up when Micelli woke and prepared for another day in the office. Sunday should be a day to do whatever she wanted. But not with an active murder enquiry. Six days and counting. She had been in the office with Pritchard and Harris until after eleven debating the whys and wherefores of what their interviewees had said.

'My money's on Kapp,' Pritchard had asserted, whose crumpled suit jacket bore testimony to being tossed on and off as they ushered the interviewees in and out, making sure they didn't cross paths. 'She's the one with unlimited opportunity. What about how she crumbled when we left her in the interview room for ten minutes?'

Helen Kapp had looked pale against the grey of her t-shirt, looked every bit her age. During the interview, she had tilted her chin upwards and met the gaze of her questioners unflinchingly, but as soon as they were out of the room she had slumped forward, head in hands and begun to sob.

'Why cry if there's nothing to hide?'

'Not going to fly,' argued Micelli. 'She's had a hell of a week with everything's that happened.'

'Like?'

'Us finding out stuff about her life which wouldn't be nice to have dredged up, and firing questions at her. How many times? Three by my count. Four if we count the first time you went to the Condor after security footage. Crying's never been an admission of guilt in my book.'

'Okay, I'll discount the crying,' said Pritchard, 'but what about her admission that she returned to Azarov's room late on Monday night and found him dead. Why didn't she raise the alarm then and there if she had nothing to hide?'

'And she removed the glass she'd used to drink from and wiped down the bottle,' said Harris. 'Pretty suss behaviour if you've got nothing to hide. I was checking out that lawyer Willoughby when she was talking, and he turned pale when she admitted she'd gone back to Azarov's room.'

'Probably thought his fees would need to be adjusted down if his client ended up on a murder charge,' said Pritchard.

'Okay, enough.' Micelli strode to the white board and announced they would now scrutinise everyone who presented with a degree of motive, some opportunity and the means to kill Azarov. 'Let's start at the top with Kross.'

The large colour photo of Kross taken front-on stared out at them. Blue eyes, blond hair, mouth turned down in a scowl. Not his best angle. And not the one that was plastered online and over the back pages of the newspapers showing his athleticism. 'Undoubtedly has motive,' said Harris. 'Here's how. He was owed money by Azarov. Had to foot the bill for his coach and masseur from his winnings after Azarov took his cut. Was asked to take bribes to fix matches, presumably arranged by Azarov. Anyone got anything else to contribute?' No one added to the list. 'And because we don't have any reliable footage from the Condor, it's possible he could have snuck in and done the job.'

'And the condom? With female saliva?' asked Micelli.

'Yeah. I can see that's not really going to work unless we have another female—hang on a minute.' He jumped up and raced over to the white board. 'We do. The mystery woman in the lift footage,' he said, pointing at the ♀? *lift* notation. 'Maybe she was the lure and Kross snuck in later?'

Neither Micelli nor Pritchard looked convinced.

'Not going to fly?'

They shook their heads.

'Possible but improbable,' said Micelli. 'Whoever killed Azarov wasn't watching tennis in a café and meeting a dodgy character trying to bribe him, as Kross did on Monday night.'

Next they considered Artur and Kristo, and agreed that although Artur disliked Azarov intensely, they couldn't see either or both as killers. Their alibi, a visit to the casino from just after seven until almost midnight had checked out, and if Kapp's statement was true that she returned to Azarov's room a little after eleven on Monday and found him already dead, they had no opportunity.

Moving onto Serchanov, who could still be in the frame for Azarov's murder even though he was now dead himself, they agreed had motive if they accepted that he wished the worst for Azarov. But again, the condom proved to be the sticking point.

'That leaves us with Bagrova. She maybe has opportunity, but there's no evidence of that. She's got the means if it's as simple as asphyxiation. And after all, someone had to deliver the sushi to his room. It didn't just appear by magic. But have we got a motive? I don't think so,' said Micelli.

'Not if we accept that she's Azarov's mistress,' said Pritchard, stroking his chin, 'but so far, we only have her word for it. She told me when I first went to talk to her that she and Azarov were going to have a holiday together up north after the tennis. She was excited that's for sure, as well as distraught that the holiday was not going to happen. But when we questioned her yesterday evening, she couldn't name the destination. Not even if it was an island or a resort on the mainland or somewhere as obvious as the Gold Coast. Claimed that Azarov had done all the bookings, and that it was a surprise for her birthday.'

'Hang on.' Micelli flicked through the transcript of last night's interview with Bagrova. 'You're right. And I know there were no tickets to Queensland or accommodation bookings in Azarov's possessions. Only an open ticket for him to Tallinn.'

'What about e-tickets though?' asked Harris. 'Doesn't everyone get them nowadays? Much easier on your phone than forgetting bits of paper when you're at check-in.'

They paused. 'Her phone?'

'First, her birthday according to her passport is in October, so it's either a very early or a very late gift. And second, when you asked her about Azarov's tattoos all she could say was that he had some. Lovers tend to know every inch of each other's body. Don't think she could have missed that star on his knee,' Pritchard said, 'especially given its significance in certain Russian sub-cultures.'

Harris chimed in. 'Or missed the one on his groin? If a star tattooed on the knee means you don't bend for anyone, what does one on the groin mean I wonder?' Micelli rolled her eyes. 'And none of the tennis contingent thought he had a mistress. It was Artur, wasn't it, who said he was too tight to spend money on a woman? For my money, Bagrova was not his mistress. And we have no idea why she declares to have been his mistress, or even why she's here in Melbourne.'

Micelli felt her phone vibrating in her pocket. 'Frank Sutcliffe, Ange. Sorry to ring so late. Look, something's come up with the tests we ran on your man Azarov. And now the next victim, Serchanov. Is now a good time to talk?'

Micelli explained that she was in the office with her colleagues, Harris and Pritchard. 'Okay if I put you on speaker phone, Frank? Lessens the chance of me getting something mixed up in the translation.'

'Certainly, Ange. This is pretty complex stuff. Of course, I'll send a report to you later today when George and I have got our thoughts down on paper in a logical manner, but here goes for now.'

For the next fifteen minutes, Sutcliffe outlined what he and George Porter, a professorial fellow from Cambridge in the UK who was in Melbourne for the international forensics and autopsy conference, had discerned by using further tests on some of Azarov's blood and tissue samples. 'I was sitting next to George at the dinner this evening and telling him that the Azarov case had me a bit puzzled. As you know, my preliminary findings are death by asphyxiation, but there is no obvious single cause for asphyxiation. I know we've discussed the plastic bag and the sushi plate, and I've told you about the reduced flow of blood back to his heart, an observation that can be seen in some deaths resulting from anaphylaxis, but there's been something else as well niggling me, something I couldn't put my finger on.'

The three detectives listened intently. Micelli was poised to scribble notes while Pritchard stood at the whiteboard.

'George has worked on several high-profile cases in the UK, including a couple where there's been poisons involved. You may be familiar with the Russian penchant for poisoning people they want to disappear? The Skripals in Salisbury? Litvinenko in London?'

The detectives replied that they had heard of these cases before Sutcliffe went on.

'The poisons used in the Salisbury case acted on the victims' nerves, and to all intents and purposes they were dying of suffocation when they were found. Fortunately for the Skripals they were able to be resuscitated, but not the poor woman who either found or was given a bottle of perfume that contained the poison.'

'I recall that case,' said Micelli, 'because the poison was in a Nina Ricci perfume bottle and it's a perfume I was using at the time. Threw it in the bin straightaway.'

Sutcliffe chuckled. 'It took some time for the woman in that case to die, which is why George ruled out Novichok as a poison used on Azarov. But he was pretty keen to see if some other form of poison had been administered. And he came up with another potential poison, gelsemium. Ever heard of it? Also called heartbreak grass, it's a flowering plant, not found in Australia I don't think, thank god, although some lunatic homeopaths use it in their potions I believe. Anyway, a dose of this stuff can cause fatal asphyxia within thirty minutes. Of course, we didn't test for traces of heartbreak grass originally. Why would we? I'm pretty sure there are no other cases listed in Australia. But given George's interest in gelsemium based on a long-running investigation into another Russian's death in London a few years back, a lot of controversy and difference of opinion amongst the profession about the cause of death apparently, he encouraged me to investigate gelsemium as a possibility. We ran some tests this evening, and bingo! We, or I should say George, came up trumps. There were tell-tale gelsemium alkaloids in the urine of both men.'

'Wow!' said Micelli. 'Can you get this stuff in Australia? Is it liquid or powder?'

Sutcliffe cleared his throat. 'Probably both. Maybe other forms too. I believe it's feasible to source it if you're a Chinese medicine practitioner, but without checking the importation rules, I imagine it'd be pretty tough to get through Customs. Course you can buy gelsemium sempervirens in nurseries, commonly known as yellow jasmine, and drops and so on online through homeopathic dealers, but it's a different species. The toxic one's gelsemium elegans.'

'Did you say it was used in the poisoning of a Russian in London?' asked Pritchard.

Sutcliffe confirmed the fact but was quick to reiterate that the coroner, after a four-year investigation, ruled in the end that the victim likely died of natural causes. 'The victim was a high-profile businessman, wealthy of course, and was threatening to blow the whistle on some dodgy Russian business colleagues. Make of it what you will, but George thinks that because at the outset of their investigations, the police didn't treat the death as suspicious, evidence that could have been conclusive was either lost or overlooked or conceivably even tampered with. Anyway, I'm sure you've heard enough from me at this point. Report will arrive later today. Hope this has been helpful.'

The detectives remained silent for a few seconds before Micelli kicked into gear. 'Pritchard, you and I are going to Bagrova's place right now. I want her arrested and brought back for questioning. Harris, you arrange backup and, this is important, I want to be informed of every act, every step, every everything. Clear? Every fucking thing.'

They grabbed jackets, phones and pistols and headed out the door.

'We could already be too late.'

The Sydney airport was jam-packed, wheelie bags, backpacks, kids aboard ride-on suitcases made to look like elephants or bees or London buses, another indulgence Janzen guessed to keep kids happy. She and Nguyen threaded their way through the throng, no time left for a lounge breakfast after their early morning meeting with Hargreaves from Sydney CID, so a takeaway coffee and bacon and egg roll bought at the departure gate was the only option. Not that the meeting had turned up anything new. Again, Gregory Anson had disappeared into thin air.

Squashing into adjoining seats, Nguyen said between mouthfuls of roll, 'He's a bastard of a man. I keep on thinking of that little girl whose picture we saw when we went to Christina's place last year. How's she going to feel in a few years when she gets to understand that it was her father who killed her mother.'

Janzen sipped on her coffee. 'We don't know that for certain. We don't even know that Anson is her father. What is she, six? If she's cared for well, she may come through all this okay. Some kids are very resilient you know. I learnt this in Drugs when we saw the worst human wreckage you can imagine, wrecks who also happened to be parents looked after by their kids as young as seven or eight. Broke my heart, those so-called families.'

'We need to get him.' Nguyen scrunched his leftovers into his empty coffee cup. 'Put him where he belongs for a long, long time. He's got to have contacts that enable him to disappear. And I don't understand why none of us, and I'm talking VicPol and New South, can find a single thing. Makes me think he's got friends in very high places.'

The flight was announced and they joined the queue. Nguyen flashed his boarding pass and noted an incoming email from Macleod. 'I see we've got the forensic results from the Valentino house. Keep us entertained on the way home.' The cabin crew completed their safety demonstrations and seatbelt checks, and they were ready for take-off.

After service and the obligatory tea and coffee, Nguyen opened his email. 'Hey, take a look at this.'

Janzen scrolled through a section titled Financial Data. 'A hospitality venue. Well, well. Who would have thought.'

'And what a fascinating set-up it is. The co-owners of the venture are none other than Sally Sinclair, wife of the Police

Minister himself, and Adriana Valentino.'

'Wonder if the wives know they're part-owners of a wine bar?'

He shook his head. 'Doubtful, I reckon.' Reading further, the report described how a former laundrette in North Melbourne had been converted to a small but lucrative wine bar two years ago with the fetching name, *Wash House*. 'How do you take ten grand a month in cash sales at a wine bar? If each glass is worth say ten bucks, then you have to sell a thousand for cash, that's two hundred and fifty glasses a week. And who pays by cash now? Everyone swipes their phone.'

'Especially the people who tend to frequent wine bars in my experience,' said Janzen. 'Okay, so they do bar snacks as well, just checked on Google. But that's still a helluva lot of money in cash.'

'Common, but. The hospitality industry pays workers cash, takes cash out of the till, or, and this is what the forensic accountants at Macleod are insinuating, it's a great way to launder money coming in from other sources, say gambling—'

'Or drugs or porn. Anything that you can't legitimately bank. But you can bank this cash. Ta dah. Officially laundered.'

'Not quite. Another layer or two and you're there. Sink some of the wine bar money into real estate. That way you don't have to declare all the wine bar income as profits for the tax man. And guess what? Valentino had a real estate business.'

Janzen clapped her hands together. 'Those Macleod girls and boys are very very good!'

Reading on, they discovered that not only were Sinclair's fingerprints all over the cash injections into the wine bar that connected him to Valentino, but his DNA had also been found at Valentino's house. Yet perhaps the most intriguing discovery of all, was that buried in the black set of folders was a code that turned out to be a safe deposit box number. When the box was opened it contained a million in cash and more than a thousand ecstasy pills, all imprinted with Anson's trademark bulldog.

'You've been to her place before, so you drive,' Micelli said, plucking a set of car keys from the cabinet in the kitchenette and giving them to Pritchard. 'No time to finesse tactics. I'll knock while you park. Hope Harris got onto back up.' They turned right out of the carpark, just caught the lights as Pritchard gunned the car left onto Spencer Street. 'Is there a back entrance that leads onto a laneway like most old houses? Be better if you go to the back instead of following me. In case she does a runner.'

He pulled the car alongside the kerb, parked it. 'The one with the black door.'

Micelli leapt out and raced up the pathway, knocked loudly. No answer. Pritchard had already disappeared down the laneway.

Hammering on the front door again, Micelli yelled louder this time, 'Open up! Police!'

Next door an old woman kneeling on the ground in her front garden, got to her feet and leaned over the fence. 'She not there. Car come.'

'She was picked up by a car?'

'She had rolly case with her.'

'How long ago?'

'One minutes. Maybe less.'

Micelli swore under her breath. 'What colour car, do you know?'

'Big like yours, but black. No see in windows.'

Micelli pulled out her notebook. Saw two squad cars pull up outside the house. 'Didn't happen to get the registration number?'

The woman shook her head, kept talking even as Micelli sprinted across the road. 'She in big hurry, speaking language I not understand. She hit man.' Micelli didn't have time to ask who Bagrova had hit, or whether the neighbour was identifying Bagrova as part of the criminal class of guns for hire.

'Thanks,' she yelled over her shoulder, before giving instructions to the squaddies. 'Black car, same as ours,' pointing to the white BMW that she and Pritchard had arrived in, now parked crookedly in front of Bagrova's place. 'Tinted windows. Haven't got the rego. Left here a couple of minutes ago. My bet is the airport.'

One of the squad cars took off. The driver parked the other squad car and both officers followed her to the front door. One used a sledge on the door. She did a quick search of the property, dialled Pritchard. 'No one here. Need to get on the road. See you round the front.'

Pritchard had the engine running when she emerged from the house. Phone scissored between shoulder and ear as she buckled her seatbelt. 'Harris, get an alert out at the airport. Essendon as well. Woman and at least one man. Give them Bagrova's passport details. We're on our way to Tullamarine. And thanks, by the way for the squaddies. Great work.'

They got onto the tollway leading to the airport. Micelli kept an eagle eye out for a black BMW as Pritchard skimmed through traffic into the right lane. The radio was crackling news from a squad car, black BMW SUV spotted half a kilometre from the Calder exit. 'Get the rego?' asked Micelli.

'Last three digits whiskey quebec foxtrot, but quebec could be oscar. Travelling at speed. Guessing hundred and thirty clicks an hour. We've radioed for a car to wait in Keilor Road, able to give chase if the vehicle exits onto the Calder.'

She called Harris and told him to get onto vehicle identification before turning her attention to a black BMW that Pritchard was drawing alongside. Windows only lightly tinted, looked like a family with a baby strapped into a car seat in the back. Another black BMW glided past them using the left lane. Blinkers on, taking the Moreland Road exit. 'Quick! Pull along beside it.' This time a woman in her fifties, bobbed hair and designer sunglasses. 'Didn't realise there were so many black BMWs on the roads these days. Must have missed the what's trending memo.'

Pritchard veered back into the middle lane, earning a horn blast from the driver behind him. 'We can't tail every black BMW we see on the road. Do we pull over and wait for positive location ID from the squaddies?' Vehicles whizzed past them both sides, more tooting as Pritchard had slowed down to 80kmph.

She chewed her bottom lip. 'Or we just go to the airport. Is there anywhere else they'd likely be travelling?'

'Might have a bolt hole in the country somewhere. Or off to a regional airport where security is not so tight. Get on a light plane and hop it up to Indonesia. Or a Pacific Island where Russia might be seen as a friend.'

She looked at him, an eyebrow raised. 'You should write books with that sort of imagination. Nah, let's go to the airport.'

As Pritchard accelerated, the radio kicked in. 'Calling all units. Suspect vehicle sighted. Rego's 1SB W0F, repeat one sierra bravo, whiskey zero foxtrot. Just over Bulla Road, near Calder exit. Travelling in right lane. Speed estimated at 90kmph.'

Micelli glanced at the sat nav. Bulla Road was fast approaching. 'Slow down.' She removed her gun from its holster, checked the ammunition. 'Don't want to risk ramming them from behind.'

'No chance of that.' He gestured towards a B-double with flashing hazard lights moving across lanes in front of them, causing him to brake. The truck shuddered to a halt on the shoulder before the driver jumped out, thick smoke escaping the cabin which immediately burst into flames as the air rushed in. Micelli looked back to see the driver straddling the metal barriers as an explosion ripped through the windscreen showering glass onto the roadway as flames began licking the cabin's top.

'Hope the fireys get there quick.' She turned back to face the front as Pritchard kept pace with traffic that had narrowly missed being caught up in the accident.

The radio crackled into life. *Suspect moving left. Turning into Airport Drive.* Again, Pritchard braked hard, moved to the left lane. Traffic more forgiving now. 'Must be locals, if they know Airport Drive.'

Micelli pushed forward in her seat. 'That's them!' She was pointing to a black SUV two cars up. 'Watch out. Don't run up their arse. This road lead anywhere other than the airport?'

'There's a lot of laybys and turnoffs into the logistics and engineering zones. You'd have to know your way round pretty well to pick the one to take you elsewhere. See, on the sat nav?' She took her eyes off the SUV long enough to glance at the screen. The SUV kept its course, cruising up the on-ramp then slowing at international departures. It pulled into a park outside the double glass doors.

'Bagrova's getting out! And there's two men. One's getting luggage out the back. Quick. Let me out.'

Pritchard swerved into a park reserved for taxis. An attendant in high-vis and a burgundy turban ran towards him, waggling a finger. Micelli flew out of the car and bolted for the doors as the SUV pulled away from the kerb. Pritchard flashed his badge and rushed after her. The departure hall was milling with people, some pulling children along by their arms, trolleys piled high with luggage. She moved fast, not running, but slicing through the crowd with precision, eyes scanning faces, hands, posture. There was no sign of Ludmilla Bagrova. Russian. Dangerous. Clever as hell. And there was no sign of her companion.

'Do you know who she flew with to get to Australia?' She scanned the screens for a clue as to which of the many check-in counters Bagrova might be queuing at. 'She could be anywhere. You do the rounds in International, and I'll head to Domestic. We've got her picture on file so Harris can send it through to the squaddies in the airport.'

Micelli had caught a glimpse of Bagrova maybe five minutes ago when she had alighted from the vehicle. Big sunglasses, silk scarf, heels like she wasn't trying to run. Not yet. But she'd seen it before. That look in someone's body when they were ready for anything, including a sprint.

The domestic terminal, surprisingly quiet after the hubbub next door. Micelli tried to blend in with the crowd, checking her watch every few seconds as if she was meeting someone and they were keeping her waiting. Once through the screening counter, she mingled with the few people heading into shops or down to departure gates. There was that familiar reek of burnt coffee and desperation, a scent Micelli had come to associate with last chances and loose ends. Her gun pressed reassuringly under her jacket, silent but ready. She approached the Qantas Lounge, stopped, checked her watch again. No one on the escalator. Or at least not as far as she could see. But she could feel it. That's where Bagrova would've gone. Her need for cover, for a mirror, for a moment. She imagined Bagrova inside, shedding layers of identity like a snake slipping its skin. Blonde wig, maybe. Different clothes. And almost certainly, a change of footwear. Maybe even a new face under the makeup. Micelli didn't need to see it to know.

The lounge receptionist opened his mouth, probably to tell her she wasn't allowed. She held up her badge, gave him a look that shut him up cold, and pushed through into a near-empty lounge. She concluded that businesspeople mustn't do much flying on Sunday mornings.

The lounge opened before her like a hidden world, a quiet sanctuary high above the chaos of boarding calls and wheeled suitcases. The air was cooler here, scented faintly with fresh espresso and polished wood. Low light glowed from sleek sconces along the walls, casting a golden hush over the room. Plush armchairs in soft leather were scattered like islands of comfort, some occupied by travellers in suits murmuring into phones, others by those simply staring out at the tarmac, coffees in hand, watching planes taxi to and fro.

But the silence inside was too clean. Too still.

Micelli unholstered her gun.

She walked further in, her footsteps muffled by thick carpeting. A marble counter curved elegantly near the entrance, behind which a concierge greeted her with a practiced smile, discreet, efficient. Beyond, a buffet stretched invitingly under glass domes: artisanal cheeses, warm pastries, delicate finger sandwiches arranged with an almost reverent care. Bottles of fine wine and gleaming coffee machines stood ready, promising indulgence or alertness, depending on the hour.

In the corner, a business traveller typed swiftly at a sleek desk beside a row of charging ports; nearby, a couple whispered over shared pastries and clinked glasses of something sparkling in a quiet toast. There were private rooms too, shower suites with thick towels and rainfall heads, nap rooms with dimmed lights and soft music playing low.

Time moved differently here. Outside, flights came and went in their orchestrated rush, but inside the lounge, the world paused just long enough for a breath, a moment, a small luxury between destinations.

Micelli moved quietly down through the chairs, past the screens playing news updates, towards the business alcove. Scanned the spaces. Her attention was caught by a sudden movement. Someone at the far end of the lounge, a tall woman, was entering the restrooms.

Micelli followed her, began to tidy her hair, leant over the wash basin, peered into the mirror. Only one cubicle was occupied. She found a lip gloss in her jacket pocket and was applying it when she heard a toilet flush. A woman, baseball cap pulled low over her eyes, emerged from the cubicle and stood next to her at the basins. Glancing up, the woman's eyes popped. Leaving the tap running she dashed out the door and into the lounge. Micelli ran after her and was in time to see her duck down behind an island bench laden with platters and tureens, trays of bread rolls and plates ready for the taking. She was not waiting for further confirmation that this woman *was* Bagrova. She muffled her voice as much as she could and radioed for back up. Approaching the bench like a cat stalking a bird, she announced in a loud voice that whoever was hiding behind the bench was to stand up and put her hands in the air.

Bagrova moved like smoke, one arm extended, the other gripping a small pistol. Micelli barely had time to register the shimmer of silver hair under the baseball cap before a shot cracked past her ear and slammed into a coffee machine, sending hot sludge everywhere.

Micelli ducked behind a leather chair. Bagrova was fast. She'd already rolled behind the wine bar, her gun spitting. A round clipped the chair Micelli had just vacated, splintering wood and sending a businessman's abandoned briefcase flying.

There were screams now. Customers were scrambling towards the exit, some diving behind tables, others frozen. Someone yelled, 'Get down! She's got a gun too!'

Micelli moved, fired, this time at the glass behind the bar. It exploded, and for a second, she saw Bagrova crouched low, eyes locked on hers.

Then a fizz. Bagrova had dropped something.

Smoke canister.

The room went white, a sharp hiss filling Micelli's ears. She backed up, coughing, one arm raised. She caught a shadow moving left. Not towards the front entrance.

Micelli gave chase, vision blurry, lungs burning. She shouldered through the fog, stumbling into the kitchen, just in time to see a service door slam shut.

She kicked it open, weapon raised.

Empty hallway.

One rolling kitchen cart loaded with produce still rattling slightly from motion.

Micelli swore under her breath, slamming a hand against the wall.

Bagrova had disappeared.

Passengers from QF415 out of Sydney trickled into the terminal. Detectives Sean Nguyen and Elsa Janzen were among them, defeated by Anson yet again, carrying bags slung over their shoulders. They moved together down the long hallway, scanning the terminal like muscle memory. Not quite expecting trouble but never ruling it out.

That's when they heard it. Sirens, muted, but nearby.

Janzen frowned. 'You hearing this?'

Shouting. A flash of red lights further down the hallway. Alarms were ringing. Loudspeakers were blasting warnings, telling people to evacuate the airport.

Nguyen was already picking up the pace. 'Something's not right.' As they rounded the corner they saw a security guard trying to cordon off the area outside the Qantas Lounge with bright yellow tape. Two paramedics wheeled out a man in a suit holding a towel to a bleeding shoulder. He was swearing loudly in Vietnamese.

Ducking under the tape, they ran up the escalator towards the lounge entrance. Janzen spotted Micelli through the diminishing smoke and the shattered glass. She was standing inside, framed by overturned furniture and shattered fixtures, one sleeve rolled up, blood streaked across her cheek from a grazing cut.

'Micelli!' Janzen called out,

She turned. Relief flickered, brief and buried under frustration.

'What the hell happened?' Nguyen was eyeing the mess.

Micelli holstered her gun with a sharp click. Her jaw was tight, breath shallow. 'Bagrova.' She was wheezing more than speaking. 'Was here. Ducked in to change.'

'What happened?' asked Nguyen.

'I engaged her. Shots fired.'

'She escape?'

Micelli's look said it all.

Nguyen swore softly.

After she'd caught her breath, Micelli said, 'She planned it. The gate, the disguise, the smoke canister. Like clockwork. Slipped through the kitchen and out a service hallway. She's gone.'

'CCTV?'

Micelli nodded towards a cluster of techs surging through the lounge, frantically pulling footage from monitors. 'Already on it. But she's smart. Probably avoided them or she's got someone wiping.'

Janzen sighed. 'Just like Anson. Always one step ahead. Come on, let's get you out of here.'

Downstairs, security guards were ushering people out of the hallways towards the airport exits. The PA system was blaring warning sirens and demanding that everyone evacuate.

Micelli, fists clenched, said, 'She won't be one step ahead for long.' Her phone buzzed in her hand. A message from airport control. Still no visual on Bagrova outside the terminal. Nothing in the parking lots. It was like she'd vanished. 'She's still here. I know it. She didn't leave. Not yet.' Micelli's eyes swept the chaotic terminal, every movement sharpening her suspicion. 'We need to call Pritchard.'

Nguyen was already pulling out his phone.

'We split up,' she explained. 'He went to International. God knows where he is now. But if I know Pritchard, he'll want in on this.'

'What about we catch our breath, wait her out,' said Janzen. 'There's nowhere else to go out here, so she'll have to surface.'

'Yeah. She's cornered. She just doesn't know it yet.'

Shouting. Screaming. Commotion near the passageway leading to the departure gates.

Micelli spun, heart thudding. There she was, Ludmilla Bagrova, pushing through a pack of stunned tourists, silver wig in disarray, no cap. Her pistol gripped tight in her hand.

Micelli didn't wait. 'Move!'

The three detectives surged into action. Bagrova fired once, sharp and desperate. Glass exploded above a perfume shop. People shrieked and dropped to the ground.

Micelli bolted after her, Nguyen and Janzen flanking. Bagrova ducked into a maintenance corridor, a warren of grey walls and flickering lights. Micelli followed hard, lungs burning, adrenaline drowning out the pain from the graze she'd suffered earlier.

Bagrova turned and fired again. This time closer. The shot cracked past Micelli's head and bit into her shoulder. She stumbled. Pain screamed through her arm. She gritted her teeth, switched her gun to her left hand, kept running.

'Micelli!' Janzen was shouting behind her. 'Stop!'

Bagrova burst through a side exit and onto a service runway, sprinting toward a refuelling truck.

Micelli was just behind her. She fired. Then again.

Bagrova lurched. Her leg gave out. She hit the tarmac hard, pistol skidding out of reach.

Micelli was on her in seconds, pinning her down with every ounce of fury and exhaustion she had left. 'It's over,' she hissed, breathing hard, pressing her forearm into Bagrova's back as Janzen and Nguyen arrived, guns raised.

Bagrova didn't fight. One leg was angled out from her body, shattered bone showing through designer jeans. Blood pooled on the tarmac. The silver wig was lying by her side.

As Nguyen cuffed Bagrova, Micelli sat back on the tarmac, clutched her bleeding shoulder. 'You're not dying on me today,' Nguyen said fiercely.

She cracked a bloody smile. 'Wouldn't dream of it,' she croaked.

Bagrova screamed curses in Russian as she was dragged away by squaddies. Micelli closed her eyes for a moment letting the heat of the day wash over her.

Pritchard arrived, wide-eyed and breathless. 'Did I miss anything?'

Micelli gave a half-laugh, half-wince. 'Next time, bring flowers.'

A paramedic crew hurried towards her. After a quick assessment they placed her on a gurney and wheeled her briskly across the tarmac to a waiting ambulance.

Nguyen knocked lightly before sticking his head into the hospital room. 'Okay to come in?' Micelli's room smelled like an expensive florist's, every surface laden with vases of arrangements. She was propped up with pillows, cradling her right arm that was supported by a sling, sipping from a plastic cup that looked like it contained orangeade. 'Family buy a flower shop?' he asked, sniffing the sweet aromas.

She attempted a smile. 'Looks like it, doesn't it. The Micelli clan doesn't waste any time or spare any expense when one of their own is down. But hey, you look pleased with yourself. What's news?'

He sauntered over to the bed and pulled out a chair. 'Guess Pritchard and Harris have filled you in about Bagrova?'

'Not as yet. There was a call, but I was too woozy to take it.'

'Briefly then. When Bagrova's gun was picked up from the tarmac, it exploded.'

Micelli gasped. 'You mean it shot someone?'

Nguyen paused.

'Cop? Alright?'

He shook his head. 'Cop. Not alright.'

She dropped the cup she was holding, a pale orange stain spread quickly onto her nightdress and over the coverlet. 'Fuck!' she bawled. 'Fuck the Russians!'

A nurse burst through the doorway. Seeing the tears coursing down Micelli's cheeks she grabbed a towel from the ensuite and began dabbing at her face.

Micelli pushed her hand away.

'It's probably a reaction to the anaesthetic,' she whispered to Nguyen. 'Seen it before. They wake up and then cry with relief they're still with us.'

'It's not the anaesthetic, it's bloody murder, that's what it is,' Micelli shouted. 'You get violent ones here too I know, but they haven't shot up your colleagues. Yet.'

The nurse backed out of the room, shutting the door as she left.

'You okay?' asked Nguyen.

She sniffed loudly. 'Pass me that box of tissues would you.' She blew her nose loudly. Dabbed at the wet patches on the bed. 'Keep going. What then?'

'Pritchard escorted her back to headquarters, charged her with murder after a tiny vial of suspected poison was found at the North Melbourne where she'd stayed. Told her there might be another charge of murder to follow. And because our colleague didn't make it, it's now possibly three murder charges. Probably get one reduced to manslaughter, but.'

She pulled another wad of tissues from the box and wiped at her eyes. 'Anyone else get arrested?'

'No sign of the men who were with her at the airport, if that's what you mean. She's been denied bail. She's refusing to speak. No one's the wiser as to her motive, but I understand Harris is ferreting away on financials. He said in passing that the business she was supposed to be in is some type of front for a money laundering outfit.'

Micelli tried to sit up, sank back against her pillows, face grimacing. 'Good work all round, I'd say. A team effort. Except for that prick Skelton. Don't miss him one bit. But you said there were a couple of things. What else do you have to report?'

'Krakauer's dead.' She opened her mouth to say something, dropped the wadded up tissues on the side table instead. 'Went into cardiac arrest. Died before the ambulance got there.'

'Wow. How did that happen?'

'Heard of Harold Cowan?' She shook her head. 'Big horse doping raid at Werribee six months ago. Been in Remand ever since. Whacked him.' Nguyen mimed a punch to the throat. 'But maybe not. There's a dispute between the two officers who claim to have witnessed the attack. One said Cowan punched Krakaeur, the other claims he was put in a full nelson. Either way, both can cause cardiac arrest.'

'When did this happen?'

'Yesterday afternoon apparently. Exercise yard.'

She rolled her eyes to the ceiling. 'Motive?'

'No one's sure, but there's a few theories going down.'

'Let me guess,' she said. 'Because he's a paedophile and prisoners don't like paedophiles.'

'Possibly.'

'That he's boasted about making porn but when he got to the bit about it starring kids, prisoners don't like people who violate and kill kids.'

'Kinda the same?'

'Maybe. What about drugs?' she said, swirling the remains of the drink round in the cup. 'Betting scandals? Money laundering? Who knows what pies Krakauer had his grubby fingers in.'

'Umm,' said Nguyen, 'All possible. Guess you've got a minute to spare?' He grabbed a paper napkin that had been left on the bedside table, drew a circle in the middle and wrote Krakauer in capital letters. 'I'm working on a theory that someone other than an aggrieved inmate ordered his killing.' Around the perimeter he began to write other names. Vincent Valentino. Gregory Anson. Simon Thomson-Paton. Elise Lanigan. Phillip Sinclair.

'Sinclair?' spluttered Micelli. 'You mean Phillip Sinclair, the Police Minister?'

'Sure do,' said Nguyen. 'We found out quite a bit about our police minister, thanks to awesome forensic work on the stuff we found at Valentino's place. Forensic accountants need to get to the bottom of a very sophisticated financial arrangement, but it looks like Sinclair and Valentino were more than mere acquaintances.'

'Wow. Are you saying that the Honourable Phillip Sinclair might be anything but honourable?'

'Quite possibly,' he agreed. She leaned forward as Nguyen set about drawing arrows between the names, then listing relationships one to the other. 'Elise Lanigan. She's represented both Anson and Krakaeur. Also been seen in Sinclair's company at social dos.' Next, he linked Krakauer to Valentino and added a connector to Simon Thomson-Paton, based on the fact that the same gun had been used to shoot them both.'

'Don't we think that Anson killed Simon Thomson-Paton though?'

'Yep. Interesting fact however.' He cleared his throat. 'The gun used to shoot both Simon Thomson-Paton and Vincent Valentino is the same gun found wrapped in chamois in Valentino's locked safe.'

She sat up. 'How did a gun used to shoot someone end up in that same person's locked safe?'

'That's what we wondered. But now Anson's in that cosy triangle. And you probably don't know that Christina, his girlfriend, died yesterday in hospital in Sydney?'

She shook her head.

'Anson was seen on CCTV not long before she took her last breath. Kind of like what happened in that Ballarat hospital last year to Charles de Havilland, if you remember. Something went wrong with his IV line, more likely someone fiddled with it. Well, something similar happened to Christina. Her IV line was tampered with. Cause of death was listed as an embolism. Perhaps too much air in the line? Just saying.'

Micelli leaned back against her pillows, scanning her IV drip. 'Always wondered about air bubbles in these things.'

'Need a fair bit to cause an embolism I was told. Like a syringe or two full of air,' Nguyen assured her. 'Yeah, I've seen the little bubbles travel up a line too. You're better off without them for sure, but a little one or two here and there is pretty harmless I gather.'

'That's a relief then,' she said. 'Any other additions to your theory?'

'Nah,' he said, 'but it'd be good to get that slippery bastard Anson wearing a pair of handcuffs. Slipped through our fingers again. No sightings since leaving the hospital where Christina was. And you know the really galling thing? He must have walked right past Janzen and me when we were in the café waiting to go back and see if Christina could be interviewed.'

'Guess New South are doing all the forensic footwork. Didn't we want his DNA?'

Nguyen explained that indeed New South was conducting a

thorough investigation at Christina's apartment and according to an email he'd received, a number of samples and items had been sent off for testing. 'Think the results, or at least some of them, will be on their way pretty soon. We know that Anson visited Vincent Valentino on a regular basis. And we do have samples from Krakauer's place, so might be able to get a match to show that Anson was there too.'

'It's slow work sometimes.'

'I know. I hate it,' he said through gritted teeth. 'Wish O'Leary hadn't been suspended.'

'Yeah. Don't we all. For any number of reasons.'

'They told me I'd find you in here somewhere behind a wall of floral tributes.' O'Leary walked towards her bed, a block of chocolate in hand. 'The twins insisted,' he said, passing it to her. 'Jack said that chocolate is the best cure for a bullet wound and Zoe said you just liked it a lot and that was a good enough reason to buy it.'

She laughed. 'Good to see you, Brendan.'

'You too Ange. In one piece at least. Any idea as to how long you'll be in here?'

'Nup. And the way I'm feeling, it can't finish soon enough. Not even twelve hours and I'm already driven mad by hospital procedures. Checks on this and that every fifteen minutes. Don't think I'm going to die. It's not like they haven't got more urgent cases.' Her phone pinged. She looked at the screen.

'Go on,' O'Leary said, waving a hand to where her phone sat on the side table. 'I don't mind.'

She could feel the heat in her face in the milliseconds she took to read the message. *Love you Ange. Get better soon. Xxxx D*

'Oh, I see,' said O'Leary, raising an eyebrow and lifting his chin. 'Miss Popular.'

'I'd kick you if I could,' she said, 'but anyway, tell me what's going on with you. How's the suspension panning out?'

'I've not had a lot of time to reflect, so stop me if you think I'm being paranoid, but this is how I view the situation.' He pulled out a chair and sat down. 'I reckon I've been set up by none other than our police minister.'

She frowned.

'I know. Big call. But think about it this way.'

Over the next fifteen minutes he outlined his suspicions as to what led up to the so-called drug cache discovery in his home, the subsequent suspension and linked these events to the coincidences that had happened over the last week. He described his missing phone, the smell of men's aftershave in his caravan and then again in his house on the night that the raid occurred. He listed the flowers sent to Claire and the guns sent to the twins and the fact that Goddings was adamant that no protection was necessary.

'If Valentino and Sinclair are, or I should say were, in cahoots, and it's certainly looking that way given the evidence that Nguyen and Janzen have dug up, including a joint business in their wives' names, that would be a cert for laundering money.' He held up a second finger. 'And given the pills they also found with Anson's imprints all over them, it seems logical to connect Sinclair to Anson, as we already know that Anson was Valentino's cousin, so there's that connection.' Third finger raised. 'Sinclair wouldn't want too much digging going on into how Valentino's ended up dead in a mineshaft, especially on a property belonging to a known criminal like Krakaeur.'

'He's dead,' she blurted.

'Yeah, Nguyen filled me in. So how many bodies is that? A few. And to my way of thinking, Sinclair's connected to all of them either in a roundabout way or more directly.'

'Do you think Goddings put Skelton on my team to somehow spy on you? I have a photo of him and Sinclair at the tennis having a very pally chat.'

He nodded. 'They're all in it up to their ears.'

'If you're right Brendan, there'll be a helluva stink. You going to do anything?'

He ran his tongue round his teeth. 'Hard road to hoe alone.'

She began to cough. He handed her the cup of orange drink.

'Anyway, better leave you in peace. Been a big day. And well done, by the way, on getting a murderer behind bars. Now talking of stinks, that might be a big one as I've heard she's actually a Russian national. Have a good night, Ange. I'll be in touch.' He leaned over the bed and gave her a quick peck on the cheek, closed the door on his way out.

She stared at the ceiling, thinking about what O'Leary had just said. Could whistleblowing be part of her career once she was back at work? What if it didn't work and both she and O'Leary ended up broken by a system that was flawed and corrupt. Not as bad as the system had once been, if she believed the stories the old-timers liked to share. But bad enough. Especially for those who broke ranks and spilled beans that those in the know never wanted to see the light of day. And it was always top down. Perhaps never more so than now.

She re-read David Romano's message. The words *Love you Ange* were worth reading over and over. She replaced her phone on the side table and switched off her light. Within moments, the ceiling light was switched on and a blood pressure machine wheeled over to her bedside by a nurse who looked old enough to be her grandmother.

'How's the pain?' the nurse asked, proffering a mini plastic cup rattling with pills. 'Something to make you sleep?' Micelli shook her head. The hype of the day's activities was catching up, but she didn't need drugs to make her sleep. Instead, she turned on the television. Watched replayed footage of the Bourke Street naked bike ride. Television crews had been quick off the mark to talk to anyone connected. All agreed that it was the best thing that happened all day. 'They're psychos,' reported a youth with a pixelated face. 'Me and me mates, like we were on our way to the tennis when we seen these girls riding bikes. Like naked girls. No clothes. Nothing. Too good!' Just one outlier. A man in a suit clutching a laptop to his chest. 'A public disgrace. The city's full of tourists and Melbourne is on the global spotlight right now, and these clowns show off. I don't think the peloton of the penis is the image we need to project.'

She decanted herself a nightcap of orange-aid, half an ear tuned to match highlights that the newsreader described as a brilliant game, smashing the ninth seed out of the park. Only two more matches before a possible lifting of the trophy, she was informed. On screen a jubilant Kross, arms in the air waving his racquet towards the crowd. Replays of key shots followed: a net volley that skimmed the baseline, a bevy of aces, and an overhead hit with so much force that the cloud of seagulls circling above the arena dissolved in a mist of squawks.

Acknowledgements

Writing a novel is never a solo pursuit, and this book would not exist without the generosity, patience, and encouragement of many people.

I am deeply grateful to the writers whose well-crafted novels have taught me, by example, how to shape a gripping story. Their work has been my guide and inspiration.

Boundless thanks to those who offered advice, workshopped ideas, and read drafts along the way. At the top of this list is Tania Chandler, whose close reading and insightful suggestions greatly strengthened this manuscript. I value her advice immensely. She is an outstanding writer of contemporary fiction and a generous mentor.

To my family and friends, thank you for understanding and support that kept me going through the tough chapters.

Thank you to those who read early drafts and workshopped sections of this novel with me. Maria Lacey, Amy Jasper, Anita Smith.

To the detectives, legal professionals, and forensic experts who share their knowledge in workshops and discussions, as well as research papers and online articles. May my hard drive never be searched for criminal activities!

To the readers who love their crime fiction dark, real, and relentless. This one's for you.

Finally, to the landscapes of Victoria—the dry riverbeds, abandoned farmhouses, and lost mine shafts—your silence and heat found their way into every page.

About the Author

Janice Simpson lives in regional Victoria, where she juggles writing crime novels, building bike trails, and running a winter words festival — often all in the same week. She reads anything that grabs her, writes whenever she can steal a few hours, and believes good conversations (and good stories) can change the world.

She has a PhD in creative practice, a love of mysteries, and a habit of taking on slightly too many projects at once.

www.ingramcontent.com/pod-product-compliance
Lightning Source LLC
Chambersburg PA
CBHW010300100726
47904CB00011B/2674